W9-AJT-899

04/2020

PALM BEACH COUNTY
LIBRARY SYSTEM
3650 Summit Boulevard
West Palm Beach, FL 33406-4198

PRAISE FOR *THIS TERRIBLE BEAUTY*

"Schumann's graceful evocations of people and place make it hard to forget."

—Maria Hummel, author of *Motherland* and the Reese Witherspoon book club pick *Still Lives*

"Deeply relevant to our current times, *This Terrible Beauty* explores the lengths to which we will go to find love and the sacrifices we make for family and community. I fell in love with these characters and came away heartened and hopeful."

—Christopher Castellani, author of *Leading Men*

"A compelling and richly layered story of love, motherhood, art, and ultimately self-preservation—this is a vivid, rapidly paced historical novel. Unputdownable!"

—Jillian Cantor, *USA Today* bestselling author of *The Lost Letter* and *In Another Time*

"Schumann's vivid focus reveals characters who crumble with heartbreak and rise with strength, and above all draws her readers in and never lets them go."

—Rachel Barenbaum, bestselling author of *A Bend in the Stars*

"Set in postwar Germany, this gorgeously written, sweeping, cinematic story is also a riveting and romantic page-turner. Get ready to put everything on hold and let yourself get lost in this sensual tale."

—Erica Ferencik, bestselling author of *The River at Night*, a #1 Oprah.com pick, and *Into the Jungle*

"A complex, moving story of love and loss, beautifully written. *This Terrible Beauty* explores the critical nature of art as a lens through which we can understand history and asks us to be mindful of the ways we choose to look at the world. This is one historical fiction fans can't miss."

—Olivia Hawker, *Washington Post* bestselling author of *The Ragged Edge of Night*

"*This Terrible Beauty* kept me turning the pages long into the night. Katrin Schumann evokes an often-forgotten time and place to weave a story that is equally captivating and fascinating."

—Eoin Dempsey, bestselling author of *White Rose, Black Forest*

PRAISE FOR *THE FORGOTTEN HOURS*

"Schumann's is a carefully constructed novel that skillfully weaves past and present, slowly planting clues that help unlock the narrative's central mystery while ratcheting up tension . . . The fast-moving plot and compelling, layered characters make for an addictive and incredibly timely read. A page-turner that also speaks to broader questions of sexual abuse, family loyalty, and the mutability of memory."

—*Kirkus Reviews*

"Schumann's debut novel brings a new perspective to sexual assault and how it affects families . . . Flashbacks to the past are intertwined with the narrative, and the slow reveal of detail will leave readers wanting more. With a surprise twist, this work is sure to please. For fans of Jodi Picoult."

—*Library Journal*

"Schumann crafts a powerfully compelling story of family loyalties, teenage friendships, and the fickleness of memory. Timely and provocative, this first novel will appeal to fans of Liane Moriarty, Paula Hawkins, and Jenna Blum."

—*Booklist*

"A riveting story . . . Schumann has an eye for detail, an ear for the rhythmic sentence, and a voice that is clear and resonant."

—New York Journal of Books

"A deeply moving story about friendship and love, yearning and passion, memory and loss. *The Forgotten Hours* is a brilliant debut from a writer of uncommon grace."

—William Landay, *New York Times* bestselling author of *Defending Jacob*

"A relevant, compelling, and compassionate look at the torture of conflicted loyalties and the slipperiness of truth."

—Jenna Blum, *New York Times* bestselling author of *Those Who Save Us* and *The Lost Family*

"As fictional characters go, Katie Gregory seems not so much imagined as compelled into being by the unique forces of the times—the perfect envoy to accompany you into the red-hot cauldron of accused and accuser. That Katie is neither of these but bound by love to both makes her conflict more gut wrenching and the possibilities more terrifying. Add to this Schumann's gift for knowing—and conjuring—her character's heart, and you have a story that makes you feel it's your heart at risk, your life on the line. You may lose track of these hours, but you won't forget them."

—Tim Johnston, *New York Times* bestselling author of *Descent*

"With an elegance of style surprising in a first novel, Schumann shows how when we seek truth about the past, the most treacherous secrets are those we keep from ourselves."

—Carol Anshaw, *New York Times* bestselling author of *Carry the One*

"*The Forgotten Hours* is a wise reminder that coming-of-age stories aren't only for the very young. Katie Gregory's need to confront her own youthful beliefs and desires is something familiar—and compelling—to us all. There is so much insight in these pages, so much compassion, all woven into a mystery I couldn't put down."

—Robin Black, author of *Life Drawing* and *If I Loved You, I Would Tell You This*

"*The Forgotten Hours* asks important questions about memory, adolescent understanding, the age of consent, and what men have gotten away with since time immemorial. Katrin Schumann has crafted a powerful tale for the #MeToo era that should resonate far beyond this cultural moment."

—Miranda Beverly-Whittemore, *New York Times* bestselling author of *Bittersweet* and *June*

"*The Forgotten Hours* is a stunning novel about trauma and shame, loyalty and truth. Ten years after an alleged crime destroyed her family, Katie Gregory returns to an abandoned cabin she prefers to forget. As memories of her last evening there bring conflicting emotions, she struggles to rediscover her ability to trust and her faith in love. Was her father guilty of the assault for which he was convicted? What part did she play in the events of that night, and can she move beyond her own guilt? Trying to unravel the answers before the heart-pounding finish will keep readers up way past bedtime. A must read for book clubs."

—Barbara Claypole White, bestselling author of *The Perfect Son* and *The Promise Between Us*

"For me, the best indicator of a good book is when you're thinking about the characters even when you aren't reading, wondering what's going to happen to them. This was definitely the case with *The Forgotten Hours*. I thoroughly enjoyed this well-written, compelling story."

—Marybeth Mayhew Whalen, bestselling author of *When We Were Worthy* and cofounder of She Reads

This Terrible Beauty

OTHER NOVELS BY
KATRIN SCHUMANN

The Forgotten Hours

This Terrible Beauty

KATRIN SCHUMANN

Published by Lake Union Publishing, Seattle
www.apub.com

Amazon, the Amazon logo, and Lake Union Publishing are trademarks of Amazon.com, Inc., or its affiliates.

ISBN-13: 9781542020800 (hardcover)
ISBN-10: 1542020808 (hardcover)
ISBN-13: 9781542000062 (paperback)
ISBN-10: 1542000068 (paperback)

Cover design by David Drummond

Map of World War II Occupation Areas in Europe, 1945: INTERFOTO / Alamy Stock Photo 4

Printed in the United States of America

For Peter & Occu,
who guided me with wisdom and love

Let us plow and build our nation,
Learn and work as never yet,
That a free new generation
Faith in its own strength beget!
German youth, for whom the striving
Of our people is at one,
You are Germany's reviving,
And over our Germany,
There is shining sun;
There is shining sun.
—East German national anthem,
Johannes R. Becher, 1949

All changed, changed utterly:
A terrible beauty is born.
—"Easter, 1916,"
William Butler Yeats

LEGEND · ERKLÄRUNG

BOUNDARIES · GRENZEN:

GERMANY
DEUTSCHLAND 1937

OCCUPATION AREAS
BESATZUNGSZONEN 1945

PROVINCES · PROVINZEN

ZONES · ZONEN:

AMERICAN ZONE · AMERIKANISCHE ZONE
BRITISH ZONE · BRITISCHE ZONE
FRENCH ZONE · FRANZÖSISCHE ZONE
RUSSIAN ZONE · RUSSISCHE ZONE
POLISH TERRITORY · POLNISCHES GEBIET

AUTHOR'S NOTE

Though this novel is inspired by actual historical events, the characters are entirely fictional. In creating this story, I have altered certain details for the sake of the narrative, while striving to be true to the realities of the era. For example, the fictional seaside town of Saargen is a composite of Saßnitz and Sagard, yet Rügen is a real island in the Baltic, bombed during the war and controlled for forty years by the Russians. It became part of the German Democratic Republic and is referred to in this book as the DDR, as that is how the characters would have thought of it. For more information on research and sources used in imagining this story, please see www.katrinschumann.com.

PROLOGUE

Chicago, Illinois
Spring 1961

There are eight beads, one for every year of her daughter's life. Under Bettina's thumb and forefinger, some of them are rough and some smooth, a few with sharp edges that catch on her skin. They're cheaply made, bright pink and blue and green and yellow, like sweets. They hang on the soft leather of her camera strap. Bettina has rolled them between her fingertips so often—hundreds of times, thousands, maybe—that each one seems to have its own personality.

As she makes her way through them one by one, she falls into a rhythm of thinking, a kind of reassembling of scenes from Annaliese's childhood. It's total immersion, being steeped in the texture of a regular life, the wondrous light of ordinary moments flooding Bettina's mind.

First bead.

At one year old, Annaliese has the full cheeks of a healthy baby, pinkened by sharp sea breezes and her mother's milk. She takes her first faltering steps, and when she succeeds at crossing the threshold from the kitchen to the front room, her gummy smile changes the shape of her face, sparks her eyes into knowing.

At two she loves to torment Eberle, the cat, yanking his tail until he turns on her, quick to betray the child's trust. Anna's damp fingers grasping at fur, pulling on bone; she doesn't understand yet that she has the power to cause pain.

When the child is three, Bettina pictures her daintily placing the fallen petals of the old *Rosa rugosa* into her mouth, barely hesitating, turning the velvet petals on her tongue, willing to try anything.

Anna is bright, unstoppable, and at age four she holds court over the other children in the crèche, pretending to read stories aloud and lecturing them with a pursed mouth. Her baby belly is gone, her legs lengthening. She will be tall.

When she is five years old, she discovers the magic of the letters on the page, their clusters beginning to create meaning and momentum; words have become stories. She holds her grandfather's dusty books in her palms, a grave look on her face. The old German script is indecipherable, but she knows now that one day she'll be able to read these books from beginning to end.

At age six she swims with a friend off the beach in Binz, the decrepit mansions towering above the shoreline, the waters of the Baltic swirling around her thighs, her muscles pressing against the current that tries to bully her out into the ocean, carry her northward, away from her island home.

Bettina hesitates, eyes closed.

By serendipity, the seventh bead on the strap is a multifaceted one, the same size as the others but from a different manufacturer. She often pauses here, rolling it between her fingers. Should this pause lead her mind in other directions, she invariably wonders, or should she keep going on her trajectory? It is the seventh bead, so that means Anna is seven years old and it is 1960, but the child is not aware of what this means. She does not know about the Cold War—though she will have learned about the revolution in Cuba, its young socialist government. This has been celebrated all over East Germany with parades, striped flags snapping in the wind. So today, Bettina's mind takes her to an image of the Young Pioneers, and she sees her daughter with a blue kerchief knotted at her chin. She is singing, her chest swelling with each inhalation, giving it her all, her voice warbling and high—her view of the world narrow, shaped by the island, by her history, by German history.

The last bead now. Eight.

At eight, her daughter is licking her lips as she scrapes the lead of her pencil across the checkered pages of her schoolbook, doing her homework. Does she still sleep in the little room that was once the maid's room in better times, long before the First World War, or has she moved to a bigger room that can fit a desk? Perhaps she does her homework on the dining room table, where two generations of the Heilstroms sat to take their evening meals.

Bettina's mind wanders like a swimmer reaching for some murky underwater spot, and she tries to bring herself back into her invented moments, grasping blindly. She has a rule when she completes this ritual: *Only good thoughts, and no regrets.*

She sees her daughter in the little museum in Stralsund, a hand-knit sweater hanging from angular shoulders, head turned toward an old photograph on the wall. She loves art . . .

Bettina snaps open her eyes. Maybe Anna loves art, but maybe she loves numbers?

She screws her eyes shut: Annaliese's lips are parted, her concentration intense, just like her mother's. She is looking at a picture, a picture of—

Outside, a car honks in the trash-strewed street. Bettina jumps up, chilled, irretrievably distracted. It's April, and the weather in Chicago is raw. If she saw her daughter on the street, she might not even recognize her. An ocean divides them, and the years have passed unobserved but for these beads, the cheap plastic a constant reminder of what could have been and what is not.

PART ONE

1

Bettina rests her bicycle against a wall and unhooks the basket from the rear. A throng crowding the square emits a buzz like cicadas, the sound swelling and shrinking with the direction of the wind. It must be years since so many people congregated here, perhaps since before the war began. She wishes she'd brought along her father's camera, but she was running late and forgot it on the sideboard. A haphazard regiment of soldiers sits on wooden chairs on a podium while a full band plays, but the music is barely discernible above the noisy chatter. Five or six officers wearing dark uniforms stand on the platform, hands on hips. Red banners hang from the cobbler's and the tailor's: *DEUTSCHLAND ÜBER ALLES*. People line the edges of the square, holding long poles with flags at the top embroidered with white swastikas and lined with heavy black fringe.

Yesterday someone slipped a leaflet under the door of her family's shop, proclaiming, *Die tausendjährige Eiche kommt nach Saargen—* "The thousand-year oak is coming to Saargen." In all the town squares throughout the Reich, oak trees are being planted as symbols of the Führer's vision for Germany. Belatedly, Bettina's island village is to get its first one that afternoon. Her father is at home in bed, unable to move about, coughing alarmingly dark streaks of blood into his handkerchief.

"Are you sure, my love?" he asked when she told him she was attending the ceremony. The whites of his eyes were the color of old egg yolk, and his lips had lost their fullness. "I don't believe what the radio is telling us. Things seem dire, no?"

What he wasn't saying was that he worries constantly about how she will fare once he is gone—a young woman alone in the world, a country gone to ruin. She took his hand in hers. "Oh, Papa. I'm seventeen! I'll be fine, really."

Searching his daughter's face, he smiled. "Hm. You always did have a strong will. Too late to change that now. But be careful, you hear? Anyway, who knows—maybe I'll live to see the end of this goddamn war after all."

Now the sky is turning the color of steel as the afternoon sun sinks beyond the horizon. Bettina hugs her coat to her body and looks around her for a decent vantage point. That's when she spots a regular customer from the fish shop, Werner Nietz. Every Friday afternoon he comes to the store, and he always chats with Papa; at least he used to. Now her father is too weak to work anymore, and Werner conducts his business with Bettina. She had long noticed the dreadful limp, his pale poet eyes. Though he is much younger than her father, he reminds her a bit of him: barrel shaped, gentle. She used to wonder why he wasn't fighting (almost all the men from the village are gone), but over time she realized the limp, of course, explained everything.

Werner is standing a few meters from her, and though surrounded on all sides by a jovial crowd, he's embroiled in some sort of argument. Two soldiers wearing filthy jackets are waving papers in his face. The taller one, his face scarred and shadowed by dark stubble, seems especially riled up. He jabs at Werner's chest and shouts into his face. Werner turns his head away, as though repulsed by foul breath. He appears so mild, absolutely harmless; what can he possibly have done to anger these men?

She begins shouldering her way toward the three of them. The soldiers are wearing the Reich's uniform, but they do not look respectable, and as Bettina approaches, she can smell alcohol—as though they've bathed in it, for heaven's sake. For years now her father has been telling her she needs to hold her tongue, that it is best for her to keep to herself. *You cannot survive in times like these unless you put your own safety first,* he insists. But this does not sit well with her. He thinks her willful, yet she is merely concerned with justice.

"Well, well, what's this?" the darker soldier says, sticking a thin piece of wood in his mouth like a cigarette. "A pretty little lady heading our way."

Werner makes a move toward Bettina, but the soldier will have none of it and grabs him by the arm. "Just a minute there, you cripple. I haven't decided what I want to do with you yet." The man, still a boy really, glares at Bettina, and she is aware that she left the house without a hat, like a young girl. Her thick dark hair is coiled in a bun at her neck, and she feels stripped naked by his eyes.

"Excuse me. He, this man, ah—we're meeting, to watch the ceremony together?" she says, making it up as she goes along. "Is there some sort of problem?"

"I see, well. We're just making certain he's not a burden on the system. You understand, of course—now's the time for us all to be pitching in. We don't tolerate anyone who doesn't pull his weight. We must all do the best we can." The other soldier's blond hair has been cut so short the ridges of his skull stick out. He raises a bottle of beer to his lips.

Bettina remembers boys like this from school, boys who were bullies and have become men who like wielding their power. How is it that the soldiers' superiors tolerate this kind of behavior in public? The darker soldier's accent establishes that he is from Bavaria; here by the

Baltic Sea in the north, he's almost a thousand kilometers from home. She smiles at him, hoping to calm him down. "Yes, I—"

Raucous cheers rise from the crowd, and the soldiers turn simultaneously toward the podium. In that instant Werner grabs her by the elbow and hustles her toward the stairs at the base of the town hall. They don't stop till they reach the top near the wooden doorway, above the body of the crowd, short of breath and dripping with sweat.

"What do they want with you?" Bettina asks, panting, placing her cumbersome basket on the ground by her feet. "Have you *done* something?"

Werner's cheeks are fevered. "Uh, it's all nonsense. Something about my not fighting."

Speakers on the podium let out a wavering note, shrill and prolonged. The mayor of Saargen emerges from the crowd, a skinny man with an imposing nose, wearing a uniform with gold epaulets and buttons that flash in the dusky light. The band strikes up a melody, and the crowd begins to sway; people are humming and singing. The harbor is only a few hundred meters away, and a breeze carries with it the pungent smell of the ocean. On the stairs next to them stands a little family: a stout woman and an older man whose arm is held out at a right angle by a dull silver contraption. He must be one of the lucky ones, home on sick leave. On the man's shoulders sits a boy of six or so, woolen socks pooled at his ankles, suspenders drifting off bony shoulders. They wear expressions of expectation and excitement on their upturned faces.

The crowd begins to part as a large vehicle backs up toward the podium. In the truck bed lies an oak sapling. The foot soldiers tug at the burlap root ball and heave the lanky tree over to a hole in the very center of the square. It is meant to live a thousand years, this oak, but even from this distance Bettina can see the edges of its tiny leaves are curled and brown, its branches sparse and thin as fishing rods.

"I'm a soldier, Mama, a soldier!" cries the little boy, pointing one finger at his mother while clutching a sticky bun in the other hand. His delicate pink lips are covered in jelly. "Pow, pow, pow!"

Everyone nearby laughs.

Seagulls swoop overhead, beady eyes trained below them. There are murmurs of anticipation when the band stops playing. Bettina raises her head to the sky, still cloudless but edged with shadow as evening approaches. There is a hum or a buzz in the air that is getting louder and louder.

But—the sound is not really a humming. No one else appears to notice, and she pulls at Werner's jacket.

"Do you hear that?" she asks sharply. "That noise?"

They lift their eyes. Just as the sound becomes a low, rumbling growl, as other eyes begin to turn upward, the crowd seems to take in one shallow, collective breath, a surprised *ahhhh!* For an interminable second, the intake of breath swallows the roar of the planes. The terrible *ah!* of recognition sucks every sound and movement into its stunned emptiness—then, commotion and screaming.

The air-raid sirens begin their wailing just as the warplanes swoop over Saargen Square. Airplanes coming from the direction of Peenemünde dot the sky like malevolent birds. An earsplitting shriek and a crash of explosive onto wood, stone, earth, bone. Another crash so loud it cuts through the whistling wind and swallows the sudden sound of screaming. Werner and Bettina fall to the ground. The air instantly goes from fresh and salty to acrid, and it burns right through her nostrils.

Bombs are dropping from the pregnant sky. Werner yells something at her, yanking her arm so sharply it hurts, but she is mesmerized: The mother picnicking with her family is crouching over the little boy. He is lying like an object thrown from a great height, and a leg is missing. The panicked crowd pushes the mother this way and that; she falls onto her side and then gets back on her haunches, her mouth open in an imploring scream. She shakes her child's shoulders, but he does not respond. The child is dead.

Bettina is catapulted down the steps; she lands heavily at the bottom and lies, inert, on the ground. Her basket is gone. People trample over her; a boot kicks her hand. A woman steps onto her torso as though she is a rolled-up rug laid out for the refuse collectors. But Bettina does not move to save herself. All these years into this interminable war, she is struck by the notion that human life is not only fleeting—a mere blink of an eye—but essentially meaningless, snatched away for no reason and given for no reason. It is the end, just as her father predicted, but not in the way he was hoping. She will die here, in Saargen, on a cool day in March.

Does it matter all that much? She thinks not. Her father is lying in their little cottage, alone, with only weeks or months left to live. Her mother is long gone, dead from influenza. Bettina is already alone in the world. The little boy is dead, Germany is dead because of a madman hell bent on destruction, and soon she will be dead too.

Someone pulls at her, and she peels open her eyes. Werner is grasping under her shoulders, dragging her up on her feet. Her wool stockings are torn, and she has lost a shoe. There is blood on her hand, but she cannot tell if it is her own. Her ears are ringing. Werner takes her hand in his, and she rises unsteadily, holding on to him tightly, and puts one foot in front of the other. They head back up the stairs.

He pulls a key from his pocket. She remembers then that he is a civil servant; he must work here at the town hall. Werner hurries her through the marble front hall. "There's a bunker," he explains, "out back. We'll be safe if we can get there." But the cavernous hall magnifies the screaming, the drone of planes, the hum and crashes, and as awful as it is to be outside where people are groveling and dying, it is far worse to be in here, to feel the walls tremble as though they're as fragile as parchment paper.

They come to a door leading outside into a garden planted with gnarled apple trees. At the side of the building is a trapdoor that Werner hauls open. Wet air rushes up from the darkness below, foul smelling.

"It's the cripple," comes a cry, and a piece of wood crashes down on Werner's shoulders, sending him to the ground. Behind him stands the drunken soldier from earlier, gasping and reeling. His jaunty cap is missing, but Bettina recognizes his dark hair, the boyish face. He raises his arms to strike again, and she throws herself at him with all the strength she can muster.

"Leave him alone," she screams, tangled in his army jacket, his flailing arms, breathing in the smell of his ripe body, the alcohol that seeps from his pores. "He hasn't done anything!"

He throws her down so easily, pinning her to the ground, digging his knees into her shoulders. "Silly girl," he huffs. "I'm not interested in . . . in *him* . . ."

Underneath her, pebbles pierce her clothes, and she rakes at them frantically with her hands, flinging up fistfuls, shredding the skin on her fingers. She screams as loudly as she can, but no one can hear her. The man begins dragging her toward the opening of the bunker.

"You're a fighter, yes, yes . . . I like that! We can . . . let's fight some . . . you and I will fuck like rabbits, and the others can all go to hell."

Bettina looks up at him and sees the pinched concentration on his face melt into incredulity. His nose is too long for his otherwise stubby features, and his mouth is slack and open but silent. He flops forward, almost gracefully. His own army-issue knife sticks out from the side of his neck, plunged in so deeply that only the deer-antler handle remains visible. Blood spurts from the wound, running in rivulets over his shoulders.

The heat of his body and his blood, warm and wet, is on her skin. He is heavy and motionless, but the blood seems alive like lava. Bettina writhes and twists, trying to free herself. She hears only the crashes, the faraway shrieks of the dying, the unending roar and whistle of plane and bomb.

"Help," she cries. "Help me!"

A handkerchief passes over her eyes, clearing her skin of debris and blood. It is Werner again, kneeling. He drags the soldier off her, the body slumping heavily as though the muscles have dissolved. Werner's round face is ashen, contorted with pain, his hair sticking out from his head. "He's dead," he says quietly. "*Herein!* Come on—get in here, quick."

Bettina stumbles into the dank bunker.

Hours later when Bettina and Werner emerge, their secret—their murdered soldier—is buried in the mounds of chipped and shattered bricks, the tumbled trees. A ringing sound pings through Bettina's head, and she cannot hold on to her thoughts. It is impossible to believe that the marketplace, surrounded by medieval stone buildings and grand redbrick businesses, will ever be normal again. There is no sign of the podium, the truck, or the young oak tree. The musicians and their instruments are gone. Paramedics have arrived, and they work quietly and quickly, turning over bodies to check for signs of life, ignoring the dead, sorting the injured men and women into two groups: those who need transportation to the hospital in Bergen and those who suffered only superficial wounds. Werner is stunned, eyes blinking. There is dried blood on his hands. Thick rays of light from torches illuminate the scene. The moon is briefly obscured by a cloud, and under the impenetrable black sky the ruined town looks hateful.

Bettina refuses treatment for her hands or the gash in her calf but accepts a ride home in a van lined with wooden benches. Werner helps her into the back, clutching at her hand in an effort to recapture her attention, his doleful eyes searching hers. "Bettina!" he says urgently. "Will you be all right?"

Before they are jostled apart, she reaches down and holds her fingers lightly to his cheek, as though he is a child. This man helped her. His eyes are kind, and he does not want to let her go. An elderly woman climbs gingerly into the van and sits next to her. A fur stole is wrapped around her shoulders, and she is hatless, her thin hair covered in dust. The van begins working its way through the blocked streets and alleyways at an excruciatingly slow pace.

The force of the blast in the town center has shattered some windows in her neighborhood, but the cottage is still standing. Her father is safe. Bettina jumps from the van and races in, calling out to him. Even here, the air smells acrid, and there is a sense of tension, of time trembling on a broken continuum where everything and nothing is normal.

Jürgen Heilstrom is sitting up in bed, sheets pulled to his chin, lips parted in a rictus of fear. Father and daughter hold each other close, sobbing. She says nothing of the soldier or what he tried to do to her or that it was Werner Nietz, the man from the shop—the one who comes every Friday—who saved her. Her thoughts are incoherent, and she cannot latch on to anything that makes sense. She has lived with war for years already, she has already experienced death, and yet on this day something inside her closes up tight.

2

Papa lives another twelve months, but he does not live to see the end of the war.

It is not yet morning on the day of Bettina's eighteenth birthday. Her eyes open before day breaks, and she is not able to fall asleep again. A week earlier her father's body was removed from the house. Her sister, Clara, has been coming as often as she can to help out, but it is hard for her to get to Saargen given the severe shortage of petrol. Before the war she was a secretary in the chalk mines, but she no longer has work. Her husband, Herbert, suffers fevers and nausea from an infected wound in his arm. There is no penicillin to be found, and the sulfonamides cause blisters so big they weep. Clara might as well be living in another country.

Bettina is trying to warm herself by the grate in the kitchen, which she has filled with twigs gathered at night from the edge of the nearby forest. After their fish shop was destroyed in the bombing, she worked only on keeping the two of them fed and warm. On making her father comfortable, reading to him from Schiller and Hauptmann, and even, toward the end, Thomas Mann, frowned upon by the authorities but adored nonetheless. Day after day she read aloud the passages from *Death in Venice* describing Aschenbach's exotic journeys. They talked of adventure and the fullness of life while hiding in the tight-ceilinged rooms of their cottage. He made her promise to be watchful, cautious, but he did not know that he no longer needed to urge her toward withdrawal. They were both waiting, praying that Hitler would be killed, that this war would be over. His daughter washed his body daily and, as they felt the end drawing close, slept curled up beside him on his sickbed, listening to the sound of his breath receding. When Clara was there with them, it was just about bearable. Now that she's returned to her village to nurse Herbert back to health and Papa is gone, the house echoes with their absence.

The fire sputters. The fisherman's cottage lies on the northern edge of a small cobblestone square called Apolonienmarkt. Dark thatched eaves cap the roof, swinging down at sharp angles toward the ground. The four-square windows and fading-green shutters distinguish it from the other houses on the square. Even though it is not in any way grand, with its long sloping roof and the small central window above the front door, it is the biggest house on the square, a sign of the status the family once enjoyed. By the late 1800s the Heilstrom men had built up a successful export business, managing the distribution of thousands of tons of fish to large mainland cities throughout Germany. But after the Great War the family's holdings dwindled, eventually leaving nothing of their business but the one fish shop in Saargen, gone almost a year now.

Wearing old wool pants, workman's boots inherited from the butcher's son, and a wool sweater, Bettina shivers in the early-morning coolness. With the entire year to go and only forty-three points left out of one hundred on her ration card, she has to manage with whatever garments she can sew or scrounge up. The kitchen faces northwest and has a window looking out on a patch of lawn, hard as flint after the bitter winter, and a small shed for the chickens. It is a utilitarian kitchen, painted pale blue with speckled honeycomb tiles on the floor and a trestle sink. There is a compact table with a chipped enamel top around which the women of the house—her grandmother, her mother, Clara, Bettina, and sometimes an aunt or two from the mainland—used to knead batter for pumpernickel bread or stuff meat into cabbage. Now she is the only one left. The front room with its low-hanging beams and mullioned windows feels too big for her, and so the kitchen is where Bettina spends most of her time.

The radio drones and then barks on the countertop. It broadcasts constant, terrifying warnings about the Bolsheviks, and sometimes when there are noises on the cobblestones outside, Bettina imagines it's the Red Army at her door, or perhaps stragglers from East Prussia fleeing the onslaught. The Führer promised them a swift victory, but it has long been clear that this is not to be the case. All the values Bettina and her neighbors have been taught to believe in—order, hard work, reliability—mean nothing anymore. No intelligent person can trust the media; everyone knows the Russians are advancing steadily westward, even if Goebbels denies it. Behind them they leave a trail of devastation; a scarred, barely recognizable landscape; and people so horrified by what they've seen and done that they no longer feel part of the human race. A neighbor's son, Otto von Donnersberg, saw it with his own eyes on his endless overland journey home. Half-witted, he tells his tales of misery and horror, and people can barely bring themselves to believe him. Yet you can see from his dead eyes that the unthinkable is happening.

Bettina's *Ersatzkaffee* long gone, the slightly bitter taste of the oak nuts lingering in her mouth, she heads into the dining room. She surveys the dishes from her grandmother glinting at her in the breakfront, thinking she should set the table today, her birthday. The blackout shades are still drawn, and the room is dark. Catching sight of a compact wooden dresser with swollen drawers next to the hutch, she has a sudden idea. After clearing a path to the door, she drags the dresser into the kitchen. There is a large hammer under the sink. Wielding the tool with both hands, she smashes it down on the dresser, again and again. At first, the hammer bounces back as though on a spring, but she doesn't give up. Hitting the edges, she hears the first crack as the wood splits. Her long brown hair hangs loose, and moisture is accumulating at the base of her scalp. She peels off her sweater and continues pounding until the dresser has been smashed into long, irregular pieces.

Surveying the damage and the mess, she grins to herself, thinking how shocked her fastidious mother would have been. She gathers up some of the larger bits into a pile and places them by the back door; she will use those later. Then she tidies up the remaining wood, sweeping away the splinters and dust. Kneeling by the grate, she feeds the fire, little by little, until it blazes with warmth. The radio is tuned to a station playing music for the soldiers, and she turns up the volume.

And then—the song! Zarah Leander's growling voice sings "Lili Marleen," and Bettina begins mouthing the words to herself. Soon she is dancing, and then she is singing as loud as she can.

It is the story of lovers hoping to reunite under a lamppost by the barracks. A song that plays ceaselessly in homes and bars and even sometimes in the streets when someone opens their windows wide enough to let the notes fly through, sweeping over the cobbles and dirt tracks and touching the exhausted islanders with a rousing, familiar embrace. Bettina danced to this song with her boyfriend, Dieter, before he was conscripted, his long arms wrapped around her and his lean body—so thin, a young boy's—pressed against hers. They kissed deeply and then laughed at their indiscretion, so certain of their future in spite of all the uncertainty around them. Bettina cannot listen to that rich, growling voice without remembering what conviction and pride felt like. She imagines herself a seductress or a lover, swaggering through a party, cocktail in hand, hope and lust and confidence transforming her into a beauty.

Bettina twirls around the small kitchen, crushing splinters of wood with her too-big boots, the music filling her up. The next song is faster, and she does a little jig. When Herbert Lange was courting her sister, Bettina and Dieter were sometimes allowed to tag along with them to the dance halls on Saturday nights. She would wear her favorite pumps, swinging herself from one eager man to the next until she was out of breath, muscles aching.

Everything had seemed possible back then. If she had been a little older and said yes to marrying Dieter before he left, maybe she would have a child to take care of now. A child—oh, the thought of a child. Would that be better or worse than being alone?

As dawn breaks, Bettina heads for the beach on her bicycle, her father's camera bouncing on its leather cord around her neck. The streets are barely lit by the cool pink of a springtime sunrise, and vagrants are milling about, half-dead soldiers sleeping under trees and on sidewalks. It seems as though the whole world is on the move as the Russians march farther and farther west, ever closer to them. Her father's last words to her as he lay dying had been, "*Versteck dich, Bettinalein.* Promise to hide." But she can't, not today. She badly needs to see the ocean again; she can't stand being cooped up inside the house any longer. Bettina is willing to risk anything just to feel the sea breeze on her parched skin and taste salt in the back of her throat again.

A few fishermen have detangled their nets, hanging them to dry between long sticks. Bettina lifts the camera and looks down through the viewfinder, taking comfort in clicking the dial till everything comes into sharp focus. She presses the button, again and then again, even though the camera is empty of film. It has been years since she has been able to find thirty-five-millimeter cartridges. After a while she starts running, just so she can feel the wind against her arms and her legs, her neck and face. Her housedress flaps around her knees like wings beating against her skin. Close to the edge of the sea, she runs as fast as her feet will carry her, clutching the Rollei in both hands. Tar-covered debris littering the sand makes her footing clumsy, but she jumps over the pieces of wood, the twisted scraps of metal. She has become a woman, and she doesn't quite know what this means yet. She runs until her side is pierced by a stitch and her breath comes in short, sharp bursts, and then unexpectedly her foot lands badly and she trips, falling spectacularly, flinging her arms out in front of her.

Something wet nudges at her shin, and in horror she jerks herself upright. It is a small dog, a ridiculous-looking mutt with yellow tufts springing from his ears. Bettina tries to stand, and a stinging pain courses up her leg. In the cove of trees not far from her, she detects a mound of fabric, olive green and filthy, next to which lies a boot. Dozens of Scotch pines, battered by wind blowing in from the north, stoop along the edge of the sand, gray and wizened. Crimped limbs have been broken by storms. It takes her a moment to realize the boot on the sand is attached to a foot, and a person is lying among the dunes in the shelter of the trees. The person stirs and sits up. It is a man, a soldier.

Her body stiffens. This is what her father warned her about; she should have known better.

Acknowledging what must be a look of terror on her face, the beach man lifts a hand and waves at her.

A wave—a commonplace, casual wave! No one waves at strangers anymore. Bettina struggles to her feet. Leaning heavily on her ankle, she winces. As the man rises and begins walking toward her, she attempts to back up. His uniform is stained in oily patches and torn at the seams, and around the sleeve of his jacket is a grubby white armband.

"Please, I don't . . . ," she stammers, backing away from him. "Please don't hurt me . . ."

The man stops. His face is fine boned and narrow, patchy with dirt and stubble, his eyes weary. He crouches down to pat the dog, and there is quiet for a time. The islanders have become so furtive, talking rapidly in hushed tones, eyes wide and mistrusting, yet this man seems different. When he looks up at her, it is with the look of an ordinary person, unafraid, unhurried. As he moves his hand over the small animal's back, his shoulders are relaxed. An unaccustomed stillness settles over Bettina. Under these circumstances, in the early morning, on a litter-strewed beach at the end of a brutal war, she finds this discomfiting yet also exhilarating.

"I . . . uh . . . I was just going for a walk," she says, and the man laughs, such a startling sound. But it is good natured, and as he rises, he lifts his rough workman's hands into the air in a gesture of surrender. In one hand he's holding a tattered notebook and pencil.

"A walk, at this early hour? Never mind—let's take a look here." He is close now and carries with him a penetrating musty odor, as though his clothes have never fully dried. His blond hair is darkened with grease. He sticks the notebook into his breast pocket. "The leg, can you put weight on it?"

She glances down at her bare feet, covered in sand, and shifts her weight onto the foot. It hurts, but not as much as before. Nodding at him, she begins to back away again.

"Good, that's good. You know," the man says, hands on hips, narrowing his eyes, "there will come a day again when we can greet strangers without fear. When children will run on the beaches, and there will be laughter, and we will laugh along with them. It will happen. We must believe this."

She scowls. What gives certain people this confidence in the face of all that's already happened? "We must *believe*? Believe what?"

"Come, come," he says. There's something so impish about his smile—a kind of uninhibited joy—that she finds the muscles in her jaw beginning to relax, and her lips draw into a hesitant smile in return. "Just look at the beauty everywhere." High above them a white-tailed eagle soars on the thermals, the fringes of its shadowed wings elegantly splayed. They track its path; then their eyes settle on each other again.

"Well. I expect the children will forget all about the war, won't they?" Bettina acquiesces.

"Aha—so I win!"

"We're competing, are we?" she shoots back. She points the camera at him and clicks the shutter a few times, then laughs aloud into the brightening sky. "Sorry. I haven't had film in years. I really miss it."

Bettina limps toward her bicycle, and the man heads back to the pine grove. The dog trots alongside her. He seems quite content, and when she hitches up her skirt and lifts herself onto the seat, he regards her levelly, as though to say, *Oh well; next time, perhaps.* Far away on the beach, the soldier in green is just a speck among the pine needles, but a small white object moves back and forth rapidly in front of his body. He is waving again.

As she cycles back toward home, she wonders where the man will go. Does he live here, or is he passing through, on his way somewhere else? She wonders what he writes into his little notebook. It was impossible to tell how old he is, but she herself feels very old, like a woman who has already lived many lives. He could have been as young as seventeen or as old as thirty. He was filthy and emaciated; should she have invited him back to the house and given him some of her food? It would have been the right thing to do, but she promised her father she would be cautious, that she would try to stay safe.

The butcher Johann is an old family friend, and after both her parents died, he started dropping by occasionally to check on her. He gave her a treat for her birthday, and later that afternoon Bettina takes it out of the icebox and places it on the counter. Half a goose breast with some spiced fat preserved in a little glass jar. Her mouth waters just looking at it. Placing some of the fat in a pan, she sears the meat, sniffing frequently to prolong the pleasure. She brings out her grandmother's plate with the picture of a stag painted on the front and a crystal wineglass and sets a spot for herself at the dining room table. She chews the meat slowly, the richness of the flavor like molasses. There is only water in her glass, but she pretends it is wine. As she eats, she thinks about humankind's mysterious compulsions. Why is it that people insist on treating each other so cruelly? Why do men behave with such pride and violence and fear?

After clearing up, she unrolls some brown packing paper used for wrapping fish and brings out a few bits of charcoal. For hours she sits on a stool in the kitchen, almost motionless but for her left hand moving back and forth over the paper, drawing. Mostly she draws faces from memory, working especially hard on getting the eyes and brows just right. Today she is copying an old sepia photograph of Dieter dressed in his Wehrmacht uniform. The rejuvenated fire keeps her warm for many hours, and she does not head up to bed until very late.

In the coming years she thinks of that day often, the last birthday she spent alone. The radio with its portents of what was about to come. The beach, littered with debris, wind whipped. The food she savored but did not share. The unexpected laughter and the pictures she did not take.

3

Chicago
Summer 1965

The overhead lights dazzled her. It was like staring into the sun or being examined by an eye doctor—all sense of depth snuffed out. Looking out over the crowd, which was growing steadily by the minute, Bettina could make out a few splashes of color but no familiar faces, not one. She stood on the platform, holding a microphone unsteadily. A headache insinuated itself up the back of her skull toward her temples.

Who *were* all these people?

George, her boss, gently took the microphone from her and tapped on it. "Hello? Hello, everyone! Quiet, please—quiet." His tone, its deep bass rumble, was an anchor. The swell of voices began to falter, and when he spoke again, a hush fell over the room. "Welcome to the Parkington Gallery," he said, flashing a big American smile. Even after all this time, that was how Bettina still thought of those smiles: *American.* In no other part of the world could people instantly turn on that kind of warmth.

Standing at well over six feet tall, George was an enormous man in every way: oversize facial features, a rounded stomach, his laugh a bellow. He had a way of commanding attention, something about the way he spoke, his calculated hesitations, and he was tough as nails, relentless in his pursuit of breaking news stories. He'd once admitted to her that as a black man, he had to work twice as hard to be heard, and she had smiled in recognition; this was something she understood. They both knew what it meant to be an outsider, to be perceived as a threat.

"We are here to celebrate this remarkable woman, Bettina Heilstrom, and her art, so compelling and timely," he said. "Art that provokes and asks questions rather than providing answers. Art that takes everything in, and everyone—wherever you come from, whatever you believe, your class, your work, your soul—Bettina Heilstrom can pick up on your essence with her camera."

A wild surge of applause fell on her like hail. Could such praise be sincere? It was hard for her to tell these things.

George gesticulated as he spoke, revealing big, leathery palms. "Over a decade ago, Bettina arrived in Chicago with nothing more than a suitcase and a camera. She came to work at the *Tribune*, cleaning the floors and dusting desks—and look where she is now. But listen: I'll let her speak for herself. Please give a warm welcome to Bettina Heilstrom, winner of the Smithsonian photography prize in the category 'The American Experience'!"

Later she would not be able to remember if she'd actually said one word of what she'd written down on the scrap of paper that was wilting in her damp fingers. Time slowed as people waited to hear what she would say. They were so patient, so generous, and this helped her relax.

She forced herself to smile broadly, without hiding her teeth. "*Guten Abend—Willkommen*," she said, addressing in this way the fact that, as a German, she was so obviously on the wrong side of history. "Thank you for having me, and thank you all for coming. You have welcomed me with a generosity of spirit I could never have imagined back when I worked in a factory on an island in the Baltic Sea."

She kept that part of her story simple. That was not what these people were here for; it did not interest them. That part of history—what had happened *after* Hitler, after the war had finally ended—seemed irrelevant to them. Clearing her throat, she tried to concentrate on what she thought they wanted to hear. How, on a cool afternoon about a year after arriving in Chicago, she had ventured out alone and had absentmindedly grabbed her Rolleiflex for company. The old camera she'd ignored for so long. The camera that, in a way, ended up saving her life.

Here she raised the camera itself in the air, holding it out under the glaring lights, the weight of it like a boulder in her palm. It had a leather strap with twelve beads laced onto it. Every corner, every dial and lever and minuscule bolt of this camera, was familiar to her. It was a bulky piece of machinery, quite outdated, beautiful with its twin lenses and engraved metal plate secured into place on the front. Box shaped, awkward to hold or sling around your body, it allowed you to flip up a viewer on the top so that you didn't have to place it in front of your face but could look your subject in the eye while shooting. A lever on one side wound the film forward, and a dial on the other focused the bottom lens. This camera had been dropped, it had been rained on, flung aside, and once it had even withstood falling on the sand. The whole thing had practically been taken apart and put together again, and yet it had somehow managed to survive it all.

"The camera is a friend," Bettina was saying to the crowd. "A reliable friend at all times. It allows you to be in dialogue, to observe, yes, but also to communicate."

That Sunday years ago, she had gone up to the Calumet River around Ninety-Sixth, drawn to explore the steel mills, blast furnaces, railway tracks, utility poles, and bridges. The industrial landscape was both familiar to her and alien, the tangle of electrical wires crisscrossing the sky like vast spiderwebs. At home on the island in the years after the fighting was over, factories had sprung up like mushrooms, and yet Rügen was beautiful in a way this city was not. There she'd had the churning Baltic Sea, the herring gulls that carved elegant paths across clear skies. The smell of salt and shifting colors. In Chicago people were overwhelmed by glass, steel, grime, faded industry.

Bettina did not say so now, but that day walking along the neglected riverbanks had been as close as she'd ever come to thinking that life was no longer worth living.

For hours she had assumed she was the only person on site, and she'd wandered around, alone but not entirely alone. Always, always an insistent, familiar voice whispering in her ear, encouraging her to look closely. To absorb and engage, to never succumb to the too-easy idea of giving up. She'd caught sight of a woman and a child standing in front of an abandoned shoe factory. The woman's pale features, the child's chapped cheeks, took her by surprise: The color among the gray tones. The . . . what was it? Softness of their skin. Their two faces contained a thousand conflicting stories.

What were they doing in this godforsaken place? Where had they come from? Were they mother and daughter? The child, a girl of about eight or nine, looked at Bettina with an intense curiosity that seemed at once arrogant and vulnerable. She was gaunt, rangy. Without thinking, Bettina had clicked open the Rolleiflex and captured what she saw: the contrast of shapes, the inanimate buildings behind the warmth of these ravaged faces. All the while, the three of them looked at one another, silent.

That day taught Bettina that she could be both invisible and seen, and this contradiction would allow her to make it through that day and each day after. It helped her learn about her new world and achieve a more intimate knowledge of its people. It had, eventually, led to this prize, this celebration. She had learned that she had not only the will to live but also the desire to achieve.

"Sometimes a moment can do this," she summed up, looking over the bleached-out faces. "Sometimes things can change in an instant because you decide to take a certain action. When we do not act, we die inside." She did not mention that she had given the mother and child the last of her money, almost fourteen dollars. That she'd decided that very day to begin carrying the camera with her everywhere she went—and that shortly thereafter, she'd picked up two colorful beads and strung them onto its strap, buying a new one every year after that on the occasion of her daughter's birthday. Deciding to open her eyes again, to allow herself to remember and imagine.

Last week after her prize was announced, the *Tribune* ran an editorial calling her work "a postmodern look at the dehumanizing nature of industry and the individual's struggle to emerge from the shadowy masses. Bettina Heilstrom skewers universalist notions of morality and human nature to reveal that we are, at our core, complex and vulnerable, brave and fearful, constrained and yet also seen." She hadn't fully understood what the words meant; when she snapped her photos, all she was conscious of was that her eye was drawn to contrasts. In the development process, Bettina worked on heightening the focus on her subject's features—the droop of the eyelid, the yank of skin at the corner of a mouth—while leaving the background slightly unclear. But what it all really meant, she wasn't entirely sure.

Standing in front of these strangers, she would have liked to talk about the irony of an immigrant like her being awarded a prize for portraying "the American experience," but she scrambled to find the right words when talking about such personal things. George had nominated her work without her knowledge, and when he told her that she'd actually won the award, she'd thought he was playing a prank. Even though her heart plummeted and her mouth went dry, she had smiled at him to let him know she had no hard feelings. That she understood he was just having some fun. He'd had to take both her hands in his and beg her to believe him. It still didn't seem real.

When she'd first set foot in this country, she had known nothing about the life she was thrust into. The vast plains of the ice-clad Midwest, the chubby-legged children, the cars with their extraordinary fins, so sharp and fluted they reminded her of the Baltic sturgeon. But that day, taking the picture of that little girl, she had warmed to the idea that it might be possible to find some sort of happiness here, so far from the people she loved and pined for, the people who suffered, even now.

Bettina meandered around the gallery, champagne flute in hand. She wore new heels that pinched and a black silk shirt she'd bought that morning at Wieboldt's on Grand and Ashland. Her slacks were undistinguished except that George's wife had once complimented her on them. Bettina didn't have much of an eye for fashion. She was thirty-nine years old, and her long hair, the color of wet earth, hung loosely around her face. The champagne tickled pleasantly at her throat. George caught her eye from across the room and raised his graying eyebrows, checking to see if she was all right. He knew that all this attention was hard for her. Bettina should have told her sister, Clara, about the event, but it honestly hadn't occurred to her that it would be such a big celebration. She'd expected a handful of colleagues, a few amateur photographers perhaps.

One after another the visitors touched her arm with soft fingers and leaned in to say how they admired her work, how much it moved them. Someone finally dimmed the overheads, and after she downed a few glasses of bubbly in quick succession, it seemed as though the faces tilted in her direction were emanating a kind of warmth, and it drew her out of herself. Bettina began to smile in a more natural way. There was music playing in the background, something modern with sitars. Everywhere now there were bright shots of color, not only in people's clothing but in their skin tones: faces all shades of white and brown and everything in between. Hair that curled and kinked and flowed in disheveled waves (on men, too—this was acceptable now). There was a woman with long white hair, her body draped in a caftan. Some of the men wore suits with pencil-thin pant legs, and a sprinkling of women were in jewel-toned cocktail dresses, cinched tight at the waist as had been the style just a few years earlier, though this already seemed outdated.

All these people, young and old, had come here to celebrate her! Bettina allowed herself the faintest prickle of pride.

"Ms. Heilstrom," said one of the men. Dark hair sprang from his jawline. "I'm from *National Geographic*. I wonder, will you be focusing exclusively on this country? Do you plan to travel and document change in other places too?"

"I don't have any plans yet," Bettina said. She didn't mention that George was putting ideas in her head, insisting that her work could make a real difference. That she had a voice now, and she had a responsibility to use it. He was pushing her to think about taking a position at *Time* magazine, but she was not accustomed to being hopeful—it made her vulnerable to disappointment. And there was a nugget of coal inside her, something toxic and vile that reminded her she did not deserve happiness or success.

"I like to take it one day at a time," she added, and this was true.

A young woman with orange feathers hanging from her earlobes asked about one of the larger prints: an old photograph from Rügen that was, actually, the invisible backbone of the exhibition. Without it, none of the other pictures would exist—and yet she had *almost* not taken that roll of film with her when she left, and the composition had almost been relegated to nothing more than an idea. Black and white, a cluster of people at the base of a stark chalk cliff face; a distorted perspective that presented the cliff as a thing of terrible beauty and the people as helpless as insects. But it was too hard to explain her work. This one—it was a picture she both treasured and despised, yet she recognized it as connected to everything she was doing now. She shrugged and clinked her glass with the girl's. "For me, it's about the shapes, I suppose. For the viewer, it may have several meanings."

If she didn't eat something soon, she would keel over. On her way to the buffet table, she recognized a number of her colleagues from the paper: Demetrius and Sarah, standing with John, the photo editor who'd allowed her to use the *Tribune*'s darkroom during the graveyard shift many years ago. There was a man in an ill-fitting olive suit behind a cluster of people at the bar area who caught her eye, but she didn't think much of it until he began moving toward her, and she realized that he was missing his right arm.

Her glass slipped from her fingers and fell to the ground, but it didn't break. There was some commotion as people fetched napkins and one overeager woman mopped at Bettina's trousers with the hem of her skirt. Bettina did not take her eyes off the man as he made his way through the crowd toward her. The sleeve of his suit was folded in half, and the excess material was neatly tucked under his armpit and pinned into place. In this country you rarely saw people with missing limbs. In her country you saw this all the time.

She stared at the missing arm and then shifted her eyes back to the man's face. It couldn't be, but it was. Herbert Lange.

"Bettina, *mein Gott* . . . I had to see if it was really you," he said to her in German. Though he did not smile, his eyes were friendly, small and surrounded by feathered creases. His mouth, slightly down-turned, gave him the look of a man about to tell a bad joke. "I don't know how many Bettina Heilstroms there could possibly be, and yet, incredible . . ."

Her breath was caught in her chest; she was unable to utter a word.

"You look well. Very well. I see you've built yourself a new life," Herbert said. "This makes me extremely happy. You deserve it."

"You're in touch with Clara?" Bettina managed to ask. "She knows about tonight?"

He shook his head. Over the years her brother-in-law had aged considerably. His flaxen hair was thin on top, but he retained that mischievous air he'd had when he was younger. Her hand flew to her face, and she wondered how changed she appeared in his eyes. Herbert and her sister had fled Germany for Chicago just one year before Bettina arrived; for the first awkward months she'd been here, she'd lived with them in their one-bedroom apartment. She hated thinking back to that time: Her fragility and neediness, the absolute shock and desperation of it. The guilt as bitter as thistle.

Her sister's marriage to Herbert had already been disintegrating back then, though Bettina hadn't known it. Until tonight, she hadn't seen him since he'd moved away with Clara over a decade ago, this time to Milwaukee, in a last-ditch effort to reignite something that had already been thoroughly doused. Soon after that, they'd divorced.

"We're not—we don't stay in touch. I didn't want it to fall apart, the marriage," he said. "It was never my intention to divorce, but you know your sister. She had other ideas."

Clara was now remarried to a man named Borvin Kuznetsov, who ran a catering business. The irony of this never ceased to amaze Bettina: Clara had left East Germany to escape the Russians, and then she'd married one.

"I'm sorry, Herbert. I'm so surprised—I don't even know where to start," Bettina said.

John, the photo editor, materialized at her side. His wavy hair hung to his shoulders, and an odor, something smoky, came from him. "Congratulations!" he said, clutching her hand. "You don't have a drink. Can I get you one? Having a good time, are you?"

Herbert stared at the man, a look of incomprehension on his face.

"John, this is, uh, my . . ." Bettina tried to find the right words. "My past brother-in-law, Herbert Lange. He is—that is, we haven't seen each other in a very, very long time."

"Greetings," John said. His eyes went straight to the missing arm, and he cocked his head. "Germany?"

"Russland," Herbert answered.

"This lady," John said, leaning toward him, "I'm warning you; she is one chill dame. An eye like a hawk. Real talent."

Herbert watched him walk off. When he turned back to Bettina, he raised his brows, revealing slivers of blue iris. "Where can we talk? I was in Berlin recently, and I have some news I think you'll want to hear."

"You mean Rügen? You were in Rügen?" Bettina's heart lurched and then fell. "Is it about Annaliese?"

"I'm afraid I know nothing about the child," Herbert said. "It's about Werner. Shall we find a bit of privacy, yes?"

4

It would be another hour before Bettina was able to leave the gallery with Herbert Lange. The music kept playing in the background, an up-tempo jazz melody suggesting in its own chaotic way that everything was cool, under control, when in fact it clearly wasn't. Its deep bass a constant thrum behind the cheery voices fueled by cocktails and art talk. She tried her best to be charming and to answer people's questions. Knowing that Herbert was waiting for her—that something was wrong—made her fumble her words and flush with confusion. More than once she gave someone a blank look instead of an answer, and she could just imagine the headline for the snippet in the Arts section of the *Tribune*: *Smithsonian Winner Snubs Fans*. Sweaty palms slipped against her skin, too warm, too close. Smiles full of teeth and braying praise. She was grateful; she really was. But the noise and the lights . . . and Herbert, waiting for her.

Finally around eleven the music died down, and George and his wife came over to say their goodbyes. "Soon you'll be leaving us for sunnier climes," he said, one big paw reaching out to help his wife, May, with her jacket. "At least professionally speaking."

"I haven't decided anything," Bettina said.

"George told me he thought you'd do great at the *Post* or the *New York Times*," May said. Her mulberry lipstick had smeared a bit, her black hair working itself loose to create a hazy halo around her face. "You're not stuck in Chi-Town forever, are you?" May was from Barbados, and the few times the two women had met, she always found a way to hint at her yearning for the warmth of the islands.

"Ach, it's really not so bad here," Bettina said. The idea of taking a permanent job with a bigger organization—of moving, perhaps, and being on staff—was tantalizing but impossible. In some strange way it seemed critical that she keep her life temporary, that she not commit her passion to anyone or anything. What would it mean if she accepted that this country was truly, incontrovertibly *home* now—that she could choose to climb the ladder of American enterprise, was willing to cast aside her otherness? It would mean she had given up on Anna.

She cast her eyes around her to see where Herbert had wandered off to. "In truth," she said to May, "I'm not very political. I think George has more ambition for me than I do."

"Bull. Life is politics. Culture is life. Every time you click that shutter, you're already deep into a discussion," George said. He handed her a tote bag, white tissue paper peeking out the top. "There's a little something inside here for you. It was delivered to the *Tribune* offices. Open it when you get home, okay?"

It took some time to say her goodbyes, and then she grabbed Herbert by his good arm and nodded at the bartender. "I'm ready," she said. "Please, let's go."

The gallery was on the south side of Chicago, in the Hyde Park neighborhood. She and Herbert stood outside on the pavement as a young man in a jean jacket pulled the iron grille over the windows of a small grocery store next door.

"Bettina, Bettina," Herbert said. "Always so serious. Remember when you used to like to have fun?"

His eyes had a glazed look to them, and when he lit his cigarette—a trick he managed to pull off with only one hand, and quickly, too—his entire body leaned forward from the knees up, and it looked as though he might tip forward. He seemed out of place in these grimy streets, the city air washing him in a kind of gray scrim. In this context he seemed like a stranger, and she found herself wanting to touch his shoulder or his hand to convince herself it was really her brother-in-law. She didn't even know where he lived anymore, let alone what he was doing in Chicago. The immensity of all she didn't know weighed on her, not an absence but a crushing burden. She wanted to sit down for this conversation.

"All right, listen," she said. "I'd better take you to my place. You need to sober up."

"Aha," he said, raising his brows suggestively.

"Herbert. I hope you're just having some fun at my expense."

"Of course, of course," he answered. "Take me home and feed me something, and we'll talk."

Under his suit jacket, Herbert wore a wrinkled blue shirt that made his skin look very pale. Even when he was younger, he'd never been conventionally handsome, but as he tried to chat in the kitchen of her apartment while she fried up some sausages, his face became increasingly animated, and she recognized in him the young man she'd known before the war. He was living back in Germany, but in the West, he explained, working as a plumbing-fixture salesman for a company in Hannover that exported gaskets to America. They had just started sending him to visit the major showrooms in the States, and Chicago was only his second stop. He held up a small, battered dictionary he extracted from his jacket pocket: he was trying to learn some English.

She served him the sausages on the old stag plate from her grandmother. All these years she had treasured this plate, and now it was once again serving a member of her family. Or at least someone who had once been part of her family. It was wonderful to feel German words in her mouth again. Often she spent whole weeks feeling as though she hardly knew who or where she was, still surprised after all these years by the intensity of her disorientation. It was only when she picked up one of the German magazines she occasionally bought, or every now and then when she talked to Clara on the phone, that a temporary calm settled into her bones.

But something was holding them back as they tried to make conversation. They had parted rather badly, and now, as much as she wanted to hear his news from Germany, the prospect of knowing actual details of the life she'd left behind was frightening. It had been such hard work to push away her homesickness, to stop thinking about her child. Work had helped, eventually. George had helped—more than he even knew. And now here was Herbert, with his secrets, his news.

The kitchenette was in a corner of the living room, demarcated by a short Formica counter and two peeling laminate cabinets. When Bettina found the place, she'd expected to stay just a few months but ended up staying more than ten years. Having Herbert sit with her where she took her daily meals made her see the room through his eyes: it was shabby and cramped. But as different as it was from her fisherman's cottage on Apolonienmarkt, this studio was the only place she could really be herself. Eventually she'd painted the walls a pale yellow (like the curtains in her old bedroom). There were pots of dracaena and cascading ivy, as well as a fiddle-leaf fig by the window that was over five feet tall. The windowsills were lined with cacti in bright ceramic containers. There was a rubber fig, graying but healthy enough, and a luscious jade plant that was supposed to bring good luck. She needed the greenery in order to survive bitter winters, the winds that howled for months on end, rattling her windowpanes. On the walls hung dozens of her photographs (unframed, tacked up with strips of tape) and a map of the United States. In the opposite corner was a large bamboo screen that she used to cordon off her single bed. The windows faced an alleyway and led to a small fire escape where, in the summertime, she'd sit on a cushion wrapped in the aroma of rosemary and basil from her flowerpots and the occasional waft of exhaust or cigarettes from the streets below.

When he was done eating, Herbert attempted to place his fork on the plate, but his aim was not accurate, and his movements seemed overly deliberate. "I was very impressed tonight, Bettina." He took a deep sip from his beer. "This career. The accolades. I've thought about you often over the years."

"Well. Thank you," she said. She took the greasy plate from him and placed it in the sink, overtaken now by an exhaustion that rolled over her like a wave.

"You know you are beautiful, Bettina, yes? I don't know why you waste your life here, living alone in this city. Don't you want anything for yourself?"

"I *like* being alone. And I have my work." She thought about the daughter she'd left behind. She had never chosen to be alone—in fact, just the opposite.

He wiped his hand over his forehead. "I don't know. Sometimes being alone is just another way of running away from yourself."

It seemed very stuffy in the room, the air in her nose and lungs too heavy and warm. She went over to the window to crack it a little. As she leaned down, she felt a presence behind her, and when she turned around, Herbert was standing with his face just inches from hers.

"You know," he said, "you haven't changed at all."

"Herbert," she said. "What are you doing?"

But she couldn't move. His beery breath on her skin, the pulse that came from having a human body so very close to hers, was transfixing. He put his hand on the round of her shoulder, and instead of flinching she yearned to lean against him, let his body support her. It had nothing to do with Herbert and everything to do with the shocking jolt of a man's touch, the familiar yet distant thrill of allowing her body to lead instead of her mind. Through the black silk of her shirt, his fingers felt heavy and slippery, and she shuddered. She understood love—she had

had it in her grasp once—and she wanted it *back*. If she only could yield a bit, soften, it might be possible again. But not with this man.

She pulled away and placed a hand on his chest. "No," she said. "No, this cannot happen, whether you're married to my sister or not." Scooting around him, she pulled out a blanket from behind the couch. "You will sleep here. You drank too much."

"Come, Betty, please—don't you feel anything?" He swayed slightly, his eyes reddened. He was a man unmoored; like her, he was looking for someone who could understand him.

"I'm sorry, I—it's just . . . you're like a brother," she said more kindly, though this wasn't entirely true. Her stomach turned over. It seemed impossible that after all the searching and calling and letter writing she'd done over the last decade, this man had actual news for her from her home. She'd been so desperate for information, and now—now she was afraid. "You can stay if you need to, but first tell me your news, for God's sake. What's happened?"

Herbert coughed into his closed fist a few times. "My mother, she's still up in Gummanz," he said. "She toes the party line, loves the five-year plans, all that . . . that socialist nonsense. The fortifications of the wall, Leonov's spacewalks, the rabid, endless competition with the West . . ." He waved his hand in front of his face as though to swat away the whole sorry business. "We spoke some weeks ago, and she told me about a friend of hers in Berlin, someone who works with Werner Nietz."

"Werner?" Bettina asked, the pulse of her heart echoing in her throat. "Werner works in Berlin?"

"Doesn't he at least tell you about the girl? You have a right to know about your own daughter, don't you?"

"That's not the way he is," she said. "I—I haven't been able to get news. And I suppose I . . . well, eventually I sort of gave up trying."

"I see, all right. So yes, he's in Berlin. He works there now." Herbert's eyes were small and swollen from the alcohol, and he seemed reluctant to talk all of a sudden.

"Herbert, please. Just say it."

"He's sick, Werner is. Cancer, my mother says, or some kind of horrible illness. I'm sorry."

Bettina gazed out into the darkness. She couldn't be certain what she was feeling; of all the things she had obsessed over, she had never considered that Werner might die and leave her daughter an orphan. "He's in the hospital? In Berlin? But where is Annaliese? She's not on Rügen anymore?"

"I'm sorry; I don't know. I—Betty? Listen, you are all right?"

A tinge of panic, but also of possibility—of *hope*—began tugging at her. She was frozen, sick to her stomach. She was going to have to do something, but she had no idea what.

5

Rügen
Spring 1945

Each day when Werner Nietz arrives at his office in Saargen Town Hall, he completes the same simple ritual. In his pocket he carries two fresh handkerchiefs. He takes one out and swipes the surface of his desk, removing specks of dust that have settled on its gleaming surface overnight. He does the same to the smaller desk, which holds a typewriter, an adding machine, and a wooden tray. Each light (there are four, including the standing lamp near the filing cabinets) is switched on, regardless of the amount of light that is coming through the large window. Before he settles down, he makes himself a cup of tisane using the electric kettle his mother gave him when he was first given this job at the age of eighteen. He'd prefer coffee, but that's impossible to come by these days.

As an accountant he is tasked with numerous responsibilities. Assessing extra taxes, for example, meting out rations, or—in recent years—typing letters about death benefits (or lack thereof) to the bereaved in the nearby villages. Werner is good at this work. He understands that his role is not one of substantial power, that it is, in fact, one of relative weakness. He carries out orders; he does not give them. In his twelve years as a civil servant, he has been promoted only once, yet he wields a certain power: surrounded mostly by elderly or crippled men and a handful of women, he is able to roam largely unchecked in the marble corridors of the town hall. Werner thus operates with a certain lack of constraint and has access to all sorts of information. Lists of inhabitants, their wealth, and their holdings. Letters of complaint to the town hall. Sometimes letters of commendation. Requests for repairs, for divorces, or for visitation rights. On occasion he is privy to information that he may not—and does not—divulge to anyone. It is a privilege to have a window into people's lives, to know so much more about them than they would ever suspect. The secrets he holds are jewels he cradles in the safety of a warm palm.

Werner swipes a paper off the telegram machine and reads it through. *No German town shall be declared open! Every village and town shall be defended and held by every possible man. Every German who contravenes his obvious civic duty will forfeit his honor and his life.*

My God, he thinks, *so it is finally happening.* The Nazi Party district leaders have been organizing squads of civilians on every block, an army of men—and even women, he's heard—and now it seems the time has come for a final resistance. No one is admitting it yet, but Werner knows this means the war is over. Their island, Rügen, lies right underneath Denmark and Sweden, straight across the lower Baltic Sea; once it was Danish, then Swedish—it was even French for a few years—and finally, for 130 years, it's been part of Germany. Now they are all terrified it will fall to the Russians. Everyone on the island is tight lipped, stunned by privation and fear. What they hear from Goebbels is not what they're hearing on the ground. When France was liberated the previous year, Werner added to his stockpile of canned food (which he hides in the cellar of his small apartment block) and acquired a gun— albeit an old one from the first war, but he's made sure it functions. He'll be damned if he's going to let the Bolsheviks string him up just for being a German citizen.

The telegram is a directive from Berlin, sent to all major cities that have not yet been overrun by the Allies. This ragtag people's army, the so-called Volkssturm, is being ordered to blow up the two-kilometer-long bridge between their island, Rügen, and the Hanseatic city of Stralsund that lies on the mainland. Any man "still breathing" has been ordered to give his life in this eleventh-hour effort to keep the Russians at bay.

Bringing the paper over to his desk, he is aware again of the dull pain in his hip, the ever-constant ache he has known since he was ten years old. The doctors told him he would need to use a cane for the rest of his life, but even as a child, and a rather timid one at that, he scoffed at the idea. It is bad enough that he moves like a machine with ill-fitting parts, like some poorly oiled hunk of metal, but to add a cane to the mix—absolutely not. He does not wish to draw even more attention to himself, and yet at all times, in almost all situations, eyes are busy tracking him—curious eyes seeking to unclothe him in order to stare at his body, twisted with poliomyelitis. Even now as an adult, well presented in a suit and hat (always conducting himself with intelligence and honor), people tend to be dismissive. They see the limp, the shortened leg. It takes an age for them to look up into his face, to actually hear what he is saying.

Rubbing at his thigh muscles with his thumbs, he digs deeply into the tissue. The pain no longer bothers him, but the memories it brings up do. The boys who poked him with sticks in the playground when he failed to rise quickly enough. The little girl who shrieked as he disrobed to swim in the ocean. And of course those blasted Wehrmacht soldiers at the ceremony in Saargen. He wonders what the new world order will mean for him, but he pushes that thought aside. A certain delirious fear, something that is probably not unlike courage, percolates through him at the thought of finally, *finally* doing something useful.

He thinks, then, of the young woman from the fish shop, Bettina Heilstrom. How he discovered deep inside himself the fierceness to act when she was in danger. In that instant he surprised himself, and her too. Werner cannot forget the sensation of pushing that blade through the soldier's skin and deep into his flesh; it entered the boy's body so very easily. What heresy, and yet war pushes men to do what they must, no? The triumphant surge Werner felt when the soldier slumped over electrified him, and that feeling lingers even now. It reminds him that he is, in fact, a man, someone with abilities and needs, a man who can make a good life for himself with the right woman at his side.

Each time he'd entered the Heilstroms' fish shop, he had not allowed himself to look at her for long; she was far too young. Not someone for him. But who *is* for him?

The shop has been closed for two years now, and for a while he lost sight of the girl, though she crops up in his thoughts every so often when he lies alone at night: the lush brown nest of her hair; that shocking moment of recognition they'd shared when she touched his cheek. Then, about a year ago, he read in the paper that her father had died. After that he could not stop wondering about her. He remembered that her family lived on the old square, Apolonienmarkt, and one day he stopped by to pay his condolences.

He's now been to her fisherman's cottage a number of times. At first he arrived empty handed, twiddling his hat in his hands, but he's taken to scouring the shops for some offering with which to indulge her. Truthfully, this takes time, and he often struggles to determine if his finds are appropriate. It's become a bit of a scavenger hunt: one week an embroidered handkerchief, the next a small bottle of schnapps. They are lucky to live on an island with animals and gardens (unlike in Berlin, where people are said to be starving); last time he visited her, he took some beets from the communal plot down the road and a bottle of homemade beer. Her face lit up, and she invited him to stay and enjoy them with her.

This girl, she emits an energy that is palpable; it changes the cadence of his breath. Perhaps it is her youth. It is possible that she is only twenty or twenty-one years old; he can't be certain. But those years do not mean so much when you have been through what they experienced together. She could be a dancer, the way she moves with such purpose and grace. A long neck, pale and smooth. Her limbs, covered in fine hairs. He thinks he can see from her demeanor that she appreciates his presence. Perhaps even that she admires him a bit. She may be young and timid, but he sees a spark of empathy in her, and he believes she could grow to love him. It might be time to make his intentions clear.

The very thought of doing this makes him begin to sweat, and he realizes that he will have to head back to his small apartment after work to change his undershirt before he makes any moves at all.

The Kübelwagen, a Wehrmacht jeep, clatters over the cobblestones, passing through the old market square three times. A loudspeaker rigged on its roof with twine is held in place by a mangy-looking boy. Each time the jeep enters the square, the same proclamation rings out from the vehicle while a gaggle of children run behind, throwing small rocks and twigs at the tires.

"*Achtung, alle Männer!*" the speaker announces, calling all the neighborhood men. "Convene at your local town hall, tomorrow, eight a.m. sharp. Calling *all men*, injured and whole of body, ages twelve and up. Bring identification papers and work boots. Those with injuries, bring signed documentation from your physician." Then there is a pause before the incantation resumes.

Werner is in the living room of Bettina's house, surveying the scene outside. The room is rather spacious, shaded by a jagged thatch that overhangs the windows. An extraordinary number of books line a set of shelves on one wall. Above the hearth, which seems to be inactive, hangs a portrait of a man with a handlebar mustache and a high forehead—her grandfather, perhaps? In his pocket Werner carries his mother Lotte's battered wedding ring.

"Oh dear. What's that racket outside?" Bettina asks, putting down a tray with cups and saucers and a pot of *Ersatzkaffee* on the table between them. Her dark hair is pinned back in a bun, and she wears a plain dress with a spotless apron tied around her waist.

"Do not concern yourself," Werner says. "It will be all right."

"But . . ." She peers out the window, leaning with both hands on the sill. "It's the end, is it? Is that what they're saying?" When she looks over her shoulder at him, her eyes are wide. They are dark, an intense brown that borders on black. Though her face has strong features, she carries a softness on her bones that some women don't grow out of until they're fully adult.

"Not quite yet," he says, fiddling with the ring. "We will make one last push against the Soviets. There were orders from Berlin—the town hall was buzzing about it all day."

"Will you fight too?"

Is that a look of concern on her face? The idea that she might be worrying about his safety gives him courage. "Bettina, dear," he starts, but his tone is patronizing, and that is not at all what he is aiming for. He clears his throat. "This is the end of one phase of our lives and the beginning of another. This . . . after this, nothing will be the same again, whatever happens. I think, don't you—that people are better off together than alone?"

He fumbles in his pocket, bringing out the gold band. "This belonged to my mother, and I would like you to have it," he says, holding it out toward her. "May I dare to presume that you do not find my company distasteful? Together we would be stronger. Together—we could face whatever may come next."

Her face is blank as she gazes at his hand. Clearly she has been taken by surprise and is struggling to think of a response.

"Your father and I were friends," Werner continues, though this is perhaps overstating things a bit. "I think he would approve."

"Is this a proposal, Herr Nietz?" the girl asks.

He continues to hold the ring out somewhat awkwardly. "Bettina Heilstrom, would you . . . I mean—I promise . . . will you do me the honor?"

"What is it that you promise me, then?"

She is trying to be lighthearted. Or is she being coy? He can't quite tell. He chooses to believe she has the capacity for playfulness, and so he smiles at her. "I promise to be true to my word. I will always—never mind the circumstances, I will do my utmost—"

To stop his stammering, she brings her face close to his and kisses him. And then—he can barely believe it to be true—she parts her lips. Her mouth tastes of nuts, and her skin smells pleasantly of soap, and this sends a shot of adrenaline through his body. He begins to tremble.

He is tired of making decisions on his own, of trusting in a fickle fate. Domesticity, the comfort that comes from family life, will be the driving force that will see them through the coming years. The war is lost, and they will spend many years digging themselves free of the horrors foisted on them by the Nazis. Werner doesn't care for politics, for the NSDAP and all the party now stands for under Hitler. He isn't moved by the rhetoric and bluster of a party bent on dominance and destruction; he believes that strength lies not in politics but in family. It seems possible that he might cobble one together for himself after all, and he knows that it will change his life in ways that he cannot even begin to imagine.

He pulls away from the kiss, grasps Bettina's hand, her bones as slender as reeds, and slips the ring over her finger. And so it is done.

6

Husband and wife are careful with each other; Werner treats Bettina with the kind of gentleness with which you might treat something breakable. Next to her at night, he sleeps peacefully, stretched out with his hands at his sides and the feather duvet pulled up to his shoulders. He does not like to be touched as he sleeps, and this suits Bettina fine. Spontaneous affection is not instinctive for her. Even after five years of marriage, Bettina is perplexed by this man's daily rhythms, his nocturnal sounds, even his odor, which is at times animalistic and repellent but also surprisingly alluring. Many hours go by as she stares at the ceiling in the darkness, unable to fall asleep, trying to imagine faraway places she reads about in the old books her father so loved.

At night, flickering images of the dead fill her mind as though they are trying to keep her company, and even though she does not want them there, they stay. Sleep remains elusive. It is not just the murdered German soldier she sees—his surprised young face—it is *all* the dead, even the enemy, the Russians and the Allies. No amount of reading or dreaming of new worlds can banish the pale, gaunt faces of all those who have been killed. Their blind eyes, slack mouths. The islanders have slogged their way through the postwar years, and yet the war seems to rage on inside her head regardless. The dreams, they simply won't stop. And she'd prayed that by now she and Werner would have children, but it has not happened.

Just a few weeks after Werner's proposal, he and Bettina were married. Her new husband gave up his modest apartment (a widow from Danzig with her three-year-old had immediately moved in), bringing along only two battered leather suitcases with him. He had no family heirlooms, no decent furniture, and only a few framed photographs of his parents, who had died years earlier, but he did request that two crates of accounting texts be brought over from his office. The old volumes sit on the overfilled shelves alongside her copies of Kleist and Goethe, next to her collection of etchings and photography supplies.

For the civil wedding ceremony at the registrar's office, she wore her favorite maroon housedress with the lace collar while Clara and Herbert looked on with bewildered expressions on their thinned-out faces. Neither bride nor groom invited a single friend or acquaintance.

Afterward in the early evening, Bettina and Werner retired to her house to share some elderberry wine and become intimate for the first time. The pain was not so great. At first Bettina found herself thinking of Dieter, the sweet boy who had already been dead for years, turning her into a kind of widow even though she'd never been married. But after just a few minutes with her new husband, she was distracted by the sensations she was experiencing, and she stopped caring whether it was Werner or Dieter who was in the bed with her; she knew only that these feelings rising up inside her were unexpected and overpowering—but fleeting too. She soon discovered that relations with her husband were infrequent and unpredictable. Werner seemed to find pleasure in her body, stroking it eagerly, but his desire was so easily sated that she did not have time to figure out what she herself should be thinking or feeling.

Each night she wonders whether he will touch her again, and while she half wishes to be left alone, part of her wants to reach for him, to try to bind him closer to her—because that is why she married him, to be close to another human being.

The factory where she spends her days is perched at the edge of a cliff, dark against the piercing midday sun. Bettina stands behind it, eyes screwed shut. The inside of her mouth tastes like a dead animal. Once again she's been vomiting, and this time it isn't because she is with child—even though she lost the baby days earlier, the nausea will not go away. A double cruelty.

Breathing slowly through her nose, she forces herself to open her eyes and look out at the vista in front of her. Twenty meters away, at the bottom of the chalk cliff on which the factory sits, the Baltic Sea spreads as far as the eye can see, up to Finland in the far north and to Poland—now also part of the Soviet Union—to the east. It is the one consolation about working here that she can step outside during her breaks and let the natural beauty of the island comfort her. The land is immutable; man might appear to dominate, but the earth resists stealthily, steadily, relentlessly. At the edge of the factory, snowy hawthorn blossoms cascade in unruly clumps. The grass at her feet is crazed with silvery seed heads. Everywhere she looks, life is pulsing.

A van inches its way toward the factory and idles for a moment. An officer jumps out to unlatch the gate, and Bettina tucks herself in closer to the side of the building. A police car follows behind the van. As the men disembark and enter the building, Bettina peers through the smeary window to look inside. At the assembly line, the foreman stands with a bunch of Volkspolizei right where, just a few minutes earlier, she was filleting herring. If only she could hear what the police are saying, but her ears roar with the sound of the waves crashing into the chalk cliffs.

She cups her hands to either side of her eyes to cut the glare. The workers—her friends, colleagues, boss, the new supervisor shipped in from Moscow—merge into one vast, shadowy mass on the factory floor. The assembly lines grind to a halt, and the workers stand at their stations, idle hands dangling at their sides. The Vopo—the local East German police—and a man in an unusual uniform surround a group of women. The foreman, Putzkammer, stands nearby with his hands in his trouser pockets, vast shoulders hunched forward. He will turn a blind eye, no matter what's going on; of that, at the very least, Bettina is certain.

Her coworkers Christa, Anne-Marie, and Stefanie huddle together, stiff white aprons smeared with blood and guts, hairnets askew. In a place where the machinery is always clanking, accompanied by the swift, precise flurry of hundreds of moving hands, everything is bizarrely still. The police hover close to the women. The odd man out wears a green-gray tunic with white piping and silver buttons that flash under the fluorescents like coins flipped into a murky pond. He has on a flat cap with a broad front brim that looks somehow familiar to Bettina, but she can't quite place it.

She senses a sudden shift in mood and presses in closer to the salt-encrusted glass. One moment, stillness; the next, a sort of trembling of the air currents. There is commotion, heads and limbs shifting this way and that in a mad jumble. Putzkammer lunges forward, and collectively the workers raise their hands as if in some sort of supplication.

Christa Kellermann has broken away and is making a run for the sliding door that leads to the cargo area. She is a heavyset woman, and in her bulky plastic boots there is no hope of her escaping. In a flash, an officer grabs her and presses against her, cinching her arms behind her. He swings Christa around and barks something at the foreman.

Bettina's heart speeds up wildly. They have come to get *Christa*?

The two women have been working side by side since the end of the war. Christa is in her late thirties, almost fifteen years older than Bettina, with an extended family of three children and two nephews orphaned during that last desperate push to keep the Soviets out. Her husband is long gone, killed when his tank overturned in Southern Italy in '43. Yet every day when Christa comes to work, her face alternates between grimaces of delight and irritation as she recounts her stories of domestic life. Her unfailing optimism takes the edge off Bettina's tendency to be quiet and withdrawn. Bettina listens to Christa's tales about her children, the endless foraging for food, for ration cards, for shoes, and then, as the years pass, for male companionship. As a newlywed, Bettina listens especially carefully to her colleague's stories of how to run a household, and on the weekends she will sometimes go to Christa's house to learn how to decorate handkerchiefs cut from old bedding. She cannot think of a single thing that her friend might have done to warrant getting arrested.

Bettina runs to the front of the factory and sees the van doors slamming shut.

The vehicle heads through the gates and turns sharp right, down the winding road that leads toward the center of Saargen. Bettina starts running after it, sucking in the billows of dust thrown up by the tires, yelling, hoping she can think of something, anything, that might make a difference. Something that will make them stop.

Finally, the van and the police car disappear from sight. For a long while she stands there, panting. She stares at the hazy spot that marks where the rise of the earth meets the horizon, beyond which the road spills out onto Seestraße. There will be people going to the market in town, picking their children up from the *Kindergarten*, walking home for their lunches. She wonders whether anyone will even notice the van. It seems as though these things have been happening more and more recently: disappearances, midnight summons, tattling neighbors, and petty-minded colleagues. Can this be right? Everyone was so relieved when the war was over, so eager to start anew, but no one had been equipped to look beyond the violence, to imagine how life would actually look under the Russians. All the mundane details of this new order are cumulative, insidious. It sometimes feels to Bettina as though God is taking revenge on the islanders for their entrenched self-sufficiency all those years under fascism.

The foreman, Putzkammer, will be looking for her by now. He'll be barking at everyone to get back to work; the long black conveyor belts will squeal and then clank into action, and she will not be at her position. Her pay will be docked; she must return. As Bettina nears the entrance, she catches one last glimpse of the water. The familiar sight of the sea takes her breath away: It is alive, made up of hundreds of shades of blue, moving and still at the same time. It never looks the same from one moment to the next. Bettina pulls the strings of hair from her face, the sleeve of her dress fluttering wildly. It looks from here as though the entire Baltic Sea is carpeted in dazzling splinters of glass.

7

Bettina waits at the house for Werner to return from the town hall. She paces the kitchen, rearranging the plates on the open shelving, scrubbing the two pans that are already spotless. In the corner by the window stands a miniature bust of Wilhelm Pieck, with his prominent nose and flaccid cheeks. Propped up against it, there's a row of stamps showing the East German leader with Stalin, to celebrate the Month of German-Soviet Friendship. A silly place to put the stamps (she always worries they'll get splashed when she's doing the dishes), but these are things Werner brings home from work, and she doesn't know what to do with them.

Her breathing has not settled down all afternoon. Moments earlier she was retching again above the toilet, her throat parched, the muscles in her shoulders straining with the effort. Eberle, her old orange tabby, winds himself around her ankles as she sits down at the kitchen table. When the click of the front door finally sounds, she stiffens. She is sure Werner can help her figure out what is going on, but she also knows that she has to get this right; he can be testy about these things. She waits until she knows he will have slipped off his light overcoat and hung his black felt hat on the rack. "*Hallo*," he calls out. Footsteps fall on the stairs, laboriously, one foot hitting the treads harder than the other.

Their bedroom is at the front of the house, with a window overlooking the square. It is the room her grandmother occupied as a newlywed, where her mother started her family, and it is where her father died. Now it is

Bettina's domain. The windows are small, as they are in all these fisherman's cottages, but the thatch that hangs over the window creates a jagged shadow that makes her think of mountain ranges. Places she has never been. Werner is standing at the armoire, the back of his shirt dark with sweat. He bends down to remove his shoes and begins stripping off his clothes. One leg is slightly shorter than the other, and he has to twist his torso awkwardly to keep his balance. Looking at him, Bettina struggles to reconcile her fear about what happened at the factory earlier with the habitual tenderness she feels when she sees her husband unclothed. They make some small talk.

"The police were at the factory today," she says finally. "The Vopo."

"Yes?" He rises, slipping on his house shoes.

"They took Christa."

His pale eyes are weary. From the very beginning of their courtship, his eyes had the power to disarm her: they are heavy lidded with bags under them, very light blue and set a little too far apart. "I see," he says, noticing her agitation for the first time. "That must have been upsetting."

"Werner, do you know what's going on? Christa, she . . ." Bettina bites at her nail and then puts her hand down. Werner does not like it when she is fiddly and distracted. "She's such a good person. A good worker, reliable. And she's so cheerful! She makes it bearable for the rest of us. I . . . it's . . . I just can't imagine what—"

"Dearest. These things happen. There must be some reason."

She sits down on the bed, which is covered in a quilt her mother stitched together long ago. Once, when her mother and grandmother were out one afternoon, she lay on this same quilt with Dieter. She runs her hand over the tidy rows of stitches, bumpy and soft under her calloused, fine-boned fingers. "You can tell *me*, Werner. If you know something? You can trust me."

He swipes his hands along either side of his head, patting down his hair. "What I can say is this. We are living under different circumstances now that the Russians are here to stay. The rules have changed, and we are still learning what the new ones are. It's imperative that we have patience, that we listen and learn. At least we're done with National Socialism—we can be thankful for that, don't you think?"

What can she say to this? Her father had never liked to talk of politics or war—as though by not talking about it with his daughters, he could will it to not impact their world. He had been such a gentle man, so simple. He trusted commerce, routine, the joys of his household; he used to love telling the girls, "Fire in the heart sends smoke into the head." When she was a teenager, this irritated Bettina to no end, and she'd sometimes secretly tune in to political broadcasts on the radio after school when he was still at work. But then came the war and the bombing, memories of the soldier who had died because of her. The smell of alcohol and misery. When the Russians came flooding into town with their sallow complexions and searching eyes, the columns of men in shredded boots and belted jackets, she had continued her steady retreat from public life.

Maybe Werner is right. Are they not pawns in someone else's vast strategic game? And they are better off than they were under Hitler— that's for sure.

This morning as she was tying on her freshly starched apron, Christa was joyous. "Finally some sun!" she exclaimed. "Let's run away, play in the sand . . ." Her lighthearted commentary always managed to elicit a smile from Bettina no matter how deeply she was lost in her own world. And then Bettina thinks of the awkward tango she witnessed, the officer with his body pressed against Christa's, shoving her through the door and into the van. The fraught stillness on the factory floor. All those eyes, staring. And yet no one dared intervene.

Werner sits next to her on the bed. Their shoulders are touching. "What do you really know about Christa?" he asks. "Is it possible there are things about her that you don't know?"

"What could she possibly have done?"

"I'll ask around, yes? But I want you to keep out of this. No nosing around, getting yourself in trouble. I'm a functionary in the government; you can't be meddling."

She plays with the gold wedding band of his mother's on her finger.

He puts a hand over hers, the skin warm and slightly damp. "Don't you worry. I want to make you happy."

"I just—"

"You're a woman now, with responsibilities. Be sensible, dear. I promise I'll look into it."

Werner pulls her face around toward his and looks in her dark eyes, his smile tentative but honest. Then he rises to go to the bathroom.

The pipes start clanking as he washes his hands. Bettina walks over to the window and, pushing aside the pale-yellow curtains, stares out onto the cobblestones. The lights in her neighbors' houses cast long, rippling stripes over the stones. In each of those homes, people sleep and eat, make love and argue. They have babies, or they don't. They deal with their shame and with their corrosive secrets. Perhaps they lost loved ones and are lonely, or they are never alone and dream only of the peace of a quiet room. All those people, all those dreams. And what will happen to Christa, to *her* dreams? How can it be that you wake up in the morning, happy about the sunshine, and then by nightfall you are gone?

The next day Christa does not return to work, nor the next. On the weekend while Werner is planting red geraniums in the flowerpots, Bettina takes a walk to the hamlet of Bobbin. By the time she arrives, she has broken into a full sweat. She mounts the small hill from which she will be able to look over the fields into the far distance and, if she is lucky, catch sight of the steely glimmer of water. At the top of the hill is a small fieldstone church, the oldest on the island. It has two steeply sloping angled roofs of bright-orange tile and a small turret that glints bluish in the sun. From afar, the stones of varying sizes look like seashells, mixed hues of cream and brown. Speckled and undulating and ancient. Brick in chevron patterns cover various add-ons, and there are windows and arches and openings of all sizes, indiscriminate and jaunty.

A small dog is sitting at the gates of the churchyard, tied up to the ironwork with a piece of frayed string. His gray-and-black fur is ragged, but he has lively eyes that study Bettina as she makes her way along the path. When she notices the yellow tufts coming from his ears, she stops in midstride. Something strikes her about this animal. The mutt sits up on his hind legs in a rote, practiced manner, pawing at the air. He is not doing tricks. It almost seems as though he's been waiting for her.

Bettina crouches down to pat him. His fur is like wire, stiff and scratchy under her fingers. He appears to be quite old. A deep unease courses through her. Does she know this animal from somewhere?

That's when she remembers. Her father had just died—she was a teenager. Running either toward something or away from something on the beach. She pretended to take a picture, and there was laughter and a young man. A soldier with talk of the future.

She stands up and straightens out her skirt, homemade from checked army bedding given to her by her neighbor, Irmgard. The womenfolk and a few old men are milling about the double doors of the church, looking at her curiously and greeting the priest as they enter. There is no sign of the soldier she saw all those years ago. Did he survive? she wonders.

As she looks around her from the top of the hill by the gates, she sees an old graveyard on a gentle hill to her left and a cluster of towering chestnuts and oak trees bordering on a meadow. On her right, the hill drops off, and hundreds of hectares covered in sea buckthorn and rape flowers spread across the valley. It is a vast and seemingly endless carpet of yellow, blindingly bright even in the muted daylight.

This is a moment she wishes she could capture with her camera. The dog, who represents something ineffable—she can't tell what exactly, but it makes her feel hopeful. And the bobbing heads of the flowers, luminous where the sun caresses them with its hot touch.

8

They have a new routine. Almost every Sunday, Bettina and Werner meet up with her sister, Clara, and Herbert for a walk on the promenade by the beach in nearby Binz. They've been doing this for the past few weeks, and it has brought the sisters together in a way they haven't experienced since Clara was a teenager. Clara hooks her arm under Bettina's and tucks her body close to hers. Bettina's sister is tall, almost ungainly, with narrow hips like a boy's and hair that grows dark in the winter and light in the summer sun. Today her face is drawn, the circles under her eyes like bruises. They are talking in hushed tones.

Ahead of them, the two men walk side by side, trailing smoke behind them like kite tails. It is such an unseasonably warm day that both men have taken off their jackets and are strolling in their shirt-sleeves. They keep some distance from each other, puffing on small cigarillos they bought from a Polish girl at the bus stop. Werner is much broader and shorter than Herbert, who is lanky and tends to stoop. As usual, Werner wears a black felt hat, which he holds on to as the wind blows over them, pulling and snapping and strafing every loose thread. Herbert is bareheaded, his hair already beginning to thin at the top. When he came courting Clara before the war, he liked a stiff drink and a good joke. But during the worst of the fighting on the front, he was shot at close range through the forearm, and the wound became so infected the arm eventually had to be amputated from the elbow down. He has never been the same again.

Old seaside mansions stand like stalwart aristocrats fallen on hard times, lining the curving shoreline overlooking the walkway and the white-sand beach. Ornately carved wooden balustrades are splintered, and gaping holes appear in railings. Entire porches that once invited well-dressed occupants to sip tea and watch the sun play over the water now list at dangerous angles. Some of the houses have no roofs at all, their interiors exposed and rotting in the salty air. Now that East Germany has split decisively from the West, some houses are used as hostels for the migrant workers shipped in to run the new factories that are beginning to replace the family farms. Mechanization, increased production, chemical engineering—these are all on the upswing; they represent the hopes of the *Deutsche Demokratishe Republik*, the DDR. Everywhere you look, there are signs that their world is changing.

Bettina likes the way the houses line up: devastated, unruly, yet hinting at a kind of perverse resilience. Because of her experience with the dog yesterday, she's brought along her Rolleiflex. She snaps a few pictures, but her heart isn't really in it. It has become harder and harder for her to decide which images are worth capturing and which are a waste of precious film. If only resources weren't so scarce. If only she could snap away and develop canister after canister and not worry about where the next roll will come from or how she will pay to have them developed.

"I'd listen to Werner," Clara is saying under her breath. "Poking your nose into someone else's business is a surefire way of getting yourself into trouble."

This is what Bettina expected her sister to say, and yet resistance rises inside her like bile. Why is Bettina so quick to take on other people's problems? It is a trait her grandfather used to comment on, his erratic brows rising with disdain, yet she has not been able to rid herself of this tendency. "But he might be able to help. Isn't that worth doing, for a friend?"

Clara shrugs, and Bettina wonders when her sister became so cynical. "Isn't he just an accountant?" Clara asks. "If he's willing, I suppose. But I wouldn't push, Bettinalein. Remember, Papa always counseled us to mind our own business: *Deine Sache, was du machst.*"

It has warmed up considerably, and Bettina peels off her prickly cardigan, letting her pale arms soak up the sunshine. The water to their right is covered in sharp-edged whitecaps. The promenade is crowded with people taking an afternoon stroll; in the past half hour she has seen the Gronwalds, old Siegfried Rattenbach, and Käthe von Kohs. Each time they pass another person they know, Clara digs her elbow into Bettina's rib cage.

"Don't you feel like a zoo animal?" she whispers. "The tiny provincial zoo of Rügen, where all the species come out to gawk in their Sunday best, one day a week . . ."

Bettina laughs. She thinks of her neighbors on the square and how much she knows of their lives. Old man Henning likes his liquor so much that he often starts in on the beer before breakfast. When she and Clara were little, they played with Ilsa Schiffer's daughter, Jane, who became pregnant at sixteen and was sent away to a convent in the south (they were the only Catholics Bettina knew). When Werner moved in, her neighbors were silent and watchful; no doubt they had been curious whether Bettina would become an old maid.

In a way, life had become even harder after the Russians took over, when it seemed as if most of the old allegiances and friendships that had survived the Third Reich were severed for good. Some of that was positive, Bettina thought (those old cronies and the young diehards who believed the insane race rhetoric, *they* were in for a reckoning), but some of it was devastating. Anyone labeled a Nazi—whether they had actually been one or not—was hauled in front of a makeshift tribunal, and soon brothers were turning in sisters and vice versa. Rivals turned in former business partners. Scorned wives fingered their husbands. Fear and uncertainty made people do the unimaginable.

And it's still happening now, just for different reasons. Clara was telling her about something she'd heard in the typing pool at the mine: a trial being conducted in central Saxony of Germans who are still imprisoned by the Russians. Over three thousand of them, some of whom had been teenagers during the war, charged with war crimes and sentenced to death. There is a price to pay for what the Germans did—Bettina knows this—but when will it end? That ordinary people like Christa are now considered a threat is unthinkable. The new regime, the Communists, promised modernity and progress, but it sometimes feels as though their lives are running in reverse, away from progress, not toward it.

"Where are we going?" Bettina calls out to the men, who are walking toward a sandy stretch of beach.

Herbert waves them onward with his good arm. "Have something to show you," he yells, his words dissolving in the wind.

Bettina and Clara shuck off their shoes and ankle socks and follow the men. The sand is cool and damp between Bettina's toes. They walk along the water's edge, past the trees, after which the beach becomes a sliver of sand, covered here and there by boulders spilling out toward the ocean.

Werner and Herbert sit on a large flat rock, finishing up their smokes, looking out over the water as the women approach. Both men have rolled up the legs of their trousers and are tipping their faces toward the sun.

"Isn't this beautiful?" Herbert asks.

"We'll have to head back soon if we want to catch the afternoon bus," Werner says, and all three of them look at him in irritation.

"I'm so warm," Bettina complains, unbuttoning the top of her blouse. They are protected from the wind by the chalk cliffs that rise abruptly out of the water on one side and the cluster of wind-gnarled trees on the other. She walks backward toward the water, flips the camera open, and raises it slightly to catch the magnificent rise of chalk above the ocean, hundreds of meters of soaring crags. The tiny people in a cluster at the foot of the cliff. A sliver of sand and water at the bottom of the frame.

Herbert stands up. He's taken off his shoes, revealing sturdy ankles covered in dark hair. For a tall man he is surprisingly nimble on his feet. "Let's go swimming!" he says, grinning at the women and horsing around. "That will cool us down."

"But we can't," Clara says. "We didn't bring our bathing suits. And anyway, it must be freezing."

Bettina points over at the trees. "We could leave our clothes over there. Go in wearing just our undergarments!"

"That would be unseemly," Werner says, casting a sharp look in her direction.

"Oh, come on. Isn't it fun to be unseemly sometimes?" she asks, pushing on his chest with the flat of her hand. "Are you never just a little unseemly? Never?"

He doesn't smile back at her. "Now you're being silly."

She was in fact *trying* to be silly, but she turns away and walks toward the trees. "I think it's a fabulous idea," she calls out.

The water is so cold it freezes the breath in her lungs. Wearing only her brassiere and slip, Bettina plunges forward into the shallows to cover herself, holding her head above the waves. She swims furiously, going farther and farther out. She could keep going and never stop until she hits land again.

Treading water, she looks up at the boardwalk in the distance, the people passing by, some of whom have noticed her swimming and are pointing. There is a little girl, hair as white as dandelion down, leaning over the railing, calling to her mother to come see. She is screeching, delight all over her face. Bettina waves, and the girl waves back, her body stiff with excitement. How old is she? It's hard to tell from this distance. A boy clutching a small red object peers over the railing and laughs along with his sister. They nuzzle each other, sharing some secret, gesticulating toward the water.

Bettina swims away, tears burning at her eyes. Taking a deep breath, she sinks down into the water, raising her hands above her head and letting herself slip downward. It doesn't matter that she's ruining her hair; who cares? The icy water is shocking on her warm scalp. She wonders whether she is perhaps doomed to never have children after all. She had taken for granted that marriage would, at the very least, give her a child to love and care for, and it is possible that this is not to be. Perhaps instead she will spend an entire lifetime working at the factory during the day and cooking a meal for two at night. That thought leaves a hollowness inside her chest that aches.

After spinning around a few times under the water, she opens her eyes. The legs of a man become visible at a distance, and she swims underwater toward the figure. For a brief moment she thinks it might be Werner after all, and her heart lifts with the possibility that for her sake, he might try to change his ways. Coming up for a quick breath of air, she dives down again and opens her eyes to the hidden world. The salt water stings, but she keeps her eyes open.

It is not Werner; it is Herbert. He has kept on his undershirt and pants, and they cling to his lean frame. Is he so ashamed of his body that he will not reveal himself, even here in the camouflaging waters of the sea?

She needs to take a breath but doesn't want to surface yet. Everything is so calm, drained of all color and form. She cannot really tell that Herbert's arm is missing. From this perspective, everything is softer, muted. Closing her eyes, feeling her lungs bursting, she considers staying underwater, letting the sea fill up the growing emptiness inside her.

9

There is a rap on the door of Werner's office, and his fingers pause above the calculator. When his superior enters without waiting to be invited in, Werner jumps to his feet. The desk is covered with paperwork, and he wishes he'd had a chance to tidy up. "Good day, Comrade. What a pleasure," he says to Franz Josef Bieder.

Invariably, Bieder makes Werner feel as though he's been caught doing something perverse, like reading a Karl May western or fiddling with himself under the desk. The man has one glass eye that fails to move, giving his face a startled look while also suggesting a certain intransigence and rigidity. Bieder appears not to notice his subordinate's discomfort. Since February, he's been working at the police headquarters in Bergen with Inspector Fröse. Some days earlier he called to ask for Werner's help pulling together information about Saargen residents, explaining that he now works for a newly established organization, a kind of modernized police force: the Ministry for State Security, known as the MfS.

"Any letters of complaint?" Bieder asks Werner. "We also need names of residents trying for exit visas, yes? Those with relatives who've already gone West, and so on."

Until Bieder took him into his confidence, Werner had no earthly idea that Germans were leaving the East at such a high rate. Perhaps a neighbor or two disappeared, but this hasn't concerned him much, at least not until now. After the war, when the Allies gave western Germany back to the Germans, the Russians had other ideas about the entire eastern half of Europe: Albania, Bulgaria, Romania, Hungary, Czechoslovakia . . . all have become Communist. What a very strange outcome that his country is now split in two, each side governed by enemies, and that he happened to fall on this side by accident of geography.

Bieder opens a folder and points at a teletype from Berlin headquarters. "We've only just gotten started," he explains, "but soon leaving the DDR will become a punishable crime."

Werner looks at the piece of paper. *Is it not an act of political depravity when citizens, whether young people, workers, or members of the intelligentsia, leave and betray what our people have created through common labor in our republic to offer themselves to the American or British secret services or work for the West German factory owners, Junkers, or militarists? Does not leaving the land of progress for the morass of a historically outdated social order demonstrate political backwardness and blindness?*

Yes, indeed, these acts are political depravity. The old order is steadily being erased—those disgraced young noblemen of yore, the Junkers with their unearned superiority, and the capitalistic owners greedy for profits, those people have been stripped of all power. Change is a good thing for the Germans. The words written by the Socialist Unity Party's Agitation Department call out to Werner as though spiked with special energy, compelling him to be strong, to direct this strength toward the right goals.

The German people, too, in particular the working class, have seized the banner of peace, democracy, and socialism firmly in their hands and will not rest until democratic conditions also prevail in West Germany.

It is a mandate, and he is being chosen to help make it a reality. Werner goes to his file cabinets and begins pulling out paperwork. Over the course of the next two hours, he hands over updated lists of inhabitants, their personal wealth, and their holdings. Requests for repairs, for divorces, and for visitation rights.

Afterward he sits at his desk and wipes his forehead with a clean handkerchief. He regards Bieder as the man packs away the last of the papers into a large carton. "Comrade, you mind my asking something? There's a woman—she works with my wife."

"Your wife?" Bieder straightens up. "Where does your wife work?"

"At the fish factory, here in Saargen."

The man gives him a small smile that barely alters the shape of his mouth and has no effect on his disconcerting eyes. "Ah, yes. You must be referring to Frau Kellermann, who was apprehended at the factory last week."

"By the Vopo?"

"By the Stasi, not the locals. I take it you're aware of this new police force, my friend? Part of the MfS."

This response gives Werner pause. Is the man saying this to lull him into a false sense of security or because he does in fact consider him a friend? Werner can't be sure; he has not had that many friends. The leather on his chair creaks as his weight shifts. "I see. The new police force, right." Werner is aware of the formation of this force—apparently called Stasi—under the jurisdiction of the Ministry for State Security; he brought home a new cap they'd unveiled a few months ago to show Bettina. He wants to ask more but hates to appear ignorant.

"Well then, Nietz. What is it you wish to know?" Bieder taps out a cigarette and places it between his lips, then strikes a match to light it, managing to keep his one eye on Werner throughout the entire process.

"I was wondering, Comrade," he tries again. He can see from Bieder's sharp gaze that this is not really a conversation between equals. He decides to take a different tack. "The interrogations—they've been successful, have they?"

"May I give you some advice?" Bieder thrusts one hand into the pocket of his suit pants. The material is shiny where his hands have slipped over the seams time and time again. With the other hand he punches the cigarette in the air in compact little thrusts. "Better to stay in your lane. Showing personal interest in specific cases is unwise."

"Of course," Werner answers. It is galling to think that Werner was right all along in his thoughts on this, but Bettina has been insisting that he interfere. He wants to please her, but he wants to please his boss even more.

"So what do you think?" Bieder continues. "If you had a choice, what would you do with her, with Kellermann?"

Werner taps his fingers lightly against the desk. "Depends what she's done wrong, Comrade."

"Her son—the oldest one—a traitor to the people. Agitating against the state. Handing out pamphlets about supposed 'wage cuts.'" Bieder takes a box of papers and places them next to the door, and Werner jumps up to help him. "As a dedicated socialist, what would *you* do with such a woman? A woman who brought up a child like that?"

"He's in custody, is he? The son?"

"No. Rolf Kellermann has fled." Bieder lets out a long string of cigarette smoke. "Went over to West Berlin in March—"

"Listen," Werner blurts. "It's of no consequence to me what happens to the woman."

"You would send her to the camps, would you?"

He barely hesitates. "Enemies of the state should face the appropriate consequences for their actions. We must be vigilant."

"That we must." Bieder grinds out his cigarette in a porcelain ashtray on the desk. He props the door open with his foot and grabs another box. "Good day, Comrade."

On his way home, Werner replays this scene to himself again and again. It seems he is inching his way up the ladder. A man of significant influence has taken an interest in him. He has married a beautiful, healthy woman, and they are working on starting a family. His future is promising. So why is it that he feels as if Franz Josef Bieder was trying to test him? And why is it Werner does not feel entirely comfortable with the answers he gave?

That night he and Bettina sit opposite one another in the living room, listening to the radio. She is embroidering one of his handkerchiefs, periodically looking up at him with her penetrating gaze, dark and somehow too intense. She mentions that a friend from work taught her how to do this. It is warm in the room, and the window is open, letting in the faint scent of freshly mowed grass. Behind her, the old books in their faded cloth covers are lined up like good soldiers, and he remembers the teletype from earlier, its reference to "Junkers" and the "outdated social order." All these books in this room, they are from another era. They represent a time that the Germans have left behind. He knows he should still be feeling energetic and enthusiastic about all these changes underway—as he had felt earlier, alone in his office—but as his wife tries to make conversation, Werner finds he cannot meet her eye.

10

Bettina begins to go to Bobbin regularly. She wanders through the graveyard, wiping her face on the hem of her shirt, keeping an eye out for the little dog. Sometimes her scruffy mutt is there, sometimes not. Often, she times it so that she can attend Sunday services; though she's never been a religious woman, she finds the earnest singing and the steely coolness of the church's interior comforting. Increasingly, she can't stand being cooped up. At home, on her knees, swishing suds around the tile floor, she becomes almost claustrophobic. She used to get such pleasure from scrubbing and washing, ironing and tidying, and now all she yearns for is the open air. To really breathe it deep into her body, to feel a kind of delectable pain when her lungs are close to bursting. It is only once she's begun to sweat on her march along the dirt road toward Bobbin and the breeze rushes over her skin, cooling her down, that she feels alive again.

The graveyard is orderly and ancient, except for a pile of upended stones under the yew trees on the periphery. Irmgard Bandelow, Bettina's neighbor on the square, has a family plot in this wild lot, the gravestones etched with the names of multiple generations. When her husband was killed during those insane hand-to-hand battles at the end of the war, Irmgard found him by the bridge to the mainland and carted his body home in a wheelbarrow. Now he rests here, under a modest blue-toned marble slab—with a rough, empty spot at the very top where Irmgard tried to shave off the swastika after it was clear they had lost the war.

That blank section of stone gives Bettina pause. Even though she thinks of herself as a simple woman, she has strong ideas centered around hard work and nurturing others. These are ideas she feels deeply but isn't especially vocal about. These days, she often wonders why she didn't think Dieter was wrong to sacrifice his life for the Führer, why she wasn't ashamed that her father wore the Nazi Party pin. She was so very ignorant then. During the fighting, she saw the world through a narrow lens: what the violence and fear were doing to her parents, her friends, her community. Is this the natural instinct of those who find their homelands transformed into war-torn countries, she wonders, or is it because she was a child? Either way, the awareness of all she didn't know is a burden and a sorrow she can't shake.

Once the Russians came, she was shaken wide awake. The aperture on the lens was yanked open, then, and there was no more ignorance, whether willful or not: Bettina and the villagers saw the pictures from the concentration camps; they learned about the extermination of entire peoples, the senseless, despicable cruelty. It had been unimaginable, and then suddenly it was no longer unimaginable. She carries with her now the indelible stain of this knowledge, the horror at what her people have done, of what happened because of a system gone mad.

She runs her thumb over the blank spot on the gravestone.

"Why the frown?" comes a voice from behind the stones.

A tall figure is leaning against an oak sapling. As though released by command, the shaggy-haired mutt comes from the man's side and runs to Bettina, yapping a few times, tightly circling her legs.

Jumping back, she lifts her foot and tries to shake the dog off. But the scratchy tongue tickles, and she finds herself smiling, clutching the collar of her shirt as she stumbles around. Her blue hat is tipped to one side, and the pin holding it in place pulls at the strands of her hair.

When she looks up again at the man, she sees herself as he must see her, and instead of regaining her composure, she starts to laugh.

"I'm glad you find me so amusing," the man says. He's wearing a fisherman's cap and old dungarees and stands with long arms crossed in front of a slim chest. His eyes are obscured under the hat, but his teeth are straight and flash at her like a signal that she should not stop; she can laugh as long as she wants to, and he will not think less of her for it.

She reaches up and pulls off the lopsided felt hat. Her crisscrossed braids are coming loose, and she thinks of how Werner would throw her a disapproving glance if he were here. This makes her stop smiling at once.

"Hm, liked you better when you were happy," the man says, putting a piece of grass into his mouth and sucking on it. "Standing in a graveyard with an expression on your face as though someone's just amputated your ear, well. Doesn't suit you nearly as well."

The tone. The air of calm. It is him: the man from the beach. "You've been watching me?" she says, unsure where to rest her eyes. If only he would take his cap off, she could see his face better.

"Don't I know you?" he asks.

Her pleasure at being remembered is so intense that her color deepens. "I think so, yes."

"The girl pretending to take pictures, yes?"

She nods. Steam rises from the thick-grown meadows, evaporating into the morning air. The dog stops his prancing and lies on his back, baring his pale belly to the sun and waiting for Bettina to notice him again and to scratch him just where he wants. The skin of his stomach is pink, delicate like a baby mouse.

The man sucks on the piece of grass intently. "I was in trouble back then. You didn't realize that, I think. I'd just run away from my regiment."

"As did so many others too," Bettina says. They address each other with the formal *Sie* rather than *du*, and it sticks on her tongue like an affectation.

"What was left of the regiment, that is. I'd been with them for two years straight. I could think of nothing but home—of the beach. Coming back *home*."

"That's nothing to be ashamed of."

He laughs again, but there is no genuine humor in it this time. "You are naive, then. There's something to be ashamed of in most things humans do."

"You're a moralist? Haven't you had enough of moralists yet?"

He tips his fisherman's cap back and reveals soft, pale eyebrows over deep eye sockets. The startling black of his eyes is further exaggerated by shadow. "Is this someone you knew?" he asks, ambling over and pointing at the Bandelow gravestone. He has the look of someone who is good at dissembling: one minute this, the next that. His head is much higher than hers, and the coolness of a slight shadow falls on her arm.

She nods again, pressing her lips together.

Taking off his cap, he runs his fingers through his hair. It is blond and a little too long, unkempt like a boy's. But his face is not boyish; his eyes are serious, the irises almost purple. The curve of his upper lip is long and shallow. In a flash he has shifted from his slightly mocking, lighthearted manner to one that makes her nervous, as though he is assessing her. She is accustomed to a judgmental look in most men she encounters—what is it about her bearing that makes even strangers defensive, when she tries so hard to disappear?—but this is different. He is both weighing his impressions of her *and* declaring himself on her side.

She tries to repin the hat on her loosened hair. "Where did you fight?"

"Stalingrad. Then Pomerania." After a pause, he spits out the piece of grass and adds, in a rush, "Almost every night I dream of it, of the killing."

She inhales sharply, flushed with recognition. "I do too." This unexpected shift in their banter slips between them easily, like an invitation she can't turn down.

"Millions died at our hands, even if we did not pull the trigger or jab the bayonet, drop the bomb. Man is rather inventive, is he not?"

"So then, you're a moralist *and* a pacifist," she says.

Taking her lightly by the elbow, he indicates with a nod of his head a small mound behind the graveyard, crowded with saplings and overgrown sea buckthorn. In among the weeds and clumpy earth lies a disorderly pile of upended gravestones. On his hands and knees, he clears the black soil from some stones and then points at one just to his left. "This one here, he'd have kept on fighting, if he could've. My brother."

"Tobias Brenner," Bettina reads aloud from the stone. A swastika is embedded in the upper right-hand corner, the image of a boat on the left.

The beach man sits on his haunches and stares ahead of him. In the shadows of the overgrowth, he could be a refugee or a beggar. "My older brother. Taught me to ride a bicycle and had a soft spot for Zündapp motorcycles and for girls. 'Watch out for the pretty ones,' he'd say, 'they'll break your heart.' But let's see—my younger brother's here somewhere too. My father dug out the stone markers, threw them in here with the others that had the swastika on them." He stands and shakes out his legs. "My father's the pastor—Pfarrer Brenner? My wife was the one who had the symbol put on them, back in—"

Bettina raises her brows. "Your wife?"

"Yes, yes, I was newly married. Just six months. Katya, she arranged the stone for Tobias, and then for Berndt, later. I was in Eastern Pomerania then."

He is talking so fast she isn't entirely following.

"Now there's just me left. And Vati. He raised the three of us boys." He looks at her so intently—as though making up his mind about something—that she cannot hold his gaze. He rubs his eyes before slipping the fisherman's cap back over his head. When he continues talking, the words tumble out. "Tobias, he was a guard at Oświęcim; you've heard of it? Auschwitz? And Berndt, he worked in Fünfeichen."

This man, so big and gentle, who seems as though he has a good heart, had *two* brothers who worked in the camps—how did he avoid being sent to the Gulag after the Russians invaded?

He seems able to read her mind. "I had impeccable antifascist credentials, having run away from my unit and all." He fixes her with his eyes. "Socialism, it'll be our saving grace. 'From each according to his ability, to each according to his needs.' Things are changing."

"You sound like my husband," she says, but actually, that's not quite what she thinks. What she thinks is that this man is focused on the theories, the ideas, whereas Werner is enamored of the machinery of it all, the levers and bolts and hydraulics of the system.

Something has shifted inside the man, and he begins to talk.

"As a child, had you known me then, well. You would not recognize me now. I was so lackadaisical, carefree," he says. "But something happened when I started fighting. I . . . I did well. I followed orders. I fired the PaK 38, with its armor-piercing shells, packed at their core with tungsten, blasting the Russian tanks, and then . . ." He pauses. "Then the tungsten ran out, and I skewered the enemy with my bayonet, blew limbs from their sockets with hand grenades."

His face reddens and sets in a way that makes her see how he will look when he is elderly, frail, when youth no longer allows him the tender hope that better things are to come. There is something about the way he talks that stirs her; he is careful with his words, deliberate. He is launching himself, without restraint, into the truth of his telling. She has never heard anyone talk in this way before—not Dieter, not her parents, certainly not Werner.

"In the end, pulling the trigger or the pin, thrusting the knife, it was really not all that hard for me. I felt little fear. No pain, no remorse."

He stares at Bettina as though daring her to turn away from this terrible confession.

She does not turn away.

"And shame? No. No shame, not then. Some men I killed were so young they did not even have stubble on their faces yet. Their families, their homesteads, their beloved pets, their loves and desires and needs—none of these things were real to me.

"But . . . that all changed. It all changed so fast I didn't see it coming right at me! We were fighting, we were in the dust and rubble, and there were these earsplitting salvos, but they were followed by a sinister silence, awful . . . a kind of freighted peacefulness, and we trudged and trudged toward the next town. It was nightfall. We were flushing out entire villages; bodies lay along the roadside. The cries, they started so quietly . . . I was barely aware of the sound; I walked past the ditch, and then"—he looks away from her now—"that's when I recognized the cadence of the sobs. It was a child I was hearing—a child crying.

"Then a shot. And no more sounds."

Her body stiffens. In one instant they have been catapulted into yet another realm, taken a step even closer to a place of such horror that she cannot take a breath.

"Those cries," he says, his face drained of all energy, his eyes unwilling to meet hers. "They touched my conscience. It was unbearable. I waited that night; God, I waited until my men fell asleep—we were in the basement of a bombed-out library. And I gathered my backpack and my pathetic supplies, and I started the long trek back to Rügen. I deserted them. I had no thoughts of what I'd do when I was home again; I wasn't thinking about retribution or punishment. Self-centered, even then! The only thought as I walked was that I had to set foot on the island again or I would explode."

A slow inhale, the air in her lungs on fire. There are no words with which to comfort or excoriate him.

His eyes come to rest on her face again, tentative, daring her to reject him. "And then I saw you, on the beach," he says.

They are both aware that he has overstepped some boundary. Her head is filled with the scenes he painted with his words. She senses that this man, this stranger, has a power inside him that has never had a chance to be put to good use—but it's not that; it's not really about power. Perhaps it's strength. Or conviction. She feels faint, as though something heavy is pressing against her, but it's not unpleasant. If she let herself, if she were less self-conscious, she might burst into tears. In the face of all his words, she cannot say a thing.

"We'll find a way to redeem ourselves," he says after a time. She can tell that he is trying to smile, that he wonders whether it was a mistake to tell her his secret. "The very least we can do is ensure everyone is treated equally. I'm not entirely sold on Stalinism—but shhhhhh, eh? We'll have to see what happens."

Politics. She is yanked back to earth and thinks of Putzkammer, the foreman at the factory, and how he likes to drone on about the proletariat. Stefanie, with her profane remarks, whispering derisively as soon as the foreman turns his back. Christa's perpetually moving hands, flashing back and forth as she wields her filleting knife. Are the socialists—the Communists—really on the side of the workers, the ordinary Germans? But then, this isn't about fairness or taking sides: everyone is aware of the steep price they have to pay for being German.

"I apologize for going on and on," he says. "I don't have that many people to talk to."

"What about your wife?" she asks.

He shakes his head. "She died."

The congregation is beginning to filter into the church. They nod at one another stiffly, and Bettina heads for the church door as the man walks away from her, toward the copse. When she sits down, she realizes that she has been holding her breath. That day the psalm is number forty-two. The small group of townspeople sings heartily, led by the strong, slightly off-key voice of Pfarrer Brenner.

Wann werde ich dahin kommen,
Dass ich in Gottes Angesicht schaue?
Meine Tränen sind meine Speise Tag und Nacht
Weil man täglich zu mir sagt: Wo ist nun dein Gott?

"When will I finally see God's face again," Bettina sings. "Day and night, tears are my only sustenance, because daily I am asked: So then, where is your God?" As she tries to follow the verse, her singing falters. It seems clear to her that if in fact there is such a thing as God, her people have been abandoned by him. The man, the deserter, claims they must learn to live as equals, but is that actually possible now that they have all been poisoned by the bitter taste of power and humiliation and fear?

11

Digging in the scrubby backyard, Werner pauses his work and looks up at the house. Bettina is preparing breakfast in the kitchen. He can see her through the back window. Reaching down to bring out the heavy iron pan in which she will cook some eggs, she briefly disappears from view. Then, straightening up again, she sweeps her brown hair from her eyes in that characteristic gesture of hers. As always, a sense of wonderment flushes through him: amazement that she is his wife, that they share a bed, that she ever said yes to him.

When she smiles, which is too rare, snaggleteeth soften her otherwise startlingly handsome face. She always tries to smile with her mouth shut to hide what she thinks of as an embarrassing imperfection, though Werner insists this is precisely what makes her beauty unique. Her body is trim and strong, and the curve of her hips suggests that behind her intensity something sensual is hiding, something that she herself does not recognize, even.

He stubs out his cigarette on the brown grass, watching her fluid movements in the kitchen, and—though he has tried so hard to control this irritating natural tic of his—he feels a flush stain his cheeks, accompanied by an urgent pounding in his chest. Each day that he avoids talking about that woman from the factory is yet another day that he is letting his wife down. It has already been a month. He heads over to the chicken coop, where the speckled Hamburgs chitter and squawk, and searches the cages. Only two eggs today.

Palming them gently, he returns to the kitchen. "Bettinalein," he begins. She stands in front of him, the wooden spatula in her hand hovering in midair. Reaching over, he hands her the eggs, still warm and encrusted with droppings. "Perhaps we could head over to Binz with a picnic later?" he asks.

Bettina carries two china plates and two small glasses on a tray into the dining room. "They didn't have any flour at the bakery yesterday," she says over her shoulder. "So there's no bread."

"This is fine," he answers, taking a seat next to her. "I was thinking. We could plan a trip sometime, you and I? Perhaps go to the mainland, stay in Stralsund for a night."

She stares at him long enough that he begins to feel heat rise under his collar. Her face is sharply angled, so when she is serious, all the energy seems drawn toward her mouth, making it turn down slightly and darkening the shadows under her cheekbones. And then, whenever she smiles, it is as though her eyes and cheeks have been loosened from some knot at her core, and her whole face softens.

Now her jaw is stiff. "What?" he asks, his mouth full of egg. "Wouldn't you like that? I can get a travel permit from work." At the mention of work, Bettina presses her lips together. "What is it?"

"I wanted to tell you that I've decided to go by Christa's house for a visit," Bettina says. "I have some food for the Kellermann children, and I'm going to drop it off. Please don't try to talk me out of it."

"You know that isn't a good idea."

"I'd like it very much if you came with me."

He lays his napkin down on the table and leans back in the uncomfortable old chair, some relic that Bettina's grandmother bought back when they had money. He sighs. Each day he is reminded, in one small way or another, that this was Bettina's home long before he became the master of the house. "No food for the Kellermanns, or we'll land ourselves in trouble, all right?"

Abruptly she rises and heads for the kitchen, taking her plate with her.

"You're making too much of this," he says, following her. As she turns around to regard him from the back of the room, her expression is so distant that anger begins to rise inside him and block his throat. He has done nothing wrong, and yet she seems to blame him for everything. She looks at him as though he were a stranger, when she herself is like a book with the pages glued together!

Bettina grabs her old coat from the rack and hooks her basket over her forearm.

"You're leaving?" he says.

"It's the right thing to do," she answers. "You can always come with me, Werner." She steps into the square, tying a kerchief around her head. The brisk early-morning air pours into the hallway as though filling a vacuum.

"But—wait. Wait, Bettina! Don't you want to know about her? About your friend?" he says, his voice bright and false.

She spins around to look at him. The knot at her core unties itself as he watches, softening her face. "You know where she is?"

"I don't have details, Bettina, though, believe me, I pressed for them." He shifts his weight from one foot to the other, trying to think quickly. "But I, well . . . I asked for leniency, for some compassion. I—you see, I wrote a letter on her behalf."

"Oh!" She takes a step toward him and then frowns. "Why did you not tell me all this before? I—I've been . . . so confused."

Her voice is plaintive, and suddenly he's deflated; how does she manage to do that to him? "I didn't want to raise your hopes."

"Where is she? Do you know?"

"I'm sorry," he says, pulling his mouth into a little grimace. Now that he has started lying, he finds he can't stop. "They won't tell me anything."

"Well, I'm grateful that you asked." She hoists the basket higher on her arm. "I should go now—I want to drop these off before my shift. Are you certain you won't come? We could talk along the way."

"I can't go," he says, folding his arms across his chest. "I have to be at work." His eyes follow her as she walks away from him, through the square. What has gotten into her? "Bettina, did you not hear me?" he calls out, and either she does not hear him, or she does and chooses to ignore him.

12

The road stretches out in front of her like a black ribbon. After she walks briskly for a while, warmth begins to seep into her muscles. She pulls the kerchief from her head. The fields of Rügen are an undulating sea of yellow. The rape flowers with their heavy pollen-speckled heads sway this way and that, bent by the never-ending winds, painting the meadows first sun yellow, then tan, then sun yellow again as the flowers shiver on their long stalks. Overhead, a lone seagull shrieks, having strayed too far from the ocean. It swoops up and down and then heads east, back toward Saargen.

Every step she takes seems like a small act of defiance, and even though she hates the thought of Werner's disapproval, after a while she feels a blossoming sense of exhilaration. Something about the beach man's horrifying story about the crying child helped her decide that she had to take some sort of action, no matter how small. By the time she arrives in Bobbin, her body is buzzing with energy. On her feet she wears men's shoes she managed to buy from a shipment of goods from Berlin, and they are large and clunky, causing blisters. But the sight of the little hillside church, with its blue-toned steeple visible for kilometers, is uplifting, and she feels more like her old self than she has in years.

Christa's house is one of the tiny thatched cottages at the bottom of the hill upon which the old church perches. As Bettina approaches, she slows down her frantic pace and shifts the wicker basket from her left arm to her right. Filled with tins of fish and two big potatoes, the basket is heavy. A rusty green car is idling at the curb to her left, and instead of turning down the dirt path where the row of cottages stands, Bettina continues along the main road as though planning to continue straight through town. As soon as she rounds a corner, she stops and turns to look over her shoulder. The car makes her nervous.

Scrambling up a small rise and through a thicket of yielding saplings, she doubles back on herself. From the narrow chimney of Christa's cottage, below her now, a stream of smoke emerges. There is no activity on the path in front of the house, and Bettina emerges from the trees and heads toward the side door. Her knock is not answered for a long time. She peers through the small window. Inside there is a gloomy hallway, its walls pocked with brass hooks weighed down with coats in all different sizes. She knocks again, more loudly this time. A face appears in the doorway that leads to the kitchen; it is Manfred, Christa's teenage nephew. She's met him a few times at the beach in the summertime.

An earnest boy with restless eyes, he stands and blinks at her. Bettina waves at him through the window, smiling timorously. Manfred unlocks the door and opens it a crack. "We've met before," Bettina says. "Remember me? I'm Bettina Nietz."

"You shouldn't be here," he says. "You know what happened, don't you?"

Bettina puts her basket on the ground. Pain shoots through the muscles of her shoulders. "It's all right; no one can see us. Has anyone told you anything yet?"

"Oh, you don't know," he says, wide eyes darting behind her, strafing the area. "Last night they brought her home. She's back."

Bettina's hands fly to her mouth.

"She's in bed. She's—I don't know." The boy shifts his weight. "She's different."

"Is she . . . was she, uh, hurt?"

He shrugs lightly. "Want to come in?"

Christa is in the upstairs bedroom under a quilt, even though it's already getting warm outside. The curtains are drawn, and the room smells of something sweet, like a rotting plant or sweat. Standing on the threshold, Bettina is gripped by the realization that after all these years of working next to this woman, she doesn't really know her heart, her dreams and fears. This knowledge rises inside her like a swell of water, catching her unawares and leaving her shaky.

"*Hallo*," she says quietly, not wanting to wake her friend. "It's Bettina, from work?"

The sheets shift, and Christa's head rises, her graying hair a mass of unruly curls. Her face has thinned out, and the texture of her skin is like sandpaper, the pewter shadows in the hollows of her eyes startling amid the pallor.

"I brought some food." Bettina comes closer. She fidgets with her kerchief and looks down at her feet. "I gave it to Manfred. Are you all right? I've been so worried."

"Yes," Christa says. "I'm fine."

Bettina searches her friend's face. "Did they—are you hurt?"

"No," Christa says, "not really."

Should Bettina ask more questions or leave well enough alone? This sense that in fact they barely really know each other makes her reluctant to pry. She pulls over a wooden chair and takes a seat. "Work hasn't been the same without you. Putzkammer's getting fatter by the minute. They must be giving him extra rations."

"I see."

"What . . . Christa, what happened?"

"The police, they were . . . it was strange. You wouldn't think it, but they were *polite*," she says, her voice barely audible. "They don't hit or shout. It's like torture. It messes with your mind."

"I don't understand. Polite?"

"It's inhuman. They ask the same thing over and over again. And I didn't ever know what it was they wanted from me." Christa closes her eyes and leans back again. She whispers, "A secret police force, just like in Russia."

Bettina places a light hand on her shoulder, and her friend flinches.

"I miss Rolf so much. He's gone, and he won't be coming back again. It's all they wanted to talk about." Christa's lips are a thin line, chalky and cracked. "What could I tell them? What on earth did they want from me?"

"You're here now," Bettina says. "And they didn't hurt you; you're healthy."

In the gloom, Christa's eyes gleam like a skittish cow's. She takes a deep breath. "But when you don't understand *why*, then you don't know if they'll come again . . . ," she says. "That's what drives you crazy."

Bettina doesn't stay long. There is a sour taste in her mouth. She brings Christa a glass of water and drinks two entire glasses herself. When she leaves the house, her basket empty, she looks in both directions to make sure the green car is not idling at the corner anymore. It seems there are eyes everywhere these days, when previously it felt as though the islanders were invisible to the larger world. For years what they did or did not do was of no consequence to anyone.

No longer. Someone or something—hawkeyed, lingering—seems to be watching them, intent on something, but what the point of all this can possibly be is not clear to her.

PART TWO

13

Chicago
Summer 1965

Herbert stayed the night in her apartment, too drunk to return to his hotel in the city center. He must have been nervous, waiting for Bettina to finish up at the gallery, wondering how his shreds of information would impact her—even though, in truth, his news was both laughably incomplete and fundamentally unhelpful. He had no more information; he didn't even know details about Werner's illness and whether it was fatal. What was she supposed to do with this piecemeal news? After he told her, there had been silence. It seemed as if he wanted to comfort her, but she didn't want that; she wished she were alone. She waited till he'd used the bathroom and then let him stumble over to the couch before bidding him good night.

After grabbing her robe from behind the screen, she went to wash her face and brush her teeth. Her fingertips were prickling as though she had become deeply chilled. She could not control her trembling, and a heavy dread lay in her stomach like a rock—what was she supposed to do now? She had been gone for more than eleven years, an eternity. There had been so very little hope of reconciling in any way with those she'd been forced to leave behind—and now . . . was a door opening? Was this an opportunity? But she had no means, no agency. No access to people, money, information, power. So Werner was sick; what did that change for her?

Slowly she unclipped her pearl earrings and leaned over the sink to look at herself in the mirror. Her dark-brown eyes were bright, their slight slant a little more exaggerated with each passing year, lending her an air of skepticism. Her skin was feverish even though she felt strangely chilled. Herbert had told her that she was beautiful, but she saw in her reflection a woman whose life was passing her by. She wondered if, back in East Germany all these years, Werner had ever remarried. Perhaps he'd been promoted again. She still wore his wedding ring because it protected her as a single woman alone in a big city. But it was also a daily reminder of what she had to atone for.

A small black-and-white picture of Annaliese was attached with a piece of tape to the wall by the light switch. The child—not yet a year old—was propped up in a metal tub in the kitchen, dark hair plastered to her cheeks and neck, eyes closed but mouth open in laughter. It was pure joy: the blurry grin, the water glistening on her chubby arms. The photo had been taken in haste and was out of focus, but it told a simple story of fearlessness and trust, a story so powerful Bettina felt it jolt her every time she looked at the picture, even now.

She undressed hastily and, emerging with her robe tied tightly around her waist, saw that Herbert was already asleep on the couch, fully clothed. She slipped off his shoes and pulled the blanket over him. It was hard to be angry at this lonely man. He had tried to comfort her when she'd first arrived in America, stunned by the hairpin turn her life had taken, and for a brief time they'd confused the tenderness of their connection to each other with something else. It was disappointment that tied them together, and a certain tentative fondness, nothing more. Her sister had been oblivious (and for that Bettina was grateful), but the marriage had failed regardless.

There was a moment back then when Bettina had looked into an empty bottle of Fleischmann's gin, reeling, her head pounding with anger and pain, but she'd found it within herself to stop turning to the bottle for comfort. What use would she be as a drunk? How could she ever make amends to her child? She discovered that, even in the depths of her distress, she did still have the capacity to make choices about her life.

By the entrance door sat the gift bag her boss, George, had given her as she left the gallery. She brought it into her sleeping area and closed the bamboo screen behind her for privacy. Herbert's breathing was heavy and regular, a little wheezy. In the stillness of night, her world suddenly seemed overly crowded and confusing, as though the many millions of people inhabiting this earth were no more important than insects. Striving toward something indefinable, working ceaselessly. It seemed impossible that earlier this evening, people had been applauding her for her work, that she had been the center of attention. It all seemed so pointless, even though a small part of her had been excited at the thought that this might mean she could change after all—she could still make something of her life.

Bettina laid out the contents of the bag onto her terry cloth coverlet. There was a bottle of Dom Pérignon—real champagne—with a silky blue ribbon tied around it and a card: *Dearest Bettina, You have a powerful voice and it is being heard! Many congratulations! With love, George and May.*

There was also an unopened envelope addressed to *Bettina Heilstrom, Photo Journalist c/o Tribune Publishing, 435 North Michigan Avenue, Chicago, Illinois, 60611.*

Inside lay a lovely piece of cream-colored, embossed paper that congratulated her on being the 1965 winner of the Smithsonian photo contest. And slipped into the folds of that letter was a check made out to her.

She could not believe her eyes: *$2,000.*

The phone rang the next morning, waking her from a light, twitchy sleep. Instantly she remembered the money and bolted upright, her heart racing. Two thousand dollars! What she could do with that money—she could hire a lawyer; she could even fly to Berlin if she wanted. The money gave her something she'd never had before: power. The phone trilled again.

It was George. He apologized for waking her. Two days earlier a fire truck up in the Garfield Park area had run into a signpost, toppling it and killing a young black woman. A photo in the *Chicago Daily News* showed protestors holding signs claiming the death hadn't been an accident, and unrest was spilling over into other neighborhoods. "There's a full-fledged riot broken out now. Sorry, Bettina. Can you come? We need action shots, good ones. Meet me at the Wilcox firehouse. Take a cab, pronto."

Bettina was not George's usual go-to on-the-ground photographer; that was Dan Markowski, who was on vacation. She dressed quickly in jeans, a men's shirt, and a pair of well-worn sneakers. She pulled her hair from her face and tied it back. Herbert was still asleep on her couch, and even when she tapped his arm, he didn't stir. Bettina left him a note on the kitchen counter; he would have to let himself out.

The scene was chaotic. She found George talking to one of the reserve firemen at the side entrance to the station. He motioned to her with one finger to hold on, and she began snapping pictures. For the next three hours she took photos with the old Rollei. The faces around her were steeped in hatred and fury, exhausted from a night of screaming and a life of being overlooked. In her crisp white shirt, with her white face, she stood out in the crowd, and George loomed beside her, often putting a hand on her protectively, his enormous presence offering her a kind of shield. But she was not afraid; she was never afraid when she had the camera. Eyes raked her greedily, angrily, seeing her as an institution, a symbol of the endless, unbearable oppression they were forced to endure. And yet there was something . . . something that joined them together, and the people could feel it, and they let her do her work.

The pressing heat of another summer's day rose around them, making the faces slick with sweat. As she snapped her pictures, Bettina considered the light on a glistening cheekbone, the scraggle of wiry hair pearled with water from a broken hydrant. She approached, closer and closer, so close at times that she could have reached out and wiped away a teardrop of perspiration from someone's cheek.

The eyes, so full of hunger. She recognized it without analyzing it. She took it all in, absorbing it into herself, while at the same time reflecting it. This was not art; this was life. Real life, beautiful and ugly in equal measure.

On the way back to the office in the cab, she already knew that one picture would stand out from the rest. It was a man with a boy on his shoulders, a skinny brown child in shorts who clutched at his father's temples, trying not to fall off in the swaying, rumbling crowd. There was a second when the father and the boy shared the exact same expression: eyes flashing in terror yet jaws set square in defiance. Mouths open, screaming. The picture would be dark (she'd have to work on that during development), but the flash of the eyes, the mirroring in their faces of their shared yet contradictory impulses—it was powerful. This would be the picture that revealed the humanity in these strangers, their indelible connection to all other human beings.

Climbing onto the bus to head back to the apartment later that afternoon and handing the driver a quarter, she realized with dismay that her hands were shaking quite badly. This often happened after assignments. She'd be calm, all her energy focused on the task of taking photos, and it was only once she was done that her body registered what she'd been through. With effort she brought herself back to the moment: the smell of her own sweat, the smoke in her hair, the feel of the city grime on her palms and face. The bus was full of people dressed in their Sunday best, heading to family dinners in other parts of the city, one last moment of communion before the beginning of yet another hectic workweek. Brown hats and felt caps. Women wearing white gloves, even in the heat. Strings of fake pearls on their necks, sensible shoes with thick rubber soles. Again Bettina thought of the check that lay on her bedside table, the two thousand dollars, and this time there was an abrupt shift inside her that jolted her, waking her up.

Yes, yes, the money . . . all day long it had been skirting at the edge of her consciousness with its promise of action, of change. First thing in the morning she would put that money in the bank. She'd call Clara and ask her advice. There were steps she could take now. Werner was sick; he might be dying, and she was going to find her child and reclaim her. It was possible; she could do it.

She ran home from the bus stop and was disappointed to find that Herbert had left; she'd wanted to tell him about her plans, the possibilities that were open to her now. The apartment was the same, a slight green tinge over everything as the late-afternoon light filtered through all her plants clustered at the window, the blanket and sheets neatly folded by the couch. Her familiar dish for her house keys, the small mirror she'd hung so that she could check her hair before leaving. How could everything be exactly the same when everything had changed?

14

Rügen
Fall 1951

The town hall is at the eastern end of the village square, where, years after the bombing, there are still gaps of architectural logic—the ghost of the bakery lingers here in the dusty pile of bricks, and there the footprint of the cellar of one of the grander buildings is still visible. From his office Werner can hear children in the streets below playing dice in the afternoons. They congregate on the corner—hands deep in the pockets of their hand-stitched shorts, waiting until the whole gang arrives—and then set about playing game after game for hours on end, screeching and laughing, a pregnant silence when awaiting the outcome of an important roll of dice. In good weather he often opens the window and leans out over the windowsill so he can better hear their cries floating up toward him. Sometimes they'll glance up and offer him a wave, excited by his illicit participation—a man in a suit interesting himself in child's play. It makes them hot with pride.

At five o'clock, Werner begins to get fidgety. He checks his watch every few minutes and pores over his accounts, his eyes seeing nothing but a mass of black lines that are supposed to be numbers. At 5:23 his telephone rings, and he jumps in his seat.

"Frau Nietz to see you," Fräulein Krause from downstairs says.

"Thank you, Fräulein. Send her up."

He stands when Bettina enters; her cheeks are glowing, and her brown eyes are clear and dark. Her breath comes fast.

"I came as quickly as I could, but I had to clean up first. That fish, blech!" she says. She wears an unfamiliar dress patterned with tiny blue flowers. It has a high neckline, which accentuates the length of her body, and short sleeves. Her arms and legs are lightly tanned. She does not look as though she spends hours in a cavernous factory under fluorescent lights. They are enjoying an indian summer and will walk to the beach together, perhaps get a beer at the café by the docks.

The fact that she went home and changed her clothes pleases him. "A new dress?"

"Yes. Can you imagine? The first in such a very long time!" She smiles, and her one crooked tooth casts a shadow on the others; this flaw in the symmetry of her face makes her seem at once accessible and unknowable.

Side by side, they walk through the square, and instead of turning left to head toward the fish factory, they turn right and make their way toward the edge of town, where the cliffs bend on creaky knees to reach the waters below. There are a few small businesses, including an outdoor café, that perch at the end of a narrow boardwalk near the piers at which fishing vessels dock. Here, unlike in Binz, the port is almost exclusively industrial. A long narrow strip of beach curves for many kilometers to the south, but it is largely unused for recreation.

Werner knows how much his wife loves this stretch of Saargen. It is where her grandfather's boat was docked: first a large seafaring trawler and then, after the first war, a one-man wooden vessel. Personally, Werner dislikes the insistent cawing of the gulls; the angry overhead cacophony is distracting. But he understands how much Bettina had enjoyed the uncomplicated pleasure of ritual as a child. She often came here after school, she told him, running as fast as she could, just so that she could wait on the piers and look out over the water for the telltale red-striped nose of her grandfather's boat. His hair and beard and clothes suffused with the smell of the sea—she'd loved that.

"We should come here more often," she says, clutching her cardigan to her sides against the wind.

He smiles to himself, having known she would say that. "There's the ferry." He points over the water and then checks his watch. "Must be the last one of the day."

She's brought along her camera and pops up the viewfinder, pointing it toward . . . he's not sure what. He sees the sea and a boat and a series of old docks, but he has no idea why you'd want a picture of that. They walk closer to the edge of the docks, where she abruptly comes to a stop, and he almost walks into her.

"Oh!" she exclaims. "It's—I think that's Manfred. And Henning, maybe?" She tents her hands over her eyes. "Yes, it is!"

Before he can react, she moves away down the uneven planks that make up one of the last piers. At the very end, a midsize fishing vessel bobs, banging its plank against the dock. Instead of walking down with her, Werner fishes inside his jacket pocket for his cigarettes and lights one by turning his back to the wind and cupping his hands in two half globes over his mouth and nose.

When he turns around again, his wife is embracing one of the men. Then a shorter, narrow-chested man shakes her hand. Werner squints to see if he can recognize them. Wearing a navy cap and a scarf around his neck, the short fellow appears to be just a boy. Bettina gesticulates at Werner, but he stays put, dragging deeply on his cigarette. Something about the scene nags at him.

His thoughts turn to the neighborhood boy Bettina was in love with when she was a teenager: Dieter. She told him all about the boy one night, not knowing that Werner didn't want to hear a thing, that knowledge, in this case, only served to weaken him. Had they made love? he wondered. He wouldn't put it past her; there's a stubborn streak in her that rankles. His wife has denied it, of course. Had the boy been handsome and brave—everything Werner is not? Images of their coupling invade his thoughts, even though he knows that she cannot possibly intend to provoke this by hugging this man on the dock in public. He throws his cigarette over the splintered wood, into the water below.

She raises her camera again, standing for what seems like a long time, picking her shots carefully. The two men are very close to her, but he figures they must be in the frame—and behind her is the sea, the beach, the cliffs, and the sky. What on earth can she be doing? Why would she take a picture with these two strangers in it? He doesn't understand her relationship with that camera. All the negatives that remain undeveloped and the stacks of old pictures (of nothing interesting, as far as he can tell) that gather dust on the shelves. It seems nosy and intrusive to point that thing at people all the time.

"It's Christa's boys. The nephew and her son—that's the little one, Henning. See?" Bettina says when she returns to him. "They've taken jobs here to earn some extra money."

The reminder of her attachment to the stupid Kellermanns irritates Werner further. Each week she has been trekking over to Bobbin, and he has already told her in no uncertain terms that she is endangering them with these visits. The Stasi is likely still watching the family. Not to mention that it's embarrassing to him professionally that his wife insists on defying him so openly. But Bettina returns to Bobbin again and again, even though the woman, Christa, has been back at the factory working again for over a year. She's fine!

"We're just friends," Bettina always insists. "It's harmless."

Now he grips her arm and pulls her toward him. "That was not proper," he mutters.

"What?"

"You embracing that man—in public."

A half smile hovers on her lips, as though she is trying to gauge his sense of humor. "They're practically children, Werner. It was motherly."

Motherly. The blood begins to pound in his ears. For too long now, he and Bettina have been playing a strange tug-of-war. She resists his efforts to make love; he can feel her stiffen when he approaches her, the bedsheet cold against his thighs. During the day she'll be in the kitchen, warm and solicitous toward him, giving him hope, and the next moment she'll be chilly and disdainful. Each kindness she shows him and each haughty glance she throws his way arouses in him a seesaw of feelings, as though he is a crippled teenager all over again. "And what on earth were you taking pictures of?"

"I—Werner, I was just . . . I don't know how to explain. Stop yanking my arm, please, will you?"

The heat of his unanswered questions muddles his mind. Surely the important thing now is to be unwavering and firm; he doesn't want her to think he is a pushover. He pulls her to the side of the café, out of the wind. With one finger he lifts the dark wing of hair that has fallen over her face. "Do you know anything about her family"—he gestures toward the dock—"or her past? You jumped to her defense without knowing whether she was even worth defending. It needs to stop. They'll be keeping track, the police."

"She's a *friend* . . ." Her words die out, but she keeps staring at him, as though making up her mind about something. He does not allow his eyes to shift away. Looking so steadily into her dark-brown pupils, he feels he is drowning inside her. Why can't he see what she is thinking, understand what she wants from him—who she wants him to be?

She takes a step back. "But . . . you said you helped her, didn't you? You stood up for her too?"

"Have I ever given you reason to doubt me?"

She regards him so earnestly, her eyes skittery, but it is impossible to tell what is on her mind.

"What is it?" he asks. "What is it *now*?"

"The changes at work . . . are you a member of the Stasi now?"

"It's not official, not yet, but . . ." He takes a few long strides, then turns and takes a few more. "There's a lot going on at the town hall that I'm part of. I've told you before, my work is important. *I* am important to our government. I have information about people—information that would not be considered favorably by certain others."

"I'm sorry, but I have no earthly idea what you mean."

"The Russians, yes, yes, so they've reorganized things. I'm ready and waiting for when they need me." Werner tries to take out another cigarette for himself and finds his fingers thick and clumsy. He has a sudden image of her leaving him, and he wants to tell her that she can never, ever think of it. That if she so much as *thinks* about it, even for a second, he will know, and he will never accept it. But as much as he wants to tell her this, the words stick in his mouth like a wad of paper. His love for her feels like a noose.

He cannot stand it any longer: he imagines he can hear the click-clicking of the levers of her mind filling up the silence between them as she wonders, *Do I trust him, or do I not?* Grabbing her by both elbows, he leans toward her and pushes his lips roughly against hers. Under his touch she is stiff and unyielding, and he takes a step forward and presses harder against her. The urge to crush the fine bones of her clavicle, to press into her with his thumbs until she cries out, is overwhelming. The stupid Rollei is in the way, and he yanks it from her shoulder and throws it to the ground.

"My camera!" she says, falling to her knees on the wooden board-walk and cradling it in her palms.

As though facing the blistering heat of a flame, he turns away from her. This time he saw it in her eyes: *pity.* "That stupid thing," he mutters. "You're wasting your time with that."

How can he explain what he wants from her? It is not complicated. He wants her respect. Her love. He wants not just her physical presence next to him but her soul.

15

In the bluish dusk, a small group makes its way toward the local elementary school to attend a Russian "friendship performance" in celebration of the harvest. Bettina is with her neighbor Irmgard Bandelow and two children who have been assigned to live with her. The older girl, Alma, is an orphan, and the younger one's mother is in an institution in Dresden. Alma walks alongside them, humming a tune to herself. In a dull black leather case, she carries a violin, which she swings back and forth. She wears a bright-blue Young Pioneer uniform, with the emblem of the rising sun sewn on the left sleeve. She is a single-minded girl, engaging in conversation only to discuss schoolwork or a simplified version of Communist political theory. At nine years old the little one, Elise, is doughy from eating too much starch, and she lags behind the three of them.

Hanging over the school's doors, a red felt banner proclaims: *Für's Vaterland ist keine Pflicht zu schwer, kein Opfer ist zu groß für's Vaterland!*

Irmgard arches her light brows. Her face is square, with wide-set eyes and a mouth that even when straight always makes her look a bit like she is smiling. "No duty is too difficult, no sacrifice too great for the fatherland?" she parrots. "Sounds just like the old days to me."

Alma overhears and pokes Irmgard in the back with the violin case. "Hush," she says. "That's disrespectful!"

"You don't remember the war," Bettina says, taking Alma's hand in hers. "If you did, declarations like that might make you uneasy too."

The child snatches her hand away. Her freckled face flushed in annoyance, she heads for a group of blue shirts huddled by the swinging doors. Little Elise slips her sweaty hand into Bettina's and pipes up, "I remember the war!"

"Of course you do," says Bettina. "But there's peace now, right? Nothing more to worry about."

Dark beer and Russian vodka are being served on long wooden tables in the hallway of the school building, and the mood is already somewhat raucous. It's common for high-grade spirits to be given to factory workers—a production incentive, according to Werner—and there's often free Russian vodka at cultural events. Irmgard heads for the table, downing one glass quickly and bringing two more to where Bettina stands with Elise. Her white-blonde hair has been carefully curled in large rolls that run along either side of her face and above her forehead, and the men in the room are casting her sidelong glances. Her shoulders are broad, her hands large and chapped, and until now it has not occurred to Bettina that her neighbor is beautiful.

Bettina takes a quick, deep slug from the glass. The vodka tastes of fresh wind and salty seas. It is not quite cold enough, but it burns her throat pleasantly as it goes down. Alma has gone off with her friends. They inch their way into the large hall, which is filled almost to capacity. A phonograph plays Russian marching music, and East German soldiers in khaki uniforms with braided epaulets and hammer and sickle medals pinned onto the lapels stand in a loose group, chatting among themselves.

The lights dim and then blast back on; the spectacle begins. Elise sits on Bettina's lap at the back, writhing in excitement. When the Russians sing together, their embroidered shirts bright under the stage lights, their voices weave in and out in multiple harmonies that are tender and rousing. It stirs Bettina's heart in a way that makes her vulnerable to hope. They strum balalaikas and tug at accordions; one man makes a harmonica sing with reedy, drawn-out notes. The audience quiets down, and Elise stops her squirming as a hulking Russian officer, well known around town for his spectacularly mean wife, steps onstage and adds his sonorous voice to the refrain.

When the musicians pause, a deep silence fills the room, followed by a sharp intake of breath, and as the singers exit the stage, thrilled whispers swirl amid the audience: "How could it be?" "Singing like innocents!" "Just imagine, those brutes, so refined!"

At the end of the performance, the school chorus marches in single file onto the stage to sing the national anthem of the DDR. The children wear their blue uniforms and stand in perfect formation, heads high and low, dark and light, hands clasped behind their backs. Alma stands in the front row, braids white under the spotlight, her face pinched with conviction. She raises the battered violin to her shoulder and begins her thin sawing.

> Let us plow and build our nation,
> Learn and work as never yet,
> That a free new generation,
> Faith in its own strength beget!
> German youth, for whom the striving
> Of our people is at one,
> You are Germany's reviving,
> And over our Germany,
> There is shining sun;
> There is shining sun.

The anthem is plain, with no complexity to its sound or rhythm, and it leaves behind a sense of unease that lingers like bad breath. Standing facing the children is a tall man in a shabby suit whose long arms motion up and down in time to the music. His back is narrow, but his shoulders strain at a dark jacket stitched together out of inexpensive materials. When he turns around to take a little bow at the end of the last verse, Bettina gasps: it is the beach man, cleaned up and hatless, looking almost nothing like the man she bumped into the previous year at the Bobbin church.

"Elise?" Bettina whispers into the warm circle of the little girl's ear. "That man. Do you know who that is?"

"Oh, him?" she says. "That's Alma's teacher."

"Peter Brenner," Irmgard whispers, leaning in. "Literature teacher at the middle school in Bobbin. Brainy, that one. Single too."

Bettina sits up straight to get a clearer view over the heads of the crowd, but as everyone begins filing out, there is nothing to see but bodies, torn woolen coats, yellowed shirts, and shabby print dresses.

Outside, a hint of winter edges the breeze and rifles through the almost-bare tree branches. Bettina stands in her little group, silent, clutching her overcoat close to her and waiting for Alma to emerge. It is disconcerting to see the beach man in this setting and even more perplexing that he has turned out to be an academic. No wonder his preoccupation with the lessons of recent history and his looking to the future for answers. But an intellectual, an artist? She had imagined him to be a farmer, in his dungarees, or a fisherman perhaps. This new image of the stranger intrigues her, and as she waits in the darkness, her breath lit up in the air from the floodlights, she replays their strange conversation in the graveyard, wondering if he thought her banal.

"Wasn't it beautiful?" Alma calls out, bursting through the doors into the night air. "How did I play? I was so *nervous!*"

"Oh, I forgot my handkerchief," Bettina says, surprising herself with her lie. She digs around in her purse. "It's getting cold—you all go on ahead, and I'll make my own way back."

The hallway and auditorium are almost empty of spectators now. It smells of beer, and the floor is sticky. In among the rows of chairs, some teachers and a few janitors are picking up crumpled programs from the floor. Bettina strides up to one of them and asks if they found a pale-blue handkerchief with white stitching on the edges. Her voice echoes in the nearly empty room—quiet but for the scraping of chair legs—and Alma's teacher raises his head and looks at her. Their eyes meet, and he smiles in surprised recognition.

"Haven't found any handkerchiefs," he says, "but you can have some eyeglasses if you like." He holds out a pair in his palm.

A sharp panic strikes Bettina, breaking into her voice and making her bold. "Thank you," she answers, "but those are not mine. Should you find the handkerchief, I . . . ahem, I live in Saargen, in the old square, Apolonienmarkt."

Her heart rattles against her rib cage. She is remembering the beach, all those years ago when she was still just a child, the freighted look they exchanged. It was so knowing, unnerving. It is so vivid in her mind that it seems to have happened just minutes ago. She wants very much to talk to this man, watch his lips moving as he tells her what his name is, hear him say *her* name aloud, see the changes flicker in his face from seriousness to levity and back again.

When she turns and leaves, she knows that he will follow her.

16

Bettina doesn't have to wait long. The doors swing open, and the man walks toward her. The audience has dispersed, leaving the two of them alone under glaring outdoor lights that illuminate their faces as though they are the last performers on an empty stage.

His suit jacket hangs jackknifed over his arm; underneath, his shirt is thin and stained. In the stark light he appears slimmer than she remembered. In the churchyard he had hidden himself in the thick overalls and a farmer's shirt. Even though it is already late October, the skin of his face is dark from the sun.

"Are you not cold?" she asks him.

"Will be soon, I imagine. If I hang around here with you for too long." He hunches up his shoulders. "Shall we perhaps go somewhere warmer?"

She considers this. What will she tell Werner when she gets home? Can she trust this man, a stranger? There is something about him that seems dangerous: a certain looseness about the mouth and eyes, a fluidity to his movements. The shadowy eye sockets under those pale brows. He appears to move from thought to action with no hesitation.

She knows that she will say yes to whatever he asks of her. "My name is Bettina Heilstrom," she says in response, deliberately using her maiden name.

"And I am Peter Brenner. Nice to meet you formally, after all these years."

This makes her smile self-consciously. Just hearing him say his name is like seeing him unclothed.

"Did you find your handkerchief?"

She nods yes, and his smile tells her that he knows she was lying.

Peter Brenner leads her down a side street. He can't take her to the pub—it will be full of people she knows. Does he even realize that she is a married woman? On her finger she wears a wedding band, as befits a wife. Almost daily she presses her husband's shirts, prepares his meals, helps him up the stairs when his legs begin to hurt . . . but she also secretly prays that Werner will be too tired to make love—and that when they do, he will not take offense at her frozen responses. They come to a door, and when the man unlocks it, they tumble inside along with the cold air.

It is a youth center, a cavernous space with posters lining the walls and tables set up where children can do their homework or art projects. Ropes hang from the ceiling in one corner, and there are bars installed on one of the walls for climbing. Bettina is amazed to see a Ping-Pong table and a record player. She picks up a pamphlet from a pile on the table and pretends to study it.

"The latest five-year plan from the government," Peter says.

It's a pale-blue booklet with an image of a family on the cover. A young girl sits on her father's shoulder, and the mother is waving, her hair rolled back just like Irmgard's. "Good stuff, is it?" Bettina asks. From the opening page she reads aloud: "Something new has happened: For the first time in German history, our fatherland is guided by a plan that considers only the needs of the people and aims at building prosperity and reconstructing of our fatherland. Only a few years have passed since the terrible catastrophe—"

"Enough of that," he says. "You're far too serious, you know."

She puts the pamphlet back down on its pile. "How do you know? I might surprise you."

"Wouldn't that be nice," he says.

"You teach this stuff? Isn't this economics? Or politics? My neighbor said you teach literature, no?"

"What's in there isn't very literary. Now, if they'd let *me* write those things, I could get people excited. Stories, art—that's how we'll change the world."

"You believe that?"

He casts her a sharp look. "You don't?"

"I can't say, really," she answers, thrilled with their disagreement, the energy of caring what this man thinks and believes. "After what's happened to us, what we've done . . . I suppose I don't really know what I think anymore."

"You can't let that happen. You must always think for yourself." He presses his lips together, assessing her. "Art, literature—it allows us to explore our equivocation, all our uncertainties—this is what makes it so powerful. It asks us to use our minds, to dream and discern and assess. To ask questions."

"You write, do you? What sort of writing—the kind that changes the world?"

His smile is small but genuine, his eyes warm; he is amused by her stubbornness. "I write plays. Political plays that everyone hates. I write poetry sometimes, but for that, well, for that I need to be inspired." He cocks his head to the side. "Poetry is romantic, no? You've got to be in the mood for it."

"My father and I used to read together. Poetry sometimes, but mostly novels."

"Ahhh, so you are in fact literate. Excellent."

"Of course!" she snaps, before realizing he's teasing. "Reading is a way to learn about people, why we do what we do."

"Yes, yes. And that is the great and terrible crusade, wouldn't you say—our eternal search for meaning. The endless battle for what we believe in. It's as Yeats said; do you know it? About Ireland. 'All changed, changed utterly: A terrible beauty is born.'"

She swallows, her throat dry. Something inside her shifts. He means there is a terrible beauty in *life*. The rightness of his words makes her head spin. She's been trying to make sense of these things, too, in her own way. "I take pictures. When I can, that is. I like to, uh . . . I try to record what I'm seeing, not so much what's happening, but what I *see*. But there's a risk in it . . . as though by capturing it, you're also diluting it; does that make sense? There's a risk in seeing, in documenting."

"Oh, no. No, no, no—I disagree. Unless we share, take that risk, what does anything even mean?" The whites of his eyes shine in the half dark, bright as a fox's. She understands better now what happened between them in the graveyard when he couldn't stop talking. He's a writer, a thinker. He was telling her his story, trying to make sense of the world. "So then, you're an artist too."

Her shoulders drop as muscles begin to loosen: he called her an *artist*; she has never thought of herself that way.

"What I really want to do is write a novel. A novel read by thousands that will change people's lives, open their eyes to the beauty and the ugliness. But alas"—he laughs lightly at himself—"that's a lot easier to say than actually do."

He heads to the record player and pulls out a disc from under a pile on the bottom shelf, then slips it onto the player. "Here we go," he says to her over his shoulder. He fiddles with the needle on the player, and music starts. "This is from the *Amis*—Professor Longhair. Listen."

This has the effect of a slap in the face: He is playing American music?

"You're surprised?" he asks when he sees her expression.

"I mean, the *Americans* . . . they, well—they betrayed us, didn't they? We're not supposed to listen to their music."

"Because they're capitalists? Or because the music is evil?"

"Both those things," she says. "But mainly because if we're caught, we'll get in trouble."

"There's something you should know about me right away," he answers, coming up to her. He peels back her overcoat. She is wearing one of her old housedresses, but he isn't looking at her clothing or her body; he is looking right into her. His eyes are almost purple. He seems to recognize her fear and hesitation but her excitement too. "I break rules. I follow rules, yes . . . but I also break them."

She laughs. "That much is obvious."

"It is?"

"Well, we're here, aren't we?"

"Should we not be?"

He throws her coat onto an old couch covered in shredded brown fabric. It is chilly in this empty place that smells of cleaning fluids and rubber balls. "Because I . . . I am . . . married."

Placing his forefinger over her lips, he shakes his head. "Listen; *listen* to this! This will make you understand why music can only be good, not bad. Even if it is made by Americans. Just listen."

This music is unlike the waltzes and polkas to which she is accustomed. Nor is it similar in any way to the popular ballads of the day. It has a manic energy, a big sound that is startling—there are horns and strings, a piano being thumped in the background, the growling notes of a bass bringing together all the seemingly disparate chords into one rhythmic, crashing tune. There is something about it that is entirely new to her, a different kind of beat she doesn't recognize.

Peter Brenner is snapping his fingers in time. His lean body bobs up and down, his knees soft. "Piano blues," he says over the raucous notes. "Jazz—anarchy in music form. But this, he has a strange style, no? Cuban influences. Recorded in New Orleans."

"How on earth did you get hold of it?" Bettina asks, unable to keep her tone from sounding disapproving.

"Old friends from Berlin. You know what he's saying?" he asks, and when she shakes her head, he adds, "'Bald head.' About a lady with no hair . . ."

This makes her smile, and he reaches out a long arm and grasps her around the waist, and she has to catch her breath.

Pulling her in tight and then pushing her away, he starts a kind of dancing that involves moving toward each other and then back again, swinging their arms and then letting them drop, turning in unison and separately. She parodies his movements, and even though it is terribly awkward, it is also fun. Usually you dance in one way: clasped to your partner, one arm around the waist and the other held up in the air like the prow of a ship. This new technique—half-together and half-apart—makes Bettina laugh so hard she has tears in her eyes. She is hurtling through the room, in and out of this man's arms, breathless, her heart pumping wildly, and yet she remains entirely in his control. His every nudge and tilt tells her exactly where she is supposed to go. Tripping a few times, she bends over laughing, only to be grabbed again and hurled in another direction. When the music stops, they stand facing each other, gasping for breath. Yes, anarchic and purposeful.

"I don't care that you're married," he says, using the informal *du* to address her. It sounds natural on his lips, as though they are old friends who share years of secrets. "I was married, too, and I was not happy."

He is serious now, having seconds ago been so lighthearted as to toss her around like a ball. Already she loves this ability in him to shift and change like a chameleon. She is tired of people capable of only one emotion at a time.

Standing on tiptoes, she raises her face to his, and they kiss.

Pushing her against a tabletop, Peter Brenner lifts her up so that she is sitting. She parts her legs, and he slips his hips between them.

They press against each other. When she breaks away, a sob escapes her. He puts one hand on her throat and stares at her. A high, thin note of tension courses through her chest and between her legs. Her underpants are wet.

Stumbling through the streets, Bettina trips over a loose stone and loses one of her rubber shoes. She stoops to pick it up and tries to slow down her breathing. She looks to see if Peter has followed her but sees only the watery light from the lampposts reflected in the buildings' windows and a dark, empty street heading down a hill. Everything on this little side street—from the shuttered art supply store to the bakery, the lindens lining the sidewalks and the wrought iron waste bins—is familiar to her and yet looks strange now, even ominous. How many times has she walked along this street as a child, then as a teenager, an adult, a married woman, and not really *seen* it? Not noticed the crumbling plaster outside Schenkov's Uniform Supply Store, the way the roofline of the old insurance building abruptly turns, creating a broken line that reaches into the navy night sky. What has previously been so commonplace as to be utterly forgettable is revealing itself to her as unknown. Have the series of uneven doorways always looked like a row of sentries, keeping people out rather than inviting them in? And the trees—have their half-naked branches ever reminded her before of the terrible pictures she saw of the concentration camps? In her panic it seems to her that every object her eyes fall upon is a reminder that nothing is really as she had thought.

Peter Brenner is nowhere to be seen, and Bettina is at once relieved and let down. After that kiss, the frantic fumbling, she could not stay— God only knows what she would have done—yet now the disappointment is almost too much to bear. After slipping her shoe back on, she hurries through the winding streets toward home. She turns into the square and stops in front of her house to adjust her shirt, which she buttoned up incorrectly in her haste to leave.

Werner is asleep. In the small bathroom she lights the water heater and runs a bath, hoping the sound of water in the pipes will not wake him up. She drops her clothes on the floor and steps into the old porcelain tub, which is only partially filled with lukewarm water.

Eventually her breathing becomes more regular again. The half of her body that is not submerged underwater is white and covered in goose bumps. Closing her eyes, she pictures his large hands, almost luminous in the semidark . . . sees them touching her. When the pulsing between her legs becomes unbearable, she slips her hand between her thighs, clenching them together tightly.

In the youth center they only kissed that one time, but in her imagination he is gentle with her, then rough. His hands are soft, then hard and insistent. He smiles, but then, like a child, he weeps. Bettina's fingers press into herself, and she utters a sharp cry as though she has been hurt, when really it is a reaction to the surprise of the explosion inside her—tender and yet so very violent that it shatters the logic of her life.

17

The conveyor belt has stopped working again, and Putzkammer is exasperated. The mechanics take it apart and discover so much wear and tear on the bolts that hold the belt in place that they all need to be replaced. No more work until tomorrow at the earliest. Anne-Marie, Stefanie, and Christa unfurl their aprons and head for the changing rooms. Christa has lost weight, and her work tunic swims on her body. Since coming back to the factory, she has stopped talking much except to offer up a perfunctory *Guten Morgen* or *Auf Wiedersehen*. Bettina misses the idle chats, the smiles, and the pithy one-liners. In the past weeks since her dancing episode with Peter Brenner (that's how she has trained herself to think about that night), Bettina has returned a few times to Bobbin (to see her work friend, she tells herself), and yet each time Christa rebuffed her in some small way—with indifference or an unwillingness to joke around or even smile.

"Christa, wait!" Bettina calls out.

Christa's haggard face remains impassive. "Yes?"

"I have some time now. Can I walk home with you? I haven't seen the children in a while. Last time I was there, you were busy, remember?"

Christa shakes her head no and steps away toward the changing rooms. "We are *fine*. We do not need your charity," she says. Then she lowers her voice. "I do not want your prying; you're not helping matters."

"But . . . I'm . . ." Bettina watches her walk away, then pushes against a heavy metal door and emerges onto the gravel where she and her coworkers sometimes take cigarette breaks. Is it because of Werner that she is being quietly pushed aside? At work now the women fall silent when Bettina passes them, raising their brows at one another in warning. Lunch breaks are quiet affairs without the customary light-hearted ribbing she once enjoyed being part of.

She is shivering. It is brutally cold, with a fast wind sweeping in over the water, carrying with it the promise of ice and snow. What is she going to do, she wonders, allowing herself to think now of Peter Brenner. She has tried so hard to ignore what's happening to her. But since the night of the friendship performance, there is not a moment of the day during which she does not ask herself, *Who am I? What am I doing? Where is he now? Will I see him again?*

Over and over again she replays their conversations in her mind. Certain that her most secret thoughts are written across her face for everyone to see, she withdraws ever further into herself. But her mind races ahead of itself, sending her into a tailspin. At night she cannot sleep, and during the day she stands next to her coworkers without being present, neither fully awake nor asleep. Instead she is in a new and frightening place where anything is possible because everything is suddenly unfamiliar. This is also oddly comforting to her: She is alive, burning up with the intensity of every sensation and every thought. Her body reacts to the slightest touch, whether the slippery skin of the herring or the rough wooden handles of her tools, as though she has never before felt these things. It makes her jumpy and nervous and thrilled all at once.

Who am I? she thinks. *What do I want?*

One night she tosses in bed for so unbearably long that she reaches out to Werner, startling him, and their lovemaking is so familiar and disappointing that afterward she creeps into the bathroom and weeps while sitting on the cool porcelain edge of the tub.

Each day her husband looks at her with those unfathomable eyes, asking something of her that she cannot give him. Of course, it turns out that she misread those eyes back when they first met. What she had taken as the capacity for soulfulness is in actuality a tendency toward self-pity. The pale color of his chest testifies to the fact that he is an office worker and barely spends a day in the sun. That he prefers the still air of an enclosed space to the wind of the beach or the dusty heat of the fields. Werner's hands are small and delicate, with carefully clipped fingernails and smooth skin. Peter Brenner has the rough hands of an outdoorsman, hands that show the veins under them in startling blue ridges. Though she knows he is a writer, she imagines him in the fields, hoisting his long body up onto a tractor, the sun beating down on his overgrown blond hair, bringing up a rash of freckles on his nose and shoulder blades. He is strong and wiry, and he towers over her.

This afternoon she has been given the unexpected gift of time, and she doesn't know what to do with herself. She does not want to return home just yet; she will fall into her old patterns of washing and ironing, and she cannot imagine busying herself with these thankless, mundane tasks. It's been months since she picked up her camera; after that day on the piers, Werner's words ring in her ears every time she tries to take a picture: *You're wasting your time with that business.* His disdain presses down on her, and she hasn't had the energy to fight this new and disorienting insecurity. Why *does* she take pictures? She never does anything with them. It's a costly hobby, and pointless.

But then she thinks of the youth center, of Peter's interest in her photography, how he called her an artist. What is she, in fact? What does she want from her life, *and what can she make of it?* She is unsure of what to do with the surges of energy that prickle and tease, making her body hum with a strange sort of exhilaration.

After she has changed out of her tunic and apron and cleaned up a bit, Bettina begins walking toward the center of Saargen. She stops at the bakery to see if they have any fresh bread, but the line snakes out the door and along the sidewalk. Unclipping her long hair, she lets it fall to her shoulders and walks on.

Then she thinks of her sister; yes, she will take the bus to Gummanz, drop in on Clara. Months have passed since Bettina was last at her house, and once the weather turned cold, they abandoned their weekly walks on the promenade. She feels better now that she has somewhere to go that is not home.

Clara lives at the end of an unpaved road, not far from the open-faced chalk pits. The house is a large multilevel structure with a fading orange tile roof. It belonged to her husband's family and was divided after capitulation into multiple apartments. She and Herbert went from enjoying the space and money that came from his stake in the mines to living in a cramped first-floor apartment where the coal heater takes up half the living room.

Outside is a pounded dirt playground with a broken wooden seesaw. Some neighborhood children dressed in coats and multicolored hats scream with excitement as they play with a stray cat they've trapped in a small box. Bettina rings the doorbell and waits. "Herbert, hello," she says as he answers the door. "Hope you don't mind I've come unannounced."

He stands against the wall to let her enter. What used to be quite a lovely entranceway is now a hall from which one door leads to Clara's apartment on the left and another leads to the Lichtenbergs' on the right. Everyone in the house uses the single bathroom located on the second floor. The stairway going up has been patched where the railings broke. On Clara's wedding day, she stood on these stairs to throw her bouquet at the assembled girls clustered around its base. Now it is dark inside, with one unshaded bulb hanging from the ceiling, and Bettina has to let her eyes adjust before she can see that the walls have been covered in striped paper, alternating brown and yellow.

Herbert shrugs. "She thought it would cheer the place up," he says. "It was the only paper she could find. Why aren't you at work?"

"The conveyor belt," Bettina says. "Broken again."

"I'm home for lunch." Herbert checks his wristwatch. "Have to go back in a few minutes."

"Clara is here?"

"She's resting." Herbert ushers her into the apartment. On the table in the living room sits his empty plate from lunch and a tray with some slices of sausage and cheese on it. "Are you hungry? There's some left here."

"No, thank you." Bettina hasn't been eating well for weeks. "Clara's all right? Is she sleeping?"

"Yes, she's in bed. Go on in."

The bedroom curtains are drawn shut, and Bettina can see the outline of a bump on the bed. Leaving the door open behind her for light, she goes over to the bed and looks down at her sister. Clara is asleep, her hands tucked under her cheek, her dark-blonde hair stringy and tangled on the sheets. Her breath is light, as though she is skimming a dream, neither here nor there but somewhere in between. "Clara?"

"Go away," Clara says in an almost whisper, keeping her eyes shut. "I hate it all. I hate him; I hate this house; I hate this country. Leave me alone. Just let me sleep."

"I don't know what's wrong with her," Herbert says when Bettina returns. "She sleeps fourteen, fifteen hours at a stretch."

Bettina takes a seat on the wooden banquette opposite him. Since their outing, when they swam so long together in the frigid ocean that all the color and feeling drained from their bodies, she's begun to think of Herbert differently. It had been devastating to see him so transformed when he lost his arm; then, in the water, when they were both blurred into new versions of themselves, she saw that he had not really changed at all. He was still the young man she'd laughed with years earlier, the striving businessman her sister fell in love with, the soldier doing his duty. He is all those things and more, just as she is more than the sum of her circumstances.

He wipes his mouth with a napkin and places a hand on the table. The open end of his right shirtsleeve has been folded over and pinned together to cover his stump.

"Everything all right, Herbert? How long has she been like this?"

"No. It's—I'm out of business, once and for all. They're merging the Sassnitz mines into the *Volkseigene Kreidewerk*. I've lost all my shares." Herbert had started out as a laborer in the mines, hacking away at the open cliff face for years and then supervising the addition of water to the sedimentation tanks. He was so inventive and driven that he'd worked his way up the hierarchy to shift supervisor and eventually manager, investing in the company along the way. "Sometimes I wonder, Betty— what have we come to? What has happened to Germany?"

"Nothing can stay the same forever." Bettina has overheard people talking in the canteen at the factory and outside the gates as they smoke cigarettes or wait for the bus. Werner is full of enthusiasm for the new police force, coming home at night teasing her with half-revealed stories. She badly wants to be hopeful.

Herbert clears his plate and tucks in the tail of his shirt. "I hear—in America? They have cars with no roofs, and you can drive with the wind in your hair. Everybody owns their own house."

America. All she knows of that country is what she has read in the papers and heard on the radio. Americans had been the enemy, but then they gave candy and food to starving German children after they invaded. Contradictions everywhere. In photos, the American soldiers seem loose limbed, constantly grinning. Is it lecherous and greedy, or are those smiles a sign of generosity? According to the local papers, they are still the enemy—shallow capitalists obsessed with money rather than progress and community.

"But this is our *home*, this island, this country," Bettina answers. "Could you live without the sea? We can't just give up."

"They're taking everything away from us," Herbert says. "Everything meaningful. What will we have left in the end?"

For days afterward Bettina can think of nothing but her sister's words, spoken in that miserable darkened room: *I hate it all. I hate him; I hate this house; I hate this country.* In the youth center, talking with Peter Brenner, Bettina experienced a moment of such urgent belief in the possibility of growth, of understanding—and yet at the same time she's been thrown into a state of quiet chaos.

She is coming to understand that the accumulation of small, insidious changes can be just as destructive as the catastrophic events that throw life off kilter. Unexpected twists have taken her so far from where she thought she'd be that she barely recognizes her life any longer. She struggles to make sense of where she finds herself. She does not want to end up in a bed, sleeping away her days, hating her life.

18

That Sunday she is one of the last people to enter the nave. The Bobbin church is almost full, and today Peter Brenner is sitting on the right-hand side near the aisle. Throughout the service, Bettina is able to stare at the back of his neck, ruddy as though from a lifetime of bending his head down in the sun. In that exposed skin, vulnerable with its deep creases and brushed by wisps of too-long blond hair, lies his very essence. When she studies it, she can imagine him as a baby, as a boy running around causing trouble, as a young man in the first blush of love. The words of Pfarrer Brenner's sermon find no foothold. Since the friendship performance, it is as though a hand or a leg has been amputated; she is experiencing a stunned feeling of loss while at the same time this man is present in her every thought and every activity. The music he played her runs through her mind at all times, and she often finds her mouth curled in a smile. There are a thousand questions she wants him to answer. She needs to know everything about him, even the most inconsequential details.

At the end of the service, Bettina exits quickly and lingers in the graveyard. It isn't long before he emerges. He walks right by her without catching her eye, heading toward the *Pfarrhaus* that lies in the glade behind the church, beyond the winter-thin thickets, gray and brambly. As she follows him, sweat breaks out on her neck and chest. Between them there is a safe distance, but already Bettina is beyond caring whether anyone sees her.

Peter enters the gate and walks into a thatched brick-and-timber structure that is attached to the side of the house where his father lives. She dawdles, then a few minutes later treads the same path. Stepping over the threshold, she is blinded by the darkness that settles on her like a damp palm over her eyes.

"I lied, at the youth center," he says.

As her eyes adjust, she sees that he is standing by a chair and a small table in the middle of an austere room. "What do you mean?"

"I *do* care that you're married. It matters."

They stand in silence. She shuffles her feet, wondering now whether he might reject her. Can he not feel what he has done to her already—how he has changed her?

"I don't really—" she begins but stops. Of course, she cannot say that she doesn't really love her husband, that she doesn't care about betraying Werner as long as it means she can resolve the unbearable need to touch Peter. Perhaps he thinks her foolish—or, worse, selfish and vain. But her body seems to recognize immediately the timbre of this man's voice, the smell of his skin. Even the way he walks seems familiar to her. Though her mind tries to wrestle with logic, knowing what she is doing is dangerous and foolish, an uncustomary clarity envelops her in his presence.

She wants to touch him. She has to be near him.

"Bettina Heilstrom," he says slowly, as though finding pain and delight in each syllable. "I hope you know we are going to suffer for this." He offers a timid smile.

"I know," she answers. When she smiles back, she does not try to mask her teeth. Let him see every flaw in her—she doesn't care to present anything other than her real self to him. She slips her coat off and places it on the chair. Removing the hatpin and the hat seems to take

124

forever. When she is done, he stands looking at her, and she wonders what to do next.

"I hate hats," he says.

She laughs out loud. "Yes, I noticed that."

"They hide your face." His voice has become low and heavy, and her mind flashes to his wife. She wonders whether he wept upon hearing of her death. Had he loved her at all, ever? None of this matters, except that she wants to get to the core of him, to know every secret fear, every secret joy.

"Do you want to go for a walk in the woods?" he asks her.

"No," she cries out.

"I've been thinking of this moment for so long . . . and now I don't know what you want me to do." He comes to stand next to her. "You're—you're not free. Do you see—I must take my cue from you."

She leans forward and places her cheek on his chest. Today he is wearing a cotton tunic, and underneath his heart bangs in his rib cage: *Thump thump. Thump thump.* The pulse works its way through the material to her eardrum and into her body. "Do anything you want to me," she whispers. "I'm asking you to. Please."

His breath is warm in her hair. He touches her chin lightly, and then, as she presents her face to him, he falls upon it. When he bites her lip, she thinks, *Yes, yes.* He slides his hand into the gap between the buttons of her shirt and touches the swell above her breast with his thick fingertips. With a quick intake of breath, she presses into him. Then, unable to wait, she steps back and unbuttons her blouse, letting it fall to the floor, and then reaches behind to unhook her brassiere. Her breasts are full and white. Touching one with her own hand, she feels a streak of heat shoot between her chest and groin.

If he stops, she will scream. If he keeps touching her, she will scream. They tear at each other. There is no going back.

Every part of her life is transformed. In the mornings when she heads to the factory, she smiles to herself secretly, trying not to give away her inner delirium. At work Stefanie tells mindless stories about her skirmishes with her mother-in-law while Bettina nods, her mind somewhere else. Even Christa, so insular and subdued, stares at her quizzically. At the dinner table, Bettina finds herself talkative and solicitous with Werner, as though by covering up the unease with words she can plaster over the damage she has done—and is doing.

She pushes away all thoughts of where this might end. None of that seems relevant; she is so strongly drawn to the present, to every sensation, to the constant thrumming of her body. Practicalities can wait. What matters is now. When she will see Peter again. When she can feel his skin under her fingertips.

They exchange a couple of cryptic notes on slips of paper and meet on the beach in the early-morning hours when she is supposed to be at the early shift, not daring to walk too closely to one another in case they are seen. They do not touch, yet as they walk side by side, there is something charged in the air, a connection between them that makes them feel alone in the world even though they know it is not so. This time they talk without ceasing, both of them, words flowing with the swift energy of water from a spring, at once meandering and purposeful. Peter tells her of the novel he has been struggling to write, his search for something "important enough" to write about. He is impatient with social realism in writing, which has recently become so popular with East German writers.

"You take your pictures not to document the world but to interpret it, right?" he asks her. "In the same way, I can't write simply to show things as they are supposed to be. Where does truth lie, anyway? Is it in the vast brushstrokes, you know—the big-picture story—or is it in the details?"

"The details," she says. "Details tell the story. The everyday is honest."

"And yet it is not enough, at least not in my work," he insists, and she is thrilled by his ambition, his unwillingness to simply make do.

Once, they meet again at the *Pfarrhaus*, and after making love, they lie together on his small bed, the air in the room heavy and pungent, and she talks about the first time her father let her handle his Rollei. Tracing circles on her thigh with his forefinger, Peter does not interrupt or ask questions. As she tries to explain how heavy the camera felt in the palm of her hand—how the world suddenly seemed less constrained, more multidimensional—she realizes this is the first time she's had the chance to talk in this way since her father died. In explaining herself, trying to understand her own motivations, she feels filled with hope and curiosity.

She knows already that it is too late, that she has forfeited control of her life: the undertow has caught her, and she is compelled onward.

But the next time they see each other, they are subdued, as though wrestling with what this connection they're forging will mean to them. How it will disrupt their lives. He has started writing, he tells her, but he will not divulge his subject.

His teeth gleam at her; he is playful, his excitement palpable, and she thinks that what they are actually doing is creating beauty.

And then she finds a list of names. It is on her dressing table in the bedroom, scrawled in Werner's hand on a crumpled sheet of paper:

Adalbert Zweig
Margit Bayer
Stefanie Krug
Silke Shröder
Nils Wolf
Beke Franse
Gisela Keller

Everyone on the list is familiar to Bettina. Stefanie works alongside her, just as Christa does. Nils was in her class at school. Silke is the ticket taker at the train station, and Beke works in Johann's butcher shop in town. For a long time she just stands there, holding it, uncertain of what this means. Has Werner left it on her table on purpose, to warn her, or is this accidental? He has been working more and more closely with the secret police, but she also believes he holds no real power. After all, he wasn't able to help Christa, was he?

She has arranged to meet Peter Brenner at the youth center in half an hour and is impatient to leave, yet now she is rooted to the spot.

There is no question of confronting Werner. Since the moment he entered the fish shop, he revealed himself to be both patient and relentless. He pursued her so insistently, and she quickly succumbed. When he set his mind to something, he achieved it. After years of being constrained by his physical limitations, he had learned to be dogged and deliberate. What can she ask him? Showing interest in this, revealing fear—it seems to her that this will only cause more trouble.

But truth is, the man also has a soft heart. In the evenings he often leans back on the couch with Eberle curled up on his chest, one hand stroking the orange fur and the other holding a book of poems. Sometimes he braids Bettina's hair for her or massages her feet when she's tired from standing at the factory all day. He is a man who dreams of grandeur only to find himself mired in the everyday. She thinks back to the early months of their marriage, their tentative outings to do reconnaissance after the Russians came. Working together to find a way to survive in their new world. The weekend afternoons playing cards and listening to Brahms and Mozart on the radio in the living room. The careful, polite lovemaking.

Guilt buzzes through her, a current reaching into every last part of her body. What has she started? Surely Werner would never do her, or anyone she knows, any harm. But she senses that there is more to him than he has allowed her to see, or perhaps than he is even aware of himself. She thinks of their outing, when he snatched the camera from her, yanked her arm till it hurt.

He is just a man, after all. A man whose wife is taking risks that would make him blanch in fury, a man who does not like to be surprised. She suspects that she has no idea what he might be capable of.

19

The streets of Bergen, Rügen's largest town, are bustling with children in uniforms running to take up their positions in the parade and adults doing last-minute errands before the shops close and the streets become too crowded to navigate. It is the first of March, the *Tag der Volksarmee*: the founding day of the National People's Army.

Werner has gathered with some coworkers from the town hall to join in the festivities. The main square has been renamed Karl-Marx-Platz, and there is a large fountain ringed with benches at one side. The redbrick houses with their crowstepped gables loom high over the square. Traffic has been diverted, and crowds are gathering for the beginning of the march. As Werner gazes at the marchers in their various uniforms, a sudden memory comes to him: The smaller square in Saargen and its disastrous tree planting during the war. The bombs dropping down on them all.

Worst of all, for him, those two soldiers who harassed him and called him a cripple. Because he couldn't fight! A sense of righteousness rises inside him, gripping his throat. He showed those bastards, didn't he? Every day since then has been better than the last, and once again he's standing amid a large raucous crowd, but this time *he* is one of those in charge.

There is a sense of order to the scene despite the sheer number of children and placards and soldiers and horses and swaying banners in red, black, and yellow. The children's infectious enthusiasm, the way their keen eyes dart about as they seek out orders about where to go and what to do, the lift of their mouths, the banter and chatter—it's electrifying. Like streaming water, they begin to disperse and sort into orderly lines. Werner muscles his way through the onlookers to the front of the wooden platform by the *Kaufhaus*, where seats have been reserved for government employees. He is with Comrades Hoffenmayer, Dagenbert, and Fritz. Leading the way, he hoists himself onto the rickety wooden steps—his leg has been hurting him today—and chooses a seat near the front.

The half-timbered houses that surround them are still damaged, chunks of plaster and brick missing everywhere, but on a day like today it is almost possible to believe the war never happened. It is clear and very cold, high winds snapping the banners on their poles and stirring the naked branches of the lindens.

Toward the back of the crowd are the unions, each group wearing sashes sewn from brightly colored nylon to distinguish themselves: the metalworkers, the carmakers, the teachers and sports coaches, the shipbuilders, the electrical-equipment union, and then ahead of them the farmers' collective. Then come the children, identical in their white shirts and red neckerchiefs, wearing jaunty blue hats and holding up banners. The older ones in their blue shirts. Their high-pitched voices rise above the din; it isn't until the parade begins that they will become earnest and silent.

In front of them are the horsemen whose steeds have been trained to prance, lifting their quivering legs high in the air and moving slowly and gracefully. The smell of horse manure is pungent; the deep clop of the horses' hooves reverberates on the stones around him. At the front are ten or twelve rows of soldiers in their blue uniforms, standing at attention, their rifles angled against their shoulders, eyes locked. A smaller group of men in white jackets and white caps stands at the very front.

The band is tuning up its instruments, and then silence. A few minutes later there is a whistle, and the band begins a marching tune. Loudspeakers from the government buildings amplify the sound as the marchers rustle and shift, and the procession begins, gently at first, to move forward. It is an army, but one of great beauty. It is not about violence or fear but about pride and hard work. The vast formation takes up almost the entire square; it will have to winnow itself down in order to make its way through the streets. A regular citizen stands on the sidelines on a small ladder, holding a banner: *Mit den Millionen gegen die Millionäre*—"Millions against the millionaires."

The parade takes a full fifty minutes to empty from the square, and all the while Werner wrestles with a lump in his throat, unwilling to give away how much the sight of all these people working together moves him. In the seven years since the Russians took over the island—and half of his country—they have transformed the local and regional authorities, injected money into the farms and factories, trained teachers and civil servants, and managed to attract disillusioned former National Socialists into the fold of a new political order. Over the years, Werner has come to understand that it was not the Nazis who were to blame for the misfortunes of his country but the capitalists with their incessant drive for power. With every year that the DDR finds its feet, further refining its systems of checks and balances, the country's economy is getting more and more robust. Many years earlier, Werner joined the ruling Communist party, the SED; on his jacket lapel, he wears his pin with pride. It shows two hands clasped together, a symbol of unity. After all, isn't that what they are striving for? Isn't there strength in unity?

So here he is, in this jubilant crowd, and those bullies who tormented him in front of Bettina, who cared about nothing but their own fun and games, where are they? Though he doesn't like to admit it to himself, sometimes he thinks with horror of the boy he killed, remembering the greasy glide of knife into flesh, but at moments like this he knows his actions were justified. He knows that to be on the side of the winners, you must protect, at all costs, what you believe in.

On his way to the car that will take him and his colleagues back to Saargen, Werner is joined by his superior Franz Josef Bieder. Now BV director of Stasi field operations, Bieder is often in East Berlin. Upon seeing the man, Werner experiences an uncomfortable tug in his gut. To compensate for this embarrassing yet instinctive fear, he smiles and nods his head in deference.

"*Hallo*, Nietz," Bieder says. His face has become fleshy with age, making the stationary eye with its glass pupil even more prominent. "Excellent. Just the person I wanted to see. Come with me, will you? I'll have my car take you back later."

Bieder's office is off a narrow corridor on the fifth floor of a handsome brick building next to the square. Vast swaths of beige polyester are drawn halfway across the windows, and light comes from a fluorescent strip over his desk. The air is thick with the opaque pall of cigarette smoke. Lined up against one wall are six large metal filing cabinets.

"Take a seat," he says, settling into an armchair and waving a hand toward the couch. "I have a proposition for you."

Werner pulls out a cigarette from a case he keeps in his suit pocket and sits down. On the wall behind Bieder hangs an enormous woven tapestry in which portraits of Marx, Engels, and Lenin appear in shaggy orange and black.

"You have been in town administration for many years, Comrade. It's a small town, but you built up your skills. You have shown yourself to be steadfast and unwavering. When the DVdI was disbanded to make room for the MfS, we had a clear directive, and we're continuing to work tirelessly at fulfilling that directive. You are aware of the details?"

"Of course, some of them. Especially the most recent ones you shared some months ago."

"Yes, and your pursuit of those persons of interest, how is that going?"

"Coming along nicely. I'm doing the research—political leanings, habits, associations, and so on. As you requested."

Bieder leans forward and picks up a thick folder, sliding it over toward Werner. On the cover it says: *Bundestags-Drucksache 12/3462, S. 97–107.* "I took the liberty of copying sections relevant to you. Part of our mission is protecting ourselves from sabotage from the outside and from the inside . . ."

"Yes, I understand. I've been in OTS for some time now," Werner says, leafing through the document. "What do you need me to do?"

Bieder explains that Berlin is launching a massive surveillance-improvement initiative, which requires funding, careful administration of said funds, and a discreet presence overseeing the finances. He gestures with his hand, taking in the gloomy office, the overflowing ashtray, and the hulking file cabinets. "How does a position here in Bergen sound to you? I work mostly in Normannenstraße now, in Berlin, and we need you here, not in Saargen. I think you've earned it. Married, yes, but no dependents; is that right?"

"No children yet." Werner can't believe what he's hearing: This would be his office?

"So we're looking into something else, Nietz. A rumor about you, something that happened during the war."

Werner's hand, cigarette clasped between two fingers, stops on its way to his mouth.

"No fear, good man," Bieder says with a bark of a laugh. "I can't say much yet, but I can tell you we're conducting an investigation, and it seems you may be in for some more excellent news soon."

Leaning forward to grind out the cigarette that now tastes like a bucket of ash in his mouth, Werner presses his lips together. The best strategy when you're flummoxed is to keep quiet. He wills his shoulders to descend, his muscles to relax. Everything is fine. Bieder just likes to wield his authority.

"A promotion is exciting, eh? What will your wife say?" Bieder stares at him with one eye as the other quivers ever so slightly. "We need you to begin your work here as soon as you can disentangle yourself from your responsibilities in Saargen." He rises and opens the doors of a mahogany closet where bottles of liquor are lined up. There is Kristall vodka with its familiar blue label, Nordhäuser, Doppelkorn, Goldbrand, and cherry whiskey. And then there are brands Werner has never set eyes on before, and it begins to dawn on him that Bieder is quite right—this is just the beginning of a life he could never have dreamed of for himself.

"I'll take a Goldi," Werner says, and when he is given the glass—pale yellow brown, no ice—he happily sucks it down in one lukewarm gulp.

But in his own home he is no king, not even a prince. That night, Bettina's brooding sister and her one-armed husband come over. No one thinks to ask Werner about how the parade went, and he has no chance to tell them about Bieder's promise of a promotion and a move to the Bergen office. Clara sits on the Biedermeier couch, her long narrow face mottled. Sometimes it's hard for Werner to see how his wife and this woman can be related. Clara is older by only two years but already looks thoroughly worn out. He used to find her quite attractive, but recently she has taken to wearing her hair down, pinned back hastily on either side, and this is rather unbecoming. And she has become far too thin, shapeless.

"I can't stand them, that filthy family in the house with us. And next . . . what will it be next?" Clara takes a breath and continues when no one offers a comment. "Doesn't it make you angry? I mean, this business of not *owning* anything?"

Werner accepts a glass of schnapps from his wife. He sits back, takes a sip, and places the glass on a side table next to him. He will let this play itself out. He has no interest in becoming embroiled in arguments about socialist economic theory when people are so poorly informed.

"Perhaps we have to think about the greater good," Bettina says, pouring a glass for her sister and then one for herself.

The radio hums softly, playing a pleasant marching tune. Werner reaches over to turn up the volume a notch. He will tell Bettina about his promotion later, after they've had a few more drinks. Clara's complaining will surely set Bettina up to be delighted about his good news.

The husband, Herbert, a shifty type who never seems to settle down, wanders the room. The two men have never felt the slightest inclination toward each other, and Werner suspects it is because he did not fight in the war. There is a camaraderie of sorts, something that cannot be celebrated but remains a reality, between German men who saw battle. A silent, tragic acknowledgment. Werner often senses this without being able to share in it. The lines of Herbert's face are deep, his complexion pitted and sallow.

"We want to tell you something," Herbert announces. "We are thinking of leaving. I have no role to play in the mines anymore. What is there—"

"Oh, that's just disappointment talking," Bettina interrupts. "Emotions. Listen, have you tried the new salt rolls they're making at Studemeyer's in town? I got some fresh yesterday . . ."

"You mean leave the island? Or the country?" Werner asks, crossing one leg over the other. His black wool trousers shift up, revealing socks and pale ankles, as well as deep-red scars that bracket his legs from the braces he wore as a child. Recently he's been experiencing painful flare-ups in his joints, but he doesn't let on. "Are you in earnest, man?"

"They'll never come back from the Soviet Union, half the men from the mines I used to work with. Either dead in the earth or dead and forgotten in some prison somewhere. You know that, don't you? They sacrificed everything," Herbert says. "And even if they get to come home again, it's not even really *home* anymore, is it?"

"We lost the war, Herbert," Bettina says. "There had to be a reckoning."

"There're all sorts of opportunities for DDR citizens," Werner adds. "Trust me—I know. You must be adaptable. Have an open mind."

But the two women and Herbert act as though he has not even spoken.

"Come help me bring in the laundry, Clara; then we can eat," says Bettina, oblivious to her husband's fidgeting. "I've some fresh sausage, and there was bread today, those salted rolls. We'll have dinner in half an hour."

"Women," Werner says under his breath as the sisters leave the room. He does not elaborate, but what he means is, *How is it they always manage to grab the spotlight?*

20

After the recent rains, the grass in the backyard is brown and soggy, spotted here and there with thick-stemmed crabgrass. A black tarp covers the vegetable patch. The sheets, towels, and clothing hang on a line that extends from the back of the house all the way to the shed. The women begin unclipping the laundry and placing it into a hamper. Each item is as rigid as wood.

"Käthe Janklow said she saw you in Bobbin on Sunday," Clara says. "What were you doing there?"

Bettina hesitates and then keeps pinching the clips open. She knew that there were a thousand eyes on the lookout at all times, that nothing was easily hidden any longer, but she hadn't realized her movements were this obvious. "That pretty church. I go there sometimes. It's—I don't know. Soothing, I suppose."

"My little sister getting religious? What a miserable winter it's been. Can we resume our walks again on Sundays now that the weather's finally going to improve?"

"At least I'm not talking about *leaving*! I'm worried about you. That day, when I came by—are you all right?"

"I'll survive. But I may not be able to stick it out here."

"Clara, really, you can't do that," Bettina says. Although she doesn't believe she can be serious with this talk of leaving, she also senses something alarming in her sister's tone. Something has shifted, and Bettina's not keeping up. She feels disconnected, but she also wants to protect Clara in some way. "Don't talk about those things in front of Werner. Please, it's . . . it's not wise, all right?"

"You're so jumpy, Betty. Everything all right between the two of you? Are you still busy trying to make babies?" Clara grabs a pillowcase, folding it and laying it down on top of one of Werner's undershirts.

"Ugh, let's not talk about that." Clara once told her about making love with Herbert, how fervent and impatient and forceful he is. Her sister admitted to feeling so out of control sometimes that she would sob afterward in a sort of crazed exhaustion, and Bettina has never been able to imagine experiencing this with her own husband. Now she feels a swift heat burning over her cheeks.

"Herbert thinks it's odd, you walking all the way to Bobbin. I'm surprised Werner lets you go."

"He doesn't own me any more than your husband owns you." What is her sister getting at? This talk of what women are and aren't allowed to do is ridiculous. But even as this irritation chafes at her, she also knows she's asking for trouble: if Clara is so curious, others must be curious too. Bettina reaches up high to unclip the last pair of socks. The holes in her gray sweater are neatly stitched, but the wool has stretched out and become slack. Around her neck is a fuchsia scarf tied into a knot. Out of the corner of her eye, she sees movement in a window of the next-door house. Irmgard, her neighbor, watching them. They exchange a wave and a polite smile.

"Stop now, and look at me," Clara says. "You're not telling me something; I know you. What exactly is going on?"

Hoisting the basket to her hip, Bettina kicks open the back door with her foot. "I don't know what you mean."

Clara moves past her and blocks the doorway with her body. She is shivering in her men's pants and thin black coat. "Talk to me," she says.

"Clara, you know—you look like a ragamuffin. Let's make you some new clothes."

"You're avoiding my question."

Bettina puts down the hamper. "Shut that door, or Werner will have a fit," she says. "Come—we'll take a quick walk to the high point." She leads the way through the patchwork of communal gardens behind the house. Each little square is carefully tended to produce as much food as possible, and on some of the land there are picturesque huts in which to rest and read a paper or putter around planting. The women wind along the path until they reach the highest spot in the neighborhood, overlooking a sweeping slope whose meadow is bordered by towering ash and European beech. Clara brings out two cigarettes from her coat pocket and lights them both, handing one to her sister.

"We really mean it about leaving," Clara says. The smoke blows away as soon as it emerges from her mouth. "We can't stand not knowing what rules they'll come up with next. Do you know they *watch* us? They follow their own citizens as though by just existing we've broken some law."

"I think Werner's involved in some of the new surveillance projects." Bettina cuts her eyes away. "The less I know, the better. You have to watch what you say in front of him, all right?"

"It's true, though—that trip we're taking to Sweden? We're not going to come back."

A surge of desolation overcomes Bettina. In some faraway part of her mind, she's dreamed vaguely of a bigger world out there while knowing she loves the island far too much to ever leave. Even though they haven't been close as adults, it makes a difference knowing she still has some family here—somewhere to go in case of trouble, someone to talk with.

But the truth is, they haven't found the right vocabulary to share their disappointments or their dreams. Clara can't be there for her when Bettina needs her. And Bettina has not even made mention of Peter, this man who has become—so very quickly—as important to her as oxygen.

"You'll live in *Sweden*?" she asks her sister rather sharply to hide the disorienting hollowness that overtakes her.

"No, in America. You should come; you really should—before they make leaving impossible. There are rumors, Herbert tells me. They're going to close all the borders, and no one will be able to leave anymore. Not even to get into West Germany." Clara takes her sister's icy fingers into her own hands. "Please, will you think about it? There's no reason to stay, really, is there?"

"No, no . . . I can't leave. The house? The island—that's insane."

"Why not—because of your happy marriage? Come on. I can sense how things are between the two of you. Something is off. But I don't know . . . in spite of it, something is agreeing with you. You look quite well. Those cheeks. Are you sure you're not with child?"

Bettina shakes her head no and takes her sister in her arms. Recently, she has imagined what it might be like to pack a bag and walk away, to take a train to the mainland and head to a new city with Peter Brenner. But instead of offering her a giddy glimpse of freedom, of the infinite possibilities of a new life on her terms . . . instead, these thoughts trap her breath in her throat, drain the moisture from her lips, make her head pound. She just doesn't want to go, not ever, and she doesn't want Clara to leave either!

"It won't be so bad," Clara says, her voice muffled. "We can write to each other once the dust settles."

As they disentangle from their embrace, Bettina finds she cannot meet her sister's eyes. The urge to tell her about Peter itches like a rash. She badly wants her sister to understand what she herself cannot quite comprehend: That her life has taken a turn, that it is bigger and fuller and more terrifying than ever before. That she is not the same person she used to be.

"What is it?" Clara asks. "Has something happened?"

"You must promise not to tell anyone, not even Herbert. Do you promise me?"

"Are you in trouble?"

"I've fallen in love."

Clara's face softens, the thin skin around her eyes covered in fine lines. "A love affair, Betty . . . now, why doesn't that surprise me? Always just a little impulsive. But—with . . . with whom? Is that why you're going to that church in Bobbin? For God's sake, it's not that old fellow Pfarrer Brenner, is it? He's ancient—please tell me you're in love with someone handsome and charming and *young*."

Bettina laughs; a rush of anticipation flushes through her. The affair is not sordid; surely Clara will see that right away? Without exception, it is the most beautiful thing Bettina has ever experienced—probably ever *will* experience—and that is what Clara must have seen written all over her face. "It's the pastor's son, Peter," she says. "Peter Brenner." In her pocket there's a piece of paper that she brings out and unfolds. On it is written a poem.

"Who's this? Paul Éluard—the French writer?" Clara asks, reading. "So this man, the son, he's a poet?"

"He slipped it in my pocket one day. I think it's beautiful." Bettina's cheeks flush. "It's about the force of love, its transformative power."

"Goodness, Betty, you've become a cliché." Clara kicks at the dirt with the toe of her old boot. "Aren't you worried about Werner, if he finds out? Especially now he's all puffed up about work and all. This would be a slap in the face for him, no? He's so proud. And he doesn't seem entirely rational to me."

This isn't what Bettina wants to talk about. She wants to tell her sister all about Peter, his beautiful hands, his freckled skin. The way he kisses her, his optimism, his love of books. How he looks at her, the sound of his laughter, deep and unchecked, and how he can suddenly turn serious. That he asks her about herself, what she wants from life, how she grew up, what moves her. But she sees that no matter what she says, the most obvious fact is that she is a married woman betraying a husband who only wants her to love him back the way he loves her.

Birds are fighting in a scraggly elm down below, and the cacophony is like a bunch of quarrelsome old fisherwomen. Frustration envelops her as she tries to figure out how to explain to Clara what her life was like before meeting Peter. How, even though she knows what they're doing is wrong, she can't act otherwise: she has lost her reason, her control.

"I was drowning when I met him," she says, her eyes stinging, "and he saved me."

The hours, the days stretch out before her, barren. Three more days till Sunday, when she will see *him* again. The silence in the house weighs on her like a damp blanket. She signed up for the late shift today, and there are chores to complete before she heads to work, but Bettina does not have the energy to do much. Standing by the sink in the kitchen, she imagines her sister's face: as a child, before she thinned out. Clara was chubby and imperious, apt to flashes of anger and moody silences. Bettina wipes her eyes and tries to suppress her rising panic. She tries to picture America but can find no images upon which to rest her frenetic thoughts. Is it true that there is never any shortage of food, that people habitually smile at each other—even strangers? As a child, she'd read the Karl May stories of cowboys and Indians, a land that has no end, thousands and thousands of kilometers. Mountains and deserts and trees and sand, cities and deserted corners and two oceans and vast lakes that never seem to end. A political system based on the idea of *freedom*, emancipation. What will her sister do there? Where will she live?

There is a light knock at the front door. Wiping her hands on her apron, she goes to answer it.

"Frau Nietz," Peter Brenner says, using her married name, his voice serious. His Adam's apple rises and falls as he peers behind her, a stricken look on his face. "It's been a while, but I believe I located the whereabouts of your handkerchief."

"*Um Gottes willen!*" she says in a loud whisper, ushering him inside. "What are you doing here?"

"You are alone?"

"Yes, I'm . . . Werner, he's at work." It is the first time she has said her husband's name in front of this man, and it burns on her lips like an obscenity. Hastily removing her apron, she regrets not styling her hair this morning. Her clothes are utilitarian, unattractive. But as Peter Brenner enters the front hall and she shuts the door behind him, she can only think of the musculature of his upper arms and how pale the skin is—so bright and smooth—of his thighs, his hips.

"What are you doing here?" she asks. "You'll get us both in trouble!"

"I had an early study hall this morning." He glances at his watch. "They won't miss me for another hour. I just couldn't wait any longer."

"Did anyone see you?"

"I don't know. I ran all the way here."

Bettina goes to the front window and peers out. The square is empty.

"I'm sorry; I know it was fool—"

"I don't care," she interrupts, her pulse racing. "I'm glad you came."

He bends his head down to kiss her, and his long body eclipses all other concerns.

21

Bettina swore to herself that she wouldn't go, but she signs out of work an hour before her sister's ferry is due to leave, feigning illness. Her stomach roils like an octopus. A small group lingers at the ferry dock in Saargen, and Bettina stands far away, near the bus stop. If asked, she can say she was tired and decided to take the bus home to Apolonienmarkt instead of walking. It's just an ordinary day, isn't it? Some couples are lined up by the ticket booth with suitcases by their sides, wearing light coats and hats, ready to cross the Baltic, take a few days off. Three workmen in dark-blue overalls wait, cigarettes clamped between their lips, faces lined by exposure to sun and sea. No one is crying or waving goodbye, because it's just a day like every other day.

There she is, Clara, in a dark-beige gabardine coat and heels. Herbert in his fedora and gray jacket, dour in the fall sunshine. They could be headed to a funeral, or a wedding, perhaps. The ferry toots its horn, and foot passengers begin walking along the sagging gangplank onto the deck. Clara carries one small suitcase and a hatbox in her gloved hands. Herbert has a compact leather shoulder bag and suitcase: their entire lives in those few bags. They walk at a steady clip among the other travelers; they do not glance around. There is no hesitation in their steps. As they climb the last few rungs and stand upon the deck, they do not cast one final look over their shoulders toward land.

They're coming back in a week, aren't they? No reason to be caught up in nostalgia or to be having second thoughts.

As the ferry toots once more and disengages from shore, the workmen cast ropes back onto the pier, and Bettina runs down to the beach. There's a spot on the sand where she can sit and watch the boat chugging north. The sand has been warming all day in the sun, but she begins shivering. She wraps her arms around her legs and leans her chin on her knees. When the ferry disappears on the horizon, she has still not moved. It is not until the light begins to fade and the gray haze over the water swells and becomes a thick mist that she rises, shaking out her stiff legs and heading back home.

The youth center is used on weekends and after school lets out, but in the mornings it remains locked and empty, smelling of paint supplies and the faintly sweet odor of sweating children. Bettina arranges to work the afternoon shifts and meets Peter there, often arriving to find the door unlocked and an album playing on the record player.

Werner is at home with a cold, so today Bettina's alibi is the annual physical given by her employer. Though she already submitted to this examination, she neglected to tell her husband, and now it provides her with a convenient excuse to be out of the house for a few hours. Each time she lies to him, she feels the weight and twist of it in her stomach. She imagines that someone somewhere is paying attention to every movement she and Peter make, that eventually someone will tell on them. But this affair is a train without brakes—relentless, with increasing acceleration and momentum. Even after Werner's promotion a few weeks ago, when he started coming home with stories about what the Stasi are up to, she cannot break it off.

The corner where Peter sits waiting for her is stacked with novels and schoolbooks, and he is scribbling in his notebook, head bent. His hand is moving back and forth over the paper, but his body is in limbo between the world in his mind and his reality. A Mozart violin concerto plays, a haunting melody that soars and crashes, and he registers no reaction. She watches him from the shadows. Already she knows his weaknesses, and they serve only to draw her to him more closely. For one thing, his greatest weakness is also his most impressive strength: This capacity to engage fully. To be drawn into something so deeply that nothing else can intrude. A sharp focus, an unwillingness to split attention.

Just the previous week he shared some of his new writing with her. It was the first draft of a short story about a teenager who drowns while trying to swim across the Baltic, yet Peter's intention was for it to convey optimism, and these paradoxical impulses confused him. "We want to be real, as writers," he told her, "to not shy away from the horrors, but we're also part of this new world. With that comes responsibility, and I worry—"

"No, no, Peter, I don't think so," she said. There is something about his doubt that she admires: it reveals how serious he is about what he is trying to achieve. "In your work you can only be responsible to yourself. Or you lose your voice, that which makes you *you*."

His silence told her she was not entirely wrong. Today she watches him scribbling so single-mindedly in the darkened corner and wonders whether he has changed his story in some way because of their talk: Did he embrace the impulse toward darkness, or is his voice perhaps intended for a bigger political conversation? If the latter, what does that actually mean? She can't know if those two things are mutually exclusive, but she is compelled to think of her own work, of the last photograph she took almost a year ago now. She remembers it well because of the jab of loneliness she experienced when pointing the lens toward the two boys—young men, really—standing on the dock. Her reason for pressing the shutter was not to capture what was there; it was what she felt as she looked at them, how the faraway clouds and the boat in the distance (out of focus, just a slash of red) seemed to undermine the carefree setting in some powerful yet inexplicable way.

They speak of this constantly, the tension between the everyday reality of life for workers and intellectuals, and the dreams for the future that promise so much but are abstractions difficult to capture in writing or in a picture. The thrill for her is in seeing her place in the world from such a different angle.

"It will be all right," he tells her, "as long as we keep working honestly. And by that, well . . . what I'm trying to say is the struggle to tell our truth must never stop. I want to do this in service of my country—"

"But doesn't that dilute it? Art with a purpose?"

"It's about believing. It's about that and trusting our hearts are in the right place, that we have the good of others in mind, too, not just ourselves. See? Work with a heart, yes; work with integrity."

All this talk about his "work" is an infinite loop of learning for her. This is the first time Bettina has considered work to be anything other than a place you go to complete defined tasks in order to earn money and be part of a community. For her, work is physical, practical. Peter's work is not like this—it involves exploration and analysis, an opportunity for expression, for sharing and testing out ideas. In particular, he explains, he loves taking popular literature and letting the kids play with it, creating allegories or drawing on mythology and rewriting. It's clear that his students adore him, writing him letters in their perfect cursive declaring their admiration.

He reads to her from one of his notebooks the text of a banner he put up in his classroom: *An education that does not awaken the youth to a sense of conscience and personal moral responsibility is not worthy of that name. —Eduard Spranger, 1947.* But her gut tells her to be wary of trying to shape the creative impulse into a sword or a scythe.

Because of this, she has come to think differently about her own desire to take pictures, or to make art, as she's come to think of it. First and foremost, she's ashamed that she has let Werner discourage her so easily. Once she brought the Rollei along and showed Peter how it works, and then, when Werner was at an overnight on the mainland, she went with Peter to the high school in Binz late at night. They let themselves into the darkroom and spent hours developing some of her old films. It was all so ordinary yet so dangerous.

Peter still hasn't noticed her in the youth center, and she realizes with dumb clarity that what they are experiencing is an illusion, or at the very least a reality that cannot continue its trajectory, that *will* take a turn of some sort, at some point. If and when they are caught, Peter will lose his position; he'll have to leave Rügen. Will he be allowed to write, to be published someday? And if she is caught, then what—will Werner beat her, throw her out? And would that be so terrible?

"Peter . . . ," she begins.

He startles, but it takes him a moment to raise his head. He massages his eyes. His worn wool pants are slightly too short, and he's got on a well-washed cotton shirt. "Sorry, I didn't hear you."

"Peter," she says, remaining in the shadows. "I don't think we can go on like this."

He puts down the notebook and approaches, slipping behind her and wrapping his arms around her waist. He smells of pencil shavings and warm skin. "Is he leaving you alone, Werner? Everything's okay?"

Turning, she rests her head on his shoulder. Her legs want to buckle under her. Lately she has been so very tired. "Don't you feel sometimes that we've been trapped—like, if there's some God up there, he's actually just playing with us, seeing how much we can handle?"

"Ach, God doesn't care about us as individuals."

"I like to think that we matter."

"Did the Jews matter to God? Is there even a God? I'm not so sure."

"So says the son of a preacher man." She pulls away and begins to wander around the room, absently touching various objects scattered around. A ball, an errant pair of shoes on a shelf, the record player. A surge of pressure thumps against her chest: she remembers so well the photos from the concentration camps, the stacks of bones, the dark eyes, hollow yet full of unheard stories. Maybe Clara was right to leave this place whose people could do such things. "When will we stop having to pay the price for Hitler's transgressions? Do we have to actually leave this country in order to leave it all behind?"

"We were all part of the party, stained by it one way or another, and we all bear a responsibility in addressing its legacy. No one should be leaving, not now. We have work to do." Peter's boyish face, with the square chin and dark eyes, is grave.

The burden of all this guilt, this endless search for meaning and redemption, is more than she wants to bear. She wants love, children, a family—a simple life, and yet even that's too much to ask. "*You* fought and killed for Hitler," she says. "Don't push your own guilt onto me."

"I'm just saying I wish she hadn't left, your sister. For her sake, for yours."

Red faced, they stare at each other.

"But I don't know what the future holds—for anyone." She is thinking of her early-morning sickness, her weary muscles. The swampy feeling in her stomach. If she is with child, that will force a decision. It's not clear to her how to move forward.

"You have to leave him," Peter says. "You can petition for a divorce."

But she can't leave Werner. Each day he drops yet another fact into her lap like a boulder intended to crush, each day accumulating more power and with that the ability to control her. He tells her that the Stasi wants his opinion on a procurement procedure, letting her know that as a member of the secret police, his actions will become exponentially more impactful. Last month he was working on a balance sheet for surveillance funds: he has access to money; she has none. A week ago her old school friend Nils Wolf was called in for questioning, and Werner had the audacity to gloat about it at the dinner table. *Anti-Soviet agitation*, he said, *propaganda against the state*. She wanted to ask if he had something to do with this, if that was why he left that piece of paper with the list of names on it for her to find.

Is he trying to scare her? At the very least he is testing her; he wants her to take sides. At times like this her fury weighs on her so heavily she feels as if she's turned to stone. If only she could yell, throw a tantrum, but this won't change a thing! Werner wants to get a rise out of her, and she cannot give in to this.

"I chose to marry him," she says to Peter, "even though I didn't love him and I knew it."

This is an argument they've been having again and again since Clara left. Finally Bettina sits down heavily on a wooden chair. Another pang in her stomach makes her wince. She does not want Peter to know that she feels unwell, that she has been vomiting for days and is unable to eat even the driest, most tasteless home-baked bread.

"You're pale, Bettina. This is going to be the death of both of us."

"I'm fine . . . ," she says, though she is not. She can't bring herself to accept this, not yet. "I'm all right."

Peter kneels in front of her and slips his hands under her skirt. He regards her with an expression that brings tears to her eyes. His fingers reach her thighs, and she parts them for him as a rush of fire makes its way through her chest and into her throat.

22

The doctor's office is in the back of an old house on the outskirts of town, a compact room with a large table and a few medical implements scattered around, leather-bound reference books stacked on the floor. Bettina stands behind a wooden privacy screen and pulls on her stockings. Her hands are rough as she yanks at the coarse material, clipping it to her garters. She struggles to do up the waistband on her skirt.

"So, Doktor," she calls out, affecting nonchalance. "Is it good news or bad?"

Old Doktor Kreefeld has been the Heilstrom family practitioner since he was a young man, fresh from medical school in Hamburg. He attended to Clara's home birth and to Bettina's. "Excellent news, my dear. Please, remind me; you are twenty-six years old—is that correct?"

She hesitates. "Yes . . ."

"It's about time, then; isn't it? Baby is about three months, give or take. You'll be due in April, if all goes well."

She continues to adjust her skirt, as though these movements, the fulfillment of this ordinary need, can stave off the reality that she is indeed pregnant. The idea is so enormous, so shattering, she cannot quite register it. It's like holding a gem in her hand and knowing that it is valuable yet feeling not even a flicker of excitement. After a moment she slips on her shoes and emerges from behind the screen. The doctor looks at her with a deeply creased brow. Tidy vertical scars mar both sides of his handsome, broad face, and he has vivid eyes under bushy brows that give the impression of gregariousness. He waves to her to take a seat and makes a note of something on a piece of paper at his desk. "Your blouse, my dear . . ."

She looks down to see the white of her breasts exposed by gaping clothing. The memory of the cold metal contraption between her legs, prying her open, brings shivers to her skin.

"You look concerned. There's no need to worry, if you handle this correctly. Just because your sister has had trouble carrying to term does not necessarily mean that you will too," he says as she fumbles while buttoning up. "But I want you to be cautious, yes? Nothing too vigorous, lots of rest. Minimal stress. Everything is good at home? Just keep calm and healthy, and this baby will be fine."

Bettina's silence fills the room with uneasiness.

"Frau Nietz? Do you have any questions?" He glances at the black-framed clock on the wall. He is probably accustomed to farmer wives and garrulous peasant folk, energetic secretaries, childbearing house-wives who enjoy flirting harmlessly with him. "Well. Let's see, shall we? You should set up your next appointment in about six weeks' time. Fill out these forms, here," he says, handing her some papers. "Your prenatal visits will of course be handled by the state."

Bettina stands up. Her body is stiff, as though her brain is unable to send the right signals to her muscles. She cannot think straight— maybe, maybe she shouldn't have the baby at all? How can she even know whose child it is? These realities are not adding up to anything that gives her a vision of how to proceed. "Uh, Doktor, I wonder—has the time passed when, when . . . ? Are there other, mm, alternatives?"

"My dear." With deliberation, Doktor Kreefeld puts down his pen on the desktop. She is on a precipice, looking at the only person who knows this truth of hers—that she carries the beginnings of a child in her stomach. A child she has longed for since she was old enough to understand that she, too, could become a mother one day. The proteins and fats and vitamins she ingests are feeding her blood, which in turn feeds this baby, every second growing bigger, every day becoming more of a human being.

The doctor is talking, but she's only half listening. "... not encouraged. Population growth, you see. Ulbricht wants to stimulate production, and for that we need young people ... unless there are mitigating circumstances, I'm afraid I cannot be of help. Excuse me for being bold, but I would think this could bring your family great joy. Your mother, *na ja* ... you know that I knew your mother rather well? She often said to me when she was ill how she dreamed of you marrying one day."

A vision of her mother comes to her: those cool fingers of Doktor Kreefeld's gently exploring her chest, asking her to breathe in, breathe out—*deeply now*—a stethoscope recording the shuddering efforts. The old man had delivered the news to Bettina of Mutti's death; had it touched him to deliver such a dire blow? He had told her about Papa's illness, too, how it could not be fixed. And now he is delivering the news to her about the child she has been waiting for these past seven years. It is then—thinking of death and life, of her mother, of becoming a mother herself—that Bettina is flooded with the bright, shocking thrill of reality: She will have a child. If she's careful, if she's lucky, this baby will be hers to raise.

"Then my mother would be happy now, wouldn't she?" Bettina says. A child; this is a good thing, a gift. She stands up and reaches out a hand to shake the doctor's. "I *did* end up marrying, finally, and it seems that I will become a mother after all."

But as she thinks of her dead mother—and of the ignoble reality of her own situation: an adulterer, pregnant—something heavy settles around her heart, calcifying as she stares at the doctor. There is a fearful truth that is glaringly obvious: There is no way she can leave her husband when she is with child, especially if the child might be his. She has no means, and Werner's been so ornery, possessive; while he always seemed predictable, lately there's been a kind of wildness in him.

Leaving would put this child in danger. She knows now for sure that she wants this child more than she wants her freedom from Werner.

Doktor Kreefeld takes her hand in both of his and gives her a long look. The two prominent slashes—one on his cheek and the other a deep scar on his chin—are dueling scars that he probably wore with pride decades ago but that now brand him a dinosaur, a relic of an era that has been snuffed out, discredited. He was a Junker, old nobility. It's hard now to even imagine a time when university students jabbed at each other's faces with weighted fencing swords, allowing themselves to be branded in this way, the slashes telling the world a story of class and education that commanded respect. No longer.

"Good luck," he says. "You must be sure to take good care of yourself, and then everything will be well; I promise." His warm touch on her skin is a passing of the baton; he is the old guard, and her child is the new.

Clara and Herbert had been gone a month when Werner begins peppering her with questions.

"Shall we all go for a walk again together, along the beach in Binz on the weekend? What are Herbert's plans—hasn't he lost his employment? Will they stay on the island or try to get jobs in one of the new factories on the mainland?"

Werner's eyes strafe her face as she weighs her answers. But she hesitates a moment too long, trying to relax the muscles of her jaw.

"When will they return? Weren't they supposed to be gone a week?" he insists. Then, after a pause, brows raised, "Tell me they weren't serious about wanting to leave. Bettina!"

She is supposed to tell Werner they are just on holiday and will be back shortly. But they have already been gone far too long, and as he glares at her, the words catch in her throat like fish bones; he can tell she is afraid, and so she turns away from him. They are both headed to work, and he already holds his hat in his hands.

He grabs her by the elbow, his thumb pressing so hard against the bone it bruises her thin skin. "If you're lying to me . . . ," he says. His burning stare tells her that he already knows they won't come back, but he wants her to admit it to him. "You will only make things worse. You cannot lie to me, Bettina; I will not allow it."

She can't betray her sister, and so she tells Werner one thing while they both know she's thinking another thing entirely. Then, on a Tuesday morning, Werner drops a letter in front of her on the kitchen table as she is cutting up the potatoes for an early dinner. Her stomach presses lightly against the wooden edge, and she's reminded of the child, as well as the net Werner has cast that's encircling them.

"What is this?" she asks.

"I told you this would happen," he says. "You've been summoned."

It is a letter from the Ministerium für Staatssicherheit, the Stasi. The letter is addressed to her and has not been sealed.

"My God, did you tell on them, Werner? Did you?"

"Of course not. But this only makes it more complicated. That—well, that I didn't say anything . . ." Two patches of red appear on his cheeks, and a gleam of sweat covers his brow; he is furious.

"What are we going to do?"

"You will tell them *exactly* what you've told me," he says, his face grim. "That we knew nothing. You will not make a fool out of me; do you hear me?"

Putzkammer grudgingly gives Bettina Wednesday off so she can go to Bergen for the interview. By the time she arrives, her dress is drenched through with sweat, and she is winded from bicycling up and down the hilly roads. To the west of town an entire area is being razed to the ground—homes demolished by growling tractors, piles of brick and sand cast off at the side of the road. Trees lie toppled, cleared to accommodate some kind of industrial development. The dust from the debris sticks to her skin. She climbs off the bike and walks it the last few minutes until she nears the town square, trying to force her breathing to slow down.

It is important that she is measured and calm. The back of her hand, wiped over her forehead, comes away gray with dust.

She has not yet told anyone about the pregnancy. It's possible that the baby won't flourish, as the others didn't; if this is the case, then she may not have to tell anyone about it, ever. Even though this would simplify things considerably, the very idea sends her into a panic. She wants this child, and she wants it so badly. The baby is Peter's—she feels this in her bones, in her blood. It is a result of their love; it must be. But she doesn't know this, of course—she can never know. A feeling means nothing. The child could just as easily be Werner's; her fevered calculations have proven this. She is delaying what she knows must happen soon: she must leave Peter.

She arrives at the old Gestapo headquarters in Bergen, home of the Stasi headquarters, where Werner has been working for the past five months. He is in there somewhere. The hulking edifice, five stories high, dwarfs the older buildings on either side and casts a slab of shadow over the square. Rows upon rows of windows, small like beady eyes, glinting even in the shade as though covered with a sheen of oil. Bettina takes a step forward and then another and another until she finds herself on the third floor, ushered into an interior room by a middle-aged woman who takes little heed of Bettina's anxious gestures.

"Frau Nietz," says a man with slicked-back hair, rising slightly from behind a large wooden desk and gesturing for her to take a seat. "Karl Joachim Lederer." He nods by way of introduction, quickly sits down again, and opens a folder, stroking the skin of his chin with his fingers. His insouciance seems calculated to make her nervous.

Bettina takes a seat opposite him, clutching her handbag on her knees. It is as though her torso has become a furnace; perspiration trickles down her neck, and she wills herself not to wipe it away. Perhaps he won't notice. Perhaps this is normal.

"Coat?" the man asks without looking up.

"No, thank you. I'm . . . I'm just fine," she answers, though sweat has soaked great dark semicircles into the worn-out cloth under her arms. Taking off her outerwear would expose her, reveal her figure, her everyday clothes, and she wants to be undifferentiated, unmemorable.

"Right. Let's get to business." He raises his eyes to meet hers. Like all men confident of their superiority, his gaze is dispassionate yet penetrating; he feels no need to look away or put her at ease. "You know why you have been called here?"

"I'm not entirely sure," she says. Werner has instructed her to answer in simple sentences. To avoid embellishing. To let silences sit.

"Well, let's get things straight, then. We are a new concern, separate from the local authorities, with distinct and separate powers. Part of an organization, centrally mandated, entrusted with the protection of the citizens of our country. Do you understand?"

"Yes, yes, of course," she says. "My husband, Werner Nietz? He, uh, he works here. I'm aware of the new organizations and ordinances." As soon as she says these words, she regrets them. Werner told her categorically to stay quiet—he doesn't want to be drawn into this!

"Yes, Werner Nietz. That's right. We've already spoken." Lederer is silent for such a long time that Bettina begins to wonder if she is supposed to say something in response. He snaps his gaze back down to the sheaf of papers on his desk and continues. "At any rate, your husband is beside the point. I have the authority to ask you anything I wish to know and to detain you at will. You must answer my questions truthfully and to the best of your knowledge. Is this clear?"

"Detain me for what?"

"We could always complete this interrogation at headquarters in Berlin if you prefer," he says stonily.

"No, please!" Bettina resolves to submit meekly. "I understand."

"Good. So. Says here that you live on Apolonienmarkt, on the square in Saargen. This is correct?"

She nods.

"Your family is *Burgher*; they have owned the house since 1872, yes?"

The man's hair has been cut very short, and his ears are as pale as a newborn pig's. They look laughable in contrast to the square line of his jaw, the steely eyes he assumes confer authority. He is like a child playing dress up, and she is filled with sudden rage at this game she is being forced to play. "That is correct," she answers.

"Well, that's all going to end soon enough," he says. "Private ownership. We're seeing to that now."

She presses her lips together. She will remain calm and friendly. She will answer his questions, whatever they are.

"Now. Your sister? Clara Lange, married since 1938 to Herbert Lange, formerly employed in the chalk mines—this is correct?"

Again, she nods.

"Served as an officer in the Fourth Panzer Army . . . and, I see, injured in 1942, discharged. Then he lost the arm. Lange, Herbert— work assessments consistently below average. Tardiness, insolence. Vocal about his point of view. Unwilling to cooperate with management."

Waiting for him to continue, Bettina concentrates on keeping her hands still on her lap. Is it possible that this has anything to do with Peter? She feels as if the mound of her accumulated sins is visible on her face like bruises from a beating. The urge to stand and simply walk out makes the muscles in her legs twitch. Werner has warned her a million times: *Follow the rules. Do not draw attention to yourself.* She can do this; she can. She must.

"Oh, Herbert, yes," she says. "He's a good man, but he's been terribly knocked about. Losing his arm, fighting in the war. Then—"

"Just answer my questions, if you would. We're not interested in reasons, just facts, yes?"

Her fear is a fresh wound pried open with each question. The sting of it is a pain she must submit to, and she tells herself again and again: *I can do this. I can.*

No, she does not know why Clara and Herbert Lange never returned from their trip to Trelleborg, and no, she and her sister were never especially close.

No, they do not know anyone in Sweden, nor have they ever been there before.

No, Clara never mentioned wanting to leave the island.

Bettina has no forwarding address, no news, no reason to believe her sister will not be returning.

No, she has received no letters. No, there was no forewarning.

No, she is definitely not concerned.

She can barely breathe. Yes, she will inform the authorities as soon as she hears anything, anything at all.

23

It is fall, and yet heat pulses around them, insects singing their relentless song, accompanied by the rustle of lingering foliage shifting, sliding, whispering. A reprieve before the sting of a northern winter wind. Bettina and Peter lie on a cotton blanket spread out in the meadow behind the *Pfarrhaus*. They are shaded by huge ash trees, compound leaves turning in the sunlight, cutting the blue sky beyond them into pieces of an ever-changing kaleidoscope. In a matter of hours, the temperature has climbed considerably. The vast carpet of meadow, its colors browning in swaths, has become brittle with the slow-shifting season.

Side by side, Bettina and Peter lie unclothed, staring up at the dappled leaves and swirling colors. They ignore the bugs that tease at their shins and thighs. Peter's forearm rests on Bettina's chest, and with his other hand he plays absently with the pale hairs on his stomach. The trees and the unruly hedges shelter them from view. Aldo, Peter's dog, rests his head on his paws as he pants, legs splayed out behind him and flies buzzing at his ears.

Lying in the meadow, she tries to push away memories of yesterday's unpleasantness—at least for now, for just a moment. The meeting at HQ, after which she was not able to return to work, her stomach so knotted up that the pain made her legs buckle. The way pretending she was fine took all the energy she could muster.

Werner, agitated because dinner was not to his liking.

His endless probing questions. What did they ask her? Who was the officer, what rank? Did Werner's name come up? How did she describe what had happened? Was there going to be follow-up?

His utter lack of interest in her feelings. Her sister was gone, and all he cared about was how it would reflect on him. And then, just before Bettina slipped on her nightdress, he came over to her and stood with his hands on his hips. "You're not going to get plump on me, are you, Bettinalein?"

The doctor's words invade her mind: *Take good care of yourself; then everything will be well.* How can she take care of herself under these circumstances? Ahead of her she sees only dead ends.

But now, here, alone in this field, all she wants to think about is Peter's long slim body, the warmth his skin radiates in the sun. They made love in the bright light, uninhibited by thought of anything but their own ardor, and in that too-brief interlude, Bettina had been able to forget everything. With the sweat of their lovemaking evaporating in the sunshine, the sounds and colors and thoughts come rushing back in. It seems to her that if she could only stay here, unmoving, she could wrap herself in dreams of the future that don't require pain or courage, that only presage joy. These dreams include a baby with downy skin and blond hair, long limbed. The smell of milk, sweet and cloying. A child with gums as pink as candy and fingers curled in sleep. Cries in the dark soothed by dulcet tones and gentle strokes.

But she can't reconcile this conflict: that she loves this man, and yet to be with him, she must risk that child's safety. Yesterday, as they fell asleep, she thought she heard Werner whisper at her back: "*Du gehörst mir.*" *You belong to me.*

Above all she must do what is right for the baby.

Sitting up, Bettina rubs her face with both hands and reaches for her clothes. Time will not stand still after all. They cannot exist in a vacuum.

"Happy?" Peter asks her, his eyes closed against the afternoon rays. When she doesn't answer him, he opens his eyes, a riot of colors reflected in his pupils, making them appear iridescent. "Or *not* happy?"

She cannot talk.

"What is it?"

"Did you . . ." Bettina worries at her thumbnail. "Tell me, did you and Katya ever talk of having children?"

He does not take his shining eyes from her. "Are you pregnant?" he asks.

Of course he would guess. He can see right into her, to the very heart of who she is. "You haven't answered my question."

"And you haven't answered mine."

Bettina lies back down. She is in dangerous territory now, but she can't seem to stop herself. "We haven't been so careful always. I just wondered, what would we do . . . ?"

They lie agitated but silent for a long drawn-out moment before Peter rises and pulls on his pants. He reaches down to his schoolbag and shakes a cigarette free from his packet. Three deep inhalations, and it is gone. Aldo rises, sniffs vigorously, and runs off.

"Katya had a child," Peter says. "Before she met me. His name was Thomas. He was three years old when we were married."

Bettina rolls over onto her stomach. The blanket is scratchy on the soft skin of her breasts. Breathing into the material, she fights back the urge to scream at him for having loved another child, a baby that wasn't his and one that wasn't hers either.

"She, uh . . ." Peter pauses. "When she killed herself, she was very distraught. There had been an accident that day, and Thomas died."

Bettina holds herself very still so as not to give away her surprise. She had assumed his wife died from some kind of illness, but she hadn't had the courage to pry. So *this* is the source of the drowning story he's been writing; this is the pain he was trying to exorcise.

"He was a beautiful child, Thomas—amazing to look at. Blond curls and the biggest eyes—blue, of course. He was in all the parades, such a good little Aryan. Katya was very proud of that." Peter hesitates and rubs his eyes hard with his thumb. "And then . . . then he drowned in the Rügendamm. Almost five years old. It was so shocking; he was a good swimmer. Just a small boy, but strong. Somehow Katya, she got his body out of the water and carried him into a smoking hut on the beach. It was late morning already . . . the fishermen had finished for the day. Thomas loved the smell of the smoked fish and the burning wood."

Sweat trickles between Bettina's breasts. Peter's white body, the taut, long muscles—she loves everything about him. She loves him for the breaking of his voice as he speaks.

"There was a lot of rope lying around, fisherman's rope," he explains. "That's how she . . ."

"You don't have to tell me," Bettina whispers, wrecked.

Peter straightens his shoulders. "The coroner declared them both accidental deaths. But I know how it really happened; I know what she was thinking. She was afraid the Russians would punish her for the work she did for the NSDAP. She was a secretary, you know, for the Nazis. And I . . . I had been gone almost two years already. But she never truly loved me anyway, I don't think. It was because of Thomas that we married."

"I'm so sorry."

"Without him, without the boy, she was afraid of not being strong enough to withstand what she knew was coming. Do you see what I'm trying to say?"

"I'm . . . I don't know," Bettina says. There's barking in the distance. A sound that echoes through the woods and peters out as it carries over the meadow.

"The children—without them there's just no point. They're what we do all our work for. They're the very reason we strive and compromise and suffer indignities and reach for the stars."

She wants to tell him about her dreams when she was little—how she would bathe her dolls in a bucket of warm water and imagine the brood she'd have one day. Babies nestling against her breasts, taking sustenance from her body. That she married Werner because she thought it might be her only chance at realizing this dream. She wants to tell him that she loves Thomas even though she never knew the child, that she knows his curls, his bright eyes, the tiny teeth and dirty palms and porcelain forearms. Most of all, she wants to tell him that she is pregnant.

But she hears, faintly, her name, borne on the heavy breeze, interrupting the buzz of the insects and the rustling leaves. "Bettina! Bettina!"

She and Peter look at each other, and she jumps to her feet.

24

Werner's leg is throbbing as he pumps the pedals of his bicycle. He *hates* this damn bike. For one thing, he has to attach a chunk of wood to the left pedal to compensate for his shorter leg, and this arrangement is conspicuous and demeaning. It makes it difficult for him to maintain his balance. But the ride from home to Bobbin is relatively quick, whereas the walk would have taken him almost an hour.

Sundays when Bettina goes to the Bobbin church, as she now does with some regularity, he does not let her borrow the bicycle. This is a matter of principle. Stubborn as she is, if she insists on this silly ritual of picking the neighboring church over the one in their very own village, well, then she can walk.

It is an unusually warm afternoon, and Werner is still wearing his wool suit from work. Rivulets of sweat run down his forehead into his eyes. He has already been to the fish factory, certain that today was Bettina's long shift, and then he trawled the streets of Saargen looking for her. When she did not come home after another hour of waiting, he became impatient and thought of that old church she liked. God only knows what she could be doing in Bobbin on a weekday afternoon, but he'd left work early to tell her the latest news, and now he is driven to find her.

A truck carrying tin barrels of milk from the new co-op rumbles behind him, and Werner waves it down.

"*Guten Tag*, Comrade Nietz!" the milkman calls out. A stubby ciga-rette sits in the slit of his mouth. "Can I give you a lift?"

Detlef Elkin grew up on the same street as Werner. Although they never played together as children, Werner had admired the boy's short, hairy legs—like pistons, with their bulging muscles. Those were legs that enabled him to win every neighborhood race. Even now in mid-dle age, his ruddy skin tone and beefy arms are signs of an enduring strength that Werner lacks. Werner lays his bicycle down at the edge of the road and motions for Elkin to hold on a moment; he needs to catch his breath.

"Congratulations on your award," the man continues. "Soon they'll be sending you off on fancy vacations to Hungary or Czechoslovakia, lucky devil."

Werner heaves himself into the cab of the truck. He reaches for a handkerchief and wipes his forehead. "Well, thank you, Comrade Elkin. How did you hear about it? They only confirmed it this morning."

"My sister," the man says. "She must have a second pair of ears and eyes in the back of her head, that one. She's a secretary in Bergen. Antje. Remember her?"

Oh, Werner remembers the sister well: a small, dark beauty who repeatedly rejected him when they were teenagers, then aged as befits a shrew, with an ever-widening rear end and a face full of wrinkles from her ill temper.

"Well, when she heard, she came over to the co-op, ostensibly for lunch—you know how it is with women! Did you know she never married? At any rate, I was just leaving to do the delivery. 'Remember Werner Nietz?' she said. 'Remember he used to. . .'" Elkin hesitates. "Anyway, she remembered you from the old days. Bit of a gossip, that one. But I'm happy to be the first to congratulate you."

Elkin drops him at the top of the hill. It is silent at the church, and there is no sign of anyone. In the graveyard out back, a small dog, some sort of shaggy mutt, scuttles about under Werner's feet, barking, tripping him up twice. He sheds his jacket and rolls up his sleeves. The sun beats down on his head. From afar, ravens sitting on the branches of a tree in front of the *Pfarrhaus* look like lumpy black fungus, but then they caw, flapping their great wings and swirling up into the air, swooping first overhead and then down toward the bottom of the valley. Werner catches sight of a dissipating cloud of smoke coming from behind some bushes and trees in the middle distance, followed by another small, dense puff.

It does not look like a burn pile; someone is over there smoking a cigarette.

"Bettina?" he calls out, cupping his hands over his mouth. He feels somewhat foolish, but he cannot help himself. He is as excited as when he'd received his *Klausur* from school: the highest-ranked child in his class. "*Bettina, bist du da?*"

Just as he begins making his way through the undergrowth, cursing himself for having worn his polished work shoes, he catches sight of her.

She emerges from behind some bushes, out from underneath the shade of a grove of ash trees. When she comes into the sunlight, the shine off her dark hair makes it appear wet. Waving, she makes her way up the slight hill toward him.

Werner's breath catches in his throat. She looks beautiful stomping through the grass like a child, hitching up her skirt in both hands. She has gained weight recently, and it suits her, softening her sharp features. Perhaps his news will make her proud. He smiles and waves, but she appears not to notice. This dampens his enthusiasm and reminds him that he has been looking for her for the past few hours. And what, it occurs to him, has she been doing at the edge of the neighboring field, smoking a cigarette?

When she reaches him, she is out of breath and flushed. "Werner! What on earth are you doing here?"

Her tone puts him on guard. During their courtship, he admired what he saw as a certain strength of mind, an inherently practical nature, but he wonders whether this is perhaps simply stubborn self-importance. He says, "I might ask you the same thing."

At this, she takes him by the elbow and steers him back up toward the little church. "Let's go inside," she says, her voice more gentle now. "It's much cooler in there. Can you believe this day! The warmth is so lovely."

The stone walls are dripping with moisture, and an earthy odor fills the nave. They walk, single file, up the aisle until they reach the wooden altar. For such a small church, the altar is quite something: a series of trompe l'oeil black curtains drape from the ceiling to the floor, flanked by a gold-and-black checkered pattern. It is a remarkable church, he must concede, small and modest but with flourishes that are awfully charming. He's beginning to see why she makes the trek here so often.

"Bettina, I had to find you. I've been given an award!" he says.

"An award," she repeats. She is staring at the painting of the curtains around the altar, her face turned away from him.

"Do you know what this means? They're having a ceremony for me next month. We'll be allowed to go away on holiday. We might even be assigned an automobile!" He is making up this last business about the vehicle, but he wants to elicit a reaction from her.

"A ceremony in your honor? But what's it for?" Bettina's cheeks are red from running through the meadows. In some ways she looks younger to him than when they first met, as though the years have been running backward for her, whereas for him they march relentlessly ahead. He would like to brush the loose strands of hair from her glistening forehead, but an intimate gesture seems wrong right now.

Drawing himself up, he reminds himself that she should be proud of him. "Well, it's to honor heroes, antifascistic heroes. They have decided . . . see, Irmgard Bandelow told them about the soldier. I don't know how she knew, but still. You must have said something a while back?"

"Wait, what? She told them about the German boy?" Bettina asks, looking at him with her piercing eyes.

"He was a soldier." Werner coughs into his handkerchief. That damn dust from the roads. When she does not say anything, he coughs again. "You know, they consider me a hero. They told me they were impressed with my humility."

"Congratulations, then," Bettina says. "But I—I'm sorry to say it's not really something I think should be celebrated."

"I wouldn't have told them myself. Never. I'm not proud of taking a life, and, well, we did agree never to speak of it . . . but . . . but Irmgard told them when they were questioning her—gathering information for the annual performance review."

"You're talking about our neighbor, Irmgard Bandelow, yes?" Bettina asks. "Why is she so interested in you?"

Her voice betrays incredulity, and this makes his heart begin to pound. She is acting like an imbecile. Can she not make one admiring comment? "Yes, of course; who else would it be? *You're* the one who told her! Can't you be happy for me, for God's sake?" He realizes Bettina is staring out of a small window to the left of the altar, and he hobbles closer, his knee aching now, and grabs her arm hard, pulling her so she has to face him. "What are you doing? Why are you coming to this church all the time?"

His wife gives him no answer.

"I came here to tell you some good news—*good news*, do you hear me?" His voice rises, and the more agitated he becomes in the face of her bovine expression, the harder he tugs at her arm. "And I want to know what you're doing here. Why were you in that field? What *the hell* is going on?" Before he can stop himself, his arm shoots out, and he slaps her on the side of her face.

This works. Her features crumple, and she begins to weep. He realizes he has not seen her cry since the bombing, and a surge of satisfaction wells up in him.

"Answer me—right now, answer! And what are you looking at out here?" He shuffles over to the window. Standing on tiptoes, he can see past the gravestones toward the *Pfarrhaus*. "Why are you not at work? Are you up to something? Do I have to beat it out of you?"

"I'm going to have a baby!" she yells, holding one hand to her cheek. "Beat me as much as you want; maybe you'll kill it!"

"You're . . . ?" He turns to her, his face flaccid with shock. A child—could it be possible after all this time? A baby!

"I came to talk to the priest—to Pfarrer Brenner," she cries. "For advice."

"That old drunk? You weren't thinking of not telling me? Of—"

"No, no! Not that." She smooths her hair away from her face. "I've been having nightmares. Awful—the baby is deformed . . . or dies . . . or is born already dead, like my sister's."

Her eyes move over his shoulder and stop on something. Rapidly he turns; next to the small window is a larger one fitted with a colorful stained glass depicting a saint with his head bowed and his slim fingers pressed together in prayer. Under the portrait a name is painted in old German script: *Sankt Markus*.

"I was frightened," Bettina continues in a rush. "And the Pfarrer, he calms me down; he makes me feel as though everything will be all right. I was looking for him—I thought he might have gone to Johann's farm next door . . ."

"All right, all right. I understand. Being with child." Werner barks out a laugh that shoots into the silence around them. His surprise has shifted into something entirely different, something that seems to have wings, that lifts him off the earth, renders him as weightless as the air, takes his heart and calms it. He has been waiting for this for so long, his anger and disappointment a result of the stunted hope that's haunted him, and now he will finally have his own family.

He tries to reach for her to pull her closer to him, but she flinches. "No wonder you've been so strange! And I was right about the belly . . . it's fine now. I understand. Did he make you feel better, the Pfarrer?"

"I couldn't find him," she whispers.

"Remember what I said when I asked for your hand?" Werner moves away and sits down in the front pew, facing the altar. He is suddenly very weary. His eyes come to rest once more on the stained glass window, and he takes in the uncannily calm nature of the saint's expression; everything is beginning to make more sense. His wife's reticence, her seeming coldness; all along she's been disappointed and afraid, just as he was. "I will take care of you. Both of you." He grins. "Our child will be so proud of us! Very proud! Perhaps it will be a boy . . . we can name him Markus, like the saint in this picture, yes? What do you say? Hmm, Bettinalein? How about a little boy for a change in our home?"

Bettina nods, but it is tentative, and she will not meet his eyes, and he knows that it will take him weeks to cajole her back into behaving like a normal wife. It feels he has once again said and done the very opposite of what he wanted.

There will be no winning her over with kindness. He has tried that, and it has not worked. As these thoughts race through his mind, his joy shifts once again, and a kernel of anger blossoms inside him and multiplies.

25

Something has changed. In the mornings, instead of asking for a fried egg or some buttered toast, Werner demands it of Bettina. His movements around the house are assured and brisk, and this somehow leaves less space for her. Each night he lays his head on her stomach and maintains he can hear a heartbeat, feel movement, even though it is of course far too early for any of that. After she's been silent during breakfast and the bruise on her cheek has begun to darken, he brings her allium he picked in the meadows, globular bursts of pinkish-purple flowers blooming on top of leafless stems. Most surprising of all, on the following Sunday when she prepares for her walk to Bobbin, assuming he will busy himself with tending to the last of the vegetables, he instead rises from the armchair in the front room, folds the paper, and announces he has decided to accompany her.

There is no chance of talking to Peter that day or the entire following week. Her body is in revolt, and she cannot hold down her food. The smell of the fish at the factory, the cleaning agents, and the tang of briny water turn her stomach. As she walks home after her shift, the bones in her legs ache with such intensity she must sit at the side of the road, catching her breath. It feels as though she is in a room with no windows, the air stale and heavy; her breath cannot reach her lungs; her brain cannot form full sentences. Each option she examines, turning it over in her mind like a gem, seems flawed and pointless and impossible.

Her thoughts have no middle and no end—they are questions with no answer, corridors in a closed-off maze. She cannot run, because where will she go?

Her panic at learning about the pregnancy has shifted again. The nervous energy is still there, but instead of radiating inward, it radiates outward. Can she keep the child safe? What should she do? Sometimes she wanders through her house, trailing her fingers along the brocade on the back of the couch, the chipped soapstone countertop in the kitchen, the stack of sheets in the closet. Her father seems to linger there alongside her as she stares, unseeing, at some familiar household object. His love for her is evident, and he is afraid for her, for her child. In her imagination he tells her to be careful, alarmed by her unruly, adventurous nature. This is the homestead she inherited, that she is responsible for. It contains the family she has built for herself; it is the place she is supposed to be. He warns her not to be rash.

She loves every last corner of this house. Memories live in each closet; a story hovers over each wooden step. Will her child run these corridors? She tries to imagine Clara, so far away, and her mind fails her; she cannot picture the reality of that new world. Clara herself had badly wanted a child; what would *she* do now if she were in Bettina's shoes? It's hard to believe that it's likely Bettina will never again lay eyes on her sister. It's too dangerous for them to be in touch, and yet she waits for something, not knowing exactly what. They'd made a loose plan involving Johann and a letter addressed to someone fictitious, but they're both aware they can't create a thread that might be traced back to Werner.

At dinner he eyes Bettina sideways, telling her about a recent raid the Stasi ordered on a printing press in Stralsund, on the mainland. "They resisted, those idiots. Looking for trouble," he says, spiking a fork into the beef she prepared for him. He expects her to ask him what happened, and when she doesn't, his fork hovers in midair.

He frowns.

"There's no point resisting, you know. None at all," he says. "Klemperer shot one of them in the chest, and when the other one tried to escape, he was shot in the back."

"But what had they done?" Bettina's voice is high.

"That's not the point."

"What is the point, though? I don't understand. Innocent people getting hounded and even killed."

"If they were innocent, they wouldn't be running from us," he says, "would they?" The way he is looking at her makes her stomach shrink into a fist.

His gaze is direct, his underwater eyes no longer wavering. Later that week he arrives home with a small gold plaque in honor of his bravery and an electric alarm clock that hums gently, never ending. Eberle mews pitifully, and Bettina does not have the energy to comfort him.

When she detects the faintest pink stain in her underwear, she stands stock still in the bathroom, her heels icy on the tiles, and everything becomes clear: what she wants for herself is irrelevant. If she tries to leave now, the fear, the lack of resources, of safety—all that will risk the life of this child. And all that matters now is that her baby remains safe.

Finally she gets an opportunity to slip a note under the door of the youth center before heading to the factory. *Meet me at the beach in Glowe today at 5pm.* She hopes they will not be under watchful eyes there, and she clocks out of work early.

It has been eight years since she first laid eyes on Peter Brenner on this very beach. At the appointed time she watches as he makes his way toward her over the sand. He has come straight from school and is wearing his ill-fitting jacket despite the warm weather. They walk toward each other slowly, and underneath her dress the smooth movement of her hips, the swell of her breasts, and her soft belly remind her that she is more vulnerable than she has ever been. She can only trust herself now; she must stand by her decisions.

They stand together amid a group of pines, and she takes a seat on a weathered log. It seems as though she has just walked ten kilometers, and she struggles to catch her breath.

"I've missed you," Peter says. "I didn't dare come by."

"No, you can't—it's not safe!" she says. "I mean, that's good. Werner, he's suspicious." She hunches her shoulders over the bag on her lap and looks at her shoes in the sand and pine needles. He must know that this is the end. "I'm so sorry, Peter. I don't see how we can stay together. I don't see any other way out of this mess."

"I'm not someone you can just toy around with, Bettina. You can't just leave me, please. Please!" His panic, his loneliness, his quest for happiness are visible in the lines around his mouth, in the bloodshot whites of his eyes. But in a few years she will be thirty years old; they can't behave like children. She is going to be a mother, God willing. This is not some game anymore, where they are merely putting themselves at risk.

"Things have gotten bad at home, Peter. I . . . it's impossible. We can't do this any longer. We just can't."

"Bettina, are you unwell?"

She looks away. "No, I'm fine. At least, as fine as I can be, considering."

Peter falls on his knees in front of her. Placing her hands on his lips, he kisses them. "You must leave him, I beg you. He doesn't deserve you."

"Stand up. Come now. I can't leave; he will find us!" She does not say anything about the baby because this will make Peter push even harder, and if she succumbs and tries to leave, Werner will not stop hunting them down until he gets this child back. He will never stop; she knows this in her heart. Hasn't he spent years telling her—showing her—that she is incontrovertibly *his*?

Who the father of this baby is will remain unknown. And yet this, too, is evident to her: Even if she were to tell her husband about the affair, he would never give up on the idea that the child might be his. If Peter learns about the child later, then he'll assume it is Werner's, too, and that's for the best in the long run.

There is one thing of which she is certain, however: *the baby is hers.*

"What's this?" Peter asks sharply, touching the faintly bruised curve of her cheek. "Did he hit you, that bastard?"

"Peter," she says softly. "Don't make this difficult."

"Then . . . what?"

Blushing, she turns away. "It's not what you think. Werner loves me, and he's not prepared to let me go. You don't know what he's capable of."

"Listen, we'll go to the police. We'll tell them about his threats, the insinuations—the lists of friends, all of it!"

"No one is going to listen to our complaints. They close ranks, those men. He's a decorated hero now. And he knows people; he can do things, to . . . to your father if he finds out, or to *you.* You could lose your job, your life even. This is serious—they've got the energy of the righteous."

"I don't care! We can move out of here. We'll make a new life."

"Aren't you listening to me? They hunt people down. They don't stop!" She drops her head into her hands. "You must find someone who is free to be with you."

"I'll kill him. I'll break his head right off his neck." Peter rises, his shoulders hunched under his jacket, face contorted. He lurches forward and reaches for a stunted pine, pushing against it with his body and then yanking it toward him. He pushes and yanks until the wood splits, then picks up a stick from the mat of sandy grass and begins beating it against the trunk. His hands fling wildly in the air, his breath hard and fast.

"Don't come to the house, ever," she says, rising. Never before has she seen him behave this way, but she cannot succumb to pity or fear or love; *she must not*. His pain is her pain, and yet she does not feel the anger he does, not anymore. "You must leave us alone; do you understand?"

His face opens up in astonishment, and he takes a step toward her, but she moves backward, away from him.

"It's not too late for us to make amends," she says, "to make this right again."

"Amends? What—"

She raises a hand. "Remember when I came to you at the *Pfarrhaus*? You said then you had to take your cue from me because I'm not free." Her throat is constricted. "I'm not asking you, Peter; I'm telling you. It's over. I'm not free. I don't want to be with you anymore."

He sees that her mind is set, and for a split second she wishes he would keep fighting for her. But he is a man of honor who has done something he is ashamed of—stolen another man's wife. He will do as she asks.

His face is drained of color. "I'm sorry, but I don't regret a thing," he says, "not a thing," and then he turns away from her.

How will the days and weeks and months unfold with this man living in the village next to hers? How could she have been so *stupid*, so very, very stupid? This is the price she pays for her willfulness.

Once she's on the road, she places both palms on the small mound of her belly and begins to run, and even though her muscles are screaming and she can hardly breathe, she keeps running toward home.

PART THREE

26

When Bettina went to deposit the two-thousand-dollar check on the Monday after the award ceremony, she was struck with the irrational fear that the bank teller might tear it up right there and then, telling her it was a forgery. The edges of the pale-blue paper as she handed it over were damp from her fingertips.

The woman barely looked up at her, not even registering the vast sum of money, and only asked, "Cash or deposit?"

"Deposit," Bettina said. "Please."

It wasn't until she'd been handed the receipt that it began to seem real: the money was actually hers to do with as she pleased. There had never once been enough in her bank account for anything more than her daily needs. Now various possibilities unfurled in her imagination like a magic carpet, leading her to her child. She exited the building and stood on the pavement in the morning light, squinting. The crowd of people heading to work paid no attention to her, and this anonymity was fine, good—it allowed her to think, to plan.

Her thoughts were chaotic, but there was an energy to them, a hopefulness that she hadn't felt since she'd set foot in this country. Her Rollei hung from her neck, and she fiddled with the plastic beads she'd laced onto the leather strap—some slippery new ones she'd bought when her strap had broken a while ago, some old. As she always did, she imagined her daughter, her everyday life. All the ordinary things that made up the seconds and minutes of a regular day, things that seemed precious only when you couldn't see them for yourself, when they were denied to you.

Right now Bettina's imagination was all she had, but maybe that would change. A crack had formed in the wall between mother and daughter, and—now that she had the means—she could try to slip through it.

After a week, the riots in Wilcox died down, but the story was still keeping her busy. Since then she'd been roaming various neighborhoods, from the old Lithuanian center in Bridgeport near the canal (now more Irish than Russian) to Englewood a little farther south, which had pockets of racial diversity but was becoming more and more monotone. George asked her to scout up north too: Lincoln Park, with its beautiful old brownstones, had experienced a rash of gang graffiti on its buildings last year. She took a photo of a building on Orchard and Dickens, a faded Coca-Cola sign hanging from the window, *Young Lions* spray-painted over the boarded-up storefront: evidence of a gang. In that one, she focused the picture on a young tree that had managed to weave its branches through the broken boards and was sprouting new leaves, weedy but green.

Change came so quickly, George always complained; it was happening when people weren't even looking. No one had taken the time to document how these neighborhoods cycled through different cultures, swapping Italian for Czech, white for black. He was thinking of a spread he might be able to place in the Sunday Metro section, and he wanted to be prepared. All the while, Bettina was distracted as she worked. Each scene she composed in the frame of her camera became a jumping-off place to imagine what could be happening in her homeland. She wondered how much things had changed in Rügen in the past decade. Would it even be recognizable anymore? Roaming the streets of Chicago, she imagined smelling the salty breeze, watching the endless sea shift and splinter in the August sunlight. She found herself thinking about the beach in Saargen as Clara headed off, the many goodbyes she'd said and the goodbyes she hadn't been allowed to say. The years she'd spent in this country trying to forget what she'd left behind became compressed into a shred of time, into nothing; they vanished as the memories rushed back in.

And Herbert's attempted kiss—his misplaced affection had reignited a painful longing in her. As she sat on a bench at the bus stop after work one day waiting for the Number 42 to take her home, she studied a Buick Skylark parked in front of Sam's Bar. It was the pale turquoise of shallow ocean waters, its long trunk sloping like an animal preparing either to sit or to spring upward, and Bettina stared at it, mesmerized: it reminded her of the Tatra they had driven for a few years after Werner's big promotion. She glanced at her watch. It was almost ten o'clock, and the sky was heavy with heat and summer dust and darkness; she was very tired. As she watched patrons go in and out of the bar, trying to imagine what these strangers were thinking, what their dreams could be, she felt unknown and unknowable. She had made so many false starts; could she still change and find a way to try again?

She didn't want to go back to her empty apartment. Rising, she made up her mind: she would take a cab home later. Inside Sam's Bar a flattering semidarkness camouflaged tired faces. Over the years she had come here a few times when she craved the company of people who had no expectations of her. Bettina was out of place, but she didn't care. Her hair was piled on her head in a french twist held together with two long pins. In her jeans and men's shirt, she felt almost young again. "Martini, please," she said, finding an empty barstool and nodding at the bartender.

"Gin or vodka?"

She rubbed at her eyes. "Gin." The man sitting next to her wore a dark jacket and a wide beige tie, his face like a clenched fist. As soon as she sat down, he smiled at her, but she rebuffed him, turning her body away. She had tried being with men a few times since coming to America, and it was always a disaster. Craving the touch of a man's rough skin, the press of his bones against her, was never enough to make the reality of a stranger's ministrations bearable. It was safer for her to lose herself in solitude.

A large black-and-white television hung at an angle above the counter, showing images of firebombings in Vietnam. Burning children, eyes and mouths distorted, running into the jungle. A mass of protestors somewhere in America—screaming, angry faces turned up at the camera and framed by long, disheveled hair.

"Man, is this country ever going to the shit house," the bartender murmured. He wore his thinning hair in a buzz cut, and his nails were blunt like corn chips. "President gets shot, women and negroes in an uproar. Fucking insanity." He filled a shaker with ice and added gin. When he shook the drink, the ropy muscles of his arms pulsed.

"There's upheaval all over," Bettina said. "Europe too. You know, there's a wall now that divides my country in two. They built it, what, four years ago? It's to keep people in, not to keep them out."

The man nodded absently. "Those kids, the ones protesting? Plain spoiled rotten. Go fight the war, and get it the hell over with. Who else is gonna do it?"

"Do you mind?" she asked, nodding down at her camera.

The bartender waved a hand toward her dismissively, pushed the drink in her direction, and started chopping limes. "It's just, disagreements don't fix themselves. Someone's gotta get out there and do the dirty business of fighting for what's right."

Bettina clicked the aperture open as far as it would go and held the Rollei steady at counter height. Sometimes, in low light, she could capture a kind of rawness through extremely low exposure. Faces were bleached out, ghostly, and the darkness of the surroundings served to conjure up something otherworldly, but whether it was ominous or inviting, she could never tell until she was in the darkroom with her chemicals, in control of the narrative. She wound through ten pictures this way, listening, and when the man next to her in the beige tie asked her if she wanted another martini, she said yes, she did.

27

Sweat breaks out on her upper lip and tickles her skin. It feels as though small insects are crawling around her mouth. Then the pain comes again, the pressure on her abdomen, between her legs, and stars explode in front of her eyes. The urge to push and release the pressure overwhelms her.

"*Bitte*, Frau Nietz!" Doktor Kreefeld says sternly. "Lie down, and try to relax. It's not time for this baby to come yet. We'll get you in a room and take a look, yes?"

The high ceilings of the hallways, the darkness of the old elevator as it cranks its way up to labor and delivery, the antiseptic smell of the examination room—these things register faintly with Bettina as she is wheeled through the hospital on a stretcher. Nurse Schmitt, with her full, soft face, her mouth drawn in tight like stitches, tries to comfort her with pats on the shoulder, but everyone knows the baby will be dead. It will be dead; it is fated.

Yesterday it stopped moving, and then today this terrible pain. It is only February, and she has two months left to go before she is due. Werner is solicitous, then angry, worried that she will fail to deliver him a healthy child. And Peter—she has been without him for months and months already! Though so full with child she might burst out of her skin, she is also as hollowed out as she has ever been. Bettina fears that she cannot bring a healthy child onto this earth. And even if she does, she is certain that it will be puny and sickly, fatherless—for having one father who has been betrayed and unloved and another who is invisible is surely as good as having no father at all, is it not?

On the gurney she is turned and pulled and pushed, then moved onto a bed. She keeps crying out, hoping someone will understand her and know what she should do. A cool, soft hand comes to rest on the side of her face, and she opens her eyes.

It is Doktor Kreefeld. "Frau Nietz," he says, his face close to hers and his voice calm and low. His scars protrude from the skin of his sagging cheeks, two ancient vertical lines from the tip of a sword. "Stop this nonsense. You will have a beautiful baby, and not today, if I can help it. You will see. All will turn out for the best. Now let's find out what's going on here."

Hot tears snake into her ears. "You don't understand! I don't think . . . this wasn't supposed to happen."

"But I do, child; I understand. Babies have a way of distilling complicated matters into something crystal clear. What you are afraid of now will disappear once you hold this baby in your arms. Try to relax." He pulls on a pair of gloves and lifts the sheet that covers her belly. "There is no greater love than that between a mother and her child, no matter what the circumstances."

He doesn't understand; of course he can't. As the pain comes again, Bettina turns her face away from Nurse Schmitt's curious gaze. Bettina is invisible to everyone, even though she is right here, the violent reality of her body unavoidable.

After a week of daily hospital visits, Werner returns to his desk in Bergen, assured by Doktor Kreefeld that his presence will make no difference to the chances of averting a premature birth. What a great relief to be out of that hospital, with its nurses staring at him as though he is somehow to blame for this disaster, and the smell—the cloying smell of misery and illness with which he is so familiar from his youth, when he was encased first in the iron lungs and then in the leg braces, year in and year out, until he could walk again. So he visits on Saturday afternoons and Wednesdays and on other days establishes a routine for himself in the cottage.

Two weeks later he receives the phone call: the baby is coming. At the edge of Apolonienmarkt, their new car is parked: a Tatra 600 from Czechoslovakia presented to him some months earlier. It is the gray of a warplane, aerodynamic—bulbous, you might say—with a strangely curved back end and rear-mounted engine. This model caused so many crashes before and during the war that it earned the nickname *killing machine*, but never mind that business; owning it is an astonishing testament to his rise in status. He drives it rather ponderously, but then his feet are too quick on the brakes. All eyes are on him as he passes through Saargen and enters the open road to Bergen. En route he passes the bus and wonders whether he will ever take public transport again. Certainly he will avoid riding his bike.

His mouth is dry like a cracker, his eyes peeled and watching the road unfurl. The baby is coming, and he will be a father at last—his luck is simply too good to be true.

Werner arrives too late for the birth. The doctor tells him that he's now the father of a healthy girl and that Bettina is doing fine.

"But Herr Nietz, I'm afraid there's more," Doktor Kreefeld continues. They are standing side by side in the wood-paneled corridor of the hospital, outside the room in which Bettina sleeps with the other maternity patients. Metal wheels screech, bumping over the uneven tiles, accompanied by a constant, rhythmic clacking of footsteps. "We have some bad news as well. We were surprised by something we had not anticipated—there, uh, I'm afraid there were twins."

The baby boy was born dead, the doctor explains, so underdeveloped that he was still entirely covered in fetal hair. He believes the child was probably dead for a few weeks already, which might explain why Bettina was feeling so poorly.

"For God's sake, man, how could this sort of thing be missed?"

The nurses disposed of the body, and for this Werner is grateful; he does not ask where or how. He does not want to see this small dead thing that lived and died in ignorance, without love. In his mind he imagines the child would have had black hair like his father's and an irregular smile like his wife's. So she had been right, Bettina: a baby was delivered dead just as she had predicted. What did it mean, this life snatched away from them, a life that would have made them an instant family of four? He decides there and then that he will never again consider the fact that it was the boy who died; he will celebrate his daughter's life in the way she deserves and never cast her in the shadow of the brother who is gone.

It's a girl, he says to himself, a daughter! A child who will slip her hand into his and listen to his stories and put thin arms around his neck at night before she falls asleep. A girl who will become a woman someday, striking and powerful like her mother, able to win men's hearts and keep a family alive.

"It's a miracle the female fetus survived," the doctor is saying. "In my forty years of practice, I have never witnessed something like this. Your wife, she was average size, perhaps a few centimeters larger than usual, but really . . . nothing to raise suspicions. There is no history in either family of twins, so as you may imagine, there was no indication of multiple fetuses. But Herr Nietz, consider this a blessing. This second child has an excellent chance of survival. She's quite small but, as far as we can tell right now, perfectly healthy."

"I must see Bettina," Werner says. "May I?"

"By all means. She is resting in here." The doctor indicates the maternity ward. "And if you wish to see the surviving infant, she is in the nursery on the third floor. But I should warn you, Herr Nietz, women, they sometimes suffer after birth. Not physically, you understand, but mentally. You must be prepared, *ja?*"

"Of course I am prepared," Werner says, turning away from the man and carefully folding up his annoyance as though it were a soiled napkin.

Bettina is fast asleep, her hair on the pillow like a tangle of reeds. Her skin is gray with two alarming patches of red on both her cheekbones. Nine other cots surround her bed, each filled with a woman who has recently given birth: some hold infants, others sleep, and a redheaded one stares with tired eyes at the walls. It is a glorious sight, so many fertile women, so many mothers who will raise their children to be good citizens. Once they are out of this room and back in their homes, these women and children will form part of the new wave that pushes this country into modernity. It's odd to feel much joy in this joyless room that smells of something metallic and cold—blood, perhaps?—but it courses through him, making it hard for him to remain calm.

The sheets are pressed flat and pulled up tightly over Bettina's chest. The mound of her belly is still visible. Werner goes to the side of the bed and studies his wife's face. In her expression he sees nothing of her customary defiance—which he both loves and despises. Instead there is a slackness born of exhaustion. To create a human being inside your own body is a trick of magic so commonplace yet also miraculous. What must it feel like to have this life pulsing in your womb, to feel the tiny feet kicking at your organs? Placing his hand on her stomach, he presses down gently; under his fingers, it is as soft as a pillow. Bettina does not stir.

In the downstairs nursery are nine babies wrapped tightly in blankets inside identical wooden cribs, only their wizened faces peering out. A young nurse takes Werner to one of the cots: *NIETZ, MÄDCHEN.*

So she has not yet been named. The child is no bigger than a doll and, having managed to extract an arm from her blanket, sucks furiously on a tiny balled fist. She has an oblong head of long, silky black hair. Purple faced, with this mass of dark hair, she is not the least bit attractive.

"They lose the hair and begin to look like humans after a few days," the nurse says. "She's a little fighter, this one; don't you worry. She'll pull through."

They will name her Annaliese, Werner decides, after a favorite aunt who used to massage his legs for him when his mother had tired of her nursing duties. Annaliese will be a strapping child, with strong, healthy legs and an athletic build, a girl who will bring her mother and father closer. This child will teach Werner to be more patient, to learn how to give Bettina time so she can grow into her role as mother.

Werner's heart is so full it hurts, and he turns his back on the nurse so that she cannot see the agony of joy on his face.

28

In Bergen some months later, Werner is staring out the row of front-facing windows toward the street below, where an early-summer rain has drenched passersby. He has recently shifted responsibilities once again and now works under the Directorate for the Protection of Public Property and Democratic Order. On the occasion of this advancement, Bieder and another associate had presented him with another new plaque for his desk, as well as—to his great surprise—a small gun called a Pistole M. It's a copy of a Russian Makarov, all black, modern looking compared to the wooden-handled pistols he used to see strapped to the hips of the Volkspolizei. Stamped with a J2211 on the left, it takes nine-millimeter cartridges, and when he shot it at the range near Prora, he'd found it easy to control, compact, and sleek.

A few years ago he'd approved budgets for arming the MfS and hadn't given them all that much thought; in peacetime as in war, appropriate armaments are a necessary part of proving power. But the idea of Werner ever shooting an actual human being—laughable! It was true that now that the whole town knew about what he'd done during the bombing, he'd occasionally found himself embroidering the story about the soldier he killed (and had stopped himself in embarrassment), but was it really so bad to feel some pride in it? He had, after all, shown bravery in that moment. Now knowing this snug pistol lies in the drawer of his desk gives him a jolt of satisfaction. He need never again be at the mercy of idiots like those Nazi soldiers who ridiculed him for not fighting. And not insignificantly, this means his work is valued, that he's finally put to bed any doubts about him that might have lingered after Clara and Herbert failed to return from their holiday. It had been a stain on his reputation; that stupid woman put his job in jeopardy, but he's overcome that hurdle.

He has just finished an audit of several of Rügen's largest towns, and though he is reasonably satisfied with his work, he is beset with a feeling of unease. If he's honest, the real reason he stays so late every day isn't because of his workload; it's the insufferable atmosphere at home. The baby seems to drain all energy from his wife; she has not reacted to the arrival of this child in the way Werner had hoped. Perhaps she is mourning the death of the baby boy. It is as though he does not know Bettina at all anymore. She rebuffs him every time he reaches for her, and he accepts this as an unfortunate byproduct of the difficult birth. But her demeanor, her physical appearance, and even her voice have changed; often she doesn't seem fully present as she wanders through the house, tending to Annaliese or preparing dinner. Sometimes Werner has to repeat himself two, three times before she hears him and responds. She never even attends church anymore, and that he finds *most* odd. Last year she was more than willing to trek all the way over to Bobbin, but now when she's not working, she just sits around the house all day.

He considers going home early and trying to persuade her to open a bottle of wine and drink it with him so they can relax a bit. Perhaps they can just talk again or read some Rilke together. But then he imagines her sour face, the almost imperceptible way she recoils when he is near her. Can't she just pull herself together? Is it so very hard to be a decent wife and a mother?

He slips his reading glasses back on; he'll tackle another file rather than head home just yet. As soon as he has some free time, he will go talk with their neighbor, Irmgard Bandelow. See if she can't keep an eye on Bettina and try to get her outside in the fresh air more. Perhaps all his wife needs is some resolute direction from another woman, one who has gone through her fair share of upheaval and seems to have come through it all with her spirit intact. Clearly, she's a decent person, and she did take in those two young girls, Alma and Elise. It appears she knows something about being a mother, even though she never had children of her own.

The fisherman's cottage is no longer peaceful when Werner is at work. The baby fills her lungs with air—one long, shuddering intake of breath—and then lets out her wails in a series of prolonged bursts, punctuated only by the short silence of her inhalation before the next round of cries begin. Sometimes Bettina believes that Annaliese is crying for her dead brother, that she became accustomed to the warmth of his tiny body against hers in the womb and now feels abandoned, but this cannot be right. She thinks she is simply a bad mother.

She stands at the kitchen counter, peeling misshapen russet potatoes for dinner, listening to the crying coming from the wicker basket in the living room. Doktor Kreefeld insists that she learn to ignore Annaliese's wails, but each time she starts anew, the milk swells in Bettina's breasts, and there's a painful tug in her groin. The cat has taken to sleeping under the back stoop, as far from the screams as possible.

She is growing so very quickly, this precious, tiny girl with the furious cry. Her silky black hair fell out and has been replaced by a thick dark fuzz that looks as though it might become wavy as she ages. Her eyes are neither blue like Werner's nor dark like Peter's but green, changing with intensity with her moods. When she is sleeping, her lips slightly parted and moist, her breath rasping in and out noisily, she makes Bettina think of Peter, and she stares at her for hours, still as stone. It is not so much that they share an obvious physical resemblance, but the baby's energy—even in rest—her fierce curiosity, the neediness combined with strong will . . . all this reminds her so much of her lover.

It has been over six months since she last saw Peter (one hundred and ninety-eight days). While she yearns for him physically—his absence creating a vacuum so vast it hurts her tissue, her bones; even her blood aches—most of all, she misses his voice. His mellifluous voice, its insistence. She did not realize how much she fed off that voice until she no longer heard it. He was always working on a play or a story, and sometimes, after lovemaking, he would read passages to her from his writing. In one way or another this had been a ritual for her all her life—as a child it had been her father reading to her; as an adult she'd listened to the radio. But with Peter it was fascinating to see the progression of the writing from rough to more polished. She found his ideas at once intriguing and intimidating. He started off so boldly that it could be confusing, and as he edited his work, he finessed his ideas and clarified his prose, sharpening and shaping and creating something of real beauty.

It was not dissimilar to what she used to do when taking and developing her pictures, but it has been years since she picked up her camera.

She can no longer bear to have a conversation with anyone, let alone with her husband. Every word that comes out of Werner's mouth seems drenched in insincerity. Even Christa has noticed and has tried a few times to draw her out at work, asking about the baby, but all the doors inside Bettina are locked, and she cannot find an opening, not even for her old friend.

She is not a decent wife, pushing Werner away if ever he attempts to touch her, and she is an inadequate mother, unable to comfort her constantly wailing child. At least having the baby seems to have temporarily released her from Werner's constant, feverish scrutiny. Before, he clung to her, alternately begging or threatening, but now he seems perplexed and unnerved by her new role. As she tends to Annaliese, he watches her warily, and she wonders why he keeps his distance when he promised to do just the opposite. But when she hands the baby over to him, he seems completely at ease. At night, he often takes the child and puts her in a big tin bucket in the kitchen filled with warm water. He sits on the floor, legs folded awkwardly, reaching into the water to prop Annaliese up and splash water on her shoulders and belly. The two of them grin at each other, splashing and laughing, and as Bettina watches, she becomes ever more miserable, the delight in Werner's eyes reminding her of her own failings.

Her body is soft and yielding and surprisingly compliant, full of automatic responses to her child that spring from nowhere, even though her mind is captive to this deadening grief. Her body aches from sleeping so poorly. Annaliese is often up at night, seeking comfort by nursing, and sometimes Bettina's mind is so blank, or so teeming with unstoppable thoughts, that she feels as though she is going mad. In the old fish shop she'd adored the rituals: getting there before the sun broke over the horizon, hauling fish from the fishermen's baskets, cleaning the floors and the windows, taking orders, even hauling away the trash. For years her routine was unvarying, and she took comfort in that as an antidote to the chaos of war. Now she moves through the routine of her life as a mother and a wife without feeling the moments go by. They are bubbles, fragile and meaningless. Every now and then, when she is in the darkness of Annaliese's room before sunrise, she can anchor herself firmly in that particular experience, but mostly she feels absent from her own life.

Finally Johann the butcher drops by. He'd admired her father, even shared some good laughs with her mother, and he loved the two Heilstrom girls, so he'd agreed (though not without some trepidation) to be a conduit for news from her sister. Clara had sent a letter to his co-op in Bobbin, addressed to a fictitious person. The envelope carries no return address on it. Inside there is sparse information, except that they have settled in Chicago and quickly found work. Herbert has started his own business, something to do with bathroom renovations, and Clara helps him with the paperwork. They have been given a small line of credit from the bank and entered into a partnership with a group of Germans who pool their savings. After one year, they are starting to turn a profit.

Oh, Bettina wants more, much more: She wants to hear her sister's voice, to tell her about Peter, about Annaliese! She wants to ask about the high rises and the accents and whether Americans really do smile all the time. She wishes she could hear about the first months of loneliness and what helped Clara survive. Does she miss the island, the thatched roofs that smell of farmyards and woods, the endless winds that blow in from the north? Does she think of her sister and what she left behind?

Not a day passes that Bettina does not wonder whether she can make it through the hours without heading toward the middle school in Bobbin, hoping to catch sight of Peter Brenner, or walking once again to church and staring at his ruddy neck during Sunday services. Doing her daily chores, she imagines his serious face—the shadowy eyes and full lips—and the thought grips her that he will storm back into her life in some dramatic way that will endanger them all. She wants this desperately while also dreading it. His features are imprinted on her mind when she wakes up and when she closes her eyes to try to sleep. He is with her as the baby's fists hit the delicate skin of her breasts while nursing, summoning energy and life from she knows not where. Peter is in her baby's cries and in her laughter. She could swear that she is able to sense whenever he is thinking of her, for she feels his eyes on her like a caress, and sometimes she will spin around, certain that he must be nearby.

The ghost of his love is like a living thing. It is a strange sensation, to feel that Peter has become part of her in a way that will never go away no matter how alone she is.

29

In the old pram, Annaliese lies staring at the sky with round green eyes, cooing intermittently as anything of interest comes into her line of sight: a bird, a puffy cloud, the earnest face of her mother. She is almost four months old and has a full face, pale from being inside most of the sunless winter and spring. Bettina has discovered that the child loves to ride in the carriage, lulled by the movement into a kind of ecstatic calm, spit burbling from her lips. Now that the weather is lovely, the sunshine broken up by the shuddering leaves of overhanging trees, they walk and walk together, hour upon hour. Sometimes Werner joins them, but he is slower than Bettina, and she loves to stride along at a good clip, aimless and exhausted. She is beginning to accept the feeling that she is indeed the mother this child has been given and that she can do the job. She must.

A few times she has tried picking up her colored pencils to sketch again, but her efforts are disastrous. She lacks the patience when she gets something wrong to apply herself to fixing it. When the baby has fallen asleep, provided Werner is not yet home, she will often pick up her old camera and turn it in her hands, grazing the bumpy, worn leather cover with steady fingers, playing with the levers. Ever since that day at the piers when he tore it from her and threw it on the ground, she's kept it in the back of her closet. It is so heavy in her hands. She loves to think of all the scenes she's captured over the years, times when she still inhabited what she thinks of as her *real* self. Peter used to ask her about it, encouraging her to commit to start taking pictures once again. "Being an artist isn't easy," he'd say, "but it *is* worthwhile. And I know you can do it; I know you have the eye."

But she is not special; she realizes that all humans have outer selves they share with the world and inner selves they keep hidden. She knows, too, that her core has dissipated like steam, simply vanished; she is a stranger even to herself. There's a dizziness that overcomes her, a kind of slide into a void. It leaves her shaky. Holding the camera gives her a feeling of substance, if only briefly, and Peter's words of encouragement, his belief in her vision, come back to her, fortifying her.

Bettina picks the baby up from the fishery's crèche, intending to take her to the ocean for a few hours, hoping that the clean salt smell of faraway places will entertain them both. Her work shift has changed, and she now scales and debones in the early mornings, relieved of duty every day by two o'clock. This leaves her with many hours of half freedom, when she and Annaliese can roam as they please before Werner returns from Bergen, expecting his dinner of *Vollkornbrötchen und Leberwurst*. Often he stays so late at work that she does not even need to feed him until the baby is already in bed.

Once she has scrubbed her hands in the communal facilities, changed out of her dirty uniform, and settled Annaliese in the pram, Bettina emerges into the sun-drenched Saargen streets and feels the warmth pouring down on her, and her feet carry her not toward the port but to the once-familiar road to Bobbin. A cotton jacket tied around her waist, she walks with bare arms, her legs too warm in wool tights. She reasons that it is the middle of the day in the middle of the week, and Peter will be busy at school, not at the *Pfarrhaus* or in the church, not playing with Aldo in the meadow.

As she nears Bobbin, her feet move with surprising lightness, and her pace is brisk. Already she can anticipate the rush of feelings that will tether her back to earth. A horse pulling farm machinery clops past her, and she waves at the man holding the reins. The occasional motorcycle rumbles by, but otherwise she sees no one.

The pram's big wheels have trouble on the cobbles, so she lifts Annaliese out and holds her close as she climbs the path leading to the church. As she enters the dark anteroom and steps over the threshold into the interior, her heart speeds up. How she has missed it here: the cool blue light that comes in through the leaded windows, the ornately painted confessionals. At the end of the small room is the painted altar, nothing changed. In the many months she has been away, her own life is unrecognizable to her, and yet here, all is the same. The feel of the hard stone floor beneath her feet and the musty air on her cheeks is a kind of homecoming.

The baby begins to fidget and mew, her tiny hands chilly. She nudges urgently at her mother's shoulder, but Bettina can't feed her in here. Outside, the sky is marred only by the swooping of the ever-present gulls. The graveyard is set alight by the sun, and the pale faces of the headstones flash. Annaliese is calm briefly, as though the intensity of the colors distracts her from her empty stomach. The cluster of saplings on the rise, where Peter showed Bettina the discarded gravestones more than three years earlier, offers a small stone slab where Bettina can sit and nurse out of sight. As she makes her way there, a shaggy gray animal—the size of a fox—becomes visible under the overgrown bushes. A scraggy head, yellow tufts on the ears visible even in the shadow of the overgrowth. Catching her breath, Bettina scrambles toward the mound.

"*Aldo!*" she calls out. "Annaliese, darling, look—it's Aldo . . ."

When she is still a few steps away, she stops; Aldo has not raised his head. He lies on a bed of pine needles and browned leaves, his nose pressed into his two front paws, hind legs stretched out behind him, as though he is running and resting at the same time.

"Aldo?" she says. When no response comes, she whistles gently a few times.

Clutching Annaliese, she kneels down and touches the rough fur on the bumpy ridge of the dog's back. Under her hand, his fur is like a hard wire brush. Sweat springs up on her arms and behind her ears. A sharp intake of breath, and she is back on her feet.

The door to Peter's quarters in the *Pfarrhaus* is not locked. Bettina bursts into the dark room. All is familiar: Piles of papers and books line the floor, the fireplace is filled with half-burned wood, and the narrow bed in the corner is unmade. On the table lie a candle, a book, and an empty tin milk jug.

"Peter!" she cries out, a hitch in her throat. "Peter? Aldo—Aldo is dead!"

The main house is silent, and she goes from room to room, uncertain what she's looking for or what she will find. Annaliese begins crying once more, this time with greater urgency, hitting her with her fists, and Bettina stumbles out through the front door, searching again for a quiet place to feed her child. Next to the jasmine bushes is a dilapidated wooden bench, and when she sits and unfastens the buttons of her dress, covering the skin of her chest with her jacket, Annaliese becomes hysterical. She throws her head back and forth, searching for her mother's nipple. Bettina leans forward so she can feel her breast inside the baby's soft lips, and a wave of grief speeds through her. The image of Aldo lying in the shadows attaches itself to the black undersides of her closed lids, and she begins to cry.

Then, a shadow: There is a man standing in front of her. Tall, rod thin, with unruly gray hair. Small light eyes, red rimmed and puffy. An oversize men's shirt hanging from stooped shoulders. It is Pfarrer Brenner, Peter's father.

"What are you doing here?" he asks. "I know you; you're Peter's girl." His pale eyes shift from her face to the baby in her arms and back again. "You've come back."

"Pfarrer Brenner, hello," Bettina says. "I . . . yes . . . we went for a walk. I really just wanted to see the church again."

"You . . . ? Well. I see you have a baby."

There's nothing she can say to this, so she remains silent.

"I wish you hadn't come. You're no good for him," the father says, taking a step away. "They'll start watching us again. It's been quiet. I like it quiet here—when no one's bothering us. Peter has been very *quiet*. He keeps to himself. I don't want trouble starting up again!"

Bettina realizes that the man is drunk. She nudges the baby off her breast and covers herself.

The father swings a finger in front of his face and places it on his lips in an exaggerated gesture. He whispers, "They came to ask me about my sermons. They wanted to know all about Peter too. I can't—I'm no longer permitted to keep preaching. Religion has become bourgeois, it seems. Capitalistic, corruptive . . ."

"Oh, I'm so sorry," Bettina says in a small voice, looking around. There is no one nearby. Last night she was unable to sleep after hearing loud noises in the square below the bedroom; moving aside the faded yellow curtains, she watched as a police car idled on the cobblestones. Two uniformed officers holding flashlights were standing at the door of the Jantzes', the stucco house kitty corner to hers. Bettina stared as the police handed over some papers to Herr Jantz. The old man wore a tattered dressing gown, his huge head of white hair backlit by a hallway light. Even from that distance and in the darkness of night, Bettina could see his wife's face crumple into tears in the yellow light of their hallway.

Now, her throat so dry she can hardly form the words, she says to the priest, "Aldo is dead. Did you know that?"

"He went off this morning. I found him a couple of hours ago."

"Are you . . . you'll just leave him there?" She shifts Annaliese onto her other side and clumsily buttons her dress with one hand. The baby has a dumb expression on her round face, her eyes half-closed.

Pfarrer Brenner stares. "Are you coming back again? I wish you wouldn't."

She bows her head. "I don't think so, no."

"He's better off without you." There is something about Peter's father that seems deeply neglected and distracted, but when his eyes meet hers again, he appears to be lucid. "You should go home now, and don't come back."

30

"The production quotas, have you heard?" Anne-Marie whispers. Bettina and Stefanie are leaning over the conveyor belt with long narrow knives poised in their hands, scooping up the fish and filleting them with expert twists of their wrists. "They raised them again. Did Putzkammer tell you?"

"What are you talking about?" Stefanie's shoulders are hunched forward. "Enough already." Typically, Stef likes to get on with work and save the chitchat for the locker rooms afterward, when the women make way for the next wave of workers. They strip off their thick aprons and gauzy hairnets, take off the heavy waterproof boots, and become themselves again, women in dresses with pretty hair; that's usually when words flow more freely. Bettina likes that about Stefanie: her ability to concentrate, to be professional, even while doing the most monotonous job. So many of the women just do the bare minimum, trying to get through their days as quickly as possible. Stefanie has integrity.

"Raising the quotas again?" Bettina says. "I don't think that's even possible."

Anne-Marie casts a quick glance toward the exit door, where the factory manager's office is. The smeary glass of his cubicle shows it is empty but for the reflection of the violet-tinged overhead lights. If ever his round face is pressed close to the glass, looking out at row upon row of aproned women standing on the factory floor, there is no talking whatsoever among them. "That's not all," she whispers. "They want us to double production, Franzie said—by next month."

Stefanie snorts. "Well, that's ridiculous. We're moving as fast as we can already."

Christa picks up her head. "Shut up, you gossips. You're going to get us in trouble."

The women ignore Christa, who they feel has become boring and repetitive with her insistence on conforming. If she had her way, none of them would speak to one another again, ever. They understand her fear but find the constant reminders of it tiresome. The women are beginning to sense something shifting—something they're finding harder and harder to ignore. It was one thing to be hopeful right after the invasion, when the Russians promised them all sorts of changes that would improve their lives drastically (after all, they'd been waiting for that since Hitler began making all those promises he didn't keep). After they discovered what had really gone on during the war—the endless betrayals and lies, the ruinous, escalating evil that had been unleashed in the camps—they were ready to believe in better things to come. Communism promised equality, and that, surely, was unimpeachable. And yet . . .

It's been eight years since the war's end, and in reality, *equality* translates into *subservience*; each woman is finding herself increasingly entrapped by the new rules and regulations, more constrained in movement and decision-making than before. Bettina is beginning to think that Communism is nothing more than an alternate version of fascism, in which the vocabulary is different but the goals are the same.

She pushes her hair out of her eyes with the back of one gloved hand. Around her, the sonorous clang of machinery creates a kind of insulation against intelligent thought. Her shift is almost over, and all she has been thinking of is taking Annaliese on another walk. Now she shifts her focus to Anne-Marie; the last thing she wants is to have to add hours to her shift and risk losing her afternoons, the freedom to stroll with the baby, to use her muscles and lose herself in the rhythm of movement. She asks Stef, "What do you mean, that's not all? What did you hear?"

"Uwe, in Berlin?" Anne-Marie says, lowering her voice further. "He said the construction workers, they've called a strike."

"The ironworkers in Bergen, they're striking too," Stef says, stopping the rapid-fire movement of her hands for long enough that a few herring make it past her. Bettina grabs them and throws them in a bucket to finish later. If you miss a single herring on the conveyor belt, everyone is fined, and the money is taken out of their salary.

The foreman's face appears in the window of his office; Heike whistles under her breath, and all the women straighten their backs and speed up their movements. Putzkammer satisfies himself that they are getting on with work, and his face disappears again; everyone turns their bodies toward Stefanie. She shrugs. "They're calling for a general strike. They want free elections in the East!"

Christa struggles to keep up her work as the fish glide past her. She looks up, her brows sharply pulled toward her nose, her mouth grim. Her graying hair is working itself free from her hairnet. "How foolish can you be?" she hisses at the women. "Have you learned nothing at all? Do you not understand that we are just machinery in their system—the fancy new system that's supposed to save the entire goddamn world?"

Bettina makes her way through the streets by the harbor, rubbing shoulders with men and women lingering on the pavement. Unease rises in her with each step she takes. It is an uncommonly busy afternoon, when usually the streets are almost empty at this time of day, everyone either at work or at home eating a big, warm lunch. She clutches Annaliese to her hip and picks her way through the crowd.

On the corner of Hauptstraße and Victoriastraße, a man stands on a wooden crate, people crowded around him. The fish shop used to be just around the corner, and Bettina used to know every centimeter of these streets by heart, every doorstep, cobblestone, tree, signpost. Over the eight years since the end of the war, the womenfolk cleared most of the rubble, piling the bricks into teetering walls, sometimes almost a meter thick, and burning the shredded wood. Today the air is filled with the melancholic cawing of gulls but also the low, insistent drone of voices punctuated by the man's cries. He stands next to what is now a government-run store selling home goods shipped over from Minsk. Visibly agitated, he holds aloft a sign that reads, *Stalin: Massenmörder!*— "Stalin: Mass Murderer."

This scene stops Bettina cold. A shiver runs up into the base of her skull and begins a dull drumbeat against her temples that will become her first migraine headache. She holds on tight to Annaliese. People jostle against her, but she finds that she cannot move.

After Stalin's death a few months earlier, businesses closed, and banners were strung up all over town declaring sympathy for the East Germans' Soviet brothers and the devastating loss of this visionary leader. But no one dares say out loud what so many are thinking: that Stalin was a monster no better than Hitler. There are whispered rumors of poisonings, corpses piled high in secret camps, newly leaked evidence of betrayals and atrocities. Werner has been launching lengthy tirades against the rumormongers, insisting they be strung up like traitors. This big talk of his rings false, but it's also unnerving.

"Have you seen the prices, I ask you?" the man on the crate shouts, pumping his sign up and down. "The prices go up and up and up. How much does your butter cost? How much is your bread? Can you even get bread when you want it, I ask you?"

Some faces are pinched in concentration, and others are slack with bewilderment. But the crowd remains quiet until the man cries: "Stop acting like animals, dumb farm animals, and look around you! You can take control—you can demand fairness!"

"Fairness?" one man shouts back. "We don't have that right anymore!"

"Idiot," a young woman with lacquered hair admonishes, "everyone has the right to fairness."

"You'd better watch out," someone calls from the other side of the street. "They'll call the Vopo!"

The murmuring rises as people begin talking among themselves. The man on the crate becomes red faced with the effort of yelling, but Bettina can no longer hear his words. They rise on the wave of communal noise. She hears "bread" and "quotas" and "pigs" as she forces her feet to move again, to take her away from this crowd, whose energy feels spiteful and fickle.

Can humans ever keep their motives pure? Politics ruins the world, and power corrupts. Is democracy the answer, then? Bettina wonders—will people make the "right" decisions, choices that stand to reap profits not only for themselves but also for others? This talk of "free" elections and complaining about the extra labor it will take to fulfill the new quotas, this endless wondering about where Communism will take the country . . . she wants to believe there's a point to it but can't. Bettina is an anemone in an ocean of sharks and whales. What can she do that would change anything, when she cannot even advocate for the life she wants for herself? She yearns for the simplicity of a love that is requited and uncontested, a love that sings as unfettered as a note from a violin. But the realities of the world do not allow for this.

She shoulders her way through the crowd. Annaliese is squirming in her arms, heavy as a sack of concrete. Out of the corner of her eye, she catches sight of something green: The Volkspolizei. Five, six, seven of them running down the street. People scattering out of their way, clutching their bags to their sides, straining to see where they are headed, relieved when the police run on without stopping. Bettina strains, listening for sounds—and then she hears them: First a scream, then another. A shout and then a shot. And then, quickly after that, another shot and another.

Annaliese hears them also, and even though she cannot possibly know what it means, she, too, starts to shriek.

31

The *Rüganer* does not run a detailed story of the riots that took place all over East Germany that day—alluding only to "mild unrest"—but someone at the factory gets hold of a West Berlin paper that makes the rounds in the bathrooms, where Bettina reads it, and another newspaper turns up in HQ in Bergen, where Werner and his colleagues pretend not to care about it.

Truth is, all over the entire eastern part of the country—a nation that was split in half and taken over by another system—furious German workers emerged to protest. They protested the rise in production quotas and demanded elections. Right there on the front page of *Der Tagesspiegel* is an image of the tanks this new country, the DDR, set upon its own people—the T-34s providing cover for the Vopo. The paper asserts tension was so high that the East German ruling party called in the Soviets for crowd control. Forty thousand people had gathered on the streets of East Berlin. Under the inside fold is a list of hundreds of casualties. These stories are instantly debunked by Werner's team, but there remains a sense of impending disorder that cannot be entirely ignored or erased.

While Werner's division isn't directly involved, Stasi are asking who was where, taking down names, scrutinizing photographs of the impromptu gatherings in Saargen, Bergen, Garz, Arkona. Government officials are beginning a sweep through the coastal regions, moving anyone who owns property to state-run holdings on the mainland. Everyone is on alert again—both those in charge and the ordinary citizens trying to live normal lives.

Because of his special status, Werner and Bettina are permitted to stay in the house on Apolonienmarkt. Each night he comes home with bright eyes and recounts to Bettina the important things he has been called upon to do. As he tells her his stories, he carefully assesses her reactions. He wants her to be proud. He searches her face for a sign that she is impressed, and he finds instead a vague, resigned friendliness.

Nothing is as it should be. His mind is churning.

Bettina is not sleeping at night, even once the child is settled and Werner is fast asleep beside her. She wanders the rooms downstairs in her nightgown, shivering despite the damp heat, hair in wild knots. The books eye her accusingly; the windows with their blank faces have no comfort to offer. The grass in the garden out back feels as lush as velvet under her bare feet, and she pads back and forth between the house and the shed, face turned upward to the night sky. If only she could sleep . . . when she closes her eyes, she again sees the young soldier Werner killed all those years ago, his incontrovertible humanity. Perhaps he would be a family man now, living on the southern ski slopes of Bavaria, a bunch of freckled, feather-haired children helping him with chores. Though she remembers her own terror—the crazed look in his eyes, his brutality—it is the pain of the future he lost that weighs on her. Her heart races to think of the millions of lives cut brutally short and how the Germans are failing to make up for the bloodshed despite their best intentions.

And Peter . . . Peter is on her mind at all times, but most of all when she is begging sleep to descend on her, willing her body to relax. It is then that she hears his insistent voice telling her everything will be all right. That it is truly possible they can fix the world, because two people united in love can overcome anything. But his tone is wrong—faint and fading—and sleep races away from her on cloven hooves, and she is back to her nightmares.

And then she sees him again.

Werner, their widowed neighbor, Irmgard, and her two foster children are standing with Bettina by the door of the cottage. There's an unruly rosebush twisting its way over the front entrance that Werner has been attempting to cut down, and the children have tucked fallen pink blooms behind their ears.

"You're welcome to these," Werner is saying, holding out a basket of eggs toward Irmgard. "Really, Frau Bandelow. Our backyard production is so efficient it far exceeds our own quotas." He laughs, and the woman joins in uneasily.

"Herr Nietz, you are too kind," Irmgard says, tucking a wisp of white-blonde hair behind one ear. Her handsome, square face has become more angular, her eyes in their deep sockets wary, observant. She looks to Bettina like a woman who does not like to live without a man. Although her clothes are drab and threadbare, she has a slim figure pinched in at the waist with a wide leather belt, and the eyes of the neighborhood men are often drawn to her as she makes her way to the market or to her work at the post office. "You know, I still can't get that widow's pension," she continues. Her husband was killed in the last days of the war, and many war widows are still having trouble collecting pensions. "They just won't budge. Poor Ernst. You'd think we deserve better, after all we've been through."

"We can make an omelet!" Elise pipes in, touching the eggs. "Or fried eggs, if we have some lard."

Standing between the two houses, Irmgard puts down her watering can and wipes her hands on her apron. Miniature daisies have sprung up in a series of small earthenware pots that she tends to daily.

A black BMW turns into the square, and as the growl of its engine makes its way past the group, Bettina catches a flash of light hair inside the vehicle. Her eyes remain trained on the car. The wheel wells are rimmed with rust eating into the lacquer.

Can it be the same vehicle she used to see parked outside the *Pfarrhaus*? Is Peter inside? The driver does not look in her direction, but she catches the self-conscious hunch of shoulders, tense hands gripping the steering wheel. His awareness of her ignites the air, and Bettina feels overheated and faint. It can be no one else but Peter.

A towheaded neighborhood child grabs Elise's arm and pulls her away. "Come play hopscotch," he says. "Can she, Frau Bandelow? I'll bring her back in an hour!"

"Yes, dear," Irmgard says. "Careful—that car."

Werner is watching this exchange with interest and cocks his head to the side. "Frau Bandelow, we've known each other for many years now, have we not? I know you and your family to be good people; I can vouch for that. I will take up the matter of the widow's pension again. You should be paid what is rightfully yours, after all this time. It's only correct."

She shifts the basket of eggs from one arm to the other. "I'd certainly appreciate a word to the authorities, if you could, Herr Nietz. Doesn't seem fair that we should have to beg and borrow."

Werner's expanse of white forehead creases into myriad lines as he smiles at her. He stands with his hands clasped behind his back, baring his teeth. There is something to this grin that reeks of false generosity. Bettina would have given the extra food to Irmgard with no fanfare, quietly leaving it on her back stoop. The weight of the air on her neck presses in on her like unwelcome fingers. The colors—grass, flowers, even the sky—are creamy and vague but sharpen ominously under the intensity of her sudden sense of dislocation. She could be nothing but an empty body standing there with these people, transported to some other realm of existence, yet her eyes and ears are on high alert, like a dog who can hear frequencies inaudible to humans.

"Excuse me . . . ," Bettina interrupts. There is a palpable absence—Peter was right here, and now he is gone—and yet also an overabundance of stimuli. Was he trying to tell her something by driving past her like this? "I, uh, I forgot to pick up our flour, from Studemeyer's? I want to bake some *Brötchen* for the morning."

"Too late for that now," says Werner. "It's past closing time."

"Oh, but . . . that's not a problem." The band of her apron feels tight on her waist, and she slips her fingers under it, fiddly and distracted: it seems to be restricting her ability to syncopate her breathing with her speaking. "Studemeyer, he, uh. Well"—deep breath as she tries again—"he usually leaves the bag in the back shed if I don't pick it up in time on Thursdays. I'll take a look. If it's not there, I'll see about trying Bechmann's."

"Really?" Werner remains with his hands behind his back, his brows arched. "Well, run off then, if you must. The baby is asleep?"

"Playing in her crib." Bettina takes off the apron and hands it to Werner.

"Come, Frau Bandelow," he says, waving Irmgard toward him. "Come inside and see how much little Anna has grown . . ."

"Lovely," Irmgard says, smiling. She gives Bettina a quick wave and then follows Werner into the house.

Bettina runs out onto the main road. There is no black BMW anywhere in sight. The sun has dipped behind some clouds, and the skin of her forearms prickles. As she pulls the air deep into her lungs, a stinging sensation travels down her windpipe. She continues running past Studemeyer and on past Marienstraße.

The Pfarrer's old BMW is parked on a side street next to the youth center. Glancing around her quickly, Bettina slips along the side of the building to the back entrance. She waits a second to catch her breath and to listen for footsteps. The pounding of her heart is a reminder of her body's mechanical systems, its astonishing resiliency: she is stand-ing on this street, flesh and bones, her body more determined than her mind.

The door is ajar. The lights are off in the shabby room with its out-moded furniture and listing pool table. The sudden darkness shrinks her world, like the shutter on her camera when it's stuck. She widens her eyes, tries to catch her breath.

There he is. Leaning against the wall, arms folded in front of his chest, wearing a mismatched suit. He appears vulnerable yet possessed of a manic, unpredictable energy. Light hair is falling over his eyes. She steps closer and then stops. It has been so long. Has he changed? His hair is longer, his jacket unfamiliar to her. On the way here her mind was a tumble of words, but now she is mute.

"Why did you come by the house?" Peter says aggressively. "Vati told me he saw you. I did everything in my power to ignore it, but then . . . then, finally—he said you brought a baby—"

"Peter . . ." In the darkness she cannot see his expression, but the whites of his eyes flash at her. "I'm so sorry. It was an impulse. I shouldn't have gone."

"We were doing just fine without you!"

She is stunned by the sight of him, the way his presence fills her up. It is clear how much this separation has cost him; she hears it in his voice. Her legs are trembling. It has cost her too; he must know that. Words refuse to form in her mind now that she needs them.

"I kept away. I did exactly what you asked me to! Knowing you are so close—I was going insane. And then, with the riots, I was afraid for you. How could you not let me know you were all right? I almost came by—I almost broke down the goddamn door of your house!" He pauses, taking a long breath. When he speaks again, his voice has changed register. "And I discover you have a *child*?"

Their confusion is like a foul odor in the air between them. Her eyes adjust to the darkness; the room is exactly as it always was. The equipment tossed into bins, the stacks of books and pamphlets. The posters on the walls and the faint smell of decay. How can these things not change when everything else in the world has shifted? In this moment she is willing to pay any price for their love.

"I'm sorry. I . . . I honestly just didn't know what to do."

"The baby, it's a girl?"

"Annaliese—her name is Annaliese."

"She is mine? Is the child mine?"

"I—listen, Peter . . . I don't—"

"It doesn't matter," he interrupts. His eyes drill into her. "I don't care. My God, Bettina. What have you been through?"

She approaches and places her hands on his forearms, unfurling them from their defensive grip across his chest. This loosens something inside him, and he yanks her in, crushing her against the buttons of his suit. She is softer now, after the baby. Burrowing his face in her hair, he whispers, "I don't care if you leave Werner or not; I have to keep seeing you. And the baby . . . I must see the baby right away. We can figure everything out later!"

The smell of him, the sweat and the skin and the scratchy jacket. Her lungs expand as she takes in his scent, breathing as though she has forgotten and just now remembered how it is done, as if she has to fill her lungs with him or suffocate. The muscles in her thighs quiver. For so long no one has touched her; she can't tolerate Werner's advances, and he finally stopped trying. Now Peter's hands grip her so hard his fingers will leave bruises on her sides.

32

With swift jabs, Werner tucks his shirt into the waistband of his trousers. The buttons strain over his belly, and he gives the material a tug. Some months earlier, when Irmgard Bandelow was asking him about her husband's pension, the protrusion of his stomach became obvious to him, and he decided that he absolutely had to lose a few pounds. He has started doing sit-ups in the bathroom in the early mornings before heading off to work. At first he was only able to do five. Now he is up to ten, yet his girth doesn't appear to be shrinking. But he keeps at it. Since he's the father of a little girl now, the idea of health has taken on an urgency he never quite felt before. There are realities he can do little about (such as the flare-ups of polio that plague him periodically), but there are also things over which he has control. Anna's green eyes beseech him to play. The trill of her laughter when they are together entices him to roll around on the floor with her. There is nothing he won't do for this child, including sit-ups.

He slips his shoes on and glances over at Bettina as she sleeps. Usually she would have been long gone to the factory, but she is taking a sick day today so she can sleep off a lingering cough. Her face is relaxed in repose; the angles, although softened, are regal, swooping from cheekbone to chin. Her lips are slightly parted. He'd like to give her a kiss, but he knows from experience that instead of waking up and smiling at him, she would snap open her eyes, surprised at being disturbed.

It is hardly her fault. He sighs and rises. Have they said one kind word to each other since the baby was born? They are so exhausted from the child's nighttime waking that they barely have the energy to be civil. Although, admittedly, these past few months she has been less morose and silent, sometimes even ebullient. Perhaps they are finally on an upswing.

After grabbing his briefcase and the key, Werner shuts the house-door behind him and walks to the side gate, where he keeps his bicycle. The Tatra is on the fritz again, having lost a chunk of its muffler this time. Who knows how long it will take to find replacement parts? Instead of riding over the cobblestones, he walks the bike through the square. As he nears the turnoff into the center of Saargen, he catches sight of a rebuilt Opel parked down a side street. It has become rare to see nicely appointed vehicles in the streets; most cars are patched-together relics, their colors dulled by years of sun and wind and salt. A rather tall black-haired man emerges from the vehicle, and Werner is surprised to recognize him.

"Comrade Bieder," he calls out, resting his good leg on the pavement and taking a hand off the handlebars to wave as the man approaches.

"Morning to you," Bieder says. "On your way to work, are you? What's with your choice of transportation?"

Werner smiles, telling himself that he is not blushing; he is not embarrassed. "In the shop. A small hiccup. You're in from East Berlin again? What brings you back to the island?"

"Yes, busy, busy. The call of duty."

Werner feels this is a little patronizing; after all, he is busy too. Also, Bieder did not actually answer his question. Just the previous week he paid Werner yet another visit. There's a new man in charge at head-quarters in East Berlin, Ernst Wollweber, and changes are beginning to ripple through to the local precincts, even outlying ones such as Rügen.

Last week Bieder came and poked around his old Bergen office (which is no longer his domain, and surely it is not quite polite to behave as though it is?). He studied the bronze plaque commemorating Werner's heroics in the war, examined the clothbound tax books lined up on the bookshelves, shuffled through the stacks of papers being sorted in preparation for the land audit taking place along the borders of the entire country. But this time, instead of delivering good news or treating him like an esteemed colleague, his insistent, too-soft voice kept asking questions, and personal ones at that.

How long has Werner been married? Are they planning on having more children? Is his wife religious? Does Bettina ever discuss politics with him? And friends, do they have many friends in the neighborhood—married? Single? What about the neighbor, Frau Bandelow—she's a good socialist? What is the real story about her husband; he was an active Nazi, wasn't he? Might it be true that he actually killed himself?

Why all the questions? Werner wanted to ask, but he didn't. Instead, he responded as best he could, keeping up the pretense that this was merely a friendly chat between one colleague and another. When he tried to divert the line of questioning to ask about the mandate from HQ that required reassessing all deeds for any privately owned property within ten kilometers of the water, he was met with an abrupt and conspicuous silence. When the man finally left, Werner had the feeling that he'd been tricked into giving away some seemingly irrelevant, unacknowledged secret.

"And what are you doing in my little town again, Comrade Bieder, so bright and early?" Werner asks, determined not to be ignored. "Not stalking me, are you?"

"Ah, Nietz," Bieder says, running a hand over his slick hair. He never looks directly at Werner, and this makes him appear high strung and capricious, when he is most likely neither. "Had a visit from someone around here that I'm checking up on. Nothing serious, just keeping abreast of what's going on around town. How's that pretty wife of yours?"

"Very well, thank you," Werner answers. He wonders what Bettina has to do with anything. He tries to think back to whether he has broken any rules; perhaps giving Irmgard part of their rations was foolish, but it can't be that, can it? Perhaps Bieder and Bettina know each other? It crosses his mind then that the man might have taken a liking to his wife from afar. Werner is infused with a sense of irritation so discomfiting that it brings warmth to his cheeks. Truth is, it's been so long since Bettina allowed Werner to make love to her that all it takes is for a man to glance at her sideways, and he is overcome with jealousy.

Bieder reads the apprehension on Werner's face. "Nothing to be concerned about, my man. We like to know what's what; you know how it is. Have a good day."

Thus dismissed, Werner hoists himself on his bicycle and starts pedaling away. In his mind, random puzzle pieces are jostling around without fitting together, and he is developing the suspicion that everyone has some sort of secret that only *he* is not privy to. People talk too much. Whose business is it what goes on in the square? He thinks of Bettina, who has gone through yet another transformation, as though she is finally settling into her role as a mother. She smiles more often in his presence, and they talk more comfortably—as they did in the old days—and yet she *still* turns away from him at night. If he tries to insist, she feigns aches and pains or concocts some story about feminine troubles. But what does Werner know about these things?

What he does know for sure is that he is tiring of lying next to a woman who seems only to tolerate him. He will have to find a way to set it straight: A wife has responsibilities. The way things are, with the baby, the house, their lack of marital intimacy—it simply isn't right.

33

The child: spidery lashes curled on plump cheeks, sips of breath even and shallow. Finally, she is down for her nap. Bettina coughs harshly into her fist, her chest heaving with a thick fluttering in her lungs.

There is a sound at the back of the house, and she goes to the landing to peer out over their small garden. The shed is sturdy, its shingles graying but solid, and the heavy-headed rosebush curtsies on the slight incline toward the neighbor. Fresh wash is strung up, inert in the uncommonly still air. Herr Hoechsler is working on his vegetable patch in the distance, wearing his red sun hat. It's nothing. But when she straightens up again, she is certain that she hears the back latch clacking open—that slight distinctive hitch as the metal runner slides over the doorframe. She clutches her dressing gown closer and pats down her hair. "*Jemand da?*" she calls out—Anyone there?—and then begins to cough again. "Werner?"

At the bottom of the stairs, she turns to the back entry and lets out a startled cry. How did Peter make it through the square unnoticed? Fear shoots through her, as if she were jumping from a cliff. "Peter—are you crazy?"

He holds out a makeshift bouquet of wild lupine, honeysuckle clover, and a few sharp pale-green grasses. "I couldn't wait a second longer," he says. "It's killing me having to wait so long to see you."

"You shouldn't ever come here! What if some—"

"I know. I'm sorry. It's just—I was careful. The bike is gone, and the car too. He won't be back for hours, will he?"

"You don't understand!"

It is shocking to have him here, filling this space that is so infused with Werner's presence. They are breathing the same air, walking the same floorboards. She snatches the flowers from him. She has a whole family life that Peter knows nothing about, and she is ashamed of it, as though by having this life she is betraying him, not her husband. "There are a thousand windows with a thousand eyes looking down on us!"

"I went to the factory to leave you a note, and they told me you were home sick," he says. "I just couldn't wait. You're still not better?"

His eyes on her skin are like a cool current along the ridges of her bones, making her shiver. She pushes up her sleeves, grabs a small vase from the shelf, and fills it with water. "Old man Hoechsler's in the *garden*! Why would you be so reckless?"

"I won't come again—promise."

He comes up behind her, close, so she feels the slight fold of his trousers on the back of her knee and the puff of his shirt at his waist; it makes her breath stick in her throat and her hands fall to her sides. Gently he presses his body into her until she feels the length of him, the curve of his chest, his hands on her hip bones. His lips come to her neck, so light, warm. Her shoulders relax, and she leans back into him.

It's been three months since they got together again, and seeing each other is even harder than before—with the baby, with Werner so prickly and unpredictable. Every moment is precarious. They try to see each other once a week, though that isn't always possible. Even with the pall of their subterfuge hanging over them, when Bettina is with Peter, all that messiness falls away. It's an illusion; she knows this, but it brings her back to herself; it seems that she can reveal anything to him, and he will still see her for who she really is. With him, she feels like a good person. She admitted how in the early months of motherhood, she was plagued by the idea that she wasn't cut out to be a mother, that she would fail at this; she spoke of the black depression that fell over her, the terrible lethargy. The guilt she felt about not telling him that she was pregnant. "I failed everyone," she said.

His eyes swam in a film of tears as she spoke. "You are a human being," he said. "You are both brave and fearful. We are doing the best we can."

Now he has taken this terrible risk in coming to her home, and yet she can only feel happiness at seeing him.

"The baby? Is she asleep? Can I see her?" Peter whispers.

They climb the stairs and go into the nursery, where the air is thick with sleep. Annaliese has turned over onto her front, her knees tucked under her torso, her padded bottom sticking up in the air. Peter bends over the crib and reaches out a trembling hand to touch her back, the veins popping blue from his deeply tanned skin.

Bettina spreads the feather duvet out on the wooden floor of the master bedroom by the window. After making love, they lie naked and sweating with the window cranked open to let in a little air, sharing a cigarette and looking out, watching the clouds flit over the rooftops. A jay squawks, and somewhere children kick around a ball and shriek accusations at one another and laugh. Peter will have to find his way out without crossing the square.

"We'll have two more children—boys, next time," he says into the warm skin of Bettina's upper arm. "A whole soccer team."

"No—another girl and *then* a boy." Bettina laughs. She likes playing this game.

"We'll have a little fisherman's cottage, just like this one, but right on the water." They are both silent as they try to imagine where they can live together without Werner's clammy shadow cast over them. "Once we save enough, we'll get ourselves a little boat too."

"I've already got a few hundred marks stored away, you know," Bettina says. "And you? A bachelor. You must be *rich*."

"Oh, I'm rich in knowledge. I can recite anything—just ask. Old stuff, Rilke, Goethe. New stuff too . . ."

She prods him. "You know what I mean. We need at least enough money to take a train somewhere, buy a few things. Not much, but enough."

"Yes," he says. "Most of all we need a good plan."

Is she imagining it, or does he not sound entirely convinced? She badly needs him to believe it's going to be possible for them to start anew somehow, somewhere. "Oh, what's this?" she asks, propping herself up on one elbow. She touches a red welt that runs up the bottom of his arm to the silky hairs of his underarm. "You cut yourself?"

"Oh, this. It's nothing," he says. "It was an accident."

"You were working on the house?"

"No," he says, getting up from the floor. The fluid lines of his flanks are faintly blue, the skin there never exposed. The physicality of him is arresting; it stops time. It telescopes her world in a way that is comforting yet also exciting in its intensity. He stoops to peer out the window at the boys playing below. "My father did it. He was agitated . . . I . . . well, he'd had too much to drink. It happens sometimes now. Things aren't going the way we'd hoped."

"He's been removed from the church?" Bettina asks, rising to stand beside him. "Is that what you mean?"

"I'm not sure what their strategy is anymore, Bettina. For the whole country. Officials told me the other day I can't include internal monologues in a play I'm doing with the children. No internal monologue! They're going to stipulate the form art should take? During the party conference, last year—*Greif zur Feder*, they said, and yes, it's all good to bring literature to the proletariat, but no internal monologues? How is it functionaries think they know what literature is supposed to be?"

"I didn't know," Bettina says, thinking of the warren of offices where Werner works. The delight in bureaucracy and order, the desire to control. It doesn't surprise her, this tightening of the reins, the denial of the scope and freedom of art. "How can you teach, then?"

"I can't, not really. And they've got me on some kind of watch list," he says. "As though *I'm* the enemy."

"Do you think—maybe we should think about leaving . . . maybe even leave the country, as Clara did?"

"No, no, we can't do that. What would happen if everyone stopped fighting for what's right and just left?"

"Sometimes we have to put ourselves first."

"We have to find another way. We must do the best we can, here, in our homeland."

She's exasperated. What other way, now? Surely they have already decided they need to be together. He risked being discovered in order to see her. The stupidity and danger of this astounds her, but she cannot imagine it otherwise, not having him near her in this very moment.

What on earth am I doing? she thinks. To silence her doubts, she kisses him on the mouth, and soon they are back on the floor, entwined, forgetting the rest of the world and its tremendous complexity.

34

Werner has just finished writing up his notes when there is a rap on the door. He checks his watch: four thirty in the afternoon; no wonder his eyes are heavy, the numbers in his columns swimming. This is the time of day when he usually stretches his legs and makes himself a cup of *Kaffee* mix. "Come in," he calls out, stifling a yawn.

Irmgard Bandelow smiles as she enters and bows her head apologetically. She is wearing a small straw hat perched at an angle on top of a collection of white-blonde buns. "Herr Nietz," she says. "I do hope I'm not bothering you. I was just at the market, getting our weekly allotment."

"Please, call me Werner," he says. "We've been neighbors long enough now, no?" They have been playing this game for the past few months: *Herr Nietz, no, Werner; Frau Bandelow, no, Irmgard.* Recently she has taken to wearing a brighter shade of lipstick, which makes her skin look pale and velvety. Once she was fleshy, and now she is gaunt; he finds it not altogether unbecoming. He motions for her to take a seat. "How may I help you?"

"I wanted to thank you." She pulls at the tip of each finger and slides off her gloves, which she lays, one on top of the other, on her lap. Her eyes take in the room, the etchings on the wall, the plaque on his desk, his fountain pen, and the large worn oriental carpet. "We were finally able to declare Ernst a casualty of war; they agreed! So I've been assigned my widow's pension. I know I have you to thank for that. You've been so very generous."

Werner taps on the table. Actually, he neglected to speak to Supervisor Helgendorf about Irmgard's war benefits, but he is loath to admit this oversight, and he smiles instead. "Frau Bandelow—"

"Call me Irmgard, please."

"Irmgard, yes, well . . . 'honor for the party and strength for us all.'"

"Of course, but thank you all the same. I was hoping I could entice you and your wife to come for dinner one night so that I might thank you properly."

It's funny with women, how you cannot force them into friendships, Werner thinks to himself. These two have lived side by side for more than ten years, and yet there is no easy familiarity between them. Half a year ago he spoke with Irmgard about his wife, admitting how very concerned he was, and she promised to keep an eye out for her. But Irmgard avoids his eyes now as though there is another person in the room, someone invisible to him.

"We'd be delighted; thank you," he says.

She flushes lightly, and with a start he understands that she is impressed by the office, by his position. He wonders whether she has been with another man since her husband died. Leaning back, he smiles at her without opening his mouth. Her regard for him gives him the urge to be chatty—ask her personal questions he knows are not appropriate—but it's best for him to be quiet now, he thinks. To let this moment speak for itself.

As she prepares to leave, she hesitates with one hand on the doorknob. "Your wife—she's not doing that double shift anymore, at the factory? Not since before the baby, isn't that right? When we talked, she and I, she was worried about that. She said she was very tired."

"Yes, she likes the extra time off, now that we have a family. Why do you ask?"

"Oh, I was just wondering." Irmgard's eyes are skittish, her face washed out in the fluorescent overheads. Her jaw is square and set, as though she's girding herself for an unwelcome chore. To encourage her, he leans forward with his elbows on the desk and rubs his fingers over his upper lip: thoughtful, earnest.

"I sometimes see her in the afternoons now; that's all. She's busy, it seems? But I'm sure you know she's quite sociable—hurries off . . ."

"In the afternoons? With the baby?"

"And she's become quite a beauty recently. Motherhood must agree with her after all." Irmgard swings the door open and blinks rapidly a few times. "If I were you, Werner, a man of your stature, your importance? I suppose I might just keep a bit of an eye on her."

Everything on the square looks quite normal, just the way he would expect on any day of the week. The front door of the house is shut, the top window over the thatched eave propped wide open, a sliver of yellow curtain shifting languidly in the breeze. When he puts the key in the front lock, he is surprised to find the house is unlocked. Quietly, he edges the door open and enters the hallway. Eberle mews and twists himself around Werner's ankles, and he pushes the cat away with his foot.

He pokes his head into the living room: empty. In the kitchen, a plate with bread crumbs from breakfast still stands by the sink. A pitcher with some scrawny meadow flowers sits on the windowsill, the delicate yellow heads kissing the marble countertop, leaving behind a sprinkling of pollen. The air in the house is turgid. Perhaps Bettina decided she felt better or needed some fresh air and took the child for a walk by the fields, or maybe even to the beach. The back door into the garden is ajar.

That's when he hears the sounds—of what, grunting? Or is that crying? By the time Werner gets to the bedroom door on the second floor, he is certain his wife has taken a lover. Why else does she rebuff him so steadily? He can count on one hand how often they have made love in the past few years. He throws the door open and bursts into the room. Bettina's clothes lie in a heap by the bed, and she is wearing only her undergarments. The eiderdown from the bed is spread on the floor, and Bettina is kneeling on it. Annaliese is propped up beside her. Her dark hair sticks out at the back of her head as though she has only just woken up from a sweaty nap. Widening her liquid eyes, Anna looks at her father. Her toes are fat as potato chunks.

"What are you doing?" he yells at Bettina.

Annaliese stops her sounds and drops the book as Bettina jumps to her feet. "We're *playing*! What do you think we're doing?"

Werner strides over to the closet and rips the door open. "I thought you were ill? Why are you undressed? You should be in bed, resting."

"Annaliese, she, uh . . . she wanted to play." Bettina's neck and shoulders are rosy, the creamy skin of her stomach and thighs smooth and beautiful.

The baby stares up at them both and starts to wail. "Where are your clothes?" he asks Bettina. "What's going on?"

Bettina grabs a blanket and holds it in front of her body as though embarrassed to be half-naked in front of her own husband. "I was just about to wash up. I—I was sweating so much. My cough is better. I think the fever broke."

Werner is offended by her false modesty. His confusion tips over into rage. "Put the child back in her crib."

"But she just woke up, Werner. She won't be—"

"Put her in the crib!" He wishes he could subdue the brutal beating of his heart; he wishes she did not have this dreadful power over him. She only has to give him a small piece of herself; he is not asking for so much! And yet it seems he is always asking *too* much.

Watching her rise and then stoop down to pick up the baby, he feels certain that he is losing her, that he cannot hold on, that no matter how hard he tries, she has already slipped away from him. She leaves the room, and when she comes back, he is ready for her. It has been so long, too long; he is fed up with her moods. He will show her who is in charge.

35

In the early mornings as dawn breaks and Bettina packs up Annaliese for a day at the crèche, Werner pretends to be asleep, and when the pram begins its squeaky ride over the cobbles, he dresses hastily and follows them all the way to the factory. One day he calls her supervisor under the guise of needing to check attendance records and is given access to everyone's shifts for the next two weeks. Bettina cannot go to work or leave work without him knowing. He thinks back to her vivid cheeks, the wide-eyed look she gave him upon returning to the bedroom that afternoon, and he is driven onward by something that feels like anger but is more like fear. He is accustomed to this—all his life he has lived with fear. Fear of being taunted, of being alone, of being unloved and unappreciated. Fear of doing something wrong and not being good enough. Of being abandoned. It's over, this way of living.

But it is not his watchful eyes that lead to the last piece of the puzzle falling into place: it is Irmgard's ward, Alma, the young politician and fiddler.

The girl comes over from next door sometimes to watch the baby while Bettina goes to the market on the weekends. This morning, Werner wrote a long list for his wife that would keep her far too busy to go off and cause trouble. Working on the vegetable patch in the back garden, he shoves the trowel into the black soil, upending worms and beetles, and as they writhe in an endless chain of impending destitution, a sense of futility overwhelms him. He's sent his wife on unnecessary errands, and she has not complained once, and this acquiescence only serves to deepen the gulf between them.

He will clean himself up. He will make tea and await her return, and they will talk again, like normal human beings. After coming inside, he begins playing *Kanasta* with Alma in the front room as he waits. The deck of cards is scattered over the low wooden table, and the girl's hands flutter uncertainly as she tries to decide on her next move. In her youth group uniform, she appears so confident and admirable, but in a drab gray dress with plastic sandals, she seems rather ordinary. "You are so good at playing this game, Herr Nietz," she complains. "I'm going to lose *again*."

"Don't give up yet. Keep trying."

"Oh, but I can't think straight. I'm flustered." Alma's hairline is darkened with sweat. "Frau Bandelow's just awful, as bad as I am. She can't concentrate for a single minute. Is your wife a good player?"

He laughs aloud. "No, no, I'm afraid Bettina's terrible at cards."

"Really? She's so imaginative, though, isn't she? And sort of patient . . . all that photography and drawing. She gave me some lovely stuff for my notebooks."

This intrigues him; as far as he knows, it's been years since Bettina picked up that old camera or pencil and paper. "You keep journals?" he asks the girl carefully. The dim light in the room makes her eyes flash like coins in a pool. "That's very creative of you."

"Thank you. I love to write and sketch—I'm way better at that than I am at numbers."

"It doesn't have to be either-or, you know."

Her pleasure at his interest in her is almost tangible and binds them like a song they both recognize. "Want to see?" she asks him. "I've got some sketches and poetry too." From a satchel behind her, she extracts a spiral-bound notebook. Flipping through the pages, she lands on a poem and reads it aloud.

He nods, encouraging her, and she then reads him the slogan *Junkerland in Bauernhand*, extolling the virtues of collectivizing the estates in East Prussia. "How do you even know about that business?" he asks. "Way before your time, isn't it, right after the war?"

"From the Young Pioneers, of course." She's paging through her notes, showing him the odd scrap of a landscape or a half-completed portrait, and—glued to one of the pages—there's a sketch that is far more sophisticated: Subtle shading using a black pencil, shredded clouds that waft in the sky above the textured thatch roof of a house. A strong sense of perspective that makes the image appear to pop from the creamy page.

"This is your house?" he asks. "The one next door?"

"Yes, Frau Nietz drew that—and she's so good at the portraits too. Everything. See? Isn't it amazing?" Alma points to a sketch, in fat layers of colored pencil, of a woman who resembles Christa Kellermann and, on the next page, a drawing of a man Werner doesn't recognize. Light hair, unkempt, a fine, long nose that dominates a narrow face. Keen eyes encircled with lines crosshatched with a sharpened pencil.

The energy apparent in the sketch is startling. "Do you know who this is?" he asks, pointing.

"Oh, him. That's Elise's teacher. Literature. Nice, isn't it?" Alma giggles. "Half the girls are in love with him!"

Werner is aware that he must tread carefully. "He teaches writing, does he?"

"Things like plays and poetry. Herr Brenner. He never taught me, but I wish he had! He runs the after-school program at the youth center too. I went there a few times." She wrinkles her nose. "I prefer my meetings, though. I like singing more than activities."

Brenner . . . wasn't Pfarrer Brenner the pastor from that ancient church in Bobbin who was ousted, some time ago? Werner had been involved in an audit of the rectory's financial status. The old man had one son who came back from the war. Two who were killed. Questionable allegiances.

Bobbin church.

Bettina used to walk to Bobbin all the time.

And Irmgard—she said something about Bettina having become so radiant. That she was more sociable.

The day he found out Bettina was pregnant, where had he found her? In the damn church in Bobbin, looking out the window at something Werner could not see.

The sketch has been executed in astonishing detail. Why would Bettina spend hours drawing a stranger? Werner rises, startling the girl. Who else knows about this man, this Peter Brenner? Does Bieder know—is *that* why he's been snooping around so much lately? If Werner could, he would head over to Bobbin and squeeze the teacher's neck between his two hands until he hears the bones cracking under the pressure. But even in his moment of torment, he is aware of how weak and pitiable he is, that he can achieve little through violence.

"Herr Nietz?" the girl asks. "Are you all right? Are you angry she gave them to me? You can have them back if you want."

It is the guileless look on the girl's face that helps him catch his breath, that cranks back the forward-churning train of emotions that would have him stumble into something foolish and thereby lose the upper hand. Nothing can be gained by revealing anything. If he can just be a blank slate, as dull and predictable as a piece of cardboard, he will make a plan. He will prevail. Reveal to those who doubt him just how formidable he can be.

He places a hand on the girl's and pats it gently. "Alma, can you stay for a few hours longer?" he asks. "I've just remembered I have some urgent business to attend to."

36

If it were just the two of them, they could buy themselves a train ticket and get as far away as possible, build a new life in the farmland to the east or perhaps south near Leipzig. But they have a child to consider, one whose babbling will soon turn to words; one day she will be full of questions. Anna may remember Werner and miss her little home on the island. And Bettina and Peter need work papers. If they wish to marry and have children, Bettina must secure a divorce. Is it even feasible for them to stay in East Germany but escape Werner's purview, his petty and maybe not-so-petty machinations? Perhaps she can persuade Werner to be a gentleman, to let her go, though this seems highly unlikely given his erratic behavior. Talk of the future brings with it a heavy dose of uncertainty and fear, mixed with the thrill of impending change.

And their situation has changed—Werner is terribly on edge. Bettina doesn't know what's gotten into him recently, but he has started demanding intimacy, and she must submit to him or arouse suspicion; she can't afford that now. Since he came home early and surprised her, she's caught him staring at her disconcertingly, his underwater eyes astute and piercing. What is he thinking? She dares not ask. Instead, she is careful. Even her footsteps throughout the house are tentative. Washing up at the sink, her movements are deliberate and slow, and when she calls her husband to dinner in the evening, her voice is modulated to suggest calm. But there is tension in her muscles that urges her toward wildness, toward being loud and insisting on snatching what she wants from life. She tells herself that she must be patient.

For three days in a row she places the tin watering can by the *Rosa rugosa* to the right of the front door—a sign that she cannot meet Peter at the youth center. If she places it by the front gate, it means they can meet in the late afternoon, and if she takes the can away entirely, it means she will come to him in Bobbin. But today, once again, she comes home after work to find that Werner has returned early from the office, this time with the Tatra. It's parked in the pebbly area between their house and Irmgard's, sitting there like a gargantuan beetle or perhaps a bullet. Annaliese clasps her mother's hand, and with the other one Bettina pushes the pram. The watering can stays by the bush.

There's a honk on the square as a truck rounds the corner, pulling behind it a contraption piled high with wooden crates. The vehicle pulls over, idling the motor, and her old friend Johann climbs down from the cab. A portly man in his early sixties with enormous scarred hands, he's been their butcher for decades. Now his land is part of the LPG, the new agrofarm. He holds out a package wrapped in brown paper and smiles at her. When she was little, he would offer her bits of bacon when he delivered cuts of meat to her mother. A smooth, bleached apron stretches over his belly and still retains soft brown echoes of blood. "Fräulein," he says, even though she's been married almost a decade. "Just returned from the big city. My sister, you know?"

"Oh, Berlin," she says. "You were able to cross the border into the West?"

"I was granted a day visa. Can you believe Nele has a grandchild now? Haven't seen her in more than four years. *Hallo, Maus. Wie geht's, meine kleine?*" *How are you, little one?* With one giant paw he tousles the black hair on Annaliese's head. "I've got to go, but I came home to find this letter. For you, I believe."

"Thank you for doing this, Johann. I know it's risky."

"Family," he says. "We need them, don't we?"

It's another letter from her sister. Bettina tucks the package of meat under her arm, waves goodbye, and heads for the house, parking the pram next to the car. The front door opens.

"Who's that?" Werner calls out. "Is it Johann?"

"He brought us some pork," Bettina answers. The truck rumbles to life behind them. "We can have it tonight. Come, Anna, let's wash your hands, shall we?"

But before she can get past him into the house, Werner snatches the letter from her. "And this?"

She forces herself to slow everything down. "It's nothing. It's not important."

The envelope jostles in his hands as though it's a piece of metal scalding his skin. He will open it, he will read it, and then he will know where Clara is.

"No, sorry. It's—actually, it's from my sister."

Werner says nothing. His look is hard to parse: he seems neither surprised nor angry.

"I just wanted to know that she is all right. I'm sorry. I miss her, Werner . . . she's my only family . . ."

"The butcher gave it to you? How is he involved in this?"

There's an uncomfortable flutter in her chest. "He—Johann—he's an old friend of my parents. He's like a father, almost. It's not as though—"

"How is any of that relevant?" Werner tucks the letter into his pants pocket. "So you've known where she is all along."

Bettina looks down. She fears she'll never see the letter. And what if Clara has written something about Peter?

"You knew where she was, and you didn't tell me."

His voice is too calm. She watches as he turns his back to her and heads into the house.

The Tatra handles just fine with its new muffler, and the next day after dinner Werner drives to Bobbin, claiming that he's meeting a new MfS recruit; in a way he is indeed working. He parks behind the church, partly hidden by a decrepit outbuilding in which lawn equipment is rotting away, a good fifty meters from where the literature teacher lives with his lunatic alcoholic father. Werner sits for a moment before turning the engine off and climbing out. He's been doing his research. He knows quite a lot about the two of them now—these sad-sack Brenner men, the only ones left.

He cannot see anything through the impenetrable blackness. The screeching of invisible birds in the dark overhead is making him tense. Rustling—of what, leaves? Two police cars had raced ahead of him and parked right in front of the *Pfarrhaus*. After the hurried slamming of car doors and some muffled banging, there is silence. If someone sees him, they will certainly wonder what on earth he is up to lurking around the woods at night. With his hands stretched out in front of him, he stumbles up a short hill through some brambles that catch on his ankles and heads toward the trees on the rise behind the church so he can see what is taking place in the clearing below.

Three policemen in khaki uniforms, truncheons and pistols strapped to their belts, stand outside the house. Their headlights carve shivering beams of light into the darkness. The house looks as though it is crouching, uneasy under the glare.

The front door is open. Werner waits.

A few minutes later, a policeman comes out, leading the old man by the elbow. They climb into one of the cars and execute a tight turn to head down the road toward town. Instinctively, Werner crouches down so the glowing beam of light does not hit him through the trees. When he rises again, he feels the old resentment rising in his chest: he would have liked nothing better than to storm into the melee below, make a huge racket, take his gun out of the glove compartment where he stashed it, and wave it around. Perhaps even take a few shots! At the same time, he knows this would not be wise—he still has to think of his end goal. If he's learned one thing over the past years, it's that it pays to be patient. To be slow and methodical.

Then they bring *him* out. A black police dog bounds past the teacher and runs in circles in the front yard, as though chasing a rabbit. In the glow from the lights of the car, the expression on Peter Brenner's gaunt face is visible. He does not look defeated—he looks defiant. It is the man in the sketch; there is no doubt at all.

Werner waits for them to drive off. What now? He cuts a ridiculous figure huddled in the woods like a common criminal. He straightens up and heads down toward the empty house. The front door is still open. Inside it smells of stale air and the sweat of two grown men. Cooked food and dust. Neglect. It is clear there is no woman in charge here. He is disgusted at the thought that his wife, so clean and orderly, might have come to this house to be with this man. Quickly, he trots through the hall and the living room and into the kitchen. The old Volksempfänger radio on the countertop is blaring. It is jarring to hear the announcer's voice, deep and calm, presiding over this empty space.

Upstairs there are two bedrooms, one of which is obviously the old man's. On the table by the bed are a copy of the Bible and a stack of newspapers. On the floor lie a few empty bottles of Kowalski vodka. The other room is as bare as a cell and contains an iron bedstead and a dresser. There are no books or clothes anywhere. Where does this Peter Brenner sleep? Does he even live here?

Back downstairs, Werner stands in the hallway, stymied. He is jumpy and exhilarated, like a child doing something he knows to be wrong. He is compelled to see where Peter Brenner sleeps, where he shaves his face in the mornings before going to teach at the school, where he writes letters or marks students' papers or eats his food. Werner pats the pocket of his jacket nervously.

He remembers having seen the *Pfarrhaus* in daylight and wondering how the family uses the ramshackle lean-to in which the chickens and pigs were kept in the old days. Now he turns to his right and sees a door.

Peter's room is actually quite large, low ceilinged, with a brick fireplace in the far corner and a coarse wooden floor covered in an old rug. Two windows face the front, and two face the back. Flowered curtains hang limply, pulled open. On a compact table sit an almost-empty bottle of beer and a stack of books and papers. The floor near the bed is strewn with papers, and the bed in the corner is unmade, a wool blanket cast aside. The walls seep moisture.

The papers on the floor have been scribbled on and discarded.

Apocalyptic, Werner reads. After that, something is crossed out with thick black strokes of a fountain pen.

The man with two faces. Perfidy in yellow, their bobbing heads full of lies.

A slob, this man! An intellectual and a poet and a slob. Werner's heart races. He takes one of the papers and folds it into small squares and slips it into his jacket pocket. It might come in handy. There is an animal smell in the room, musty but also acrid, like the smell of a sweating horse. Does Peter Brenner bring women into this room—has *Bettina* been in here? Being here in this place where he lives and drinks and writes and sleeps makes Werner feel diminished and impotent all over again.

A deep throbbing begins to radiate through his jaw. *Everything will be all right,* he tells himself. *I just need to think.*

There is a faint rap on the front door of the *Pfarrhaus,* and Werner jerks his head toward the sound. It seems there is no back exit to this room, and he will have to go either back into the main house or out the side exit, in plain view of the front door. Werner reaches into his pocket and pulls out a pair of panties—very small, for a young girl. He lifts the thin mattress and shoves them underneath. An insurance policy for the future, in case he needs it. He will not allow himself to be made a fool of.

Flipping off the light switch, he heads back to the main house. At the front door stands a woman a little older than he is, hair pulled back with a clip. Her blonde hair is heavily streaked with gray, her pointy face like a skittish bird.

"Excuse me," the woman says. "Marie—I'm Marie from next door. Johann is my husband? The butcher. I just wanted to check—I think my nephew may have called the . . . the Vopo."

"I'm done in here," Werner says, shutting the front door behind him. She thinks he's from the local police force? Foolish woman. The way he stands in front of her, with authority, takes away her right to ask who he is or what he is doing. "The men have been taken to the police station in Bergen for questioning. I'm with the Stasi."

"Is everything all right? What have they done?"

"I'd lock your doors if I were you." Werner sees fear flicker across the woman's pinched face, loosening her brows, slackening her lips. "Those boys, they were bad seeds, all of them. I'd watch out for him—"

She recoils. "You mean Peter? Why?"

"Yes! Do you have children, daughters? I'd keep them well away from him; that's all I can say for now." Werner lowers his voice, the growl of it reverberating in his throat. "I shouldn't say anything, but he's under investigation. We have it all under control. But be careful, mind you. We can never be too careful, can we? And I'd keep an eye on that husband of yours too." He strides away as quickly as he can, given his limp. The woman is following him with her eyes, surely, wondering who he is. But he knows that as long as he walks with purpose, speaks without hesitation, and states allegations as fact, sooner or later everyone will forget their loyalties, their memories and personal experiences . . . and the seeds of distrust will begin to flower.

37

It happens one day ten minutes after she returns from seeing Peter at the youth center. Waking up that morning, she did not know that she would not lie back down on her bed again that night or any night thereafter. Werner took the child on a walk to see the beekeeper on Seemannstraße, and when Bettina gets back home, she begins watering the roses in the front yard. She is flushed from lovemaking, her lips swollen and smarting. Her heartbeat has yet to resume its natural rhythm. It was hot and rushed, and they heard noises outside that made them stop—holding their breath. This has served to strengthen their resolve: they must leave soon! Just a few days earlier Peter and his father were picked up by the police and questioned for almost three hours straight, well into the night. Two men wearing the green uniforms of the Stasi asked Peter about his writing, his allegiances. They doubted his support for the system, and no amount of explanation assuaged them.

"They've turned on me," he told her. "It's time to make a plan."

But they have no plan yet, and as she bends over, watering, Bettina hears her daughter in the distance. Lusty, gurgling shrieks of anger. Anna is cinched in the crook of Werner's arm, her fists coiled like ham hocks, sweat silvering her cheeks. When she sees her mother, she leans her body back wildly and reaches out for her. Bettina straightens up. Something about the way Werner is walking through the gate tells her instantly that there is trouble ahead.

"*Na, kleine,*" she says, rubbing palms suddenly slick with sweat against her cotton skirt.

Werner is wearing his summer linens, the slack in the weave causing ripples where there should be none. He won't even look at her. With one hand firmly on Anna's back, he does not break his stride. "Follow me," he barks.

"I'm just . . . I'm watering . . ."

He disappears into the house. If only her body could stay there in the garden, in the process of executing menial tasks. If only she could ignore the tone of her husband's voice, the implication of his reddened face, and the way he was gripping their child in his arms. It is all so ordinary. And yet it is clear that after this stunningly ordinary moment, something profound will change. The anticipation in her stomach is like a bleeding ulcer. She follows him inside.

"You are leaving this house today," he says to her. The baby is sitting on the worn carpet in the front room, a slant of light coming through the mullions and casting a latticework of shade onto her bloomers. Anna is hiccuping and focused on the cat, who sits immobile and smug, waiting for the moment when he's had enough and will swipe at her with his claws. Bettina takes all this in. She's not quite present; a woolly feeling has enveloped her, as though time is altered in some permanent way.

The child. Bettina wants to pick her up but does not move.

"Did you hear me?" Werner says. "You will leave this house today."

The second time he says it—in that imperious tone—Bettina is jolted from her stupor and makes a move for Anna, but in a flash Werner has scooped her up again. Bettina freezes. She badly does not want to make her baby cry—if she hears that cry again, if *she* is the one who causes it, there will be no fixing this; she knows it. She will be doomed.

"Let's put her upstairs," Bettina whispers. "In the crib."

"What? What did you say?" Werner says. "Didn't you hear me the first time?"

"Please, let's not—"

"You are a lying whore." He is speaking now in a tone so low and gentle that Anna, in his arms, turns her face toward her father and places a small hand on his cheek. The words are soft, slow, and nothing has ever sounded as ominous.

"Werner, the child . . . ," she says.

"You will never, ever see her again." Werner kisses Anna's cheek. She looks over to her mother, aware now that something is wrong. Her eyes are intent, lips parted. She is teething, and a trickle of saliva runs down her chin, staining her shirt in a dark half moon.

Bettina begins to back up. "You're scaring me," she says. "I won't talk to you while Anna is here. I . . . I . . ." But Werner pushes past her and begins to labor up the stairs. It would be possible for Bettina to wrestle the child from his arms, but then Anna would be alarmed, and she'd scream. It seems very, very important that Anna not sense the terrible power of their anger, of their insidious, poisonous fear. So Bettina waits at the bottom of the stairs in the hall, next to the dish on the sideboard holding the Tatra keys, the graying lace doily her grandmother stitched, the mirror whose wonky reflection reveals a world trapped in a snow globe. The urgent pulsing between her legs has not stopped, and inside her a coil of self-hatred unfurls: the beautiful ache of sex revealing itself as dangerous. There is no one to blame but her, and she must face whatever is to come.

His preternatural calm is more intimidating than if he were screaming. Anna is in her little room, and Werner paces the master bedroom. "I saw you this afternoon on Hermannstraße. I watched you enter the youth center. I saw Peter Brenner"—Bettina sucks in her breath sharply at his name—"that teacher. Peter Brenner from the middle school. The writer with the crazy father and the dead Nazi brothers. Yes, I know all about him. I waited with your child in my arms until you came out again, you damn whore. I know you've been having an affair. I have *proof* now, Bettina. We took photos—don't even try to deny it."

Is it worth telling him he's mistaken? Should she try to find a way to explain why she would sneak around on a weekend afternoon in a place she clearly has no reason to be? His will is towering and formidable—she will have to climb a mountain a thousand kilometers high, claw her way up a cliff of ice. "Werner . . . ," she begins, taking a seat on the bed and running her clumsy fingers over the coverlet. But she doesn't know how to save herself.

"You don't have anything to say?" He regards her with a mixture of disdain and something that looks like horror—or maybe it's just surprise. He expected her to fight back. Perhaps he is hoping she will tell him that he is wrong.

"I'm so sorry," she answers. "You don't deserve any of this."

"How long has this been going on? How many—is it . . . how long has it been? Tell me," he stutters. He needs to know if it's possible that the child isn't his, but he's afraid to ask.

This is where, later, she will think she went wrong. If she had told him that the child was not his, that it was Peter's, perhaps his anger would have turned—perhaps it would have grown to include Anna as well, and then Bettina would have had a chance to keep her child. But instead, with his barely contained fury pushing against her, she takes pity on the man. What has he ever done to her but tried to take care of her?

Also, she cannot deny him the possibility that the child is his because she herself does not know. She shakes her head. "I was so unhappy, Werner; I was like an entirely different person. I made decisions I regret." He will no doubt think she is talking about the terrible months after she had Anna, but he continues to simply stare at her. She tries again. "I don't know if I can explain—it was as if I was possessed. I didn't even recognize myself anymore."

He snorts and cuts his eyes away from her. This is not the right thing to say, but it is true, more true than she can hope to explain. She simply did not know who she was until she met Peter. The person she thought she was at nineteen, when she married, and at twenty-five, when she struggled to make sense of her life, is not who she is now. There was no solid foundation upon which to build a love for Werner. But how is she supposed to have known this until it was proven to her? It took falling in love to reveal to her how wrong she had been in her choices as a young woman.

She clasps her hands so tightly that her knuckles are leached of color. All these justifications ring hollow to a husband who has been deceived, though this does not make them untrue. Yes, she had finally determined she must leave him, take the child, and start anew with another man, but she had not yet thought through what she would say or do when faced with his devastating disappointment, his righteous, undeserved pain. "Werner . . . I'm . . . I truly mean it—I'm so very sorry for the pain I've caused."

"It's convenient to be sorry, Bettina. And anyway, it's beside the point. I forgive you. You are a human being . . ."

Her heart lifts—can this be true? He can let go of his need to punish her?

". . . and no one is perfect. But in this case, Bettina. In this case you behaved like a prostitute. You are not the woman I thought you were." He begins pacing again, and this time his movements are jerky, and his left foot is dragging a bit. "You're not special, Bettina. You are ordinary. You are weak, and you are ordinary, and you have no self-control."

"You yourself said—"

"You will leave Rügen. I want you out of the house. I can't continue here in this community when my wife has been parading around with another man. Do you understand me? You will leave here today, and Annaliese, she is staying with me."

Bettina jumps up and hurls herself past him. In the small room where the maids used to sleep, Annaliese is trying to pull herself up in a huge wood-slat crib, pumping with her thick legs, hanging on the railing with both hands. Dark-brown curls stick out in clumps, and her mouth is open wide in a glistening smile at seeing her mother again.

Bettina snatches her up, breathes in her daughter's sharp, musky odor. But when she turns to race back down the stairs, Werner is standing in the shade of the doorframe, and in his hands he is holding a gun. The room is so quiet that she can hear the wash snapping on the clothesline at the back of the house.

38

Annaliese lays her head on her father's shoulder and closes her eyes. She does not understand that in his right hand he's holding something designed to kill and that he is pointing it at her mother.

Werner lurks behind Bettina as she packs her things. Time and time again she clumsily drops her clothes to the floor. Her brain cannot function properly; she has no idea what she will need. How can she, when she does not know where she is going? Her breath is short, as though it's losing its way before reaching her lungs. "You can't just take the house," she says. "It belonged to my grandparents!"

"Pack," he says, waving his hand toward her.

"You have no right. She's my child too. You can't take her from me . . ."

But he's not listening; in fact, he seems almost unconcerned. The muscles of his face are relaxed, his expression neutral. How can he be so sure she will do as he says? The fury inside her is a small screaming voice, silenced by the roar of her fear. She wonders if he would dare hurt the child. Does he suspect that he may not, in fact, be her father?

There is a fickle current in the air, something that quivers with menace, and it makes her wilt. She has one suitcase, and it is filled with all her clothing.

"Go downstairs. Take what you want of your family's things."

"Please, no . . ."

"You don't get a say in this. Take your things now, or leave them here; I don't care."

Downstairs, she surveys the long narrow front room, crammed with furniture and knickknacks collected over decades. Books are shoved against one another, as watchful as sentries. There's a black-and-white sketch Bettina made of her mother, the eyes as big as sinkholes. Her sharp gaze appears to assess her daughter and find her sorely lacking. Should Bettina take her grandmother's stag plates, stacked in the breakfront? Ridiculous—she cannot carry them, and anyway, they will certainly break. But she *loves* them! They are a part of her childhood. The tiny stags leaping over tufts of grass, the trees arching in toward each other—as a young girl she memorized these patterns while eating her sauerbraten. Extracting a linen napkin from the bureau, Bettina wraps one blue-and-white plate inside it and pushes it into her case.

The camera sits on one of the higher shelves, and Bettina thinks she will leave it there. What good has art done her these last few years? It seems frivolous and foolish, a hobby for people who have nothing better to do than amuse themselves. But then she remembers that there's a roll of film in it, and one day after seeing Peter some months ago, she took photos of Annaliese while she was in the bath. Even though she cannot believe—not at that moment, not yet—that she won't see her child again, she rises on her tiptoes and grabs the camera. There are some rolls of film on the shelf, and she grabs a few of those too.

What will become of Annaliese? The cat meows disconsolately. Bettina grabs him and holds him close to her face, his thick, silky fur pressing against her nose. "*Eberle,*" she whispers. "*Eberle!*" He lets out a long, drawn-out wail and scrambles out of her hands, skittering across the floor.

Footsteps betray Werner's approach, and when Bettina sees that his arms are empty, she cries out. "Where am I supposed to go?" she asks.

"Go to your sister. Get out of Germany." His voice is flat, uninflected. The gun looks puny in his hand, pointing down at the floor.

Maybe it's a toy—black, shiny, snub nosed. He would never pull the trigger, would he?

"This can't be legal. It's my house."

"Bettina, I had no idea you could be so stupid. It's not your house. It's not in your name. And who would care even if it were? You've lost your rights. Your behavior has cost you all of this. And I thought you were clever . . ."

She will take every invective he hurls at her. She will swallow it all gladly, if only he stops behaving in this strange, measured manner. Let him hear her out; let him soften his heart toward her. "I know, Werner—I've been so—"

"You've got five minutes, and then I'm calling the police." He makes a sound with his pursed mouth like a professor disgusted with an especially moronic student. "Tsk, tsk. The house belongs to the state. You do not own it, you cannot claim it, and who do you think they will allow to inhabit it? Comrade Werner Nietz, part of the Directorate for the Protection of Public Property—or you, a philandering agitator?" His laughter is thin and mean. He raises the pistol and points it at her. "That's it. Your time is over. Leave."

At the door, she says, "Can I at least say good—"

"Leave. Now!" And that's what she does. The lock turns over behind her with a hefty click.

Bettina runs to the youth center and finds both doors locked. It is almost six o'clock, and the sun is suspended in a gauzy haze. The leaves on the trees lining the street make an insidious rustling noise that slithers into her ears, and it won't stop. The bus—still four or five blocks away, down the street—is so loud it seems to be thundering alongside her, every turn of the wheel and application of the brake reverberating in the thick evening air. The sounds are invading her body like a virus, pushing her breath, her energy, out of the way. Her coat, boots, wool hat, and mittens are all back at the house, waiting for winter-time to arrive. But where will she be when winter comes? The money she stashed away in an envelope in the rice jar in the pantry remains there, dusty and useless. If only they'd had more forethought, more self-control.

The idea of leaving Annaliese behind is ludicrous: Bettina will never willingly do that. What does Werner think he's going to do with the child when he goes to work? What would Werner tell her about her mother, why she has disappeared? Of course, Bettina doesn't have her sister's letters with her, so even if she wanted to find a way to leave the country, she wouldn't know where to go. On the street corner close to the town hall is a phone booth, and she slips inside, leaving her battered leather suitcase on the curb. She dials the number of the *Pfarrhaus* in Bobbin. It has been over two hours since she and Peter parted ways, and he'll surely be home by now.

The phone rings and rings.

The walk to Bobbin is endless, unshaded. Dust creeps into her shoes and granulates under the soles of her feet, making her skin blister. Two vehicles pass her, and neither stops, even though she is a woman on the street alone, lugging a suitcase. The band of her skirt is tight, and the sweat gathers there, trickling down her thighs. Already she is covered in sweat and dirt. Stunned, she does not cry or panic; it does not seem possible to her that this can be anything more than grandstanding on Werner's part.

When she finally reaches the church in Bobbin, the purring sound of idling cars emerges from the woods. She stumbles. Entering the deep black shade of the trees, she leaves her case and clambers up a small rise and down a slope covered in tangled vines. Her foot gets stuck, and she must dig around the undergrowth to retrieve her shoe. At the edge of the trees, she gets a clear view of the *Pfarrhaus*. Two police cars are parked by the front door.

Of course. Of course Werner would never have allowed her to leave and have also given Peter his freedom. Werner knew full well she would instantly go to her lover, that kicking her out would push the two of them together. She squeezes her eyes shut: How long has he been planning this?

She slogs her way through the overgrown meadow toward Johann the butcher's farmhouse, arriving so drenched in sweat it's as though she's been dipped in the sea. But the house is locked, and she slides to the ground by the entrance, sitting in the dirt, waiting. The sun is lowering in a sulfurous sky, and with the encroaching darkness she panics.

Christa's house is at the foot of the hill, and when Bettina stands at the door, she begins to feel as though the air around her has turned to water. It is pressing on her from all sides; it is rushing at and around her, emitting a sound like static. It is warm, too warm, and has a muscular sort of power that makes her knees want to buckle.

There is a small window in the door covered from the inside with a patterned curtain. A hand pushes the curtain to one side, and Christa's face appears.

The two women look at each other blankly. Then, frowning, Christa drops the curtain, and she does not open the door for her friend; instead her footsteps fall—barely audible in the sickening roar of the strange, pressing air—and she walks away.

The next morning the sand is cold under her cheek, and Bettina's eyes are plastered shut. Dawn is breaking, and the sky is a pulsing, luminous pink tinted with orange streaks. Before she registers that she has slept on the beach, that she is shivering, her skin covered in sand and goose bumps, she remembers that Werner is in her house with her child.

In the cold morning air, she no longer feels woolly-headed or numb or as though she is drowning. Instead she is filled with a crystalline fury, one that shoots through her veins sharp as a dagger. No one can take her life away from her.

She dusts off the sand from her shins, slipping her feet back into her polymer shoes. Sweat from the long walk yesterday has dried on her skin, and she smells unclean, and this further infuriates her. Who does Werner think he is?

Back at Apolonienmarkt, Bettina sits on her suitcase in the crevice of an alley opposite her cottage. She will wait as long as she has to. Werner will leave for work, and she guesses that he will have hired Alma or Elise from next door to watch the baby for the day. All Bettina has to do is wait, and when he is gone, she will take the child and the money; she will try calling Peter again; she will slip him a note under the door of the youth center. They will figure it out. She will never, ever give up.

Just before eight o'clock, Werner exits the house. In his hand he carries a rag, and he runs it along both flanks of the Tatra, stepping back to study it before climbing in and backing the car out. A long time passes. Patience is what Bettina needs now, patience and determination. The sun has already edged past the thatched roofs, and its rays are spilling over the cobblestones as she makes her way to the front door of her home.

It is locked. There is no answer when she knocks. The spare key is not under the rock by the *Rosa rugosa* where they've always kept it. She heads to the rear and tries the back door. It is also locked. After digging up a rock from the border of the vegetable garden, she smashes the window on the door and hooks her arm around the wooden frame to reach the handle from the inside. Glass scrapes her forearm, but she feels nothing. Fat drops of blood splatter the tile floor, the red so intense it is like a living thing.

The house is silent. It makes no sense. Where did Werner take Annaliese? Bettina's calm begins to shred at the edges, but she hangs on to the core, because if she loses her ability to think, she will lose everything. The glass jar with rice in it stands in the pantry among the sugar and flour and baking trays, and she digs into it with two fingers to retrieve the envelope that is stuffed inside, folded in half. With this money maybe she can hire a lawyer—even if she loses possession of the house, she can at least fight for her daughter. She has rights as a mother. Adultery does not make you a criminal. Two of Clara's letters are in the drawer of the sideboard, and she grabs them.

A dull thud comes from the front of the house, and she holds her breath. It could be kids in the square, or maybe even the clack of her neighbor shutting her door. Before Bettina has a chance to put away the glass jar, just as she realizes that it is actually the sound of footsteps—multiple footsteps, inside the house—three men enter the kitchen. They are dressed in white cotton overcoats and brown shoes, and one is holding a large laundry bag. Two of the men grab her, fingers slipping on her bloody arm, and yank her wrists behind her back. The glass jar drops to the floor and shatters. Metal encircles her wrists and shuts with a click.

Her brain hasn't caught up yet—what are these men doing in her house?—when they begin to drag her through the kitchen and down the hall. In the mirror, she catches sight of a crazy woman with thick brown hair, wild and unkempt, flanked by grim men. They jostle against each other, her soft curves banging into their sharp hips, elbows and hands grappling, shoving, pulling. One of the men looks out the front door and then motions the others to follow. He opens a door in the side of a small white van, and there is her leather suitcase, already in the back. Just as she thinks, *I should scream—someone will help me!* she catches sight of a woman standing in the front garden next door.

It is Irmgard Bandelow, her neighbor. Her blonde hair is in rollers, her lips painted red. She is as pale as milk and appears to be crying. In her arms she is holding Bettina's child.

39

The men shove her into the van, release her hands, and cuff her to a rail along one side of the interior, where a metal bench is attached. Only after they have been driving for a while does it dawn on Bettina that they are not taking her to Bergen—she'd assumed they were delivering her to Werner—but must be taking her off the island. There are two small vents in the back through which she tries to peer out, but she can see nothing but a blur of browns and greens.

Banging on the partition elicits no response. She sobs so uncontrollably that at one point she chokes on her own breath and begins to cough violently. The van speeds up and slows down, and occasionally low and steady murmurs from the front cab become audible. They stop for a while, maybe as long as twenty minutes, and the need to go to the bathroom is so urgent that Bettina begins banging again, screaming to be released. She is not released. Urine runs down her legs. After that she is calmer. Nothing she does will change what is happening to her.

When they finally arrive wherever it is they were headed, the men find her slumped on the bench, half-asleep. One of them lets out a snort. "Ugh," he says, unlocking her from the rail. "I told you we should've let her out."

"Orders were to get here before dark. Who cares?" the other one says. The smell of dried urine is cloying, and the men's faces are pinched in disgust. They have taken off their white coats and are dressed in uniforms with red epaulets and multiple pockets, belted at the waist. "She's a goner, anyway." His face is narrow and feline, handsome in a stingy way, his long blondish hair slicked back. One eyebrow is dissected by a scar.

"Please tell me what's happening," she says. "Where are we? Where are you taking me?"

"*Halt's Maul,*" the first man tells her. *Shut up.*

The third one, a rotund fellow, hands her a small roll.

"What the hell, Franz?" the first guy complains. "That's fraternizing."

"She's gotta be hungry," he says.

Bettina bites into the roll, which is thickly buttered and has a pale slice of cheese in it. Her mouth is so dry the bread barely makes it down her throat. "Water?" she says. "Please, can I have some water?"

The tubby officer hands her a can of Asco Cola.

By the look of the sky, it is sometime in the late afternoon. They are standing on a wide street flanked by large buildings, with jagged edges where the bricks were blasted away during the war. A weary patina covers everything. A teenage boy rides by on a bicycle, cap low on his forehead, trousers tucked into boots. Down at the end of the street, a group of people stand outside a supermarket, and an old man is walking a dog. It is dirty and cold, a city packed with people. In the near distance, a sign reads, **HALT! HIER GRENZE**—"Stop! Border crossing." In the far distance, behind a squat white building, three enormous flags stir slightly: the United States, France, and Britain.

It can't be, Bettina thinks. *We're in Berlin.*

The policemen lead her into the white building. One of them brings along her valise, a file tucked under his arm. They place her in a windowless office and shut the door behind them.

The officer sitting behind the desk has the suspended look of a man dragging himself through an enormous list of to-dos. He regards Bettina with no curiosity, pale-brown eyes taking in her attire and her fallen features. Absently, he fingers the file the guards gave him and then flips it open and breaks his gaze. There is a stack of papers clipped together inside, an envelope, and a small blue booklet, which he holds up between thumb and forefinger: her identity card.

Bettina sucks in her breath.

There follows an exchange that she will later remember with searing shame. The officer's lack of interest in her situation is in direct contrast to her desperation. She is being expelled from East Germany. Werner Nietz has initiated a mandate to release her to Western authorities and revoke her right to reenter the country. Should she attempt reentry, she will be arrested immediately. "You may indeed choose to stay in this country, Frau Nietz, but if you do, you will be rounded up and sent to Hohenschönhausen," the officer tells her. Even Bettina has heard rumors about this prison: a vast complex tucked away in some Berlin neighborhood where dissidents are rumored to disappear for years on end.

Her desperate pleas gain no purchase. There is no trial, no judge, no justice. "Why not let me stay? I don't understand."

"Why would we want people like you in this country?" he asks lightly. "It's a privilege to live in the DDR, a privilege you don't deserve. You belong in the West. We don't want your type."

As Bettina sobs into her filthy hands, the officer breaks his detachment. "Woman, control yourself. It's the price you pay for your bad decisions," he snaps. He raises himself to his full height and leans over the desk to hand her the envelope and her identity papers. "Read this."

The letterhead is from the Ministerium für Staatssicherheit, Bergen, Rügen. It has been signed by her husband and his superior, Franz Josef Bieder. It lays out conditions for her release to West Germany: *Bettina Heilstrom Nietz will renounce her marital and maternal rights. She will leave the DDR and in so doing agrees to never return. Should she be apprehended anywhere at any time in the East, she will be arrested immediately, as will Peter Ludwig Brenner, age thirty-one, domicile Bobbin, Rügen.*

"Do you understand this stipulation?" the officer asks her. "I have been told to clarify this, to be sure you fully understand the conditions of your release. This man—this Peter Brenner—will be instantly arrested and sentenced to five to ten years' labor at the SDAG Wismut uranium mines in the Ore Mountains. He will disappear; do you understand? And *you* will be the one responsible. We have him under surveillance already."

She cannot look the man in the face. There is a metallic taste in her mouth.

"You have a choice," he continues. "Will you protect him and leave the country, or will you stay in the DDR? What will you choose?"

She'd like to drag her fingernails across his face, take his throat in her hands, and press her thumbs through the skin. She'd like to scream for mercy, but she knows it will achieve nothing. She rocks back and forth on the chair. The officer hands her a fountain pen so that she can sign away her life, and when she has regained control of herself, that is what she does.

A wooden placard in front of the guardhouse warns citizens in four languages that they are leaving the Russian sector and entering the Allied zone, which has long since reverted to West German control. Behind her a gaggle of women are arguing, and two construction workers have their heads bent toward each other in deep discussion. There is tension in the curt movements and scattered looks of the small crowd. Bettina is accompanied by yet another soldier; this one—a machine gun hanging from his shoulder—grips her upper arm and pushes her ahead of him.

The border guard grabs for her papers without taking his eyes from her.

"Can you hurry up?" a woman in line behind her asks sharply.

The soldier continues to stare at Bettina, as though trying to remember if he has seen her before. She resists the urge to wipe the sweat from her chin. When he returns her documents, she walks past the interrogation rooms, the black-and-gray German shepherd, and a group of workers waiting to be allowed through. Her strides are halting, as though she is an old woman. Her mind is filled with one image, with one word that ricochets around blindly: *Annaliese, Annaliese, Annaliese!*

The air smells of car exhaust and dust.

Her daughter will grow up without her. Bettina will live without her child.

PART FOUR

40

Chicago, 1965

Eleven years earlier, her sister sent her money for a plane ticket, and Bettina embarked on a flight leaving Tempelhof Airport. The next morning she stepped out into an alien world.

"You'll be a prisoner in your own land," Clara had insisted over and over again. "Here at least you'll have a chance at being free of him. There's nothing you can do there, Betty. Come, come to America, and you can rebuild! Then you'll be fighting from a position of strength, not weakness."

Was it the right decision? She had finally decided, almost instinctively, to head to the only place on earth where she thought she might find a bit of tenderness, something that might keep her alive. In those deadening months she'd been in West Berlin, she had twice come close to attempting reentry into the East, only to stop at the last minute when she considered that it was also Peter's life that was in her hands; she could not only think of herself.

Once, after she made an appointment with a state-employed lawyer, a man bumped into her so brazenly in the streets that she was knocked to the ground, and she was convinced that she was being followed. There was no crossing the border, sneaking back in. She became obsessed with the idea that death would be a release—that being so close and yet so far from the child she'd abandoned was a torment too terrible to bear—and that's when she began to seriously consider her sister's proposition to join her in America.

But those early months in Chicago had presented their own set of problems, which could not easily be overcome. Herbert's doleful eyes flicked over her endlessly, seeking comfort of some kind; they were two broken people desperate for something undefinable. His growing infatuation repelled yet also ensnared her. In the railway apartment that she, Herbert, and Clara shared, he would touch her shoulder lightly as they passed each other, and she'd feel sick. This was not desire, she knew; it was a misplaced yearning for human warmth, and yet she could not control her longing for it. She badly wanted to abandon all reason and lose herself, but nothing—not getting drunk or being kissed—helped her find a numbing resting place. Herbert secured her a job in a metal fabrication shop sweeping floors and cleaning up the grease from the lathes, and for weeks at a stretch she managed to avoid being alone with him. Her weight plummeted, and Clara started to fret. "Eat, eat," she'd urge, the lines between her brows like scars. "You're going to disappear."

In the spring of 1955, barely six months after Bettina arrived, a friend of Herbert's asked him to move to Milwaukee to manage a warehouse that sold copper pipes. "You must go; it will be good for you," Bettina told her sister. Clara and Herbert had begun bickering viciously, and they needed an excuse to start anew. "And anyway, I want my independence." This was only a half truth, but Bettina knew it to be critical: they could not go on living together. It was a relief when Herbert decided he and Clara should give it a try. Neither of them protested when Bettina insisted that she stay behind. With that, she found herself alone again.

She spoke little English, and each weekend she trekked west across the city by bus to the Immigrants Protective League offices at Hull House. There she took a language class along with Czechs, Ukrainians, Poles, Bulgarians, and Italians. The ladies at the office stuffed into their wool and cashmere coats gave them a warm meal at lunchtime. Occasionally Bettina helped serve the food, and eventually they began paying her a little something to work into the evenings. It was through the IPL that she met an older man from Swiebodzin, Poland (a former dentist), who'd found his way into the labor union and told her about the job cleaning the *Tribune* offices. It was a relief to no longer be inhaling fine metal dust all day, particles that scratched her throat and stained her handkerchiefs when she coughed.

Night work meant she had the freedom to walk the streets during the early mornings when the unusual quality of the light made the ordinary pulse with fragile but discernible energy. She began to roam endlessly through the neighborhoods. Because she could not sit still. She could not sleep. Walking was the only way to still her spinning mind.

For three years she worked with the lawyers at the league to petition the government of the DDR to reinstate her parental rights and allow her to be reunited with Annaliese. But she didn't have her marriage license or her daughter's birth certificate, and she was in a foreign country. She had little money and no knowledge of the law.

"It's a totalitarian regime," they told her with kind eyes as she wept in their offices. "There's little we can do."

Bettina dreamed of her child constantly. Sometimes they ran and played, enjoyed a picnic of quark and apples on the beach. Sometimes Annaliese was drowning in the waves (like Peter's wife's little boy, Thomas), and her mother was helpless to save her. In all those dreams Bettina's child was frozen as she had been in the fall of 1953: an almost one-year-old with thistle hair and a mouth that babbled only nonsense. This child never grew up. She could not talk and tell her mother if she was happy and loved. She laughed and cried, her green eyes lit up with delight or frustration, but her limbs never lengthened; her face never thinned out.

In those early months, thoughts of her own death gave Bettina some comfort; after all, she had the option to hasten it. There was not a day when she did not consider this. It wasn't just that there seemed no point in eating and defecating and sleeping and talking—participating in the endless cycle of a pointless life—it was having to live with the pain of her self-recriminations. She'd had so many chances to live her life differently, and yet because of her choices, her child was doomed to grow up without a mother. Bettina would walk along the shores of Lake Michigan and imagine stepping off the edge into the frigid waters. Drowning would not be such a bad death. She had thought about it that afternoon with her sister in Binz, and now it seemed to her that it would be a gift.

But she could not do it. As long as her child was alive, she, too, must keep living.

It was not long after this that she took her camera with her as she went to explore the shuttered factories and caught sight of the mother and child—the day that showed her that it was possible after all to lose herself again in the act of taking pictures, and that doing so gave her a reason to keep going. That in a small way she could, perhaps, help others.

Bettina continued to try to find a way to get her child back. The United States government did not acknowledge that the Soviet zone had become a separate country. There was no chief of mission for the eastern section, since technically the country did not even exist. Newspapers rarely reported on what was happening there, and when Bettina could get her hands on a German paper at the library, it was invariably out of date and never contained any information that was of use to her.

She stumbled on a group called the International Commission of Jurists, German lawyers who'd started investigating human rights abuses by the Soviets after partition. A couple of years earlier, in 1953, the ICJ's president was abducted by East German intelligence agents and executed in Moscow. But even though the West German consulate managed to get hold of the West German government report for Bettina, it had no bearing on her small-scale problems. It seemed no one could help her.

Still she managed to breathe in and out, to survive. After finding her studio apartment, she moved out of the boardinghouse she'd been in for three months, bought a few houseplants, and tried to sleep through the night without waking in a sweat. She cleaned the *Tribune* offices, skirting her duster around ashtrays filled with crushed Kent cigarettes and desktops littered with cans of RC Cola. She bought two plastic beads, then, as February came and went, another one, and began the ritual of imagining the life of her child without her.

The shadow of Peter's love dogged her during her waking hours. On the streets she would turn suddenly, aware of eyes burning through the back of her dress, certain that he was right behind her, certain even that she had caught a whiff of his unique smell. Day after day Bettina tromped along the streets, and whenever she glanced up, she was astonished that the unending sky was the very same as the one over Rügen. Should she have stayed in Germany, risking prison and hoping that when she was released, she would be reunited with her child? But it hadn't seemed right to consign Peter to imprisonment because she could not face leaving Annaliese.

Had Werner kept his promise and allowed Peter his freedom? Sometimes when she was on a bus or on the L, the steady drone of the motor sent her into a sort of stupor from which she would emerge bewildered and angry. In her imagination she'd be lurking in an alternate life, one where her family was made up of her, Peter, and Annaliese and where guilt was a thing of the past. She could feel so viscerally the sense of purpose and unity: They would make a home together, something simple, small, but with some paint and a few nails, they would make it beautiful. They would have a yard for Annaliese. Maybe water nearby, maybe not. Their faces would be creased from laughter, the skin coarse from being outside. They would have more children; it was not yet too late. But when she woke from her reverie and saw only the drawn faces of the other passengers, and the dim memory of disappointment sharpened again, she would bite her lip and look hard at the shining foreign city outside the windows and wonder what her life meant now that everything she loved had been stripped away.

41

At the *Tribune*, she got into the habit of picking up the previous day's paper when her shift was over. She'd sit at one of the journalists' metal desks in the newsroom, a lamp switched on against the darkness of the night hours, a well-thumbed dictionary and a piece of paper at her side. She looked up every word she didn't know and wrote it down, and before long she had a ream of papers that she would study later, before falling asleep. Those days, she barely spoke with anyone except the lawyers, and after a while even those conversations dried up. When she did have a chance to speak, her voice was raw and unsteady. Whenever John, the photo editor, and George, the head of the news division, came in early to cover a story, they'd find her poring over the paper, and they soon got in the habit of chatting with her while drinking vending machine coffee or taking a cigarette break. They both had an avid interest in politics and asked her all about her country, especially keen to hear about the experience of being a German after losing the war.

The two men were endlessly interested in things she'd never thought about much. Eventually John started quizzing her from her painstaking notes, and they shared a laugh at her accent. Once he leaned forward and kissed her unexpectedly, and she was so taken by surprise that she pulled away; it wasn't possible for her to be intimate with a stranger. It was hard to believe an American man could want someone like her: a broken woman who had left behind a complicated life. But then, no one knew her story. They knew her as the young woman who lurked in the shadows cleaning, the serious one with the heavy accent who rarely laughed.

Yet these men saw her as a human being, a person with ideas, and so she began to see herself this way too. And when she had the Rollei with her, people allowed her to slip briefly into their lives without even realizing they were doing so. She would gaze directly at them with the camera at heart height and snap picture after picture, and although they knew she was documenting them, no one seemed to mind.

Once, she caught sight of a group of black boys playing in a broken fire hydrant on a summer evening when the heat hit ninety-eight degrees and the humidity was so high that the air they breathed seemed as heavy as wet wool. Their glistening skin and shrieks of joy, the incredible beauty of their physicality and playfulness—it all drew her in. They ranged in age from about five to fifteen, with long skinny bones and splayed bare feet. She spent well over an hour taking pictures, and they not only let her but came over and began peppering her with questions. They found her accent hilarious. They wanted to know where she came from, what she missed about living next to the ocean. Why did the camera have two circles in front? Why was she taking pictures of them? This perplexed and delighted them, to be the center of her attention.

Those were the photos that prompted John to offer her use of the *Tribune* darkroom. She had saved some money and was having film developed at a cheap place downtown, and he caught sight of the pictures pasted in her notebook as she was studying her words one morning.

"Man," he said. "These are *good*. You know these are good, right?"

Her cheeks went hot. "I thought they would be better." It came out as "zay" instead of "they," so she repeated her sentence slowly, correctly, making John laugh.

"That's because they've been developed badly," he explained. "You know how to use a darkroom?"

She nodded; her father had taught her at a friend's house before the war began, when supplies were still readily available. For months she'd been dreaming about asking if she could ever use it on a slow news day. Now she had her chance. From then on she developed all her film there, learning to manipulate the intensity of shadow, the brightness of light. How to sharpen a feature and mute a distracting detail. It wasn't long before George started asking her to take photos of people at certain events and paid her for each picture that he published.

Being invisible had become the norm for her, and she'd enjoyed being able to disappear. It was fitting; who was she to have a voice, to live a full life? Wasn't this a kind of atonement for her actions: first, betraying a man she'd promised to be loyal to, and second, choosing to leave her only child behind so that she could have her freedom? When she had the camera in her hand, it lessened the burden of her self-loathing in a way that did not feel entirely selfish.

Now, Herbert helped her try to uncover information about Werner Nietz. His mother went to the town hall in Saargen and made friends with the clerk, who started talking freely after being offered a schnapps one day after work. It turned out that Werner had been sent to Normannenstraße in Berlin nine years earlier to work at the head-quarters of the MfS, the Ministerium für Staatssicherheit. As far as the woman knew, he had been remarried for a while. She had heard nothing about any kind of illness, and there was no documentation in the files.

Against her better judgment, the clerk also looked up Peter Brenner. His father, Pfarrer Brenner, had died six years earlier, in 1959, and there was still no pastor attached to the Bobbin church. Religious services were restricted all over the DDR now. Also, Peter no longer worked at the Bobbin school; in fact, there was no trace of him anywhere. Herbert's mother called a few of the other local schools: Binz, Sellin, Bergen, Göhren, Baabe. Nothing. She tried Stralsund on the mainland, but none of the school districts could locate any information, or they were not willing to share it with her. It was possible that he had left the island or even the country.

It was also possible that Peter was in prison.

Bettina went to the German consulate in Chicago and spoke with a supervisor. They advised that she try calling the consulate in New York, but that was a dead end. She told the Immigrants Protective League that she wanted to travel to Berlin. "Well, yes. It's possible, once you're on site, that you might convince someone to talk," said an elderly man wearing a waistcoat and bow tie. "You might be able to get into East Berlin and petition them to tell you something."

Werner had warned her what would happen if she returned—but did that warning still stand all these years later?

The day was fading, and the downtown streets were trash strewed, crowded with people leaving work. She was headed home, walking under the rumbling L, past the homeless men in dirty tartan jackets, the stream of businessmen in hats and sharply cut overcoats. She tilted her face upward briefly, and a flash of silver caught her eye: a glass door ahead had been opened and shut, catching the light on its oversize hinges.

It was a record store. Above the door hung a sign that read **Moody Blues Discs**. Cupping her hands on either side of her eyes, she pressed her face against the front window to peer inside. There were rows and rows of tables full of LPs, comfortable red chairs clustered in a corner, where a couple of people sat reading magazines, and a young woman with cropped black hair standing behind an old-fashioned till.

It was the till that held Bettina's attention. The woman rang up a customer, and the heavy drawer slid open; suddenly Bettina wanted nothing more than to hear the ping of the drawer and the tap tap tap of fingers on the till's stiff keys. After the bombing, when she'd returned to her family's fish shop to look for the sign her grandfather had painted, she'd searched and searched for the old till among the piles of bricks and the shreds of wood. That it could have been destroyed seemed impossible: it had been so very solid, weighing a ton. Now she longed to feel in her hands again the heavy push and pull of the drawer as its springs guided it in and out. A tug of nostalgia for the sawdust and the scarred wooden countertop, the crates that held eel and *Forellen*, yanked at her.

She entered the dark interior of the store.

Lingering in the aisles, she observed the other customers. It was a mixed group, as was typical in her neighborhood, with Hispanic children hanging on to their mother's skirts and a compact Japanese man with jowls in the bluegrass section. Years ago, Bettina had picked up a record player at a yard sale, but the only records she owned were Bach's Brandenburg Concerto No. 1 and a single by the Beatles called "A Hard Day's Night" that George had given her in an effort to introduce her to pop culture. She listened mostly to the radio; it had been her habit all her life.

Handwritten signs were taped onto trays that held hundreds of albums: classical, country, Motown, jazz. Everything was sorted alphabetically. Flipping through the cardboard covers, she got to *PR*. Then *PRO*.

There it was. Professor Longhair: the album Peter had played for her almost fifteen years earlier.

The young woman smiled at her as Bettina handed over a few dollar bills and some change. When the drawer popped open, the bell on the till rang crisply, but Bettina barely noticed; she was in a different world now. Walking back to her apartment, she felt suspended in time, as though she could barely take a breath.

It was hard to get the needle in the right place, but she found the song that Peter had played and listened to it from beginning to end. The energy of it, the raucous, playful noise, its complicated rhythm, was just as startling as it had been years earlier. She had thought that hearing it again might crush her, that it would grind the pain of her loss further into her heart, but instead a slow and steady fury built inside her.

She played the song three times. Then she picked up the phone and bought her airline ticket.

42

Telegrams, along with files sent by messenger from surrounding precincts, stapled-together handwritten reports, and dozens of black-and-white photographs and contract sheets lay in a balsa tray on the secretary's desk outside the offices of the director of domestic surveillance. Each day, Comrade Janklovitz looked through the stack of paperwork to flag anything important for Werner Nietz to peruse. In his early days on Normannenstraße, Werner would painstakingly look through all the material himself, a cool frisson snaking up his legs as he read, the act of thumbing through these items somehow intimate and unsettling.

But there came a time when the papers flooding in became overwhelming, and he needed a trusted subordinate to sift through it and separate the mundane from the critical, the impactful from the merely perfunctory. The day he caught sight of a faint *B* on a telex from West Berlin (the paper quality easily distinguishing it from East German missives) was not a special day, and he was not paying particular attention to his duties. In fact, he had just returned from the doctor's office (they needed to see if the cancer had reached his lymph nodes) and was absentmindedly standing at Frau Kellermann's desk, waiting for her to return with a cup of coffee for him, killing time and absorbing the news he'd just received.

That innocuous *B*: he caught sight of it, and his eyes moved on— and then flicked back to the word. Bettina.

He picked up the sheet of paper and, having left his reading glasses on his desk, held it a few centimeters from his eyes. On it was typed: **Bettina Heilstrom.**

Damn, he thought, his heart revving up. God dammit, this was what he'd been afraid of for the past decade.

IN WEST BERLIN. MUST SEE YOU URGENTLY. CONTACT ME IMMEDIATELY. STAYING AT INSEL HOTEL. WE MUST SPEAK. BETTINA HEILSTROM.

The hubris! The unbelievable hubris of this woman. He stormed into his office, slammed the door behind him, and grabbed his glasses. No additional information. Sent earlier this morning. An order summoning him. His breath caught in his throat like a marble.

His office was far more spacious than his previous one in Bergen and was carpeted in a yellowish shag with a blond wood closet system covering an entire wall. Inside were shelves crammed with files and boxes of recording equipment (he was often sent prototypes of devices to try out). The window looked out toward the street, which disappeared into the near distance of gray concrete sidewalks and denuded trees, apartment houses filled with people striving to live well and serve their country. He took a slow breath in and let it out while counting, then did it again. His logical mind was telling him not to revert to his old ways, but the tone of this self-talk was shrill. The nylon lace curtain hung in the corner of his vision, and he had the urge to grasp it and yank as hard as he could, pulling the rod from the wall and bringing the whole contraption to the ground. Instead he breathed in and out as slowly as he could.

It had taken years to exorcise this woman from his mind. The child, Annaliese, had cried so insistently for months that Werner had been swamped almost instantly with regret about what he'd put into motion: yes, he had wanted to cause Bettina pain (the way she had caused him such pain!), but more than that he'd wanted to be a good father to the child—that perfect, innocent creature who looked at him with eyes shining with devotion and trust. The joy of taking care of her had, over time, eclipsed his bitterness. And now, just like that, he was transported back to a place he thought he'd long left behind.

Frau Kellermann came in with his coffee. "No interruptions," he barked at her, and she scurried away. The coffee was black and oily, so hot it steamed up his eyeglasses, and as he drank, trying to regain a modicum of control, tears burned his eyes.

He saw her standing on the dock, pointing her camera toward those Kellermann boys. She was high-stepping through the overgrown meadow, her dark hair loose, brushing her face. Her arm, lying against the sheets, was smooth and white, and as she slept, her mouth was slightly parted, teeth just visible. As a girl she stomped up the steps of the town hall, and as a woman she brought him dinner on her grandmother's crockery. Her face, so serious in repose. The snaggleteeth that gave her face its alluring asymmetry, that made her human. They were supposed to grow old together. At this point she was still a relatively young woman, not quite forty by his calculations. Perhaps she was ill, too, and wanted to beg his forgiveness before leaving this earth. That was not going to happen.

She had gone to America, to that sister of hers. He could not help but wonder whether she had changed, her face rounder (or perhaps leaner?) and her manner less guarded, her habits those of an *Ami* after all these years in their midst. Did she wear reading glasses, have silver strands in her hair? Had she been broken by the consequences of her behavior, or was she even more brazen than ever?

The minutes ticked by as he stood at the window, staring blindly into the distance. Then he pulled himself together, buzzing in Frau Kellermann. He dictated a note putting on alert the border crossings at Bornholmer Straße, Chausseestraße, Brandenburger Tor, Friedrichstraße, Heinrich-Heine-Straße, Oberbaumbrücke,

Sonnenallee, and Invalidenstraße. In the bottom drawer of his desk at the back, along with some artifacts from his old office in Saargen, were a few photos from the house on Apolonienmarkt. It had been years since he'd been pulled back into the pain of remembering, and now he reached in there and hauled the pictures out. Later he would find a better likeness of her, but he needed to alert the borders instantly in case she was already trying to cross into East Berlin. The prints were faded, but there was one in which you could see her face, its angles and the shape of her eyes. Her hair was loose, and she wore an old housedress. He clamped his teeth together and handed the picture to Frau Kellermann.

"This will do for now," he said. "Call up her file for me, would you, and have it sent over to the records department. And distribute this immediately. Highest priority."

Hadn't Bettina built a new life for herself after all this time?

What was her life like?

What did she want from him? *Why now?*

Berlin smelled steely and urban. The rainwater rushing along filthy curbs, streaming into cracks in the boulevards, gave pulsing life to the acres of paving stone and concrete. It was so different from Chicago, a city of sleek skyscrapers lining the riverside: the buildings here were gnarled giants, colossal and imposing. On the long walk from her hotel, the sky broke open to release slivers of rain, and by the time she arrived at the Ratskeller, Bettina was wet all the way through to her undergarments.

Would she have recognized Werner on the streets of Berlin had she bumped into him on the Kurfürstendamm or Unter den Linden? He sat at the far end of the café, head bent over a newspaper. Though she did pick him out of the crowd, it was the wide brow, the shape of his head; everything else about him seemed foreign to her. He wore a blue shirt and a navy jacket. His torso was considerably slimmer than she remembered, and the wire-rimmed glasses perched on his nose were long and rectangular, the kind a beatnik might wear. Had she clipped his shoulder in walking, she doubted she'd have realized it was her former husband.

Yesterday she had received a telex from him at her hotel with the name of this café and a meeting date and time. In that moment it had not seemed real, and the prospect of being face to face with this man once again had made her knees go weak. She'd needed to sit down. She would see him—he had agreed to meet . . . this fact was incredible. It was a good sign, surely, but if she couldn't pull this meeting off, when would she get another chance? It was so important that she find a way to connect with him, to see if he would be willing to put their daughter's interests above his own. Inside her there was a heaviness that felt as though it would send her spinning if it tipped off kilter.

The glass entryway pinged with the sound of rain pelting the roof and windows. The clerk at her hotel had told her that the café was well known as a spot where East German functionaries came on day passes to take meetings with West Germans. Now that there was a wall dividing the city, it was harder to come and go from East to West and vice versa, but passage was still possible. The café was bustling, and though it was barely nine o'clock in the morning, the room was drenched in a haze of bluish cigarette smoke. To calm herself, she let drop *Der Tagesspiegel* with which she'd covered the Rollei on the way over, unclipped the camera's stained leather case, and flipped up the viewfinder.

Looking down, she located Werner again and turned the crank on the camera. Before she'd even taken the picture, it was clear to her what she would focus on in the darkroom: heightening the sharp corner on the left frame of his glasses, revealing the eyes scrimmed by lenses. He was situated much farther away than she preferred her subjects to be, but there was a powerful sense of intimacy even though he didn't realize he was being photographed. She would emphasize the tunnel of hazy detritus—people, tables, waiters, food, ceramic cups, crumpled napkins—that led to this man, sitting alone reading his paper. The act of waiting revealing in an unexpected way the permanence of shared humanity. The world could change, it could shift on its axis, and still people would wait, uncertain and on edge or fizzy with anticipation and hope.

Werner fumbled with his coffee cup, tipping it over and spilling coffee on the tablecloth and his pants leg, and gestured to a waiter impatiently. The crank turned as Bettina took picture after picture. Her fear was shifting as she watched him, slowly sharpening itself against the rock of her deep-seated anger and turning into something different, something much more useful: resolve.

He had taken too much from her, this man, and she was going to get it back.

As she approached him, Werner looked up and stood abruptly, knocking his hip against the small round table. His face flushed deeply. She forced herself to keep moving toward him; she could not allow herself to falter under his greedy gaze, his palpable alarm. Once he was erect, it was obvious that his new slimness was not in fact a sign of healthy activity and energy: His back was curved quite severely, and deep creases emphasized his jowls. The color of his skin was off, too, yellow at the center of his face and pale at the edges. His eyes were red rimmed behind the modern spectacles.

"Bettina," he said, and as she slid her chair away from the table to sit, his eyes caught on the camera in her hands. He did not offer her a cheek or a hand. His eyes were large as he slumped back into the chair, a man who had counted on one thing only to discover something else entirely was happening.

"Werner," she said, the heaviness inside her shifting.

"Don't tell me you still take pictures," he said, pointing to the camera.

Her clothes clung to her like the skin of a lizard. Water dripped from her skirt onto the cool skin of her shins. She turned the camera toward him again and cranked the lever, all the while keeping her eyes on his face.

"Did you just take a photo of me?" he asked. "Is that what you just did?"

"No, with this? No," she answered, and inside her there bloomed a fleeting sense of satisfaction at besting him. He had written this camera off from the very beginning—too bad for him that he didn't know its power. She sat down and unraveled a large linen napkin, drawing it quickly over her face, wet from the rain. Having snapped his picture, she was reminded that in a way she owned part of him and always would, because he had loved her, and she had not been able to love him back. It was true that she was at his mercy, but he was at her mercy too.

The creamy half moons of his fingernails glinted as he played with a cigarette and then, taking his time, lit it with a silver lighter. He was working hard to appear at ease. "Why—why in heaven's name are you still wearing my mother's ring, Bettina?" he asked. "How could you?"

"Oh, I—I should have taken it off; I wasn't thinking," she stammered. "It—well, it protects me."

Smoke from his cigarette curled up toward his nostrils. "You need protection from what?"

It was hard to tell if he was goading her or genuinely didn't understand. She didn't want to start in on the details of her life, her work at the newspaper, whether she had found love or not. The purpose of this meeting was not to explain herself to him. But she needed to do whatever possible to cajole him into being his best self. "I'm, uh. I'm single. A single woman who works in a newsroom," she said flatly. "I'm one of only two women there."

"And you haven't found a new man yet? With all those men around you all day?"

"I haven't been looking for a man."

He was curious about her; he wanted to know the details of her life, and this made it obvious that she was the one in control here. But uncertainty gripped her; she didn't know how to play this out. All she really needed to secure through this meeting was an agreement that she could see her daughter again. One step at a time. Just one step and then another. This had seemed possible when she was in the States, buying her ticket home and imagining her future, but now in this smoke-clogged café, it seemed absurd: Why would he give her anything? It was obvious that she was making him angry and defensive.

The waiter hovered nearby, and she ordered a black coffee. In front of Werner sat a plate of sliced sausage and black bread with pickles. The shine of his forehead was split by furrows that ran from one temple to the other. "What is it you want exactly? You flew all the way here to see me—you said it was important, and I'm here. I'm assuming this is about my daughter."

My daughter. But Anna was hers too. "Come now, Werner, please. I'm here with good intentions."

"I'm supposed to trust you? Ha."

Her coffee was hot and strong, and it scalded the top of her mouth. She ran her tongue over the instant swelling. "Werner, are you ill? I've heard rumors. If you're ill, it changes everything, doesn't it?"

"You, with a whole new exciting life—working, taking pictures. Worried about me; fancy that." He pressed his lips together and swiped at them aggressively with his napkin. "You dare come here and confront me, after all this time . . . I thought I made myself clear. Any court of law would agree that I'm the wronged party. Your rights have been dissolved. There's no point in begging."

"I'm not begging. I'm here because no matter what you think of me, I'm still a mother. I want to know how my child is. I want to know how *you* are. It matters to me because it affects Annaliese. Werner, you don't look well; you—"

"I'm quite well; thank you. Very well, in fact. Did you know that I have four children?" He smiled at her for the first time, a tight smile that showed no teeth.

"Four . . . children! Goodness. I . . . I'm happy for you." When she brought her coffee cup to her lips, she was dismayed to find her hands trembling. The skin under one of her eyes began to twitch. For a long moment, she couldn't come up with more to say about this extraordinary news. A family—he'd had more children? She had to admit to herself that she'd never considered this might happen.

That meant her daughter had siblings . . . and a new mother.

Once, soon after her own mother died, Bettina had fallen sick with the flu, and Papa had been worried that she, too, might succumb. Long nights sweating in bed, her skin slick and clammy, hallucinations making her believe that objects were no longer solid, that the ground was as mobile as shifting waters. She felt this same sensation now, sitting here: The people and the tables, the crockery and lights and the clock on the wall, were not part of her reality. They receded from her, hidden behind some kind of scrim; the world was one of transition, illusion, mutability, one in which nothing could be counted on. Her stomach turned over.

"You know we're not living on Apolonienmarkt anymore?" Werner said. He ground out his cigarette and began talking rapidly, spitting out the words. He'd been promoted to supervisor. He'd moved to a large apartment in Berlin, turning in his life on the island for a life in the city, working toward the betterment of his country. He was a director now, as she no doubt knew. *A director.* Politics wasn't a sacrifice when you were working to improve the world for your children!

Could she say the same about what was happening in America? he asked with gusto. This foolish man, Kennedy, and his "*Ich bin ein Berliner.*" Werner snorted. What about the social unrest, the riots? The rampant use of drugs so people could drown out their fear of nuclear disaster? No, in the East they were working steadily to build themselves a solid social and political system, fail safe; they weren't trying to dismantle society piece by piece. In the East they didn't have race riots, people turning on each other because they could never be satisfied, always needing something more.

Sips of breath. In, out: *Keep going. Don't let him take over.*

"And your wife?" she interrupted quietly, placing a hand on her stomach. It was important that she get the words out; she couldn't let him take the reins. "Your family is with you, here in Berlin"—*deep breath; do it! Do it now; say it!*—"and Annaliese is here too?"

"Yes, yes, my wife, my family, of course they're with me," he said. His pale eyes stared at her, and this time when he smiled, it was broad, revealing his teeth. It seemed, perhaps, that in the face of her distress, he was having some fun. "Remember Irmgard Bandelow? We've been together for eleven years."

He whipped out a photograph from the pocket of his jacket: Six people, adults and children, in front of a brick building with a wide staircase. There was a sign hanging above the door: *Lenin-Schule.*

He pointed at the children. "Annaliese, Petra, Kurt, and Henning," he said.

Her heart lurched again. There she was, the child Bettina had thought about every day, whom she had last seen as a baby, now a young girl with long thin legs. Willowy; angular features and almond eyes; heavy, arched eyebrows. Did Anna's earnest expression mean she wasn't happy? Her hair looked strange—too large and strangely coarse—and she was wearing a sack-like brown garment and oversize work boots. Everyone else was dressed in normal clothes, and one child was in a wheelchair.

"Is that—right there?" Bettina said, pointing. "Is that her? That's Annaliese?"

"She was in the school play. Celia, in *The Threepenny Opera.*"

The face was so different, and yet the eyes, the expression. This was her child, grown, growing, almost a young woman already. The fussy baby, the toddler, long gone. It was a punch in the gut to imagine all the time Werner and Anna had spent together, the endless hours and days, the laughter and meals and hubbub of a regular life. While Bettina understood that it was far better that Anna had a family who loved her, the pain of knowing this—and that she was not a part of it—was as sharp and sudden as a blade slicing through her muscles.

"And you, Werner," she said. "Can you tell me how you are? Are you ill? What's happening?"

"Oh, I'm fine. It's nothing. It's just—it's from the polio. No reason to think I'll be dropping dead anytime soon, much as you might welcome that." His lips pressed together so hard they began turning white. It would be impossible to get him to be honest, she realized. He needed to protect his life from her. She could offer him nothing but disruption.

But she couldn't allow this meeting to pass without asking if Werner knew anything about Peter. Didn't she have some sort of responsibility toward him too? The memory of her love for him was as vibrant and insistent as it had been a decade earlier. Her fingers dug into the fabric of her skirt. "I must ask . . . I wondered, what we talked about? Your promise to me, when I agreed to leave, you said you wouldn't get Peter in—"

Werner jumped up. "How dare you ask about that man?" Patrons from the tables on either side looked over at them, curious about the commotion, staring. He threw down his napkin.

"But I—"

"Why would I not keep my promises?" Werner barked. He grabbed a cane and pushed his chair back. "Why would you think I'm not a man of my word? When I've only ever been true to my word, when my word is *everything*."

She grabbed his forearm. "You can't go. Werner, please, I beg you."

He snatched his arm away. "Don't touch me."

"You took everything from me, *everything*. I have nothing."

"That's not my fault, is it?"

"But it is . . . you're the one who decided it had to be that way. You!"

They stared at one another as the other patrons slowly turned away, red faced, embarrassed by the raw look on the faces of these strangers, the terrible, trembling moment they were witnessing. And into that lacuna between Werner and Bettina, there flowed a silent stream of invective and pleading, of unspoken pain so sharp and hope so eager it could be mistaken for the shredded remnants of a kind of tenderness.

Losing his balance, Werner lunged to one side awkwardly. He raised both palms in a gesture of desperation: *back off*. As he walked away from her—limping, too thin, afraid of ghosts—she had the sense that nothing was quite as straightforward as it had seemed, that it was possible she had never known or understood him at all, and that she never would.

Outside, the streets gleamed in the continuous rain. Werner was already gone, whisked away in a car across the border into the East. As Bettina walked, she was deaf to the sputtering of the cars and buses and blind to the careless gaze of passersby swaddled in rain jackets and hats.

The look they'd shared after that last exchange had revealed something new and unsettling that she couldn't quite put her finger on. He seemed to have done something he felt guilty about. The possibility that Werner had, in fact, broken his promise to her caused rage to swell inside her, and as she walked on, she thought she might be capable of doing him physical harm. But this, too, was laughable: he had vanished, and she couldn't get to him. Her temples throbbed. Clutching her camera to her front, she passed through various neighborhoods: residential areas with towering apartment blocks, scarred with bullet holes and graffiti, plane-tree–lined avenues. Great pockets of land remained empty, the bricks tidied up, most of the destroyed buildings swept away.

It was still broken, this city, and now it was split in two by a wall.

This wall, four years old already, dissected the street in front of her. In a daze Bettina climbed a ladder to a wooden platform to look out over the truncated boulevard that ran, on the other side of the wall, in a straight line to the horizon. The plainness of this concrete barrier slicing the city in two was stunning: an expanse of yellowish gray, hideous, patched together. On this side there was graffiti—slogans and cartoon images—and on the other side dusty earth, tamped down by the sudden rains, studded with wire and watchtowers. There were large prefabricated concrete slabs upon which rows of concrete building blocks were stacked, hardened mortar appearing to drip sloppily between the seams. The wall varied considerably in height and design, and it almost seemed as though drunken workmen had hastily patched it together. At the very top, Y-shaped pieces of metal were attached at intervals, strung with barbed wire. She'd read somewhere that four million East Germans had fled to the West before the wall was built. Shoddy or not, it was achieving its purpose: controlling the flow of people in both directions.

To her left was the old Brandenburg Gate. The goddess of victory on her chariot was brutally charred and broken, like a violated woman saddled with useless tools. What had been a busy thoroughfare in the heart of Germany's capital city had become a yawning, deserted square to the east. How had it come to this, her country being divided, with her daughter on one side and her on the other?

Her head was packed with competing images, jostling against one another, Kodachrome slides in a jumble. The boy, the young one in the wheelchair she saw in the photo. Were the children cherished in that household? Anna wearing that awful wig, acting in a play (that was something she hadn't imagined as she'd clicked the beads on her camera strap). Anna in a Bertolt Brecht play, trapped on the other side of this monstrous wall. A squat white building at the border, years ago, where she'd been forced to sign away her rights. (What was it like now; would she be able to make it across the border if she tried?) Irmgard . . . their old neighbor. Her square face, the blonde hair. What kind of mother was she? Bettina remembered the ravaged look on her neighbor's face as she held the child when Bettina was taken away. The woman had been a kind of friend, looking out for Bettina from time to time. Did she love her Anna, her stepdaughter? Was she gentle, patient?

And Werner—the color of his skin. His misshapen body and the terrible limp. It was evident that he was sick. Was he going to die? Part of her thought he deserved to die for his single-mindedness, his capacity for cruelty, and yet she also knew that Anna probably loved him dearly. That his death would cause her pain, and this was not something Bettina could wish for.

By the time she made it to the Tiergarten, the rain had stopped. When she'd lived here for those months before leaving for America, most of the park's trees had been razed to make room for vegetable gardens, and the ground had been pitted with craters and covered in debris. Now supple trees stretched limbs toward the watery sun. Stopping at a bench, Bettina sat down. A shiver ran the length of her damp body. All those years she'd worked so hard to forget were now telescoped into a single black hole; in the face of all this, her life in Chicago felt very far away, implausible and insignificant. So much had changed and yet so little too.

And then another detail from the picture Werner had shown her came to her mind—*Lenin-Schule*—and she had an idea.

43

A week after Werner had had Bettina exiled, the local Volkspolizei turned up at the house on Apolonienmarkt. Along with four others, an officer with a severely shorn head revealing a bluish scalp crowded into the front hallway. He carried a briefcase and a folder and had tucked his cap under his armpit upon entering. "We will be recording the dimensions of the rooms, reconciling it with our documents. I'd like to see the *Grundbuch*," the man said, asking for the house records before glancing down at the papers in his hands. A confused expression crossed his face. "Comrade Nietz. I apologize. I see you're with us—in the Operative Technical Sector. I failed to check before heading over. Apologies, uh, I'm not entirely sure of protocol."

It was evening, and Werner had been preparing to try to put the baby to bed. He'd changed out of his suit and was wearing a cotton tunic on which Anna had thrown up after rejecting the carrots he'd cooked. "Head of accounts for the OTS since last year," he said wearily. "Supervisor of the greater Pommern region."

"In the regional offices?"

"Yes. With a possible move to the BV."

"I see, hmmm. MfS district administration?" The man seemed uncertain, as though Werner was now claiming too much credit for his position. He made a notation on the paper. "I'm afraid I still need to check that deed for the house, Comrade Nietz, per orders. As you likely know, we're overhauling our inventory of all privately owned property."

Werner dug the paper out of an overstuffed file tucked away in the breakfront. Those first awful days when Bettina was gone, his lifelong propensity for bad timing and bad luck had finally become clear to him. For *weeks* before he kicked her out, he'd been hearing talk in the office that property owners close to the water and the borders were to be evicted. He'd made inquiries about the house and his position regarding ownership. At that point he'd simply been seeking authority over Bettina, some sense that he was in control. But when he saw her with that man Peter Brenner, when he realized what had been going on behind his back, it was as though he'd been smacked in the face with a plank of wood. Furious at himself for his idiotic blindness, he'd reacted swiftly and with great purpose.

But his unwavering certainty had lasted all of two days. The baby cried incessantly for her mother, and for the first time the idea of raising this child alone terrified him. If only he hadn't been so very rash. Now they'd sent over this local baboon who didn't even seem to understand who he was, and for all Werner knew, he'd be kicked out, or some other family would be assigned to move in with them.

The policeman satisfied himself that the document was in order. "Your wife? Bettina Heilstrom Nietz . . . may I ask where she is? She is listed here, on these papers."

Werner cleared his throat. "She's not here presently. And I don't know that her whereabouts are your business."

"Comrade, let us sort through the information as best we can, yes?" The man's eyes rested on his, causing Werner to shift his gaze away. "When are you expecting her back?"

"I'm not entirely certain."

Steady creaking came from the men above them as they moved back and forth over the old floorboards. "Do you wish to file a missing person report?"

Werner clasped his hands in front of him. "Well, I suppose . . . ," he started, but he was interrupted by the others coming back down the stairs.

They poked their heads into the front room, their faces unreadable. "Finished," one of them said.

The head officer closed his folder. "Comrade, you must know—you have five days, and then you will need to file a report, or your wife will be considered a *Flüchtling*."

"She is," Werner said. Saying this made it even more permanent. It opened the door for the life that would come next. His colleagues at the MfS knew and supported him, of course (they were the ones who'd picked her up in the van), but now it was a matter of telling the local authorities. Of beginning his life without her and making it official. Annaliese began protesting her imprisonment in the kitchen, stuck in the high chair with the overcooked carrots, momentarily distracting him. "She's emigrated, gone to the West."

The man scratched at the bristle on his skull with a pen. This news did not seem especially shocking to him. "You'll need to file that paperwork, then, Comrade," he said. "It's a travesty, isn't it?"

Annaliese's shrieks got louder, and Werner took a step backward.

"Best attend to that," the officer said, making to exit with the others. "You have your hands full."

A month or so later, he arranged for Irmgard to watch the baby again, and as he handed Anna over for the day, she smiled at him, revealing her slightly graying teeth and the beginnings of what would become deep creases at her eyes and mouth. He thought back to that day she'd come to his office with her white gloves and coiffed hair, and he began to recognize the possibility of an altogether different future.

"Frau Bandelow," he said. "Why don't you join me tonight for a drink?"

Out of propriety, Irmgard declined the invitation. When they saw each other again later that week, she pursed her lips before conceding that yes, it would be a pleasure to share a drink with him. As she walked back into her house to fetch a cardigan, Werner watched her movements. She seemed to be a woman who had seen a thing or two, someone who was independent yet also traditional in a way that Bettina had never been. Werner wiped his hands along the thighs of his dark trousers. Inside his chest there was an unfamiliar prickle of excitement. He had the brief and pleasant thought that he could reinvent himself if he so chose, that maybe his errors in judgment would be washed away by a tide of sudden good luck.

When Irmgard joined him in the living room ten minutes later, she brought along a bottle of Goldbrand. "I'm so sorry I don't have an unopened one," she said, "but I thought it would be better to bring a little something rather than turn up empty handed."

Her lips were freshly reddened. Thinner than Bettina and shorter, she had narrow shoulders and a face that had clearly been quite pretty once. A large tortoiseshell pin held her hair off her face. Werner thought of Bettina's gleaming curtain of dark hair, how she had often worn it down even though he found it untidy. This woman seemed to be everything that Bettina was not.

Irmgard liked to tell bawdy jokes, and her humor made Werner laugh in spite of himself. She was especially fond of poking fun at the regime, and the fact that he found humor in her risqué remarks encouraged Werner's altered sense of who he was and who he could become. After the third glass of *Weinbrand*, they were sitting side by side on the Biedermeier couch. The sleeve of her cotton dress was touching his jacket. He slipped the jacket off and laid it on the armrest.

Leaning toward her, he planted a kiss on her cheek. She turned toward him immediately and offered her mouth. The woman was hungry for attention; her mouth was soft and wet and inviting. Werner placed a hand on the side of her breast, flattened out under the pressure from his own chest. He tried to slip one hand under her skirt, feeling with his fingers the thick nylon hose covering her legs, and she pulled away from him and slapped his face, laughing good-naturedly.

They kept this game up until late wintertime, when Werner decided what to do. He had held the authorities off for this long, but he knew that eventually they would assign him some rowdy family to share the small house. Did he want a life in which it was just him and his darling little Anna, living among strangers who would never be family? His love for Bettina had been so all-encompassing that it had almost obliterated him. He was wary of this—of the intensity of love, the way it made men vulnerable—and he was tempted to turn away from it for good. But this woman, Irmgard, she was so alive under his fingers, her heart pulsing just beneath the skin, her body pressed against his. She wanted to live and laugh, and it seemed she also wanted to be with him.

One night, when he and Irmgard had made it into a supine position on the couch after Annaliese had been put to bed and they'd shared their customary rounds of drinks, he felt himself harden under the pressure from her thigh, and he whispered into her ear, "Come live with me, Irmgard. Let's make a life together. We'll have a family. What do you think?"

44

At the Central Registry of State Judicial Administrations not far from her hotel, Bettina met with two men charged with investigating the expulsion of dissidents from the DDR. When she'd called from Chicago before deciding to come to Berlin herself, they'd opened a file on Peter Brenner. Every now and then they were able to apply some "leverage," they'd told her. Invariably there was something the East Germans wanted from them, and sometimes the Western government would offer an exchange of goods, money, or documents in return for information.

"Please sit down," said one of the investigators, Karl Mannheim. He had a severe side part and was continually laying the flat of his hand over his springy brown hair, inordinately concerned with keeping it in place. "We managed to dig up some information on Peter Brenner."

Bettina took a seat, the vinyl cover sticking to the backs of her knees. "You found him?"

"Frau Nietz," the other one said. He was standing by the window, backlit, the dark outline of his torso visible inside his illuminated shirt. A young man, he had cushiony flesh and features that melted into one another. "I'm Helmut Kreisgut. Pleased to meet you. Herr Mannheim and I are glad you could make it."

"Call me Fräulein Heilstrom, please; I prefer it . . ."

The two men exchanged glances. "Of course, we can call you whatever you wish," the chubby one said.

Her temples throbbed. Kreisgut took a seat at a coffee table near her and opened a file. In his presence she felt old, and it struck her that the past decade had actually sped by, that what had seemed like a slow-moving cargo ship churning through unfamiliar territory had in fact been a speedboat. Soon she would be middle aged, and what would she say about her own agency, the steps she had taken to have the life she wanted? It was hard to believe that she had no idea what those years had been like for Peter—how he had taken the news of her leaving, what kind of life he had been able to build. She wanted so badly for him to have had another chance at love, but sitting here with these men, so stiff and unaccommodating, she feared the worst.

"This man, Peter Brenner," Kreisgut said. "Can you tell us a little about your relationship with him?"

"To give us some context so we can begin thinking about next steps," the other one said.

"Next steps?" she asked, placing her hands under her thighs to keep from balling them into fists. "Please tell me where he is. I think I have a right to know. I've been in touch with you for the past four weeks, calling you almost daily. You either have an answer for me or not. Just put me out of my misery, will you?"

"I'm afraid it seems your friend, he's been arrested for political agitation."

Shutting her eyes and holding her breath, she brought her hands together in her lap and clasped them tightly: so it was true. It was true! He was in prison. Her fingers began to swell under the pressure, and she gripped even harder, trying to keep herself tethered to something real, trying not to cry out loud. "When did this happen?"

"He received a ten-to-fifteen-year sentence."

"As far as we can tell, he was held in Hohenschönhausen for eighteen months—"

"In Berlin. You're aware of this place? It's for so-called political agitators."

"We believe he could have been sent to a forced-labor camp. That's why we've been having trouble tracking him down," Mannheim added. "We've assigned some investigators on ground to figure out where he might be. There are labor camps in the DDR, you know. People just disappear."

She snapped her eyes open and stood up, the blood rushing from her head. "So it's been two years already?"

"Fräulein, you should sit." Mannheim patted down his hair.

What was she supposed to *do*? How was she supposed to go on? She fell back into her chair. That day when she'd told Peter on the beach in Glowe that it was over, she'd believed she might be able to save them both. Then, leaving Germany, she'd comforted herself that at least she was guaranteeing his safety—he would be able to live a "normal" life, the kind of life he deserved. "We have to get him out," she said. "As soon as possible!"

Mannheim's gaze was flat. "He's been published. Seems he wrote a novel. Someone smuggled it out of East Germany, and it's garnered quite a large following in Europe. It's been written up in the papers here, and someone in the East must have put two and two together. He published under a pseudonym, but that sealed the deal for him at home, I'm afraid."

"My God," she said. *"Forced labor?"*

"There are hundreds of political prisoners in the East," Kreisgut said. The folds of his face shifted gently as he spoke. "With the rise of the MfS, we find ourselves increasingly stymied. They've got a pretty streamlined system—"

"It was Werner," Bettina interrupted, her heart pounding hard in her ears. It felt as though, in the very center of her brain, behind her eyes, a knot was forming, pummeled on all sides by the raging of her blood, and this knot, clenching in on itself, would never unravel as long as she lived. "I know it was him."

The bookstore around the corner from her hotel had a stack of Peter's books on a table in the middle of the main room in front of the registers, and more on a shelf labeled **BESTSELLERS**. Under the pseudonym Paul Edward—a reference, she was sure, to the socialist poet Paul Éluard—Peter had written a novel called *When Eyes Are Watching*. The manuscript had been published by the West German imprint Rütten und Loening. It had lingered on the bestseller list for almost three years already. The hardcover showed a young man's back as he walked toward an indistinct horizon, the colors faded as though day had barely broken. On the back cover was a series of quotes from reviewers at the major newspapers as well as a few writers, but there was no author photo. The bio claimed that "Edward" was an East German socialist and teacher living in a town on the border of Poland.

Written in an extraordinarily modern, experimental voice that is as rhythmic and approachable as the best from the old canon, When Eyes Are Watching *dares to argue that when guided by our hearts, we can transcend petty politics,* wrote *Der Spiegel*.

On the inside page there was a dedication: *Für meine geliebte Bettina*.

With both hands on the table, she steadied herself and waited till the roaring in her head quieted down. He had not forgotten her.

It took her almost all night to read, and when she was done, she closed the book and laid it against the skin of her chest, under her nightshirt, and shut her eyes to conjure up his image. She saw him as he had been that day at the church, Aldo at his feet and a stalk of grass between his teeth. She saw him in the youth center, scribbling in his notebook, immersed in another reality. In his narrow bed, his gaze blurry with desire. At the beginning of his story, she'd thought Peter was espousing the philosophy of the absurd—his protagonist was senselessly, relentlessly faced with one profound loss after another—and with ever-increasing panic she'd read on, filled with dread at the idea that he had become a fatalist, that he'd stopped believing in man's power to affect his own fate. But as the story progressed, as the hero faced down his tragedies and lost the woman he loved, she came to see that Peter was in fact celebrating man's agency, revealing not that the individual was powerless but that he was powerful. That no matter what befell him, his spirit could not be crushed if he refused to let it be. It was magical, astounding; the narrator stands at the edge of a cliff, staring down into the roiling waters, and his heart soars with joy: *like a gull gliding on the currents of the wind.* Joy at having loved and having been loved. At having lost. Joy at the very fact of his existence.

It was a message for her. Peter was speaking directly to her, and he was telling her that she must no longer accept a life lived in this in-between state, half here and half there.

She must take every opportunity that presented itself to her, accept the uncertainties. Bitterness against Werner, the desire to cause him pain: these feelings would eat her up if she let them—and she didn't have to let them. This was her choice. She had to fight to keep her soul intact. This was what Peter had done, wherever it was that he now found himself.

She could not wait until morning. Bettina got dressed and went downstairs to call her boss, George, collect from the hotel lobby. It was early afternoon in Chicago, and though he initially seemed distracted, eventually he settled in to listen to the whole story. She told him about Annaliese, about Peter being in prison somewhere in the East. He had written a book, she explained, a book that Americans should read. At the very least, the *Tribune* could consider running a story on this. She asked him to go on the wire services and look for stories in the *International Herald Tribune* on Paul Edward. "It could be important. This could become part of your cultural conversation," she insisted, tripping over her words. "Part of *our* cultural conversation."

George agreed to try to get her a press pass through which she could secure a day visa to enter East Berlin. "As soon as possible, before this guy has a chance to block entry," he said.

"Oh, I'm sure it's too late for that. But I'm going to find a way."

George thought he could get a friend from the AP wire services to give her one of their passes, at least temporarily. They had a variety of personal identification papers that might work for her—they needed to find a woman with her approximate height and coloring. It could work, but he didn't sound sure.

If she got across, he said, it was critical to be discreet yet to shoot as much film as possible. He couldn't guarantee the *Tribune* would run a spread in the paper, but if she came back with some great images, he'd see what he could do. Maybe publicity would do the trick for her friend Peter. Though the building of the wall had already been well documented, maybe she could catch some good shots from the other side to run alongside a story about her daughter being trapped in a Communist regime.

"The media's got more clout in these cases than those functionary types or the lawyers," George said. "Public opinion counts. But we need good pictures, really good ones."

Now that she'd won the Smithsonian prize, any media outlet would clamor to get their hands on photos that revealed the source of her inspiration: her homeland, her lingering sense of disenfranchisement, he said. Could she possibly track Annaliese down? A picture of her would make all the difference. Something that showed how circumscribed, how small and controlled, life was in the East. Also, there were rumors that the German government had bought the freedom of a handful of political prisoners with West German currency. Perhaps that would work for her friend? And could Bettina get anywhere near that East Berlin prison to take some pictures? Rumors about the secret police were rife among journalists, but the American public had no inkling of what was going on. They could draw parallels with what was happening in the US, George said, getting excited now—this essential struggle for control, the inevitable chaos of change. The universality of man's desire to impose his political will on others.

Bettina was done with the political rhetoric—it meant nothing to her—but maybe this would make it possible to turn the tables, and she was willing to try.

45

George connected her with a Berlin-based journalist named Frederika Gurlinsky who worked for the Associated Press. At five feet, seven inches tall, she was an inch shorter than Bettina, and her hair was cut into a sharp black bob over which she wore a gray beret, tilted at an angle. They met at a grocery store around the corner from the AP offices and walked to a nearby park. At some point during their walk, she slipped the press pass and an ID into Bettina's bag.

"The guards rarely stop me, especially if you go through at Bornholmer Straße. That's where I'd go if I were you," Gurlinsky said, looking straight ahead. "But whatever you do, don't draw attention to yourself. God knows, if they confiscate this pass, it's worth its weight in gold . . ." She hesitated. "My supervisor would *kill* me if he knew what I was doing. This had better be important."

"It is, I promise," Bettina said.

The reporter cast her a quick sideways glance. "You'll have to do something about your hair. And take this—" She took off her beret and walked over to the edge of the path, where there was a large iron trash bin. She dropped a wad of paper into the bin and let her beret fall onto the ground. "Pick it up on your way back."

"I don't understand," Bettina said, feeling foolish, as they continued along the path. "What are you doing?"

"You can't be too safe. Just, it's smart to be careful." Gurlinsky buttoned up her coat to the top and fiddled with the button. "So listen. There's a driver we trust; he's never taken me, but some of our guys like him. He can ferry you around for a day or two. There's counterintelligence; you've got to be careful, all right? You could be followed; I mean, it's likely. Just expect the unexpected, okay—they might suddenly eject you. Be prepared, *ja?*"

Later at the hotel, after having picked up the beret on her way back and bought a pair of scissors and hair dye, Bettina stared at herself in the bathroom mirror in her hotel room. She would try to cross the border tomorrow; she had everything she needed. Raising the scissors, she stared at her reflection and began cutting.

The driver was a slim man of about fifty, with excess skin in his jowls and below his ears. His shoulders were bony, caving inward toward his chest, over which a zipped-up leather jacket stretched. He wore a black wool cap not unlike the fisherman caps they used to wear in Rügen, which afforded Bettina the opportunity to open up a conversation. He'd been given it by his father, he explained, who moved the family to Berlin in the 1930s. "The heyday, though that didn't last too long. But it was better than staying up there on the Baltic," he said. "Our choice would've been get bombed or go on a long trek south—neither very good options."

The silence between them acknowledged the complicated fact that he was of the age to have served Germany in the war.

"I'm Andreas," he said, looking at her in the rearview mirror.

She smiled tightly at him. He'd be with her all day today, and tomorrow, too, if she was allowed back in. "Frederika Gurlinsky," she said. She was self-conscious with her strange black hair, her pretend name. In her head she kept repeating: *Act normal. There's no reason for him to suspect a thing. Just act normal.*

"So what's your interest in the East?" They were driving in an old Mercedes with a boxy shape and stiff shock absorbers. Her driver took a left and then a right before stopping at a light bordered on either side by soaring new buildings dotted with balconies. The cooing of city pigeons entered the open car window like a somber melody. She rested the Rollei on the car door, snapped a picture, and rotated the crank before turning back to Andreas.

"Spent some time here as a child," she said. "May I be frank with you?"

"Of course."

"I think this country is badly misunderstood," she said. "I want to show people what it's really like here—normal life in the East. We're all just people, aren't we?"

The previous night as she waited for the black hair dye to take, Bettina had studied a detailed map of Berlin and found the Lichtenberg district, where Hohenschönhausen was supposedly located, and also Magdalenenstraße and Normannenstraße, where Werner's office was. While she hadn't caught the name of the street, he'd mentioned that he lived within walking distance of Stasi headquarters. But most important, the photo he'd shown her had revealed the name of Annaliese's school: Lenin-Schule. He hadn't realized that in showing off to her like that, he'd inadvertently led her right to the girl.

It wouldn't be prudent to tell the driver to take her there directly, but she could work her way toward that neighborhood. School would be out in a few hours, and all she had to do was drive around haphazardly, snapping pictures—and find a way to end up at Lenin-Schule when the closing bell rang at one o'clock.

At first glance these neighborhoods did not seem so very different from the West. Women in head scarves pushed unwieldy baby carriages, and men carried briefcases; workers wore their heavy boots and hard hats. But once she started turning the crank on the Rollei, the differences became as sharp and noticeable as an image coming into focus in a tray of photographic chemicals. For one thing, apart from some residential structures along the bigger thoroughfares that seemed to be new, it quickly became apparent that many of the grand old buildings were heavily scarred with bullet holes, their facades pockmarked like teenagers with devastating acne. Around every corner lay immense piles of bricks and building debris that hadn't yet been cleaned up. The city was on hold; it had barely moved forward in time. In a few streets private homes had their roofs torn off, the neglected rooms exposed to the elements, the various intimate artifacts of family life long ago pilfered. Rooms where once people had loved one another were now simply shadowed boxes, emptied of meaning and of life.

The stores carried signs with the same old-fashioned lettering that had been common on the island in the old days. In the windows, artfully arranged tableaux revealed cans of preserved ham and cookware, mannequins in crisp uniforms. Andreas drove her down Suermondtstraße, past the palace (really just a small manor house) and then down Gehrenseestraße; she had no sense for how close they might be to the prison, and he did not venture down the side roads. Street after street there were run-down apartment blocks and rows of dingy stores; there was no wall indicating something ominous hidden behind it, no barbed wire or watchtower that she could spot. Could she ask him outright about Hohenschönhausen? she wondered. Both George and the woman, the AP journalist, had warned her not to trust anyone, but she was dying to know how it could be possible to hide a prison in a city like this. They drove and drove as she pretended to be looking for a particular kind of window frame to photograph.

They passed a few grocery stores. She suggested the driver let her off at a local restaurant for an early lunch, but he insisted on taking her to his home. It was not unpleasant to have company, and she agreed, thinking she probably had no real choice anyway. Andreas lived in a development in a village outside the city, and when she entered his backyard, her legs weary from being crunched up in the car, she was shocked to realize that the wall ran right through his yard, not ten meters from his house. It took her breath away. The two of them sat at a metal table in the garden under a small umbrella, the uneven gray expanse of wall topped with loops of barbed wire directly behind them.

Andreas's wife, Heike, brought out a tray of *Königsberger Klopse*, meatballs in a lemon-caper sauce with boiled potatoes. While Heike was dour and watchful, remaining almost entirely silent during lunch, Andreas peppered Bettina with questions, and she found herself rather liking him. His mouth turned down in his flabby face, but his brows arched upward in an appealing show of curiosity and camaraderie. When he complained mildly about being overworked, she encouraged him to spend more time at the vegetable patch in the communal gardens.

"*Ja, ja*," he said, patting the small mound of his stomach, "*Ich esse schon genug Bohnen.*" *I already eat enough green beans.*

He shared that his family's holiday destinations were predetermined by the government, and she told him about a trip along the edges of Lake Michigan, how Americans strapped on sneakers and ran endlessly alongside the water simply as a pastime, to let off stress. She let him assume she'd been visiting for work.

Andreas laughed at the idea of this aimless running, but his wife looked alarmed. "Those capitalists," she muttered, unable to remain silent at this odd, indulgent behavior. "Always such relentless competition. Never stopping moving forward. Where will it all lead?"

It was 12:51 p.m. when they arrived at the Lenin-Schule in Lichtenberg. Bettina asked Andreas to pull over and park opposite the school under the speckled shade of a linden. The unexpected warmth of the day brought sweat to their foreheads, the vaguely feral aroma of the city pungent in the air around them. Berlin was landlocked, and on days like this the air was trapped between buildings, rank. There weren't enough trees. As Andreas sat at the wheel, waiting, his eyes fluttered closed. The weight of Bettina's meal pressed on her stomach, but she was fully alert, sitting forward in her seat, eyes peeled.

Less than ten minutes until school let out.

"Have a cigarette break if you like," she said. "Stretch your legs. I'm going to take some pictures of this playground."

Loading new film into the camera, her fingers were as unwieldy as rubber batons. The image Werner had shown her came back to her: a distinctive child with earnest, slightly drooping eyes. The last time Bettina had felt this anxious was when she'd taken the microphone at the Smithsonian award ceremony. But now the stakes were so high that the earlier turning point paled in comparison. She used the camera to scan her surroundings, glancing down through the viewfinder at the metal playground set on the square and the wooden double doors of the building covered in peeling red paint. The bell rang: the school day was over. Her pulse began to race. Within minutes the doors opened, disgorging children in white-and-navy uniforms with red kerchiefs tied at their necks.

The children screeched and chattered, clutching the straps of their boxy backpacks, tumbling down the stairs into the school's front yard. One after another, boys in blue shorts and girls in A-line skirts. From across the street, the kerchiefs around their necks made them look like a flock of redbirds. Down the stairs they came and came, until the doors shut behind an impressively busty woman wearing a straw hat.

Bettina scanned the children as they ran toward their mothers or began trooping down the street toward home. She pressed herself against the side of a plane tree, even though there was of course no chance that Anna would recognize her. She'd been a baby when Bettina left, not yet walking or talking. The years had swallowed up so much, blocking out a whole swath of her life.

A cluster of girls gathered at the swings, socks pooling at their ankles. They were too young, weren't they—waiting for their mothers, maybe? Surely Anna was old enough to walk home alone.

Bettina could hardly take a full breath. She peered into each of their faces. A corrosive tide of uncertainty began rising inside her: perhaps she might not recognize her own child. She stared, edging closer. Mothers came and called to their children. Boys kicked around a soccer ball. One by one, children began peeling away from the others, heading home.

The sun beat down on Bettina's gray beret, and she pulled it off her head. She worried at the nail of her thumb, her camera hanging limp around her neck. Twenty minutes later, all the children had either walked off or been picked up by their mothers.

And the playground was empty. Her daughter was nowhere to be seen.

46

Andreas drove her around, trying to make conversation, but Bettina did not respond. If she tried to talk, she thought she might begin to sob, and she needed to stay in control. There had been far too much crying these last few days. She peered out the window at the passing houses and the people on the streets, blurred and uninteresting, lacking any sort of distinctive quality, as though they'd been flattened or drained of all color. She could not bring herself to take any more photos; the very act of recording reality, interpreting it, seemed senseless.

What had she been thinking, that she could just come over to East Berlin and claim her child?

"Where to now, Frau Gurlinsky? Would you like to see the river?"

The fact that she'd chopped off her hair and dyed it this black color—that she was pretending to be someone else—seemed risible now. "Anywhere," she said. "I mean, yes, all right. Perhaps the river."

He drove her to the Spree, and she walked along the river's edge. Andreas went with her a short distance, keeping quiet now, pausing at a concrete bollard. It wasn't very attractive here: there were squat factories and chimneys emitting fuzzy ribbons of smoke, overturned trash barrels and papers fluttering in the gutter. The sunlight seemed only to highlight the ugliness. Surely the river's edge should be pretty, especially in the sun; there should be trees and grass, children dipping their toes into the water?

The wall emerged from the water, a grotesque gray monster.

The wall, this false division of a people, *her* people, her home-land. She couldn't wrap her head around what had been lost. When she thought of the future, she wanted to imagine it filled with children running and playing and laughing like those she'd seen earlier, ready to conquer the world, unsaddled with past grievances, and not yet hungry for power. Their energy, their charming, bumbling momentum, their curiosity—those were the things that made life worth living.

This barren, dirty river and this pathetic wall made her want to die. There was nothing here to give her any hope.

"Can we go back to that school for a bit?" she asked the driver. "I'm tired. I think I just need a few more pictures of the play structure."

"Of course," he said. He stared at her for a moment. "Whatever you want."

At the school she left Andreas at the car again and walked around the playground, pretending to take pictures. He was lingering by the car, smoking a cigarette, pacing and looking away, and she walked briskly to the end of the street and rounded the corner. Once she was out of sight, she started running. She wasn't sure where she was going, but running felt good. There was a terrible pressure in her chest, and sweat trickled down her neck. People looked at her askance.

But there was nowhere for her to go, and after a minute she stopped, gulping to catch her breath. More slowly this time, she rounded the cor-ner and headed back toward the car. A tall boy was standing by the edge of the schoolyard, holding some books and talking to a girl with blonde hair. A smaller child was playing at their feet, digging in the earth with a stick. Bettina walked by them.

"Petra," the tall girl said, leaning away from the boy. "Watch out! Mami won't like it if you get your skirt covered in dirt."

Bettina took a seat on a bench nearby and watched them. About ten minutes later two more children joined the group, and one of them seemed about Anna's age. Bettina sat up straighter and then picked up a newspaper from the ground and pretended to read. Looking into her viewfinder a few minutes later, she could see the children without seeming to be spying on them. Her body was a live wire, unpredictable and dangerous; she couldn't be sure that she wouldn't burst into tears or start yelling.

Because it was her—it was definitely her. Bettina felt it in her bones.

Her instinct was to crush Anna in her arms, and a brief fantasy played itself out in her mind in which she saw the two of them talking and Anna happily getting into the car with her, heading away from this life and straight into Bettina's.

The child was so beautiful: gawky limbs, long and slim, her skirt rising above bony knees. A violin case dangled from her fingers, and the other child carried a guitar; they must have been practicing together after school. As Anna spoke to the boy, she swayed back and forth on her heels and waved a bare arm around to emphasize her point. They appeared to be arguing about a book.

"It's just boring," the boy was saying. "Can't they make this stuff more exciting?"

"Not everything can be an adventure," Anna began, but Bettina couldn't catch the rest. Her hair was springy, with round curls that fell below her shoulder blades. It was the kind of hair that would take hours to dry and, when tangled, would be almost impossible to comb through. It was hard to see any resemblance to her or to Werner, and with those dark curls she seemed quite different from Peter too. Her eyes were spaced far apart, and Bettina remembered so well that gaze of hers from when she nursed at her breast. Intense and warm, deeply engaged. But what was shocking was Anna's smile; Bettina could never have anticipated her child would smile in this way—it entirely changed the shape of her face. She seemed to like this boy and would periodically lunge backward as though worried she was getting too close, and then she'd grin at him and inch her way closer again. When she smiled, her cheeks pushed up into her eyes, and she showed almost all her upper teeth. It was as though she gave her whole self to the act of it.

Bettina watched, mesmerized. She stood up and moved a little closer. The children paid no attention to her. The younger child was humming a tune to herself. It sounded like the national anthem, perhaps, or a lullaby.

"Oh," said the boy suddenly, and Bettina shifted the camera down. He pointed at her. "What's that?"

"It's a camera, silly," Anna said.

Would she remember the camera from when she was little? Bettina raised it again and held it out toward them, her heart clattering in her chest. "Would you like me to show you how to use it?" she asked. "It's a Rolleiflex. My father gave it to me. It's quite old but works like a dream."

"I'm Petra," said the little girl, running up and standing very close to her with her hands behind her back and her belly sticking out. "May I touch it?"

"I'm Klaus," the boy said. He hung back, trying not to be overeager.

"I think your fingers might be a little dirty," Bettina said to Petra. She turned to face Anna, hardly able to breathe. Would the girl recognize her? Would they share a look that would change everything? "And who are you?"

"Annaliese," her daughter said. She, too, had come close and was peering at Bettina's hands. She smelled of warm skin and something salty. Bettina ground her teeth together and told herself to stay calm.

"Here, I can show you how it works." She flipped the viewfinder up and then down and showed them the double lenses at the front and how the crank worked. The children peppered her with questions about choosing what to shoot, how to focus, the development process, how many pictures she took and why. They seemed at ease, their bodies relaxed and supple.

"Papa showed me some things from work," Anna said. "They were cameras, I think. But they were tiny. People aren't supposed to know you're taking pictures."

"Annie, you're not allowed to say that," said the little girl, Petra. "He said it was a secret."

"Are you sisters?" Bettina asked.

Petra nodded. "He's just a friend," she said, pointing to the boy.

Anna put her hands on her hips. "We're just like sisters," she said, "but we have a different mother."

"Why do you always have to say that?" Pink spots emerged on Petra's cheeks. "It's not nice."

"It's perfectly nice, *Mausie*," Annaliese said, leaning down and putting her arms around the girl. "It's just that I know everyone's wondering why we don't look anything alike."

"Her mother died," the boy said. "She was on a boat and went out and got caught in a storm and never came back. And no one ever found her body, and it's possible it washed up on shore somewhere very far away, like Sweden even."

Anna looked up, her fingers stroking Petra's wispy blonde hair. Bettina worked hard to control the expression on her face, but inside her it felt as though her stomach had flipped over. She could say something now, right now. She could say: *It's possible your mother didn't die, isn't it?* But that would be the same as saying: *People you love have lied to you.* Anna's face would crumple, or worse, she might retreat in fear. Right now the girl seemed unconcerned, not at all self-conscious. It seemed as if she had told this story many times.

"I used to live on the ocean," Anna said. "She loved the ocean, and if you have to die, I think it's not a bad way to die. Anyway"—she rose to her full height again and squared her shoulders—"we share a *mutti* now, don't we, Petra, and she gets angry if we're too late, and practice ran long today. We'd better go." The sun hit her face as she spoke, revealing a cluster of freckles on her brow and nose. She gave Bettina a courteous but dismissive smile and grabbed the two backpacks and her violin case. "Tomorrow, Klaus."

Anna's interest had waned as quickly as it had been ignited, and she and her little sister turned away and began walking down the street. Her child, so mature, so fatalistic. Too stunned to do anything else, Bettina nodded goodbye to the boy and hurried back to the car. Maybe if she could just figure out where they lived, she could come back and talk to Anna later, or she could find a way to tell her that she had some important information—give her a chance to steel herself.

"Andreas, do me a favor, will you?" she asked, sweat prickling her upper lip. "Drive behind those two girls, but not too close?"

"I'm not sure . . . ," he started, but when she drew out ten American dollars from the pocket of her jeans, he snuffed out his cigarette and climbed in the car. "Suppose it can't hurt," he said.

Anna and Petra walked quite a long way down a large-tree-lined boulevard and then into the side streets, winding their way in and out of the minimal shade. They swung their clasped hands between them as they walked, their heads tilted toward one another the entire way. When they reached Schottstraße, they stopped outside an apartment block with multiple entrances opening up onto a grassy bank. A few water fountains and benches were dotted around under unruly bushes. Andreas parked down the street and across from the building.

The child's words were still ricocheting through Bettina's head: *dead, ocean, not a bad way to go.*

Dead.

Werner had told Annaliese that her mother was dead. This shouldn't have been such a surprise, and yet Bettina realized that she'd always assumed he would tell Anna that her mother had deserted her. That he would want to obliterate his daughter's feelings for the woman who had betrayed him. The sorrow Bettina carried with her about leaving her homeland was tinged with shame about the child feeling abandoned, unloved, discarded. But it wasn't like that at all; Annaliese seemed at ease with the fact that her mother was gone. She carried no shame. She didn't seem to have unanswered questions or doubts.

With her camera, Bettina captured the deep blue of the sky against the top of the apartment block, with its rough edge of crumbling concrete. She captured the two girls as they stopped at a fountain, situating them in the lower edge of the frame and allowing the vertical flight of balconies that punctured the facade behind them to soar out of the top left of the picture. The act of taking these photos made it possible for her to maintain her composure, but when she stopped and saw that the girls were talking to a woman with one very small child on her hip and another in a wheelchair, her tears began to flow.

It was Irmgard. Her face was relaxed and free of makeup, her blonde hair twisted into a high bouffant.

Anna knelt down in front of the wheelchair. Her face broke into a smile, all teeth. She took the child's two small hands in hers and waved them in the air, laughing. The little boy reached out to grab her hair, and she pulled a mock frown that was disarming and lighthearted. Looking up toward Irmgard, she asked her something and then unstrapped the child from the chair and lifted him up. He was about three or four years old, extremely thin, with a big head of tousled brownish hair that he leaned on his sister's shoulder. Irmgard pushed the wheelchair ahead of her, and the four of them began walking away, down toward the end of the street.

Werner had found real love; it was all around him. He had built the family he'd always wanted.

Andreas turned to look at her over his shoulder, but she could not tear her eyes away from the family. "Drive; please drive!" Bettina whispered. Her breath burned in her throat; it stung her lungs and rattled back out through her mouth and nose. Her eyes streamed, and she did not wipe the trails from her cheeks or the sweat from her hairline, and her tears did not stop, even when Andreas bade her goodbye at the border or when she arrived back at her hotel an hour later.

47

For most of the morning, Werner sat with seven other men in a windowless conference room at MfS headquarters. The outside facade was pocked with the distinctive checkerboard pattern made by endless tiny rectangular windows, giving the building its nickname: the House of a Thousand Eyes. On the table in front of each of the men—directors of various regional Stasi units, as well as a few upper-level functionaries like Werner—sat a black phone and a pad of paper. These phones were high frequency and could not be tapped. Each man wore an almost-identical dark suit. They were discussing the new guidelines that had recently been issued by Mielke. Werner had already learned that these policy reviews could last for days on end. Today their task was to draft another new set of directives for the "operational control of persons," also known as surveillance, and he became involved in a lengthy and dull disagreement with Herr Schmidt on the use of eavesdropping devices and camera surveillance in schools and the vast cost of all this equipment.

The phone call came right in the middle of the meeting, and Werner was relieved to have an excuse to rise and stretch his aching legs. He had the call transferred into the hallway where Frau Kellermann sat, and he picked up her handset. She continued with her typing.

"*Hallo, Nietz hier,*" Werner barked into the receiver. He motioned to the secretary to get him another coffee.

"Kassendorf. We thought you'd like to know: we have been tracking some unusual activity, uh, around the border area, and—well, it seems to perhaps involve you . . ."

"What do you mean?" he asked. A few days earlier, right after his meeting with Bettina, he'd submitted a photograph of her taken by a DDR operative at the Ratskeller. It had been an overcast day, intermittently pouring with rain, and the picture quality was not very good. His copy of her old government ID was a much better likeness but very outdated.

"We successfully accompanied a subject—FJG, number 22392—who entered the DDR through the Bornholmer Straße crossing at 8:12 yesterday morning," the man said. "A Frederika Gurlinsky, a reporter on assignment. It's routine. She comes over all the time; she has an aunt here. There's someone in her office who gives us the heads-up."

"I don't see what this has to do with me."

"We had word—Nietz, you should see these notes with your own eyes. It's personal—we recommend you read it immediately. Our department has sent over a copy of everything we have to your office."

"I see." Werner accepted the coffee from the secretary and put it down on her desk. "I'll attend to it immediately. Meanwhile, where is Gurlinsky now? Has she exited?"

"Yes, and no further attempts to cross at this time," Kassendorf answered. "Do you want to change directives? Pursue the subject?"

"I'll let you know when I've read the files."

He begged off the rest of the meeting and headed back to the fourth floor to his office. His enormous desk was bare except for a small crystal inkwell Irmgard had given him on their fifth anniversary, as well as a manila folder. After all these years, he still appreciated her levelheadedness, her natural instincts with the children, her extraordinary generosity in the bedroom. Seeing the inkwell as he worked was a reminder of all the positive things that had befallen him in the past decade—the way he had managed, against the odds, to remake his life into something worthwhile. Even though they had their troubles with little Kurt, the family worked well together. Werner's position afforded them certain material comforts (a modern wheelchair, for example), and they spent most weekends walking together in the forest in Potsdam or boating on the Havel. Their apartment was in a grand building with high ceilings and large windows. They never wanted for fresh food and enjoyed a daily bread delivery, regardless of shortages elsewhere.

It was a good life, this one they had cobbled together, even though he was too busy for his liking. The amount of paperwork he dealt with in his position was astounding. The Stasi workforce had grown exponentially since the inception of the Ministry. Werner was in charge of finances for not only OTS, which protected the government against saboteurs, dissidents, and intellectuals, but also Department N, communications security. These comprised six departments each, and each of these departments was established in every region of the country, which meant 180 discrete budgets were under his purview.

And yet . . . and yet seeing Bettina had shaken him so badly that he'd barely slept since seeing her. There was something about that woman, a feeling that overtook him at unexpected moments. At the café he'd had a profound and disorienting realization that she was not in fact responsible for the feelings she aroused in him. What had she said? *I've lost everything.* Indeed she had, and because of him. She was an ordinary woman, yet he could not think of her without his heartbeat galloping. Now he was saddled with the niggling idea that this was not really her fault.

The file in front of him now, from the Main Administration for the Struggle against Suspicious Persons, was crammed with photos and reports. Attached to the front with a paper clip was an index card with a black-and-white picture of a woman with cropped black hair and a sculpted face with pronounced cheekbones and direct eyes. For a second he thought it might be Bettina. He began flipping through the pages rapidly, but it was all the ordinary stuff: date of birth, crossings, articles filed for the AP and other outlets, personal details (school, marriage, habits), names of friendlies in her press office, and so on.

He didn't need to see the typed form at the back to begin to understand what was going on. He felt very, very stupid.

A few typed pages, dated the previous day, had been added to the file. This woman had crossed the border yesterday, the second crossing this month, no red flags yet. There was a black-and-white photograph, taken from a distance, of her exiting a Mercedes and approaching a house. Her build was similar to Bettina's. The hair was odd—cut to the chin, blunt, and very dark. The second photo showed her face more clearly: it was his former wife.

He picked up the phone and requested Bettina's file. And then he continued reading.

She had been driven around Lichtenberg, Prenzlauer Berg, and Marzahn. The driver, Andreas Ottenfeld, filed a detailed report on their activities, including the fact that they ate *Königsberger Klopse* in his back garden and that she seemed overly focused on the wall (visible from their yard). Then Werner saw the problem: a familiar address on the list of sites, Rummelsburger Straße.

He sucked on his lip, then pulled the chair closer to the desk and leaned with both elbows on the wood, reading. FJG #22392 requested that the driver stop opposite a school, the Lenin-Schule, in a spot where the car would not be visible to the students. She instructed him to "entertain himself" and proceeded to take multiple photographs of the building, the yard, and presumably the children. They stayed thirty-four minutes, during which time she became visibly distraught, including afterward when they toured the riverside briefly. She insisted they return to the school and continued to observe the playground. Then FJG #22392 approached a group of children approximately between the ages of six and twelve and spent fourteen minutes talking with them.

One of those children was determined to be Annaliese Nietz, daughter of Werner Nietz, head of finances for OTS.

Upon returning to the vehicle, FJG #22392 was distressed and asked Ottenfeld to follow two of the girls as they walked to Schottstraße, where she observed them for eight further minutes. The children were met outside the building by a few members of Director Nietz's immediate family. During this time FJG made no effort to hide the fact that she was crying. Attempts at eliciting an explanation were met with silence.

Damn. *Damn!* He'd allowed himself to become vulnerable. What a fool; he had underestimated Bettina's nerve.

He thought back to last night, when he returned home from work . . . Annaliese had seemed quite happy and normal. She'd chatted as usual about her day, telling them she'd come top of her class in a science test and completing her chores unperturbed. She did not mention meeting a woman, did not seem upset or distracted. Right before bed she came to Werner in her long cotton nightdress with the flower pattern, her hair wet and smelling vaguely medicinal, and plopped herself onto his lap. She was too old for that sort of thing, but still she asked for a story, and he gave her one: it was about being a child of the sea.

What should he do? he wondered. Despite his agitation, he could not help but imagine what Bettina must have felt, encountering her child again after such an eternity. And in spite of himself—in spite of the danger it presented to him—he felt some small pleasure that she had seen the girl, that she had witnessed for herself just how lovely she was, how perfect in almost every way.

Many years earlier, Franz Josef Bieder had built up a file on Bettina Heilstrom Nietz. There were reams of typewritten notes, various administrative details, and the names of the surveillance officers assigned to her. Copies of Bettina's birth certificate, their marriage license, and Anna's birth certificate. There were a few letters that had been intercepted, when Bettina was still in Saargen, sent from her sister, Clara Lange, to an address in Bobbin, and a few reports typed up during the years of their marriage, including when she insinuated herself into that business with her coworker Christa Kellermann and began trekking to Bobbin constantly.

Werner read, again, a detailed log of her comings and goings to various events, such as the Russian friendship performance at the middle school in Bobbin, where it was noted that she met with a teacher named Peter Brenner; Werner's chest tightened at seeing this name written down again. She was also noted to have frequented the youth center when the place was ostensibly closed, and there was documentation on her interrogation in Berlin in 1953, along with a photograph of her in a room, signing the papers that secured her release.

None of this was news to him.

Werner picked up the phone again. He issued an order to assign three agents to go to the Insel Hotel in West Berlin instantly and not to let her out of their sight. Under no circumstances was she to be permitted reentry to East Germany. All Berlin borders were to be put on high alert. Should she attempt to cross the border again, his orders were to apprehend her immediately and contact him, day or night. He wanted the phones in her room tapped; she should not be speaking to anyone without their knowledge.

They were going to have to figure out a way to get the photographs from her. She worked at a newspaper, she'd told him; this was very bad. He could not allow her to take photographs of the child back to America with her. She would make some kind of scene, dredge up the whole sordid story of their past in the media. Times were tense; he couldn't be sure this kind of unwanted attention wouldn't knock him off his spot at the agency. There was always someone in the wings, waiting for his chance in the limelight. Nothing was ever stable.

Fanning the reports over his desk, he cast his eye one more time over the attachments and notations. There was a smaller piece of paper stapled to the very back of a report; he'd been distracted by that last

photograph of her and hadn't seen the attached note. The heading read
Haftbefehl—"Order of Arrest." And the name that came after that: Peter
Ludwig Brenner.

His skin went cold. So the Stasi had cross-referenced these two. It
had been a long time since he'd bothered to look at their files, either
of them. The man had been arrested—*of course* she must assume it was
his doing.

This time he called the records office to request Peter Brenner's
files be delivered to him immediately, but they were kept at
Hohenschönhausen, not HQ. He decided it was time to call in a favor
and dialed his friend Rataizick. After hanging up, he gathered together
the papers, slipped the file into his briefcase, and grabbed his jacket. The
cup of coffee from earlier sat on his desk, a caramel-colored film staining the upper edges, untouched. He locked the doors behind him and
instructed his secretary that he would be gone for the rest of the day.

A Russian ZiL with tinted windows took him to Genslerstraße, where
the prison compound lurked behind a long perimeter wall topped with
barbed wire, tucked in behind larger apartment blocks. First the car
was allowed through a long boom gate. Beyond that were a series of
squat concrete buildings and a few high-rises housing Stasi personnel.
They passed through another high wall overlooked by octagonal guard
towers.

Werner entered the prison through a side door and flipped his
pass out of his jacket pocket. The guard clicked his heels. "Afternoon,
Comrade Nietz," he barked, pressing a button behind the desk.

"Here to see Siegfried Rataizick," Werner said. "Section fourteen."

"*Jawohl*," the guard answered.

Werner nodded at another guard in a blue uniform. At the end
of the hall, instead of mounting the stairs to Rataizick's office, he

descended two levels to the area known as the U-Boat. He was limping a little, his right leg radiating pain from the ankle to his hip bones. A boiling, greasy queasiness overtook him, and he paused, catching his breath, trying not to throw up. The cancer was spreading; he'd suspected it for months. Now it was a matter of ignoring the discomfort, of embracing the time he had left. The doctor had said it could be anywhere from two years to ten, and maybe this time he'd be lucky—who could predict?

At the end of a long corridor, he came upon a door marked *Vernehmungsraum*, the interrogation room. Inside a small unlit control room was a windowpane that looked into an adjacent cell, where a single bulb was illuminated. On a wooden stool fastened to the floor sat a man whose long body was folded into itself like a piece of origami. His head hung down so that his chin was resting against the gray material of his prison uniform, his long legs crossed and tucked underneath him. His arms were fastened behind his back.

A few minutes later, a guard delivered a file stuffed full of papers, marked *PLB #7833082*. Werner pulled a chair over to the window, sat down, and began leafing through Peter's dossier. Werner had been so happy to move to Berlin, to be off the island where this man lived— happy to banish him from his thoughts once and for all. He'd kept his promise to Bettina: he'd never made use of the girl's underpants he'd tucked under the man's mattress that day, "just in case." He hadn't needed to. Bettina was gone, and he had a new woman in his life and a child, with more to come; it was better to leave the poor idiot to his own devices and let him hang himself if he insisted.

But there had been years of surveillance, he saw now, continuing long after Bettina left. Copies of leaflets from the workers' strike in 1953: *Utopia Can Be a Reality! We Demand Transparency! Socialism Is Rooted in Truth!* A small booklet, nicely printed with a pale-green cloth cover, with the name Peter L. Brenner printed on the front. Inside, poetry.

A handwritten note:

As for men in power, they are so anxious to establish the myth of infallibility that they do their utmost to ignore truth.

—Boris Pasternak

Another small booklet titled *Berliner Brautgang*, by Wolf Biermann. A sheaf of mimeographed papers clipped together, labeled *Pinocchio's Original Tale: A Play in Three Acts*. A notation in pencil scribbled on its front sheet: *May 21, 1963*. Then, clippings from a few West Berlin newspapers:

> An entirely fresh voice in Pan-German literature—*Die Post*.
> A romantic take that does not stint on the sobering realities of postwar life in East Germany—*Neues Deutschland*.
> A fearless exposé of the wrongheadedness of our country's search for redemption—*Die Welt*.

The man had written a novel, it seemed, published in the West and highly lauded. Werner had known Brenner was a teacher but hadn't given much consideration to his subject matter. Since his move to Berlin he had been preoccupied with other things; he did not read modern novels and, embarrassingly, had not been aware of this book or the stir it had caused. It appeared that almost two years earlier Brenner had been apprehended; he'd been questioned for six months, had been moved to a facility in the suburbs, and was now in transit to a labor camp in the south.

When Werner looked through the window again, Peter Brenner had not moved. Both men remained still until Werner realized from the rhythmic rise and fall of the man's shoulders that he was asleep. Werner banged his fist against the thick glass, making a clunking sound: Peter raised his head, throwing his shoulders back, alert now like a deer. His eyes in their deep, dark sockets scanned the room, but there was no one.

48

Bettina could not fall asleep even though in the past week she'd slept no more than fifteen hours in total. Again and again she came back to two images: the sisters from behind, walking down the street with their hands linked, and the small child in the wheelchair over whom Anna had hovered with such evident adoration. A limited slice of the child's life that elicited in Bettina both pain and a sharp sting of joy. The pain of understanding that she played no role in this scene, that her presence in Anna's life was not only unnecessary but could do her no real good. The joy of knowing that the girl was carefree, unburdened with complicated memories or confused feelings. What did a mother most want for her children? For them to be safe. To be happy. To feel loved.

And yet she felt as though she'd been flayed.

How badly she wanted to raise her daughter and teach her how to see the world. But what she *should* do—it seemed now that that might be entirely different than what she wanted. Perhaps what she should do, in fact, was absolutely nothing. Werner was ill, but was that enough of a reason to snatch this child from the only family she'd ever known? The girl had a mother. She had a sister and brothers. Her family was *real*. What Bettina wanted was not of much relevance here.

This harrowing fact made her head pound, and she spent half the night in the bathroom, sitting on the edge of the tub, holding a cold washcloth to her face. It had seemed possible, briefly, that she could go back in time and claim what had wrongly been taken from her. But this was not about her.

Bettina woke up with swollen eyes. Her skin was blotchy, with pale-gray and mauve undertones around the eyes and mouth. It was early, but clusters of people were already gathered in the lobby, standing around or drinking black coffee at the tables; a few men in dark suits and hats, others who looked foreign, one wearing a leather coat. A woman sat in the phone booth in the corner, and Bettina thought she should try to call her sister later, even though calling internationally would cost a small fortune. For the past few days she had been paralyzed, and Clara might help her decide what to do. She would put things in perspective.

There was a large pharmacy on the corner, and she headed over there without eating breakfast or getting herself a coffee. As she neared the exit after buying a bottle of aspirin, she caught sight of a balding man in a brown linen jacket and a flat cap. He wore sunglasses and was looking away. But when she turned from him, she noticed in her peripheral vision that he immediately turned back toward her. She strode down the street, a sudden hammering in her ears. In the hotel, she slipped off to the right and stood behind one of the pillars, and a minute later there he was again.

Still wearing his sunglasses, he looked around the lobby before making his way to the back, toward the elevator. Bettina waited a full five minutes before rising to return to her room.

Later, when she called the Central Registry of State Judicial Administrations, she thought she heard a gentle click on the telephone as she picked it up, as though someone on the line were hanging up, though that made no sense here in the West. Instead of asking her questions over the phone, she decided to go to the office and see if she could meet again in person with Kreisgut or Mannheim.

On the way there, a tall, rather portly man followed her along the street and onto the bus. He was handsome, wearing a dark windbreaker, his face broad and unlined. She chided herself for being paranoid. Stopping in front of the bureau, Bettina thrust her hands into the pocket of her jeans and waited. There were two men now—the other one slimmer, with a mustache and elongated silver eyeglasses—heading toward her. They were upon her too fast for her to make it through the revolving doors, and the one with the mustache grabbed her Rollei with both hands and tugged as hard as he could while the other man yanked her arm behind her. She struggled and screamed, kicking them, clutching the precious camera.

They could not have it—they could not take this from her—the photos of her child were all she had left now, and they were hers!

The leather strap was caught around her neck, and just as it began to slide painfully over her earlobes, another pair of hands entered the fray, and a whistle was blown into her eardrum, and it was like a shriek inside her head, and she covered her ears with her palms and screamed, and the men released her as if she had caught on fire. They began to run, and two uniformed West German policemen gave chase.

The police at the station near the Spree were alternately bored by her story and incensed. In truth, she was no one special: tens of thousands of people had left someone they loved behind the Iron Curtain. They explained what they knew about the surveillance patterns in the East, emphasizing that once someone was flagged by the MfS, they were pursued until otherwise instructed. It was not unheard of for undercover agents to snatch people off the streets of West Berlin.

They were in a kind of cold war, they said, where the fighting was secretive but relentless, where the enemies were often from the same country, sometimes even the same family.

Bettina had few options. She could fight for her daughter through the court system, but given the stature of her husband, his role in the *Ministerium für Staatssicherheit*, it was unlikely this bid would be successful. And even if it was, the ruling would be hard to enforce: Annaliese Nietz was a minor living with her biological father in a repressive political system.

Stop, stop—she waved a trembling hand in front of her face. Her arms had been yanked in the wrong direction, and the muscles in her upper arms ached. The headache from earlier had descended from the crown of her head and taken up residence around her eye sockets. The fluorescent lights were so bright they made her eyes pulse uncomfortably, and she was having trouble focusing.

Back at the hotel, she switched rooms to one on a higher floor and lay down on the tidy coverlet, her bag packed and in the corner. Truth was, she was no closer to solving her problem than she had been before arriving in Berlin. Werner had lied to her; he could not be trusted. Any ground she gained would have to be in spite of his efforts to keep them apart; he would not help her. She thought of Peter's book and struggled to rid herself of the poisonous thoughts about Werner that led only to a black hole of grief and helplessness. She could not change him. He was right that she had made the choice to marry him, she had teased him with the possibility of winning her love, and she'd snatched it away from him in the most shameful way possible.

And yet. At the café she had seen in him a veiled tenderness, despite his boastful talk when he showed her the photo of his family. Clearly he adored them. He had failed to make Bettina love him, but he had found others who did. Irmgard, as she held the baby, as she talked to Annaliese, had seemed content, relaxed in a way she had not been back in Saargen when she was alone, a widow with no children. Those two had found one another, against all odds, and had built a family together. Did Bettina want to destroy that too?

That sweet look Anna had given the boy in the wheelchair. The way she had glanced up at Irmgard, asking permission to pick him up. The evident warmth of their bond. If that was broken, it would be almost impossible for her to get back. Anna would miss out on the boy's childhood, and on the childhoods of her other siblings too. What would that do to the girl—would it harden her soul in a way she would never be able to fix? This went directly against what Peter had been trying to assert in his book. It went against what Bettina knew, in her heart, to be noble.

She lay fully clothed on the bed, her cheek against the pillow, face toward the wall. Over the past decade, her camera had shown her a world that was vast and infinitely varied, in which people struggled to find their place, whether geographic or emotional, a place they felt at home. Everyone suffered. Everyone was clawing his or her way toward the very same goal.

We all want the same thing, she thought as she drifted to sleep. And she wasn't sure if she could be granted her wish if it was at the cost of her child's happiness.

49

Werner watched Peter from behind the mirrored window. Over the years he had been in this prison many times for meetings, participating in endless hours of conversation about budgeting for prisoner maintenance and proper surveillance. Never once had he engaged with the prisoners themselves. He had never even observed them, at least not up close like this. Sometimes they'd be trooping through the prison yard as he was chauffeured into the complex, and occasionally an inmate would be the one bringing in refreshments for longer meetings. In all these interactions, Werner had not said a word to any of them.

A senior guard turned up with a set of keys and confirmed that authorization had been granted for Werner to enter the interrogation room. Another few minutes till the stenographer arrived. The guard opened the first chamber, let him in, and left. The door clanged shut behind Werner. Werner then used the key to open the second door, and when that one shut behind him, a buzzer sounded.

Peter was sitting upright on the stool, his eyes open and clear. He was haggard, with graying stubble and a hollowness under his cheekbones that made him look old, though he was younger than Werner by at least a decade. His blond hair, bedraggled, was dark at the sides with streaks of gray throughout, very thick—Werner's mind went instantly to Anna, to Bettina, to their thick hair. He pushed the thought aside, as he had always done. He could never know for sure whose child she was, and he had long ago determined that it made no difference to him. The room was like an ice chamber, a tang like wet metal in the air. There was also the pungent smell of a man's sweat. Werner felt wildly overheated yet had goose bumps on his forearms. He put down the briefcase on a table, got himself a paper cup from a side table, filled it with water from a pitcher, and drank it down in one long sip.

Peter gazed at him. "Werner Nietz," he said quietly.

"Are you thirsty?" Werner asked.

"Yes," Peter said. "Thank you."

He held a cup of water to Peter's lips, and after he drank it down, Werner refilled it for him. The air in the room was so close it felt as though neither of them could draw one full breath with the other man there, just centimeters away.

"Can you tell me, please"—Peter hacked into his fist, then looked up at Werner with reddened eyes—"what happened to her? To Bettina."

"I'll be asking the questions," Werner said, throwing his cup in the bin. "Not you."

"I have to know. Please, I need—I just need to understand. It's driving me insane. Can you understand? I must know . . ."

And then, to Werner's horror, the man's face crumpled in on itself, and he began to weep unabashedly. Thick blond brows came together, pulling skin with them, pinching his face into a terrible grimace. Until this moment, Werner had thought seeing Peter Brenner in cuffs would be glorious. He had wanted to come here to remind himself who had come out on top in the end. On the way over, anger burbling in his chest, he'd expected a triumphant surge as soon as he laid eyes on him, but that had not happened. Instead, he was baffled: Was the man genuine?

Werner took a seat at the table and studied his hands. "Brenner, you lack a moral backbone," he finally said, his voice steady and low. "I'm not surprised you ended up in here."

Peter remained silent, and they looked at each other for a long time. Werner thought of the men in the room behind the mirror, listening dispassionately; it bothered him. "You stole a man's wife. You took what wasn't yours," he finally continued. "You're a pig."

But it didn't feel good, insulting the man in this way. Not while he was crying. Werner remembered when he was a teenager and the boys who'd played on the school soccer team called him a cripple, how he'd bitten back the tears, how they seared the back of his throat.

"Did she die? I heard rumors," Peter asked. His lips were cracked and dark in the center, his eyes bloodshot. "Can you at least tell me that?"

Werner had inadequately prepared for this exchange. It would have been far, far better to have had some sort of game plan. Knowing he was so close by, Werner had been compelled to come see the man in person, but now that he was here, his motives seemed sordid.

He stood up abruptly. This was not going to be possible: he could not talk with this man in front of other people. He could not countenance the interest or lack thereof on the part of the guards, the stenographer, those listening in. This was *his* life they were talking about; these things had happened to *him*. He nodded toward the window, and a moment later a guard appeared at the door.

"You're leaving?" Peter asked, wild eyed. He tried to stand, but his arms were attached to the back of his chair, and he could barely rise. "Wait, wait, you—"

Werner ignored him and left. Once outside the room, he informed the guard that he would be taking the prisoner outside into the yard. He would keep him handcuffed and write the report himself upon completion of the interview. After showing him his badge, he held out his hand for the keys.

"Comrade, that's highly unusual," the guard said, drawing his brows together.

"You take orders from me, Fuchs," Werner said, staring at him. "Give me the keys immediately."

Something peculiar was dawning on him. There was some of Peter in his little girl; he had seen it as they sat in the interrogation room staring at one another. The shape of their faces, even the lean build of their bodies. The eyes a little wide apart, a malleable mouth. All these years he had understood that it was possible Anna was not actually his, but now, having seen Brenner in cuffs, he was beset with unease that felt not unlike shame. What did this mean, if it was in fact true that Peter was her father? He could have the man sent away for good, and the problem would be erased. Anna didn't know and need never know. But he thought of Bettina in the Ratskeller, that freighted look they'd exchanged, infused with all the pain they'd caused one another. What happened to Peter didn't matter to Werner all that much, but he hated that Bettina might think he hadn't been true to his word.

After all, he was an honorable man. He prided himself on being rigorous and correct. It was important to him that Bettina understand that he was not a liar and a cheat, as she likely believed. Because, in fact, he was a man who kept his promises, as every good man should.

Out in the yard, the September afternoon had cooled down considerably, and there was a breeze that blew the clouds above the horizon line, striations of white like cotton candy in a blue, blue sky. Werner had developed the habit of noticing the texture and colors of the sky whenever he was outdoors. It was something Bettina had always remarked on when they were together, and he'd been charmed; he'd never paid attention to these things before.

Peter Brenner's hands were still fastened together behind his torso, and he walked beside Werner with his face tipped upward. He squinted hard. The light was very bright, and even Werner had trouble adjusting after the dark of the prison interior.

"Ahh, the air," said Peter. The vague sound of the city—cars and some sort of gentle buzzing—drifted alongside them as they walked. "I thought you were leaving. I am . . . I'm so very relieved."

"You are *relieved*?" Werner said. Though he'd once seen Peter from afar, he'd never actually spoken with him, and he was startled by the gentleness of his voice. He had imagined him to be a blowhard. Where was the man's anger or his fear? It was mystifying to Werner; anger would be so much easier to deal with than this disquieting acquiescence. Some of the reviews of Brenner's book had puzzled over this same thing: the writer's apparent lack of bitterness, as evidenced by his protagonist ultimately deciding against suicide. This was thought to be revolutionary, enlightened, revealing a refreshing lack of cynicism. It was hailed as a movement that urged forgiveness over self-righteousness.

"Oh, yes! Not knowing is the hardest of all," Peter said. "And they both just disappeared. There were times when I didn't think I could keep going."

"Well, Bettina is certainly gone."

Peter stopped walking, his eyes watery holes in a gray face. "So she is—she really *is* dead?"

Werner took pity on him and shook his head. He recognized in his expression something of the emotion he himself experienced when thinking of Bettina. "No . . . no. She lives in America. For a long time now."

A low groan escaped from Peter. "America! I . . . it's just, I thought she might have committed suicide."

They allowed this to sit between them as they walked along the perimeter wall.

"So. You wrote a book, and it landed you in prison," Werner said, indicating the walls and the guard towers with his hand. "Why would you draw attention to yourself in that way; don't you know better?"

"Isn't this your doing, my arrest?" Peter kept shuffling ahead, his shoulders bent forward like an old man's. There was a guard not that far from them with a gun strapped over his shoulder, and another on the wall to their left, pacing, watching them.

His anger swooped back in just as quickly as it had dissipated. "Brenner, God dammit. I kept my word. I promised Bettina—if she left, I wouldn't interfere with you, and I didn't. You were already in the system; I had no control over that. They'd been watching you for years."

"I wanted to kill you when she disappeared," Peter said. "I should tell you that."

"And yet you didn't, did you? So it seems we live in a civilized society after all."

"The only reason I didn't . . ." Peter stopped and looked him in the eye. "I couldn't. I was too afraid. I didn't know what might happen to her if I hurt you. And anyway, I was the one who'd started it all."

"I suppose I should be grateful, then." Each time Peter spoke, his candor chipped away at Werner's understanding of who the man was. He didn't know what he should be feeling, but what he'd *thought* he wanted to feel was triumphant.

"And Anna? Where did you two go?"

The child. The child who was Werner's—and yet was perhaps not really his. Everything now revolved around her, really. His priority was to protect her, to keep her safe in his family, with her brothers and sister, living the simple routine of her emerging adolescence. "We're here now, in Berlin. I have a family. She has siblings. She's a happy child, healthy and inquisitive."

Peter made a strange sound in the back of his throat. "After, right when Bettina disappeared, I went back to Apolonienmarkt, you know. I saw you with the baby. I thought, at least . . . I thought, I can see her every now and then, little Anna. I can watch the two of you walking into town or playing in the grass together, or maybe on the beach in the summertime. I don't know. I comforted myself with knowing that she wasn't that far away, even if I'd lost Bettina."

"And what did *I* lose? Did you ever think of that?" Werner let out a disdainful puff of air. "Did you think everything you wanted was yours for the taking?"

"Oh. No, no—I never thought that. I know it's terrible, a terrible thing for you, but when I met her . . ." Peter stopped once again to readjust his arms behind his back, grimacing. The gray of his prison uniform was stained at the pits and knees. "At first I wasn't thinking much of anything except, well. That it was imperative I see her again. I knew it was wrong. I knew that from the very beginning. I was always . . . no, I still am very sorry for that."

Werner didn't want to hear it—and yet hadn't he felt that same magnetic pull when he'd first met Bettina? Wasn't there something about her that had drawn him in, despite knowing even then that she would likely never love him? "And you had to take what was already mine? Haven't you had someone else in your life?"

"I might take issue with her being 'yours.' Do you think Bettina will ever belong to anyone, really?"

Werner waved away the distinction. "So you have no family; is that right?"

"I had a wife, a long time ago. She died. And a son, he—"

"A child?" Werner wondered why he hadn't noticed that in the files. "Where is he now?"

"They both died. And he, the boy—his name was Thomas—he wasn't mine biologically, but it didn't matter. That never matters once you fall in love, and me, I fell in love with him the minute I set eyes on him."

Werner had to turn away in the face of Brenner's palpable sorrow. So the man was an idealist, a dreamer. This was a trait Werner would have sneered at publicly but one he knew, privately, that he shared. An unsettling feeling almost like camaraderie prickled at him. "Your crime, then," he said, "the reason you're here? It's because you wrote a book. Tell me, is it a love letter to my wife?"

"That's not how the authorities see it," Peter said. "They say it's a tirade, that I want to bring down the system. But I was simply asking questions that are important. We have to continue assessing, figuring out where we're going wrong and what we're doing right, don't we? This attempt to silence us, it's not sustainable. We're individuals, all of us. Our culture won't accept the suppression of art, of dialogue. Don't you see that?"

Werner did not feel inclined to argue this point. He saw little value in art. When Bettina had carried that old camera around with her everywhere, snapping photos, he'd never been able to think of it as anything more than a pointless hobby.

"And they didn't like the play I'd directed," Peter continued. "*Pinocchio*. The old version—too much moral complexity, apparently. He's a rogue; he's beaten and executed. I thought that was interesting for the children to explore—what happens when you don't behave; is the punishment commensurate with the crime?"

"Ah yes, I can see where the problem lies," Werner said, laughing lightly. "Moral complexity is most certainly frowned upon."

Peter turned to him. "But what do *you* think?"

"I'm afraid I'm not in a position to have personal opinions about these sorts of things." He thought of Bettina's father's books, how he enjoyed reading them even though they were out of favor. He motioned brusquely to one of the guards to come over. "I must go now. We've talked enough."

"But wait, wait," Peter said. "What will happen to me? Where will I be sent?"

"You should have thought about that *before* you smuggled your book out of the country."

"You're not an evil man," Peter said. They stared hard at one another as the guard trotted toward them.

Werner frowned. He broke the gaze and tugged at his jacket sleeves. "Of course not."

"I'm glad you're not the one who had me locked up. That you kept your promise to her."

The guard prodded Brenner, and they walked back toward the entrance to the cellblock. From some other part of the complex, a siren sounded, the notes high and lingering, a plaintive wail.

Picking his way along the river, Werner studied the meandering barbed wire fence that split the waterway in two, one side east, the other west. Looking to his left, he traced with his eyes the outline of the fence as it emerged from the water and met up with the wall. Barbed wire, metal fences, and slapped-together bricks. He didn't like it; it was all very well to make rules and enforce them, but keeping an entire nation captive seemed a sign of weakness, not strength. Because he had approved the budgets, he knew there were bombs buried in the water, dogs who patrolled no-man's-land, sharpshooters in the towers. It would continue to grow and grow, this wall, reinforced with hundreds of tons of mortar.

This part of the riverbank was highly industrial. He passed mounds of chemical waste and stretches of earth pounded by large freight movers heading to the loading docks. For a few minutes he rested on an upturned plastic tub and looked out over the water. The river was quite wide here, and a few rusty barges were tied up to the dock.

Close by, a guard tower stood, and two soldiers leaned over the edge, smoking cigarettes. The tips of their guns poked over the railing. Werner waved, and one of the men nodded his head in response. He was thinking about the picture he'd glimpsed in Bettina's file: her eyes had had no life to them; her face was drained of all color.

Truth was, he loved her still.

It galled him, and yet it was such a familiar feeling, like a friend he knew well and could count on. It was something true and immutable, something he would carry with him to his grave. Why this was so, he didn't know. He wanted her to think of him as honorable. He yearned for her respect, her gratitude even.

The car ferried him back north to Normannenstraße, and he sat himself down behind his desk. Embedded in Werner's mind was a paragraph he had memorized long ago from page two of the directive Bieder gave him when he'd left Rügen: *Hate is simultaneously a lasting and strongly motivating force in behavior. It must, therefore, consciously be used and made stronger in clandestine work as the driving force behind difficult operative assignments.*

Indeed. Hate made you loyal, and loyalty was the most respected trait in the DDR. It gave you energy and made you ruthless. But was that enough to ensure a good life? Of course it was not; he knew this. At home tonight he would sit at a large round table with Anna, Petra, Kurt in his special chair, and baby Henning on Irmgard's lap. They would eat cold cuts, and he'd drink a beer or two. They might play a board game or cards, and later he'd crawl into bed—aching and tired—next to a woman he loved who seemed to love him back.

Hate did nothing for them.

Today had reminded him of this important fact: Werner was actually one of the lucky ones.

50

For the next few days, Bettina did not leave her hotel room. The Rollei was locked in the safe downstairs, behind the reception desk, and she did not answer the phone or report back to George about the photos she'd taken in East Berlin. She did not change out of her clothes and only got up from bed in order to go to the bathroom. On the second day she ordered herself some breakfast, but otherwise she lay on the nylon coverlet, trying to decide what to do.

Before leaving, she had peeled the old photo of Anna in the metal tub from her wall, and now she stared at it until the image swam in front of her eyes and ceased to mean anything. Her fingers were sticky from the tape on the back. The picture had faded so much that it seemed not to represent someone real any longer, just the ghost of a person. There were two other pictures Bettina loved that she'd salvaged from the old rolls and brought along with her: one of Anna as an infant in her crib and another of her swaddled in ridiculously thick woolen clothing that barely allowed her to move. Bettina lay on the hotel bed looking at them for hours, but they aroused in her only confusion: This child was gone, and there was a stranger in her stead. Was it possible that Bettina would never get to know the real person, Annaliese Nietz, daughter of a mother both brave and fearful, a woman of contradictions?

With a marker in hand, she reread Peter's book, underlining sentences that spoke to her. She cried so violently that her throat ached with the effort, and it was not possible to cry any more.

It was over. She knew she must stop fighting for Anna.

Some part of her was relieved to have realized this, to be giving up. It would have to be all right. Anna would stay content and oblivious; it was what was best for her. If Werner was ill, the girl had a support system in place. But Bettina had not yet determined how this decision would affect the trajectory of her own life, let alone the near future. Reading Peter's book again, it felt as though she were having a long argument with him about love and forgiveness, about hope and creativity and moving on. She imagined him as he wrote it, in his room at the *Pfarrhaus* or in the youth center, thinking of her. And now Peter was in jail. How could she try to heal from giving up all hope of Anna? How could she go back to Chicago as though everything were normal, worrying about her "career" or even what she should photograph next?

As she struggled with these doubts, the black shadows under her closed eyelids turned to bright yellow, a blinding flash of color, and she saw an image of herself in the rape fields, lying on a scratchy woolen blanket with a man who was not wearing his shirt, his skin reddened by the sun and blotchy with freckles. In this dream, Peter lifted his arm to reach out to a tiny child, a little girl with dark hair not yet one year old, revealing skin as pale as the underside of a fish. They were marooned in a sea of yellow, and whether they were really there or not, whether they were old or young or even alive, whether they were physically close or far away from each other, it seemed to her that as long as the spirit of their love continued to shift over the flower heads, they were still together on some plane of existence.

She could not give up on him. She could not simply go back to her life.

A large pad of paper embossed with the hotel insignia lay on a table by the window, and on the evening of the second day as the sun sank behind the grimy buildings of West Berlin, Bettina rose from the bed, found a pen, and began writing a letter to Werner. Her fingers were connected not to her brain but to her heart, she told herself; she must allow her heart to speak without censorship. The rule she made for herself was to write without stopping or rereading. She would write until she had written everything she had to say to him.

She wrote about how she knew, the day of the bombing in Saargen, that Werner was a man with a good heart, but she should never have married him. He'd had a right to be happy, and she had not been the woman to make him happy. She wrote that she had not deserved to lose her child, that he had been needlessly cruel. Her anger spilled out, and she let it. The words she wrote became spiky and smaller and tighter as she unleashed her bitterness. She was lonely, and she hadn't expected her life to turn out like this. She wrote about the life she had missed, the steep price she had paid.

And yet—she was not thinking so much anymore of what she had lost, she told him. Seeing Annaliese had rocked her understanding of what the three of them deserved or didn't deserve. She could see that their daughter was growing up to be an incredible young woman. Poised, alert. Thoughtful. She played music and was creative, had a family she clearly loved. If anyone deserved anything, it was this child. And what was it that was currently most vital to the girl, that fed her confidence and her imagination, that was helping to shape her into the woman she would one day be? *Her family.*

Bettina thought they each deserved their hard-won happiness. Perhaps one day Werner and Irmgard would see fit to tell Annaliese the complicated story of her past, and the child could make up her own mind about whether to seek out her real mother or not. That would be up to them.

As for the photos she had taken, they were precious, invaluable, and she would keep them to herself. Anna didn't deserve to be drawn into an international story of intrigue and repression when she was so cheerfully forging ahead with her life, the ordinary life of a young girl still starry eyed and eager.

But Bettina had one request.

It was the only request she would ever make of him.

Now she *was* begging—now she was on her knees, begging him to hear her out.

Could he find it in his heart to give her this one gift: to find Peter Brenner and release him?

In the lobby, hotel guests glanced at her sideways as she exited the elevator, feet bare on the cold tile, her dark hair tangled after days of neglect. Just as a clerk began to approach her, a concerned look on his face, Bettina slid behind a pillar and put one finger up. *Give me just a second. Just one second.*

On a two-seater couch there sat a man wearing a black hat and a sports coat. Next to him was a woman in heels and a beige suit reading the newspaper. On a bench in the far corner, a boy of seven or so was playing with a small toy Bettina could not quite see. And then, close to him but not with him, there stood a young man, no older than twenty perhaps. He shifted weight from one foot to another, rubbed a finger over his wristwatch. He lifted one shoulder, then the other, looked behind him, checked the time.

Moving quickly but with soft steps, Bettina picked her way across the lobby toward him. By the time he had stiffened in response, registering with alarm that she was acknowledging his presence, she was standing right in front of him.

"Give this to Director Nietz immediately," she said. She placed the envelope in his hands and held his eyes steadily. "Did you hear me? This is important. Go. Now."

As though it were possible to simply *will* people to do good, Bettina spent the next days thinking back to the early weeks of her married life. How she and Werner had yearned for simplicity and regularity, for safety. How they'd prayed for an armistice, for the chance to capitulate and rebuild. White sheets began floating from church windows; a hoisted scrap of white cloth hung over the town hall door. Each night as darkness fell, Werner and Bettina talked quietly in the house, waiting for soldiers to arrive, not knowing to which army they would belong. Would it be the Americans, who (they dared hope) might bring with them the faith of a people so new—their country barely 150 years old—that they were still motivated by the naive belief that people around the world would embrace their enlightened ideas on democracy and capitalism? Or perhaps it would be the French or British, those stodgy old colonialists, accustomed to the push and pull of peoples fighting against one another and against their conquerors. But it had been much worse. It turned out that on the mainland, below Stralsund, Rokossovsky's armies were pushing north. It would be the Russians.

Werner had returned one morning with the news that the Red Army was on the outskirts of Bergen. Though the bridge to Stralsund had been destroyed, this did not deter them. He and Bettina set about scouring the place for political artifacts from the last few years. They found some old pamphlets and two pins—one with a gold swastika and the other silver on a red enamel background—that Werner had been given at work. These items were taken into the garden, burned until they were unrecognizable, and then buried next to the bomb shelter, as deep down as the still-hard earth would allow.

Tanks soon rolled into Saargen, accompanied by a constant low rumbling that echoed in the empty streets like an oncoming storm. A regiment of Russian soldiers marched in an uneasy formation in front, and vehicles filled with administrators followed close behind. There were no crowds to greet them. Old Hans Janslav took off a young Russian soldier's head with his ancient hunting rifle before he was mobbed by exhausted soldiers. Bettina and Werner had already been crouching in the storage room next to their bedroom for eleven hours when the pounding on their door began. The air inside was thick with the smell of body odor. A small receptacle for waste was already full.

During those long hours, Bettina held on to Werner, and they spoke only sporadically. In the dire reality of the fast-approaching end, this human body next to hers, the beating heart, the clenched jaw and kind eyes, meant everything. Looking at her husband's crooked legs stretched out on the wooden floorboards, his barrel torso bent under the low, sloped roof, Bettina had been thankful for his presence. Waiting, waiting together for their future to begin. Waiting for an altered life, for what they thought would be freedom. They clutched each other, their bodies covered in sweat, and prayed to a god in whom they did not believe that the Russians would go away.

But the Russians had not gone away. Not ever.

Two days later there was a knock on the door of her hotel room. Freshly showered, her hair wet, Bettina opened the door to see the clerk standing in the hall.

"You've been waiting for this, I believe," he said, smiling.

Her lips quivered as she tried to smile back at him. Before tearing open the envelope, she stood by the window, open to let in some air, and promised herself that no matter what was in the letter, she would be all right. He could not make or break her life, not anymore. Once, they had relied on each other, and now they had cobbled together their own separate destinies. But it was possible, not likely but possible, that he understood that she had loved him in her own way, and while she could not hope to fully understand him or forgive him, she would in so many ways be forever indebted to him, no matter what choices he now made.

51

The car idled at the curb in the early-morning hours, in a street so still that only the birds, dark gray against a gray sky, agitated the sleepy quiet. The river wound lazily just a few hundred meters from them, a black muscle slinking through the divided city. The banks here on the western slope fell steeply toward the water, overgrown by weeds that, in the morning darkness, looked impenetrable and unruly. Sitting in the back of an unmarked police vehicle, Bettina leaned her forehead against the window. No one spoke. There were two agents up front, occasionally straightening from their slump when the radio crackled, otherwise immobile and silent.

> SIX AM SHARP AT GLIENICKE BRÜCKE. NO
> PHOTOGRAPHS OR WE WILL ABORT. RELEASE
> CONDITIONAL ON COMPLIANCE: NO NEWS
> REPORTS OR PUBLICITY.

There had been no names in the telex from Normannenstraße, no indication of why or how Werner had engineered this, and as the time ticked by, she felt this release was as precarious and unlikely as snow in June. Perhaps Werner just wanted to play games—raising and then dashing her hopes. Whether he was capable of that or not, she didn't know.

Six o'clock came, and the men in the front seat began checking their watches every few minutes.

"Never punctual," one of them murmured.

"Do they ever pull out? The East Germans?" she asked. "Promise, and then not show up?"

The men exchanged a glance, and one of them turned to her. "To be honest, it's the first time for us," he said. "We don't really know what to expect. Let's just keep waiting. We'll stay till we hear something to the contrary."

Bettina fiddled with the collar of her shirt. Over her lifetime she had learned all about being patient. There was nothing to be gained by railing against reality. In her lap, she held Peter's book, and from time to time she leafed through it to read the sections she had underlined.

> *Hannes knew that death is not always recognizable.
> "There is death in life," Rilke wrote in 1907, "and it
> astonishes me that we pretend to ignore this: death,
> whose unforgiving presence we experience with each
> change we survive because we must learn to die slowly.
> We must learn to die: That is all of life." Hannes hauled
> the bag over his shoulder: He would not do this. He
> would not live as though already dead. What was the
> point?*

> *Each memory, a gem of limitless value. The light of
> which illuminated not only the sadness but the unend-
> ing goodness too.*

"There is beauty in sorrow," the man said to Isadore, but then he laughed, a braying so obnoxious that the ticket taker cast him a suspicious look. "I'm sorry," he added, "we're all doing the very best we can, aren't we?"

A slow sharpening, a darkening of shapes, coming into perspective: figures in the distance, crosscut by steel girders and a tall iron fence that closed off the mouth of the bridge. The two policemen lurched forward simultaneously. One of them grabbed binoculars.

"Is it him?" the other one asked.

"I don't know," his partner said.

"I've got to get out," Bettina hissed, yanking at the door. "I can't breathe."

"Stay here," the one with the binoculars ordered sharply. "Do nothing! No surprises."

They sat, the three of them, bodies tensed and compelled toward the bridge but held in place by doubt. Bettina took the binoculars and peered through them.

Was it him?

A man walking, wearing a black anorak that swallowed his upper body. His gait uneven but determined. He walked alone, arms stiff at his sides. In one hand he carried a small bag.

He was close now—so close she could see the light hair darkened at the sides, the pallor that radiated from his skin. The pull of disbelief tugging on his features. His eyes scanned ahead frantically, his head moving a little from side to side.

It was him. It was Peter.

Guards in uniform and an official in a black suit clustered at the gate, and then it swung open, and Peter Brenner walked through. The time it took for him to confer with the men, to look up and past them to her vehicle, and, finally, to disengage and make his way toward her was the time it had taken her to live her entire life.

She climbed out and took a step toward him. He stopped and furrowed pale brows. Raising a hand to her dyed hair, she frowned a little. Of course she didn't look like herself. "It's just a bad haircut," she said.

His stunned smile stripped away the years and made it seem as though she might be able to bear a lifetime without her child. He was very slender, and there was no strength in his embrace. But in a way nothing had changed—the smell of his skin was familiar; the sound of his voice saying her name made her want to weep.

"Bettina, Bettina . . . ," he said again and again, as though testing the taste of it on his tongue.

Reaching for her hand, he pressed her fingers hard against his mouth. "I can't believe it," he said. "How is this possible? What are you doing here?"

His face was gaunt, his neck too long now that his graying hair was short, but the eyes were dark and full of life. He looked skittishly at the others pressing around them now, their voices loud and intrusive. She caught the fear in his gaze and saw his mouth turn down; she knew he was remembering Rügen, the beaches and the ocean, the life he had led, and wondering what was to come now. This happened to her sometimes: She'd catch a whiff of sea air and think of her fish shop, the old wood that gleamed like a woman's freshly brushed hair, the wide white beaches. And then her mind would turn to the fish factory, and she'd hear the terrific screech of the machines, the fuzzy pop of the loudspeakers readying for an announcement, and she would know that that life was over—and good riddance to it.

They would talk. She would share with him the impossible ideas that might now be possible, the life they might have together. Perhaps his book would be published in America; he could write, and she could take pictures, and what a formidable team they would make! If she took the job with *Time*, if they moved to New York City . . . but she saw his skittish eyes on the others, the tension in his jaw.

They embraced, clinging to one another as though only now understanding this was real. "I saw her," Bettina murmured into his shoulder. "I saw Annaliese."

They held still in each other's arms.

"I think she's happy."

The silence between them was filled with all they had not said to each other in the past decade. They would have to find their way toward each other one word at a time.

"Last week, he came to see me. Werner," Peter whispered back to her.

His voice had not changed, but he talked haltingly, and she held her breath for fear of saying something wrong. She was perplexed: last week? "He . . . you saw him? When?"

"A week ago, maybe more. He said he hadn't been aware, you know. That I was in prison."

She pulled away slightly. "Do you believe him?"

"Does it matter?"

Did it matter? She pressed her lips together, and a rush of something hot and light went through her, something like joy or relief. Something that released a deadening tension in her chest, made her want to laugh. "I read your book," she said. "You must keep writing, Peter."

After a moment she stepped back and took his hand in hers. She was calmer now. Peter's single traveling bag was placed in the trunk of the vehicle. It contained everything he owned, and it was almost empty.

They settled into the back seat, leaning against each other. The trip to her hotel seemed monstrously long, and they were silent. She thought of Apolonienmarkt, the *Pfarrhaus*, the summer meadows—all the places where they'd stolen time to be together. As the car pulled off the main road, the city streets became choked with people heading to work. They stopped at a traffic light. Bettina rolled down the window to peer out, and Peter leaned over as far as he could toward the fresh air and breathed in deeply. A quivering halo of fresh sunlight hovered over everything.

As they gazed out the open window, his body pressing into hers from behind, Peter brought his hand around her shoulder and slipped it into the collar of her cotton shirt. The air coming in from outside was cool, but his hand against her skin was hot. With this one gesture he reclaimed their right to happiness.

EPILOGUE

Radical Changes in East German Academia

Brightest Stars Allowed to Study Abroad

By the Associated Press

January 21, 1977

New York, NY—In an unprecedented move, the repressive regime of the German Democratic Republic (GDR) is allowing young academics to study abroad.

Minister of Education Helga Labs indicated Friday that the country is granting special visas and scholarships to four outstanding science students seeking advanced degrees.

Herman Gutig, 25, from Leipzig, will complete postgraduate research in biomedical sciences at the University of Wolverhampton, Wolverhampton, England.

Jan Kleboviz, 26, from Dresden, will pursue a PhD in nuclear engineering from the Massachusetts Institute of Technology, Cambridge, MA.

Annaliese Nietz, 23, from East Berlin, will begin PhD studies in environmental engineering at Columbia University, New York City, NY.

Käthe Mann, 28, from Schwerin, will complete a dual international masters in mathematical informatics at University Cathleen de l'Ouest, France.

Previously, East German athletes have been granted permission to travel outside the GDR's borders to attend special events. This is the first time East German students

will be allowed to live abroad for
extended periods of time.

"These young stars will return with
the latest tools to help strengthen
our fine homeland," Labs said.

ACKNOWLEDGMENTS

My family left Germany when I was two years old. It's often the case that children reject their parents' influence, especially in families that straddle different cultures, and I'm so grateful for the patience and commitment my father and mother, Peter and Occu Schumann, modeled for me. German school on Saturdays; transcontinental drives from London to Freiburg; lengthy, vigorous hikes; frequent nudity (without embarrassment!); punctuality—I resisted all of it, and yet it made me who I am and drove me to build a life with stories at its center. Thank you for sharing what it meant to live through your extraordinary experiences. Thank you for taking me to Rügen.

Much gratitude also to my aunt Jane Laack, ninety-four years old and strong as ever, whose deep love of the island is infectious—and whose stories would make your hair curl. My German relatives, including Herbert and Gerda Fritz, not only helped fire my imagination but endlessly impressed me with their fortitude and sense of adventure.

Eve Bridburg, executive director of GrubStreet: I'll never forget the day you called to say that against your better judgement (you were inundated with work), you'd read the first few pages and *just had to know what happened.* I'm so grateful that you believed in my ability to tell this story—it's what gave me the energy to keep at it.

Thank you to Erin Harris, my incredible agent, who continues to surprise and delight me with her attention to detail, commitment, and know-how. She is both a dreamer and a doer. Huge thanks to Jodi Warshaw and the team at Lake Union, who took a gamble with this story. Your enthusiasm for the characters and the time period is gratifying. Tiffany Yates Martin encouraged me not to shy away from pivotal turning points, gently and assuredly helping me deepen the book. I am grateful to David Drummond who—twice now—has designed the most compelling and beautiful cover an author could dream of.

Kathleen Buckstaff: How can I ever thank you sufficiently? Whenever I worried whether this story would move readers the way I hoped it might, all I had to do was think of your ten-minute-long voice mail, that unbridled outpouring of support, your absolute certainty that this story was worth telling.

In the early days before I found my GrubStreet community, I was lucky enough to have a few generous and insightful readers who are themselves gifted writers: Hugh Kennedy, Billie Fitzpatrick, and Erica Ferencik—thank you for the hours you've spent with these characters. Tom Jenks and David Colson pushed me to keep trying to get it right. My dear friend Kristi Perry provided moral and creative support, as well as good laughs—thank you! Jennifer de Poyen, Christiane Alsop, Anne Marie Welsh, Jennifer Perini, Susan and John Howard, Amy Beckwith, and Lynne Griffin were astute and insightful readers, and I'm immensely grateful to them.

Once again I've been so heartened by the generosity of authors who took the time to help me. Warm thanks to these novelists who, despite touring with bestselling books; teaching; and managing pregnancies, summer vacations, and deadlines, supported *This Terrible Beauty*: Rachel Barenbaum, Jillian Cantor, Christopher Castellani, Eoin Dempsey, Erica Ferencik, Olivia Hawker, and Maria Hummel.

I wrote much of this novel in the Writers' Room of Boston. What an amazing resource: a quiet place to work full of dedicated, talented people. Also, many thanks to the Virginia Center for the Creative Arts and the Hemingway House in Hull, Massachusetts, where I toiled on rewrites in a magical setting.

During the many years of researching this book, I was inspired and informed by writers, historians, and filmmakers too numerous to thank here. Please see my website (www.katrinschumann.com) for a more detailed list of the talented people who fueled my work—from novelists such as Bernhard Schlink (*The Reader*), Jenna Blum (*Those Who Save Us*), and Eugen Ruge (*In Times of Fading Light*), to nonfiction writers such as Anna Funder (*Stasiland*), Jana Hensel (*After the Wall*), Timothy Garton Ash (*The File*), and Joel Agee (*Twelve Years*), to directors of movies such as *Good Bye, Lenin!* (Wolfgang Becker) and *The Lives of Others* (Florian Henckel von Donnersmarck), to researchers at the German Propaganda Archive at Calvin College, to name just a few.

I was lucky enough to have teachers whose impact on me was profound and lasting, especially Dr. Richard Cooper from Brasenose College, Oxford, who filled me with enthusiasm for beautiful words, romance, and history, and Penelope Nelson, my fifth-grade teacher from PS8 in Brooklyn, whose enthusiastic encouragement to be true to myself stuck with me as I was trying to figure out where I belonged after leaving America when I was eleven.

And where would I be now if it weren't for my partner in crime, Kevin O'Marah? You make everything possible. You listen hard; what a precious gift. Your steadfast belief in me fuels my work and my life. Ubuntu, my love.

BOOK CLUB QUESTIONS

1. Do you think this book is more a love story or a political one? In what ways do the public and private angles play off each other?

2. The novel's title, *This Terrible Beauty*, is from a line in William Butler Yeats's poem "Easter 1916," which is about the steep price people pay in their brutal yet valiant battle for independence. How do you think this connects with East Germany's struggle to define itself after Hitler? In what ways do you think it might also apply to Bettina's personal troubles?

3. In this story, we follow closely as Bettina and Werner try to rebuild their lives after the devastation of World War II. Are these two lost souls good for each other, or do they hold each other back?

4. We are told that Irmgard Bandelow scraped off the swastika from her husband's gravestone at the end of the war. What do you think about punishing people for the crimes of their country? Should soldiers like Peter Brenner ever be forgiven for their actions?

5. What does the fact that Werner is threatened by Bettina's photography say about men of that era in general and about Werner in particular? Do you find it frustrating or understandable that Bettina capitulates, given how independent she was as a teenager?

6. What do you think it is about Peter that is so irresistible to Bettina? Is there any justification for what she does?

7. Many characters in *This Terrible Beauty* have an appreciation for art: the Heilstrom family loves to read the classics, Werner is drawn to books, Peter writes, and Bettina ends up becoming a successful photographer. Why are people in all different circumstances drawn to creating art? Do you think creative acts can have political impact?

8. Bettina, Werner, and Peter all embrace Communism. Each has different reasons for being drawn to this system, politically and philosophically. What are those reasons, and how do they reflect on their characters?

9. Are there any points in this book where you feel sympathy for Werner? If so, when and why?

10. Bettina is deeply tied to the place of her birth, Rügen. How do you think life on the island shaped her personality—and how did world history shape her? After ten years in America, she still feels like an outsider. Do you think this experience is true of all immigrants, or is it particular to Bettina?

11. The two male protagonists—Werner and Peter—both change significantly over the course of the novel. How do they change, and is it for the better or worse?

12. In the 1960s, America was experiencing race riots, assassinations, and the escalation of the Vietnam War. How does this contrast with what was happening in East Germany?

13. Do you think Bettina is right about her decision in the end, regarding Annaliese? Is it true that *family* is what a child really needs, above and beyond anything else?

14. Imagine the story continuing after the last chapter. What do you think the newspaper article suggests about what might happen to Bettina's family?

15. If you read Katrin Schumann's first book, *The Forgotten Hours*, you might think these novels are very different. But the author sees a strong connecting thread between the two stories. Can you identify it?

ABOUT THE AUTHOR

Katrin Schumann is the author of the *Washington Post* and Amazon Charts bestseller *The Forgotten Hours*. Born in Freiburg, Germany, she lives in Boston and Key West. She is the program coordinator for the Key West Literary Seminar, teaches at GrubStreet in Boston, and was an instructor in PEN's Prison Writing Program. Katrin has been granted numerous fiction residencies and is the author of several nonfiction books. Her work has been featured on *Today* and *Talk of the Nation* and in the *London Times*, among others. She studied languages at Oxford and journalism at Stanford. For more information and to sign up for her newsletter, go to www.katrinschumann.com.